About Henri d'Mescan / th

Infamous writer and theorist Henri d'Mescan emerged in pre-war Europe as a cultural critic, enjoying considerable acclaim until his June 1947 conviction by a French war crimes tribunal for the purported authorship of a set of collaborationist documents collectively known as "The Vichy Papers."

Escaping execution (his actual collaboration in question), d'Mescan disappeared from the world stage until the later 1950s, when the experimental writer Henry Mescaline was discovered—and the 1964 publication of *Hallucigenome: A Henry Mescaline Reader* cemented Mescaline's place in the nascent consciousness-expanding movements of the period.

Following the 1967 death of his academic patron, David Schneiderman, d'Mescan/Mescaline entered a period of intense seclusion to construct his legendary unfinished epic: "Post-America," which is, as one critic notes, "heir to 'Finnegan's Wake,' 'Gravity's Rainbow,' and the 'Tibetan Book of the Dead.'"

The 2006 fine-art limited edition of *Multifesto*—with sandpaper on its cover—edited by theorist/fiction writer *Davis* Schneiderman, and academician Phoenelia Yeer, brings together pre-War d'Mescan prose, his Henry Mescaline prose, and for the first time, excerpts from the previously unavailable "Post-America."

This new edition, *Multifesto: A Henri d'Mescan Remix*, presents the 2006 material with additional texts, critical materials, commentary, and framing materials.

"**DAMN EFFECTIVE**…d'Mescan captivates you with his confusing characters the way few authors can."
Tim Clunky, author of *The Hut of the Red Octopus*, *Verve Cliché*, and *Breakdown: Superstring Theory and the Threat to Democracy*

"**GUT-WRENCHING**…Davis Schneiderman's complex psychological thriller picks up the reader and **SPRAYS** her in the face with **WINDEX**."
Hans Dialectic, Saturnine Evening Post

"**A MAJOR WORK…MAGNIFICENT…POWERFUL**…If books about writers and editors and the women who love them were given medals or monuments for authenticity, insight, and honesty, Multifesto would most likely be considered."
The Supermarket Gazette

"**THE BOOK OF MORMON** meets **THE X-MEN** crossed with **TERMS OF ENDEARMENT**"
Jerkus Reviews

"The **MOST** impractical, incoherENT, ANd inaccessible way to teach d'Mescania I have never read, largely because my copy was lost in the maIL."
JT leROY, enormously famous author

"HenRI d'M-Who?"
Henry MEescaline

MULTIFESTO:
A HENRI D'MESCAN ~~READER~~

edited by

DAVIS SCHNEIDERMAN and PHOENELIA YEER

SPUYTEN DUYVIL
NEW YORK CITY

ISBN 978-1-933132-36-5

Front cover photo and back cover photo courtesy of Nicole Haramis. All others courtesy of Hans Dialectic, and, where noted, Sapphoe VanBattene and Charles Gideon.

Carlos Hernandez [a.k.a. Arc-Zen S. Denarhlo] co-authored Section 21, "Fex During the Occupation of France," in the manner described therein. This section is used with his permission.

Thanks to the following publications for publishing excerpts of this text: *3AM Magazine, 3rd Bed, Absinthe Literary Review, Collage, Diagram, Fiction International, Gargoyle, Happy, In Our Own Words: A Generation Defining Itself, Magazine Minima, Near South, Notre Dame Review, Pindeldyboz.com, RealPoetik, Spread, Mad Hatters' Review, to the QUICK,* and *Unpleasant Event Schedule*

Remix edition design by Vasiliki Gerentes

Special thanks to Kaisa Cummings for her help in assembling the Remix.

Library of Congress Cataloging-in-Publication Data

Schneiderman, Davis.
Multifesto : a Henri D'Mescan Reader / edited by Davis Schneiderman and Phoenelia Yeer.
p. cm.
ISBN-13: 978-1-933132-36-5
1. Experimental fiction. I. Title.

PS3619.C4472M86 2007
813'.6--dc22
2006022050

For Phil Schneiderman [father of us all]
and Kelly Haramis [who puts Phoenelia Yeer to shame]

Table of Contents

Part III: The Post-American Years

Spuyten Duyvil's Note on the Less-than-Perfect Past (II):..........286

Archival Documents

Critical Reception

Remix Editon

Pre-face to the new edition, 2012:
MULTIFESTO: A HENRI D'MESCAN Remix

by Henry Mescaline

1. the irony of my being asked to introduction write the
2. the still wars we at are
3. the william walsh of wasted words
4. the fact of the copies 50 edition fine-art, limited 2006 in sandpaper-bound cover
5. the molly gaudry of malicious gall
6. the impossibility sheer of my being the person same henri d'mescan as
7. the you have an account twitter fake
8. the ben tanzer of bewitching temerity
9. the after fine-art maurice girodias tod thilleman delay publishing edition commercial
10. the alissa nutting of avaricious nonsense
11. the edition commercial never about published when sputyen duyvil went olympia press
12. the james tadd adcox of jeremiad-tasting admixture
13. the old beatniks maxim that die never just they mold away
14. the lily hoang of loony half-truths
15. the david/s schneiderman (x3) phoenelia yeer and henri d'mescan are the cupidity of
16. the matt kirkpatrick's jerboas of masturbating kinkiness
17. the spuyten duyvil back to never forget publish a henri d'mescan reader, multifesto
18. the kathleen rooney of killjoy ruefulness
19. the remix is a everything
20. the matt bell of mutilated bull-droppings
21. the time passed into this multifesto now, a henri d'mescan ~~reader~~ remix
22. the roxane gay of recalcitrant glibness
23. the occupy all manuscripts is # the world future
24. the crapulent salinity of craig saper
25. the adrien brody janey smith story that writes under these names
26. the someone who under writes these names
27. the guy in all us debord
28. the someone who under writes
29. the someone who writes you under

Foreword:
Hors d'Oeuvres d'Mescan,
or the Homme-lettes That is (In) This Book

by Craig Saper

1. Introductions

The definitive collection of Henri d'Mescan's multifarious works, *Multifesto* (2006), tried to cover all the works authored by that author's apparently multiple incarnations—including those of American Beat writer Henry Mescaline—but the editorial disputes and cacophony of competing editorial voices in that volume has led to the necessity of this current volume. This volume remixes the initial project, which was already a novel drama of critical editions, collected works, and editorial annotations, in an effort to de-sediment (the name of the strategy that Jacques Derrida preferred over the term deconstruction that he disliked) the margins of d'Mescan's oeuvre once and for all (or saving that impossibility, to open *Multifesto* to further explorations of multiple collective authorship and pseudonyms). (see Saper, 2001 and 1997; and, dj readies, 2015; see also Schneiderman, 2010).

Although one might see this remix project as an effort to create a "firm context" for the umbrella term (*Multifesto,* the first), under which at least one of the two editors organizes the d'Mescan oeuvre from his first writing in wartime Europe through his late, unpublished collection Post-America, this entire enterprise in both editions has as much to do with what I have elsewhere called *posthumography*, the poetics or style involved in publishing texts posthumously, as it does with *editography*, the genre of editorial anecdotes, annotations, and disputes.

The publishers have honored me with their invitation to introduce this volume in the context of my work on posthumography, the case of Allen Smithee, and the music-performances of multiple-use performance identities such as Monty Cantsin and Karen Eliot. Drawn to my recent work on revitalizing biographical anecdotes as legitimate scholarship, the publishers also share with me an appreciation of how editors' anecdotes—as a genre of literary texts—profoundly inform the interpretation of literary texts. This volume and *Multifesto*, the first (2006), explore the poetics of this play between authors, editors, and the texts generated among that multiplicity. The genre, so brilliantly illuminated by Davis Schneiderman, paradoxically builds on the seeming rejections, in

xv

contemporary literary theory, of examining the biographical and editorial contexts surrounding literary texts.

With that scholarly significance, it is worth tracing the events involved in the d'Mescan editorial project—more than or para-editorial project—through its posthumographic or editographic poetics. In 1966, a man known as *David* Schneiderman, a university professor and primary editorial director of Spuyten Duyvil's now defunct precursor Atom Press, published "the canonically influential *Hallucigenome: The Henry Mescaline Reader* (1964), and apparently secured the purported author Henri d'Mescan's acquiescence for a future collection to be one day called *Multifesto*. Many years later, and by a bit of serendipity the first of (what I claim are) two *Davis* Schneidermans began work on this project.

One suspects that the first Davis Schneiderman was not up to the grand achievement of original *Hallucigenome* editor David Schneiderman, never mind the responsibility to the great American Beat writer Henry Mescaline. In fact, the later Davis Schneiderman was but a pastry chef, later a *sous-chef*, and eventually a food writer. It was the similarity in names between David and Davis Schneiderman (not relatives) that serendipitously led to the latter becoming the editor of the Henri d'Mescan collection, *Multifesto, the first* (2006), because of confusion in mailing manuscripts to D(avid). Schneiderman.

It strikes one only in retrospect that the publisher later realized that it should open the floodgate to other editorial voices, and that has led to the current volume that remixes and annotates the original *Multifesto* (2006) volume. Further complicating matters, a second Davis Schneiderman, a prominent fiction writer, academic editor, Chair of the English Department at Lake Forest College, and one of the prime movers of the &NOW organization, is credited (perhaps incorrectly) in the subsequent rave reviews of the *Multifesto* work. This *Davis* Schneiderman, the third person in this discussion, is also credited with a handful of experimental novels including a recent broadside, *Blank*, which is both largely blank and has been therefore called the "ideal book for the 21st Century." This Davis Schneiderman has been nominated for a Pushcart Prize, has worked with DJ Spooky on *Blank*, and saw his complex novel *Drain*, about the disappearance of water in Lake Michigan, reviewed to strong critical reaction. This Schneiderman's work has appeared in numerous publications (including *Fiction International, The Chicago Tribune, The Iowa Review, Exquisite Corpse,* etc), and he is a well-regarded contributor to *Big Other, The Nervous Breakdown,* and *The Huffington Post.*

Add to this mix of dis-conjunctions, mistaken identities, and hall of mirrors-multiplicities involving one Phoenelia Yeer—a doctoral student specializing in Henri d'Mescan and his multiple and pseudonymously published works—who collaborated with one of the Schneidermans on the *Multifesto* project. Although she left the project in a cloud, the publishers kept her introductions, annotations, and credited her as the co-editor. This desperate Yeer, a half year from a tenure decision, in dire need of substantial publication, jumped at the offer to assume joint editorial duties on the first release of *Multifesto: A Henri d'Mescan Reader* (2006); and, she offered her current research on Mescaline during the first official meeting with the editor, the first Davis Schneiderman. Confused? I will distinguish here between the three Schneidermans as vieux (David), deux (Davis I), and sous (Davis II). And, to Phoenelia Yeer as Yeer.

Further, this cloudy conflict between the academic Yeer and the food-writer Schneiderman, left the publishers in a constantly evolving dilemma on how to organize the writings, how to equitably share the responsibilities, and other editorial problems. On the one hand, there was the literary huckster, either deux or sous, who had gained "a small measure of previous notoriety for reprinting Shakespeare's sonnets with Duchampian facial hair placed on top," and on the other, Yeer, who was described increasingly as unhinged and denounced by her co-editor as delusional.

Let me try to clarify the issue by explaining, first, their agreement (that is between Yeer, sous, possibly deux, and likely vieux). They agreed, initially, that d'Mescan was, in fact, both "Henri d'Mescan" and the American Beat/experimental fiction writer sometimes allied with his name, "Henry Mescaline." Later, Yeer accused sous of conspiring with deux to fabricate the connection, and elevating vieux in order to place him (or their) self (or selves) as the all important editors and introducers of the (fabricated) writer. Schneiderman(s), sous and deux, laughed off these increasingly hostile claims as the delusions of the Yeer; she was acting-out: much like a character in the novel situation of *Multifesto* that Yeer claimed was written by sous or deux (or that they were one and the same). These attacks begin in Schneiderman's first section, "Introduction: in p a r t s…"

2. Structures

From this editor's perspective, the conflict between the academic Yeer and the food writer Schneiderman, left the publishers in a constantly evolving dilemma on how to organize the writings, how to equitably share the responsibilities, and other editorial problems. The legitimacy of all the previous editors was called, severely, into question. Even David Schneiderman (vieux) assumed the responsibility of the *Hallucigenome* collection "solely on the strength of his sports jacket and putrid tobacco pipe." This links directly to deux's notion of distinguishing between the telling (plotting) and tale (story) (see his introduction to *Summary Execution*), as crucial to understanding literary meaning, which seems an unacknowledged nod to Roman Jakobson's linguistic theories, which in turn influenced all contemporary literary and media Structuralist theory.

There is in d'Mescan and *Multifesto* a Joycean quality, with Kafka-esque overtones, as reflected in Yeer's story about the Electric Bartender ("Introduction: *Abstractions* [1937]"). Further, d'Mescan (or was it Mescaline?) often uses the visual design of the page to make editorial commentary part of the novel and essential to the literary meaning. For example, the author writes in the margin (almost in Talmudic, multivocal style) surrounding his masochistic (cringe worthy) pornographic story. There is also an undercurrent of the (writing) machine as in the use of the railway metaphor indicating society as an outmoded machine, as with the Electric Bartenders, body machines, and much more. All these machines suggest a self-destructing machine destroying itself in a pleasurable dis-integration of the outmoded and failing culture that d'Mescan inhabits. Machines are threatening, artificiality castrating, and outside of pain and pleasure—just as writing moves beyond the confines of a singular voice.

The editors, or at least Yeer, add intrigue to these machinations with the claims that d'Mescan was a collaborationist with the Vichy government. Of course, the sous Davis Schneiderman's version of pre-war Europe casts the perhaps Mescaline-authored "Vichy Papers" as frauds, forgeries—supposedly collaborationist documents supposedly framing Henri d'Mescan. Let me paste excerpts from a series of footnote passages typifying the below-the-lines editorial dispute in *Multifesto*, *supposedly scripted by deux or sous:*

> The connection between Henry Mescaline, American writer of experimental fiction, and Henri d'Mescan, (unjustly?) convicted war criminal, moves from the margins to the center. David Schneiderman attempts an explanation: "So I assumed that by linking you, Henri, directly to Mescaline, I would succeed in drawing you out of the shadows. The reader of course, if she is unwilling to entertain the thought that you are one and the same,

will move into the more delightful hypothesis that Mescaline is little more than a morally bankrupt opportunist, which of course, we both know to be the truth."

For one of the Schneidermans the hypotheses that the man executed in Paris at the close of the "Identity Trial" in 1947 was not Henri d'Mescan, but rather, the imposter who both composed the "Vichy Papers" and became the recipient of the death sentence—thus precipitating the work of Henry Mescaline; or in an unlikely scenario that Yeer briefly entertained (out of spite perhaps), that the "Henri d'Mescan" traced by the government was not the original, but perhaps the imposter. After her initial slip from sanity, Phoenelia clung to the theory that Henri d'Mescan, whom she carelessly labeled a guilty war criminal, had been a Nazi collaborator, and thus, rightfully sentenced to die. Yeer had moved on to a theory that David Schneiderman, the loyal editor behind *Hallucigenome*, fabricated the entire collection in order to blackmail d'Mescan into assuming a new identity, or to rescue him, despite him- self, from the Nazi stigma that haunted him.

She never came clean on which scenario might fit, and after we had been separated from some time, as we tried to meet our obligations to Spuyten Duyvil and to d'Mescan while simultaneously searching for the child we had never seen. Yeer fabricated the even more absurd scenario that we had somehow fabricated the complete Henry Mescaline and David Schneiderman corpus. The career of experimental writer Henry Mescaline will project an abrupt and tragic end with his seizure by angry riot police in Chicago during the 1968 Democratic National Convention. Covering the events for the radical, Situationist International arm of the *Ladies Home Journal*, Mescaline will flee the 22,000 armed officers, National Guard, and federal troops ordered by Mayor Daley during the police riot, and in exasperation, will pound on the door of a small house in hopes of eluding the authorities. The occupant will shout an inquiry as to identity of the person at the door. Mescaline, full of the bravado that signified the best of his work, can shout "Mr. Mescaline" in reply, and will be then allowed entrance by the tenant, a student at the University of Illinois-Chicago completing, (coincidentally) doctoral work on Mescaline's distinguished career.

Unfortunately, in the course of their discussion over high tea, Mescaline will certainly criticize the student's central thesis that

Mescaline's current fiction will at best pander to a crack-in-the-pan craze for flash fiction, cross-correlated, in this author's case, with a base and so-called "postmodern" fascination with repossessing dyspeptic clinical spaces traditionally used by the autocratic armies of patriarchy—with predictably self-referential creative production. The student, under increasing pressure to complete his project, will be unable to avoid restraining Mescaline in an elaborate cocoon of duct tape and plastic wrap before reading the entire dissertation aloud while rapping Mescaline's shins with a ball-peen hammer. After lulling him to sleep with what can only be described as the impenetrable, faux-ramblings of a excessively masturbatory academic intellect, he will drag Mescaline's body onto the front lawn, where Mescaline will then be trampled by neighborhood children before his removal by federal agents to a "detainment" facility. There, truth be known, life will flood out of him completely and with obscene speed, although witnesses may claim to perceive some vestigial movement, where his body shutters as if in orgasm for a single millisecond, with a distant pulse penetrating the callused layers of a witness's skin, just as the end of prose poem might resonate on any particular day for any particular reader, puncturing the oily epidermis of reason and fear.

I will reserve judgment and let the reader decide these issues, or how, exactly, to unpack them, "just as the end of a prose poem might resonate on any particular day for any particular reader" upon reading the remixes of this new volume. The effect of these various strategies is to create a kind of *palimpsestous* text of editorial voices, authorial commentary, and various mirroring pseudonyms. The manuscript builds up a residue on the Henri d'Mescan oeuvre (coincidentally, that author's name is an anagram for Schneiderman) until only traces remain of the initial oeuvre. We are often left with what d'Mescan (or one of the editors describes as "the un-peopled vacancy of random archaeology" rather than the fullness of a singular authorial intent in one person).

3. Multiples

Alluding to the entire Henri Mescaline case, Mark Amerika explains that his "creativity" informs "the experiential quality of the struggle that persists throughout an artist-medium's life as they continually fine-tune their body (their *body-image*) *as* instrument" (Amerika, *ReMix*, 2011). It was this body-image, according to sous, deux, or vieux that "made almost liquid by fear with its unifying image of the camera gun" that suggested that the "imposter's corpse" was at the center of [the Socrates-inflected d'Mescan] "death scene" that "confirmed that the man, [presumably war criminal d'Mescan,] whose body was buried in the outskirts of Montmarte was not the d'Mescan [at all], who was instead present in the gallery on that final day, incognito, helping to prepare the imposter's body for its punishment. Some evidence indicated that this executed double was d'Mescan's pre-war translator Hans Dialectic."

For her part, Yeer, with empty body-image bags piling up, holed up in the, now shuttered, Wonderland Motel in Ithaca, NY, close to where I am writing this introductory essay, plotted out the rest of her conspiracy. Whether Yeer was delusional or not, Spuyten Duyvil thought it best to include David Schneiderman's introduction to the *Hallucigenome* (1964) section of *Multifesto*, the first (2006), without direct editorial comment—from either Davis Schneiderman or Phoenelia Yeer, because their conflict was counter-productive to the reader who simply wished to complete *Multifesto*.

Who actually wrote this strange text?

David Schneiderman working as the experimental fiction writer Henry Mescaline? Henry Mescaline as his autonomous "self"? Henri d'Mescan as Henry Mescaline? Yeer? Vieux, Deux, or Sous in a series of odd-toned editorial arabesques? Strange lines differentiate the prose styles in later section of *Multifesto* from the earlier d'Mescan material, and you are left, just as a word might leave its referent to assume only local, immanent relations, to ponder the distinction between "author" and "editor." In the current remix volume, the notion of the collective editorial voices as palimpsestuous seeks to de-sediment the extension of the oeuvre's chalked out lines like the marking at a murder scene— surrounding a body of work.

Finally, there is one Dr. Davis Schneiderman. In my haste to complete this introduction in time for publication, I could not track down if the Davis Schnederman food-writer/chef was indeed connected to the prominent Lake Forest College Professor and Chair, or just one more coincidence. Since, the latter is a prominent academic and administrator, who I knew years ago, I doubt any connection despite the prior suggestions in this essay. I will also add that Davis Schneiderman is no Davis Schneiderman, let alone the Davis Schneiderman. Or, as Gertrude Stein would no doubt feel: a Schneiderman is not a Schneiderman is not a Schneiderman.

Craig Saper (csaper@umbc.edu) is a professor and the director of the Language, Literacy, & Culture multi-disciplinary doctoral program at UMBC (University of Maryland Baltimore County). He is the author of *Intimate Bureaucracies* (as dj readies, 2012), *Networked Art* (2001) and *Artificial Mythologies* (1997). He has edited, and written afterwards for, Bob Brown's *Words* (2010) and *The Readies* (2009), and he co-edited an anthology on *Imaging Place* (2009). He has guest edited special issues of *Visible Language* (1988) and *Style* (2001), and co-edited two special issues of *Rhizomes* on "Drifts" (2007), and on "posthumography" (2010). He wrote the introduction to Sharon Kivland's *A Disturbance of Memory*, II (2008). His curatorial projects include exhibits on "Assemblings" (1997), "Noigandres: Concrete Poetry in Brazil" (1988), "TypeBound" (2008), and folkvine.org (2003-6). He has published two artists books *On Being Read* (designed by Diane Fine, 1985) and *Raw Material* (2008), and he is presently writing a biography of a poet-publisher-impresario-writer in every imaginable genre, Bob Brown. More on Brown: http://www.readies.org

Works Cited

Saper, C. "The Political Economy of the *Allen Smithee Case*," in The Allen Smithee Case, ed. Stephen Hock & Jeremy Braddock (Minneapolis: The University of Minnesota Press, 2001), pp. 29-50.

Paper: Saper, C. "Auteurism, Ghostwriting, Pseudonyms, and Fronts: The Politics of the Alan Smithee Case," featured speaker at the conference on "Specters of Legitimation: Alan Smithee as Auteur," U Penn, September, 1997.

dj readies. "Sociopoetics of Forged Identities: Getting Intimate With Monty Cantsin, Allen Smithee, and Karen Eliott," Ed. Yeer, Phonelia. *The Legacy of Intertwined Networked Nomenclature.* (New York: Atom Press, 2015).

Saper, "Scratch & ReMix Machine, Paik in Amerika," in Mark Amerika's "Open Remix Online Exhibit and Catalogue," in conjunction with Amerika's *Remix The Book* (University of Minnesota Press, 2011), n.p. (http://www.remixthebook.com/scratch-remix-machinepaik-in-amerika).

Schneiderman, Davis. "Posthumography: a response and review" Boundaries of Publication: Posthumography issue. Ed. Craig Saper. *Rhizomes.com* (2010): 20.

About the editors of this volume:

Davis Schneiderman is a multimedia artist and writer and the author or editor of ten print and audio works, including the novels *Drain* (TriQuarterly/Northwestern), the *DEAD/BOOKS* trilogy from Jaded Ibis [including *Blank: a novel* (Jaded Ibis), with audio from Dj Spooky, and the forthcoming *[SIC]* and *INK*]; and the co-edited collections Retaking the Universe: William S. Burroughs in the Age of Globalization (Pluto) and *The Exquisite Corpse: Chance and Collaboration in Surrealism's Parlor Game* (Nebraska). His creative work has appeared in numerous publications including *Fiction International, The Chicago Tribune, The Iowa Review, TriQuarterly*, and *Exquisite Corpse*, and semi-regularly in *The Huffington Post, The Nervous Breakdown*, and *Big Other*. He is Chair of the English Department at Lake Forest College, and also Director of Lake Forest College Press/&NOW Books. He edits *The &NOW AWARDS: The Best Innovative Writing*. He can be found, virtually, at <u>davisschneiderman.com</u>

Phoenelia Yeer is an Assistant Professor of General Rhetoric, Writing, and Composition at SUNY Vestal, and trustee of 49 original letters between Henry Mescaline and his 1960s Atom Press editor, David Schneiderman. She is co-editor of the current collection, *Multifesto: A Henri d'Mescan ~~Reader~~ Remix*, and has written extensively on collaborationist artists and literary inhabitations. Her critical study, *Psalmanazar and Chatterton: A New Dialogue* (Ossian Books, 2001) won the prestigious Charles Bertram prize for scholarly publishing in 2002, judged by James Macpherson. She has lived near Reykjavík, Helsinki, and Kigali, although originally from Altoona, Pennsylvania; she lives with her daughter and polydigital cat.

Note: This text appears on a small card inserted in the 2006 fine-art, limited edition of *Multifesto*.

How this book was made:

Gilles Deleuze and Felix Guattari note that "[t]here is no difference between what a book talks about and how it is made," and so this book was made in the following manner: each edition was hand-stitched from the silk of the Madagascar Pineworm, first sighted by humans in the late 1600s: "Behold! A pineworm, within this enchanted isle of Madagascar, methinks!" (from *The Strange Tales of Men of Great Musculature*....[123 additional words in title]). Later, in a containment facility in the Mongolian Steppes, a series of wild howler monkeys, trained in the finer points of synthetic abrasives, attached the emory cloth using a mentholated variety of aerosol spray glue. The fumes caused a cohort of the beasts to exhibit improper attitudes toward the books, and the resulting splashes of errant glue stain, the mild marking of the cover, and the occasional staple—all came to represent the compromise between the simian urge to mutilate and the desire of the monkey handlers to limit such mutilation. Nonetheless, one dying capuchin (who watched the proceedings with great interest), signed a dire warning to his masters: "Other books...rubbing ... book this ... destroyed ...dire warning!" His handlers deciphered this strange syntactical voicing to indicate two important vectors1) that the sandpaper cover *will* destroy other books, and 2) that, so fragile is this device, any unnecessary bending of the cover while reading may in fact *loosen* the sandpaper. Better, the monkey signed, to open the book as if the text were hardcover-bound, so as not to bend the sheath. Regardless, these texts were soon deployed, transported across the world in a rickety steamer, and now, at the end of their journey, are held, warmly, by your presumably mammalian fingers.

This definitive collection of Henri d'Mescan's multifarious works—*Multifesto*—decades in the making, covers his multiple incarnations only as a parachute, descending slowly from the atmosphere, might appear to momentarily blanket a forest. Through the tireless campaigns of Spuyten Duyvil's two editors (more on *those* two in a moment), this text includes the heretofore-unavailable documents of d'Mescan's pre-WWII output, along with a sample of the "Vichy Papers" that precipitated his 1947 death sentence by a French war crimes court. This is no small accomplishment. Charting also the work of experimental fiction writer "Henry Mescaline" and the subsequent production of his later years—again using the Henri d'Mescan nom de guerre (that reclusive elder statesman of twentieth-century letters)—this project ultimately establishes a firm context for the twenty-year epic known only, in partially viewed pieces, as *Post-America*.

Speculation among the power-lunching literati runs cold-to-hot as to whether d'Mescan will continue his critical, literary, philosophical, and historical shenanigans once his case is publicly revealed—opening the waters for future complementary tomes. Dive deep. Yes, dear reader…d'Mescan is certain to remain his willful silent self, a translucent bottom feeder blind from decades below the surface. Occasionally, as in *Multifesto's* final sections, he *will* go so far as to actively participate in the preparation of his manuscripts; at other less expressive junctures, he makes his presence known through the proxy statements of various pseudonyms or imposters. Through the shadowy murmurs of literary ventriloquism. We thus remain unable to coax him into reality according to our desires; he refutes such logic with every word.

Spuyten Duyvil practice holds that prefaces such as this

one (as in *Spin cycle* by Chris Stroffolino or, further back in time, *The Fairy Flag & Other Stories* by Jim Savio) should be left to our authors and editors. Our views and ideas, biases and preferences, are best disseminated by what we choose to distribute and manufacture, rather than what we might interject directly into the work. Our readers are not simpletons who must be bludgeoned with context. Yet the truly bizarre circumstances surrounding the production of *Multifesto: A Henri d'Mescan Reader*—a project embroiled in countless legal battles, contract lapses, and now, to Spuyten Duvils great legal dismay, several unfortunate character assassinations, requires a brief statement (composed under a certain amount of duress). Given d'Mescan's continued silence, Spuyten Duyvil must bear responsibility for the proper invocations.

And so, we invoke.

Oh great Sebek the Unholy, crocodile-headed god of Shedit, Crocodilopolis, patron saint of Henri d'Mescan, locate our two editors Davis Schneiderman or Phoenelia Yeer. Will the rot of their decomposing bodies fume through the ventilator of a hidden writer's garret? Rise, oh crocodile tooth, wear your ruby scabbards and splash the waters of the mighty Nile onto our backs. Bathe us in the light of your elusive moan and draw the scales from our eyes...

Ok, enough of that silliness (much more to follow).

d'Mescan's mythic foibles aside, we have every reason to believe that the three main participants of *Multifesto: A Henri d'Mescan Reader* dropped deliberately out of sight, perhaps in simple exhaustion from the sheer complexity of their work:

In 1966, a man known as David Schneiderman, university professor and primary editorial director of Spuyten Duyvil's now defunct precursor Atom Press, noted critic, philosopher, and editor of the canonically influential *Hallucigenome: The Henry Mescaline Reader* (1964), apparently secured d'Mescan's acquiescence for a future collection to be one day called *Multifesto*. [Schneiderman was a literary huckster, gaining a small measure of previous notoriety for reprinting Shakespeare's sonnets with Duchampian facial hair placed on top.] Their agreement held that d'Mescan would adhere to both controversial identities: "Henri d'Mescan" and experimental fiction writer "Henry Mescaline." In return, d'Mescan negotiated proprietary review rights for all *future* editorial introductions to his work. His yarrow sticks could not have been any more proleptic; on August 1, 1967, while grading an unseasonably large stack of student papers in his Vestal College office, Schneiderman was overcome by intense heat behind his left ear, a veritable cauldron of wax churning in a mass of chicory flavored singe; before he could so much as reach for the phone, the burn had given him a fatal heart attack. His office was closed for a year, before a steady stream of new adjunct professors occupied its mass of cluttered filing cabinets, and somewhere, deep within the metal drawers, the nascent *Multifesto* collection lay buried, cast in a disorganized file on the cutting-room floor.

Fast forward thirty years to the winter of 1997, editorial assistant and Spuyten Duyvil historian, *Davis* Schneiderman [no relation[1]], makes contact with one Phoenelia Yeer,

1 No relation to *David* Schneiderman, although the similarity precipitated a 1985 glitch in Spuyten Duyvil's auto-mailer system, generating a form letter to Davis Schneiderman, then a professional chef at New Yorks prestigious "49" restaurant, requesting an update on the *Multifesto* project (defunct, of course, for 18 years). Upon receipt of the document, Davis, also an accomplished food writer, presents himself at the Brooklyn office of Spuyten Duyvil, and through a series of accidental identity mix-ups, found a places on the payroll—in charge of the now-renewed collection. This almost unbelievable circumstance has been entirely favorable to our organization, and we officially approved Davis's appointment in 1993, updating the Byzantine computer system to prevent such future "glitches."

Assistant Professor of General Rhetoric, Writing, and Composition at the newly christened SUNY-Vestal based upon her brief note, "David Schneiderman: A Forgotten Name" in the March 1995 *Tableaux of Higher Education*. The desperate Yeer, two seasons from a tenure decision, in dire need of substantial publication, jumped at his offer to assume joint editorial duties on the 2006 release of *Multifesto: A Henri d'Mescan Reader*; coincidentally, she offered her current research on Mescaline during their first official meeting at a local steakhouse—centered on the fact that David Schneiderman's office still holds his correspondence with d'Mescan/Mescaline, *in a series of forty-nine original letters*. And just maybe, she noted halfway through a bottle of Chianti, she has recently come to occupy this very office. They were lovers within the month.

And so the subsequent (violent) conflict between Yeer and Schneiderman most likely stems, in part, from our obsessive desire to force these two to unravel the mysteries of d'Mescan. Spuyten Duyvil is not above acknowledging this, in retrospect. Never should we have allowed *those* two to seduce each other through an almost grotesque textual affair, to be caught in the throes of a passion that might turn on the revelations of a footnote. Oh yes, we hoped they would break the proprietary rights of d'Mescan with a trenchant academic discovery—but perhaps the extravagant private suites, the constant attention we offered, pushed things *too* far. We must admit to picturing their no-doubt awkward lovemaking during our editorial meetings, the way Yeer's arms would flap to her side while Schneiderman's tongue caressed her...and so we feel some small measure of responsibility for the tragic events.

And yet, in order for the reader to follow the at-times confusing materials collected in *Multifesto*, the result of our ill-conceived attempts, we must briefly explain the structure:

For Part I—"The Pre-American Years"—Schneiderman and Yeer submitted substantial co-authored introductory materials in early December 1999, several weeks *prior* to their unfortunate split while visiting the Mescaline archive in the small town of Future, Missouri, on the banks of the Mississippi River. They were to write as one voice—and Spuyten Duyvil was not informed of the separation until three months later [March 2000]; we thus erroneously assumed that the other editorial introductions from Part I that we received in the January and February also followed this co-authored method. We subsequently decided to alternate their introductions, painstakingly separating individual ideas from their original co-authored work to best determine in what order to arrange the future, individual introductions. Nonetheless, as both Yeer and Schneiderman refused to cooperate with each other, significant editorial confusion reigned.

A technical problem plagued Part II—"The Un-American Years." Yeer and Schneiderman, both of tempestuous natures, never progressed far enough in their joint process to submit co-authored materials about the crucial Henry Mescaline period [or David Schneiderman's 1964 anthology of Henry Mescaline's fiction, *Hallucigenome: The Henry Mescaline Reader.*] We were thus left without even a glimmer of consensus. After several difficult board meetings, Spuyten Duyvil determined to follow the previous logic, continually alternating their introductions in the now-established pattern. Yet, we could now assign specific sections to a specific editor, and although, we could no longer depend upon their collective research, the editing and introductions of Part II ensure that that the reader is treated as fairly as possible to an even distribution of contrasting viewpoints.

For Part III—"*Post-America*"—Spuyten Duyvil remains, according to our legal counsel, contractually restricted from commenting. We thus defer, as per this apparent legal obligation, to whatever Henri d'Mescan chooses to note. (See Sections 22+).

Readers, this woefully incomplete explanation must be completed in the text itself, and we leave, for you, this intricate pleasure. The collective silence of d'Mescan, Schneiderman, and Yeer can strike us as less of an organized conspiracy and perhaps, we hope, only the quiet that descends, again like a parachute, after particularly traumatic events. This is the same statement we will repeat to the authorities if we are again questioned, during what, in the naiveté of their inquiries, seem always to be the first time.

And so it will be from Spuyten Duyvil's offices inside this insulated Brooklyn garret that we launch this incendiary collection—a daring and erotic tome for the pleasure of a culture that knows firstly how to enjoy itself, and, secondly, how to cover its own tracks. With it we will establish Henri d'Mescan in his rightful place, because we, Spuyten Duyvil, have been positioned by fortune to liberate his desires from the airtight bell jar of ancient professors and critics, prosecutors, and judges who damage to his work from their erogenous safety zones. For far too long, Henri d'Mescan has been a demon in the myths of lesser writers. Today, we spring him from those anonymous cells of writerly DNA, and, in doing so, introduce to the reader a life so fantastic that it inspires the lowliest among us to discover our own, perhaps equally anachronistic futures.

—Spuyten Duyvil[2]

---

2 Spuyten Duyvil in no way condones the rampant use of footnotes. In rare instances where we are forced to interject, the note will be followed by this mark— (Spuyten Duyvil)—to differentiate it from other notes.

When the enigmatic, obsessive, at-times noisome figure of Henri d'Mescan emerged from the hedges of the pre-war European cognoscenti, he could not have known that *his* production would eventually blossom from the ashy soot of earth into the most enticing specimen of the twentieth century. Davis Schneiderman—the name we respond to—birthed in the last messy segments of the twentieth century, labored eternally under conditions so difficult that even the hardiest blooms withered. Then, in the vestibules of various uncomfortable torture chambers [at times a restaurant kitchen, at times Spuyten Duyvil's insufferable garret]. Now, a mere broom closet of patchwork texts and dog-eared postcards offering fuzzy volcanoes and undefined landscapes, where we worked that awful day, January 19, 2000; quarantined in the SUNY-Vestal office of our ersatz co-editor [disappeared, gone, with our daughter!], the ghost of our former love, the ever-absence we called simply, Phoenelia Yeer.[3]

***

A bouquet of lilies appeared along the spiral staircase of the first meeting in 1997. Exhilaration as our trembling feet

3 Where is she we asked? Couldn't this entire process have been simplified if the introductions spoke in one voice, rather than—well, flip ahead to the next sections. It was almost as if we had a restraining order out on each other. We could imagine being separated from a close partner, forced to endure her misleading introductions from remote locations, through the conduit of an unfeeling third party, a corporate entity, and then, forced to respond in the same way. Communication, except that of the most confused nature, remained an impossibility. We tried to accomplish a specific project in this way and well...it is clear why we were *forced* to use the occasional footnote.

stepped over the rickety platforms toward Yeer's home, another lightless garret set high in the industrial town center, among burnt-out factories and the rumbling dirge of vibrating freight trains. Bearing a scepter of this virgin flower, we announced our presence with a knock; our knuckles mashed against the rotten wood as a brittle stone might strike a curtain of moss. Before the stunning Phoenelia Yeer parted her door, that first time, before we presented her with the same arrangement of lily sprigs that had thrilled Anthony of Padua, our body melted into an uncharacteristic mass of primordial goo. Spores of unseen mold grew strong in the dark hallway, the dust of dead insects pushed into each stone fissure along the spiral stairs. Her lips emitted the sweet reek of an interconnected global futurism, a faith in the machines of our age, a faith that her current *misinformed* [and why not say it? DANGEROUS] version of Henri d'Mescan—as Nazi collaborator and international fugitive—embraced all too easily. She was ripe for correction.

This delicate Phoenelia Yeer, poisoned from years of graduate school into a relentless zombie, spouting Derrida, Foucault, Baudrillard [she suffered from theoretical Tourette's], from cadres of self-important professors trumpeting the useless gangrene of indeterminacy, yes, this one here, yes her, grew to think that *our* book *Multifesto* [and why not say it? MY BOOK], should "resist and radicalize" some indecipherable problematic she attributed to the "One-God-Sun-God" version of **CON-FLICT**. Who knew that her research might threaten Yahweh himself? She screamed like a banshee, refused to acknowledge transcendent love even as our lips kissed soft punches into each others flesh. Together, we rose above such petty semantics, but she never left the dirty earth. And Yeer, now? On the run still, with no lily bulbs to plant, no set identity to be found in European theorist Henri d'Mescan or American fiction writer Henry Mescaline—all of that faded, we fear, into the mad ambiguity of escape. No final meaning to receive, she said, dangling over the void in those final weeks before Future, Missouri. Her sullen breath was perilously close, and if we had with but one hand gripped lightly to a crumbling shelf of soil and bitumen at the decisive moment, then…well, we firmly believed, *just as we had always known*, that our duty to raise others from the pit would eventually kill us all. This is not self-importance, but preservation of the species. Ourself.

***

Lily blooms both beautiful and intimate assaulted us so often that the scars of the twentieth century—electric railroads, microcomputers, et al—seemed a river of stinking sewage cut only by the passing pleasure of a fragrant sprig. And yes, of course, an essential **CONFLICT** allowed that story to proceed. The order of the daily business commute [increased productivity] becomes the order of Auschwitz [*Arbeit macht frei*]. Yeer, like most post-structuralist, deconstructionist, third-wave feminist, anti-rationalist, postmodernist [now we were diseased!] hacks, yes hacks, would absorb with sickening credulity the seduction of her *preferred* meta-narrative concepts. All "indeterminacy" had to do was shuck its pants, and she'd be ready to stroke the cock of "meaninglessness." Faith in nothing, little *chickie*, is still faith. Of course, our training in classical modes ensured that we would agree to her basic axiom—this postulate of **CONFLICT** undetermined and shifting—but we asked her to consider whether a knot of complications did not mean the same thing once it became unwound. While we despised Auschwitz, we must also get to work each day.

***

Our initial **CONFLICT** surrounded 1947's infamous "Identity Trial" of Henri d'Mescan. An "indeterminate" [ha, ha] scoundrel assumed d'Mescan's personas as one might don a cheap suit. Identity thievery paid color back to the original: each falsehood lightened this pseudo-d'Mescan's pigment, bleached his uniform until this rogue, dragged into a French courtroom to be tried as a Nazi collaborator, shimmered like the translucent bottom dweller he was. While the general public [from decades of misinformation] had long convicted d'Mescan of having penned the virulent pro-German propaganda now known as the "Vichy Papers," Phoenelia Yeer knew, yes she did—*just as we had always known*—that these documents were mere forgeries, inventions of inventions, digests of countless unpublished diaries cut from some other context. Sampled by this imposter in the figure of a fascist intellectual made only from semantics and mirrors.

Yes, Yeer always knew, *just as we had always known*, that d'Mescan's only novel from this period, the splendid *Outsourcing* (1939), actually *corroborated* his innocence. Still, the vicious prosecution attempted to present that document as "evidence" of d'Mescan's willful complicity. d'Mescan penned *Outsourcing* in the late 1930s, cross-breeding the mechanistic phonemes of German annual reports, splicing the reaction of primary investors and stockholders—using scissors, paste, and multiple typewriters to continually fabricate new arrangements—until the nouns of the German military-industrial complex had no choice but to betray its verbs. In I.G. Farben we read "final solution"; in Volkswagen we smell the musty metallic timber of "Treblinka."[4] And so d'Mescan's eloquent self-defense from the trial of his doppelganger, included in this collection as *The Trial and Death of Henri d'Mescan* (1954), pre-

4 We had planned to include an excerpt of *Outsourcing* in this space, but Spuyten Duyvil's minority German shareholder Humleich Bower Verlag, Inc., ordered through their attorney that sections of *Outsourcing* be withheld from this collection, pending a WWII slave-labor reparations lawsuit utilizing the text as evidence.

sented the necessary evidence. Against this, *just as we had always known*, Phoenelia Yeer withered in a consumptive gaze.

***

Both the chirping voice of the cicadas and the glorious tongue of the nine muses reminded us of that fragrant lily, white aroma wafting through the chambers of the nose. We first discovered sweet Phoenelia embossed on a keyboard of cloud and moss; her legs spread between springs of the winged-horse pasture, pressed up from the underbelly of the soil. Together we drank from the waters of a mournful oblivion, delighted in soft QWERTY folds, forgot our shame under the naked carapace of heaven's sullen alphabet. As with all labors of intense connection, this work encouraged her confusion: Was the man tried in 1947 *as* Henri d'Mescan a patriot, an imposter, or a collaborator? Did the American experimental writer, Henry Mescaline (emerging through the efforts of that *other* Schneiderman, *David*) have any association with either wartime d'Mescan? These questions held infinite permutations, but together, for a time, with the help of our gentle fingers, Phoenelia no longer doubted the sinister uses of d'Mescan's corpus. She no longer denied his need to escape a State-ordered death in France, to assume a new identity in post-war America, to become "Henry Mescaline" just as the bell of the flower become itself only in full bloom.

***

Our vision of wild ducks carried her stiff body through the air, over candy dreams and absinthe pathways, and, oh, how to explain Phoenelia's loss of sanity, of consciousness beyond such brazen images of our own making? Perhaps the slip occurred during those long afternoon stretches when we left her alone to discover some strand of the complex story we had *already* identified. A common practice—the teacher charted a path for the student, carrying the single white lily announcing the death of a friar or the foundation of a church, so that the disciple will follow of her own accord.

In time, the deep-breathing rhythm of our respiratory circuits caused our chests to feign collapse; we slept in separate beds, in different rooms cut-apart by the never-ending hallway, individual spaces that looked the same as our communal reality but demarcated themselves from happier times through subtle tricks of her bulbous eye: Yeer's words, once smooth from the bubbling brook of her throat, clung hard and fast to the chin, dribbling ineffectually to the floor; her editorial prefaces, once capable of cutting through the kudzu of prejudice against d'Mescan, lost all semblance of definition, or form. She refused to maintain that d'Mescan had been maligned, that he was a *victim*, that words and images conspired against him at every juncture, that an invertebrate cadre of National Socialist and French collaborators strategized ways to replace their crumbling backbones at the expense of his pristine character.

Yeer mutated into a bare twig as the cruel winter wind ripped plumage from the carcass of the year, and after their fall, this gnarled branch colluded with other fallen bark bowed into a calligraphist's curve. We knew, always, that **CONFLICT** created all meaning, but never, no we never guessed, that Yeer would become the enemy.

***

Phoenelia Yeer existed in a sort of parallel universe, trapped within sight, but far from reach. Nothing could save her from the cold chemical wash of her so-called postmodern epoch. Concerned for her health [and also for *Multifesto*], we knew that her salvation waited eagerly for spring: for flowers to descend in angel flutter once more, for buds to poke through the cold ground in an unspoken promise.

And so in that dead winter of 2000, with only memory as a guide, we tracked her to seedy chat rooms, the amniotic cabarets of hyperspace, coordinate points on an ever-expanding grid of portal providers—to remind her once again, by our edits, that d'Mescan held the position of the most important resistance writer under the grip of the National Socialist program—of those under the palm of all dogmatic control systems.

This was not simply a matter of our need to complete the legacy of *David* Schneiderman. But perhaps it started with him, over a century back, when that hapless doppelganger of 1888 began his slow tromp through history, blissfully unaware that two generations later—*our* body would inherit the burden of his genes. Perhaps he found himself trapped as Yeer had been, in the regressive gyre of d'Mescan's rotating beacon. Perhaps those forty-nine letters set the stage for his death, the heat of the world collected in his left ear because he could never *write* his way out of this dismal office. Yeer may be a lost cause, but we could not abandon our daughter, or our d'Mescan.

***

Thus, this long-overdue "Reader"—*Multifesto*—chronicling thousands of interchangeable worlds, billions of prepared snapshots, the unfolding narrative of those forty-nine letters. Only seven remain unseen. We have searched everywhere, behind the walls with the insects, inside the hard drive with the tiniest robots, even in that secret compartment of the file cabinet, yes, we found that right away, sweet Phoenelia; but we could not find those seven shiny parcels.

And so we set out after her.

She crisscrossed the continent with her bundle—the child she called Dial-Up Networking. The child we never named. We scanned roadside stops for traces of her phantom corona. She scrawled on napkins at the motel bar, "our arteries hardened with the pulse of the people" and we felt our breath again on her neck. Sometimes we were close enough to hear the child cry, close enough to double back to this office. Close enough to find the child that had never known its father.

David Schneiderman could never be far from Yeer, either, in this place—for here he inhabited those seven unopened letters just as a crocodile inhabits its muddy marsh, opening its world jaws to a polychromatic sunset at the nadir of the universe. Have we not heard the murderer's snarling noises? Still, no doubt, a child had been constructed somewhere, our child, just as a bloody puddle spilled across this office carpet, the scene of some horrible murder [yes, murder!] the murder of David Schneiderman by the forces of those like Phoenelia Yeer, just as Henri d'Mescan lived on in a network of infinitely reproducible cells.

***

Listen closely, Phoenelia Yeer, Henri d'Mescan, David Schneiderman and know that we approached, that we contained legions inside of our bodies. For that was us, following ever closer. And despite ourselves, we found her most exciting.

20

3) Listen closely—do you hear the one about the man who *tastes* almost the same as the other man? The scars along the inside of your wrists make the question incidental to your rope burn, to your crisscrossed musculoskeletal system bound and tethered to your chair, tendons swollen. Your flesh becomes a purple-stained contour map between the latticework of the leather shackles, an eggplant-patch checkerboard soured by this mystery man's spittle. He zigzags elsewhere, no doubt studying the authorial technique of a third man, who may also exist as a fourth and possibly a fifth man, depending on which manifestation of the first man most effectively pulls tight your bondage straps.

4) Unfamiliar? In the throes of your dizziness it becomes possible that this cohort of just one man, or, of all men, possesses the extraordinary ability to expand and contract like a metallic accordion spliced through a tape loop, the holy rosary of man or man-y men and hair and bone and shaving cream and phlegm and flesh and stiff parts circled over the bathroom rug, blood running from one or several noses, ears cleaved in a balm of distilled wormwood. All *this* gruesome violence for the pleasure of that *next man*, who, with unbelievable forwardness, listens too closely, severed ears pressed against the horrible back-shift of tenses caught on a rusty reel to reel—and who may indeed be just one of many near-identical other men.

You tell yourself (in confidence), that you cannot survive such onerous restraint.

5) After all, it isn't long before your birth name and rank

attaches itself to the shoddy office door—Phoenelia Yeer, Assistant Professor of General Rhetoric, Writing, and Composition (an unholy triad) at SUNY-Vestal—that those forty-nine sacred letters emerge from the primordial muck. Treated unkindly by a variety of pestilential office insects (the angular bookworm and the silent, inky-headed anopheles of the Lower Zambesi), as well as several quasi-seasonal floods from the Susquehanna River, these missives wedge below an almost invisible corner of the office's overstuffed filing cabinet. Up from the false-bottom mystery of a magnetic tether: Charlie Chaplin's reverse movement through the enormous gears in *Modern Times*—second per frames 24—into your fleshy cold hands. Warm and backwards, you go crazy from love.

6) Forty-nine waters mix in the muddy marsh, choked in a lily bloom. Forty-nine nourishing elements inhaled as vapor, transferred into your burning heart. Forty-nine faces shift into forty-nine times forty-nine permutations. Forty-nine blackbirds and man-y men are one. Forty-nine psalms read by forty-nine friars upon the death of their forty-ninth brother. Forty-nine paths to righteous action according to the I-Ching, book of changes, of the forty-ninth hexagram, KO. The Lord is the shepherd of forty-nine sheep. Forty-nine folds over forty-nine pages. Forty-nine stamps on forty-nine letters—and *you* shall not want. Forty-nine ancient biographers overrun with muttering sickness, rolling forty-nine paper scraps around forty-nine death bullets with forty-nine disappearing spells—*Abracadabra, Barcodebar*—impacted into the jejunum of the forty-nine mummified reptiles. From these forty-nine intestinal parchments, you receive forty-nine secular beatitudes: Concretes of Lemnos through Phylogolus of Carthage, Johnson through Boswell, Cervantes through Menard, Joyce through Ellman, X through Haley, etc. Here, with forty-nine letters, the process

takes an indirect course: Henri d'Mescan through Henry Mescaline through David Schneiderman through Phoenelia Yeer, countered by the alternating rants of Henri d'Mescan through Henry Mescaline through David Schneiderman through *Davis* Schneiderman—who wants, more than anything, to possess the original packet of forty-nine. Forty-nine crocodiles show forty-nine times forty-nine teeth in a smile that runs the length of the Nile.

7) Winter—circa 1999, forty-nine years from mid-century, the distinct possibility of some dime-store second coming loosing its liquid bowels over your already brown-stained keyboard, your tattered *The Riverside Shakespeare* ("The Winter's Tale" annotated by a schizophrenic freshman). You perch a seasonal affective disorder (SAD) light on the edge of a composition-reader-stuffed bookshelf. You want no part of the scatological rapture. A bust of Pallas hovers above the lightless window in a labyrinthine sub-basement of twirling corridors, caged torsos draped in hounds-tooth jackets, mouths spilling resinous pipes of moldy tobacco across cracking spines. You work slowly, one inch per hour, writing one *good* paragraph per month in your manifold "box," in your "cell" below the planet. Graduate students copulate wildly in their shared offices, wiping with rough hand towels from the industrial restrooms, while you and your colleagues rip down tubers suspended just below a carapace of dirty ceiling that floats inside a concrete membrane between your work and your life fading fast into the glow of the unevenly flickering SAD light. Translucent fish and blind albino spiders crawl over each other and digest rubber mealworms, squirming on indoor-outdoor carpeting that reeks of dirty tile and broken intercourse.

8) Stories have a way of sucking you inside your own body.

Like ego-defense mechanisms. Like history. Bodies constructed in privileged positions. Bodies writhing blindly in a mosquito-netted canopy bed. Bodies grasping for a piece of flesh that bunches in the automatic grasp of your fingers long enough to insist that Henry Mescaline and Henri d'Mescan share the same bones, the same skin. Insisting their orgasms play along the same frequency of lung and ligament. Stories and bodies whisper together in their sleep, offering their secret rhythm that rises gooseflesh in the dark and crumples to dust under the cold grey sun—and you are told once more, by that odious *man*, how Henri d'Mescan had been wrongly tried and accused as a Nazi collaborator, and blah de fucking blah…Dewdrops stutter along the husks of un-mowed lawns, along the fiberoptic blades of grass—your partner Davis Schneiderman thrashes the tiny pistons of his pelvis.

9) Forty-nine times, in the white-hot glow of the postcard sun, you see an army of flamingos balancing on ash-grey legs devoid of ocean pigments; their wings flap; they flood the lagoon of your sleepy medulla oblongata in white crimson jerks while Henry Mescaline composes angry missives to push his editor David Schneiderman away, under the water, into the deep red tide. That evening, reading that letter, when Lucifer falls from earth to sky for a brief but divine revolution, *David* Schneiderman's only crime is to prove the innocence that Mescaline claims for his war-criminal self. Who may or may not be the same person who closes his eyes as the stars begin to fall. On crutches, on nights like this, you walk with three legs in the theatre of your mind, unable to find a seat.

10) If the archangel Gibreel arrives with a check from Publisher's Clearing House and a sonogram printout of your holy belly, you would yawn just so that your mouth consumes

the camera eye with a shot of creamy tonsil before completely swallowing the viewing public. Most of this correspondence between David Schneiderman, scion of a defunct academic trust now represented by the publisher Spuyten Duyvil, and Henry Mescaline, the experimental writer whose work you never read, at first—well, most of it concerns a book within the book of this collection: *Hallucigenome: The Henry Mescaline Reader*, a 1964 entry into the literary milieu of Yvor Winters and Lionel Trilling, James Thurber and Malcolm Cowley. The tome does little to draw attention to *its* body through your fingers. It wears no shiny, embossed letters calling the Eisenhower years into account, no noxious drawings of army brats fresh from a spooge on the Korean peninsula. Nothing in the author Mescaline's name, or in that of the editor—David Schneiderman—to suggest the significance of the book in the hexagram of your life—your KO, distilling the waters of the muddy marsh, and you never *ever* drink the *agua* down here below the filing cabinet.

11) Under this metal ceiling, Mescaline's collection, edited by David Schneiderman, occupies a nether-state like the end of James Joyces *Finnegans Wake*, where the two woe-men turn to stone in the liquid of the murky word. You annihilate the universe as arteries harden with the pulse of the people. Beware of an earlier back-tense shift. Not uncommon during your graduate work. Between drunken assaults against the petit bourgeoisie. Between carefully orchestrated trips to the thrift store, when you must pretend, with authority, to be an authority on certain books. Books you have never read. Books you will never read. Books that do not exist. The minor authority of the authorial.

12) The fire, choked by the lily bloom, invades the waters of

the muddy marsh before you have even heard of a man or many men called David Schneiderman. Nod your head anyway. Judging solely from his correspondence—well, then the whole thing becomes interesting. David admits somewhat grudgingly in Letter 22 ("Their illegitimate generation of distracted, you-me-mine-obsessed consumers"), that at least two-thirds of his work started out a fabrication... And you so *desperately* want to believe that the CIA funds Abstract Expressionism as well as post-war university American Studies programs. Bill de Kooning on the dole. Larry Rivers assassinating Castro in a swirl of droll color so that everything mixes together in *one great big bootiful bwob.*

13) Forty-nine letters tell forty-nine times forty-nine stories, and forty-nine factorial more tales trace so many histories. From the latter 1950s an unidentified person—soon to be known as Henry Mescaline—not only takes the trouble to assume a new American identity that obscures his life as Henri d'Mescan, but also, fabricates an heirloom set of pewter spoons representing the lost continents of Lemuria, Mu, and Bimini; genealogical records dating back to the grandfather of the assistant head blacksmith on the Mayflower; fecal samples preserved in a series of pressure-sealed mason jars; charitable donations to various foundations that provide charitable donations to various smaller foundations; several years worth of backdated garbage including used syringes and soiled napkins; and a startling array of absurd sexual quirks and self-pitying Oedipal complexes caught in *flagrante dilecto* on the flip side of a privately pressed 78 record. So possessed with it all is this Henry Mescaline, that one of the forty-two already-opened letters becomes worth quoting in some detail:

The source of your trouble, Schneiderman, in

the *Multifesto* draft will be, as I predict, plural
and promulgate: callousness, insensitivity,
phonecianism, didacticism, tetragrammatol-
ogy, slavishness, racism, spite...things which
most of us will be guilty of at some times in our
lives, but those which a serious editor will
labor to keep out of the work. You will play
your reader, your publisher, and your subject
cheap...

David, with regard to my past as a resistance
member and accused Vichy collaborator with
the Germans, I will repeat myself again: It cannot be my desire for you to do what I will not
do myself. Why wipe clean a slate that will
never be dirty? I will be me, Henry Mescaline,
when this has ended, and no one else. Never
again will I consent to this sort of collection.
Your precious *Multifesto* can disappear completely for all I care. It remains a question of
sanity with me. (Letter 26 "Soft-but-dried flesh
and anthrax-infested brain structures.")

14) For the medieval Cabbalist scholar-thief known only as
Volanis (1389-1501), numbers become harbingers of mystic
correlation: "Assumption and harmony manifest the divine
numeral, neither accident of nature nor discovery of man—but
rather, numbers reminds us the planogram of heaven. *Of how
far we have fallen!* Is not everything interwoven into a series of
countdowns, intermingled into a twist of roots which mimic
heaven?" Numbers represent perfection. And from a place of
imperfection, we count: "Of the eleven secret names of G-O-D,
the sephirot: Eheie, Yah, El, Elohim, Eloi Gibor, Eloah, Jehova,

Saboth, Elohim Sabaoth, Shadai, and Adonai, so go the forty-nine manifestations and tangles of multiplication. Some will cast us from the garden, others will merge and mix us in facsimile."

15) Several of the forty-nine letters imply that Henry Mescaline deliberately fabricates his own "damaging" biography, so that David Schneiderman might discover it by accident, a crow picking obliviously through the Jonestown carrion. Drunk, again. At the Kool-Aid vat, again. David Schneiderman, of course, antagonized by Henry Mescaline's refusal to cooperate, finds himself even more fixated on the thesis that Mescaline so cleverly plants. Mescaline's plan for the David Schneiderman-edited version of *Multifesto*, as noted in one of the later letters (dated July 1, 1965):

> ...will be to extort compliance to a narrative of will, which chooses to jettison the facts in order to reclaim a measure of autonomy by which I can revel in the basic human figure of dignity. I intend to twist your arms into pretzel knots; collapse the house of cards that throttles your lungs. You, *David*, whose house is that of the Lord, must compose a "Reader" containing not only the collected works of Henry Mescaline the fiction writer, *but also the works of the lost Henri d'Mescan*—the only person who will be capable of fabricating Mescaline so convincingly in the wake of the post-Vichy Identity Trial...In your editorial work I will find your future self—the literary editor—who may as well unearth a new original version of me in the process. Check the grave of sorry

Henri d'Mescan, and you will find a corpse far from decomposed." (Letter 34: "We can see nothing but clouds of darkness and inky silt.")

16) You read the forty-two *open* letters to sounding brass and tinkling symbol. If the future has already arrived and you have already opened the remaining seven letters, they will always remain unopened, in the present, for you. You cannot read the future in a book until you understand the grammar of time travel. Steam will not work. Any order arranged can be letters...but you always proceed chronologically. Metal staples bind the future to the floor of a filing cabinet.

17) *Finnegans Wake* for example. James Joyce maintains that his readers should spend a lifetime studying his works. Only *one*? As he loses *dinosboozy* for his eyesight, he goes *pigeony linguish* to his amanuensis, Samuel Beckett, once yelling, "Come in," to a caller, which Beckett takes as integral part of the nonsensical dictation. Mohammed with *The Koran* or Joseph Smith with *The Book of Mormon*, your young Sammy, bound by scarves into a wooden rocking chair, feels the sacred absurdity of his master's text. "Come in," stays in the *Wake*. Oh yes, there's the part at the end where the two lady-voices (who have been creating and revising a universe throughout their discursive exercises), triumphantly, turn to stone. So, that's the joke—if you haven't devoted years of study to *Finnegans Wake*...next time youre at a cocktail party, turn to the *bompramifazzio* next to you and wow them: "Rupert's base innuendos and excessive ingestion of diseased goldfish remind me of the end of the *Wake*, oh you know, where the two woe-men turn to stone..."

18) Before the dim light of literacy shines upon the general

populace, when only the priests and fathers and kings and fathers and lords and fathers might string thoughts into signs, so ABRACADABRA is a "spell." Place directly on wound. Next day, write ABRACADABR, sans final A. Place directly on wound. And so on, and so o, and so, and s, and, an, until a gash on your body completely disap...

19) In Letter 37 ("The grayness of editorial abuse renders everything that much sharper"), Mescaline drops all pretense of independent existence from the fugitive Henri d'Mescan, reverses the suppositions of Letter 34, and *now* accuses *David* Schneiderman of fabricating all of Henry Mescaline's fiction and attributing it without permission to the exiled and uninvolved Henri d'Mescan. *This* David, argues *this* Mescaline, shamelessly capitalizes on the strong link between a war criminal and the public's need for personal redemption. A homemade world where everyone's guilt sits on the end of a fork. You can almost see the outraged Henri d'Mescan, Panama hat shading the equatorial sun, chowing down on over-cooked breakfast sausages, consuming reports that trickle in about "his" innovative fiction emerging under the Henry Mescaline guise in the States...perhaps he sees a way back to the disgraced past. "Bartender," leaving a tattered bill on the table with his strong, black glove, "make it new!"

20) A certain number of the forty-nine letters gurgle over with this brand of mixed confession:

> No, I will not disapprove. Whether I can
> approve, I don't know. Benevolent neutrality, in
> your words, may be it. I'll be glad to read the
> manuscript with the idea of correcting factual
> errors and with the idea of pointing out jarring

notes, "devout agnostic" and "scion of the
ambisexual, interplanetary philosophy set" but
I can't pretend you've come even close to the
correct star system. The details will be presented, the texts excerpted, but the context will all
be wrong. Everything anyone would want to
know about me will fade into *your* image (an
image I will never ask you to construct or resurrect regardless of this brand of necrophilia
that has made *Hallucigenome*). I will abide by
this version of the Henry Mescaline persona,
for now, but have no intention of allowing this
temporary relation between your creation and
the "me" known as "Henri d'Mescan" to con-
taminate the entire line. In short, I will defend
my chromosomes from the whole genetic
sideshow, as well as your salutatory pandering,
whenever I deem it necessary, seeing as we will
soon share certain...uh...attributes. (Letter 3:
"Every narrative will build upon its past influence, in order to transmit an alteration of that
past.")

21) Forty-nine letters and David Schneiderman assumes literary executor responsibilities for a growing Mescaline franchise,
solely on the strength of his sports jacket and putrid tobacco
pipe—until d'Mescan winds his way through the slums of
Panama City, some drunken Pizarro Cortes Balboa chewing on
gold doubloons and sunning himself under cacao trees. Much
of South America acts as a teleportation station, a parallel port
for the unwanted molestations of its avuncular partner, the
United States. One moment you sit along a strand of the god-
dess Ix Tab's shiny web, stuck on a gossamer filament of pal-

metto and silt, burning snifters of native rum and snakes the length of garden hoses bandying playfully through your intestinal track, and the next, you look charred, a nice even brown color, somewhere in the southern U.S., hauling molasses on a barge toward Baton Rouge, hiding in the steam room of some paddleboat monstrosity as the mighty Mississippi crooks its way up the continental armpit. You can always be sold down the river. d'Mescan in the Amazon, Mescaline in the mud. Small towns dot the riverbank in tiny periods, indeterminate commas.

22) Maybe the editor loses his nerve, so to speak. Maybe ruddy old Henri d'Mescan becomes clever Henry Mescaline who everyone suspects to be the cleverer Henri d'Mescan? Maybe Schneiderman-the-editor decides he doesn't care for authors who can't keep their yaps shut, their pens down. Maybe Frankie "Know-Nose," and Sammy "the Sign" Marinara teach him some general linguistics will a ball-peen hammer. Maybe he even loses his tongue once your eyes go out in soft flicker scripts.

23) Maybe *David* even loses his hands, fingers freeze; he can't open his last few letters because his ear is on fire. But that's no reason for *you* to balk. Maybe the editor loses his nerve, so to speak…seven letters from Mescaline unopened upon David Schneiderman's death. The earlier letters from Mescaline received meticulous annotation from David Schneiderman, with every indication that he suffered terribly under their cruel yoke, but these seven—seven that undulate in their hidden bundle with vast potential energy—remained sealed beneath the endless muck…?

24) Martin Heidegger's *Being and Time.* You have not opened

the letters. Thomas Pynchon's *Gravity's Rainbow*. You have not forwarded them to Spuyten Duyvil. Even *Don Quixote*. Working on the lamb. Little left to chance. Just nod yer head as if you know exactly whats going on and the entire parcel remains hidden. Imagine everybody in the audience naked, buried in an inaccessible vacuum as you lick your soft lips with a tongue changing slowly to stone.

25) Until you patch into that dingy office by the cruel trajectory of academia, even the first forty-two letters, decades of salty dust, a thick sheath of surface electricity, remain unopened since their original annotations. Maybe your ear grows hot like a warm hat kept on by a roaring fire that catches on the yarn and pushes like a furnace into the inner cochlea. Maybe it's August 1, 1967. Maybe you scribble "no urinal thought" in the margins of a student thesis on the Nazi complicity of your favorite subject—Henri d'Mescan. Maybe the research for this planned collection finds itself scrapped on the cutting-room floor of your tiny office, locked in the false bottom of a rickety filing cabinet until you accidentally discover its contents on November 19, 1997—exactly two months before your first contact from the conveniently named Davis Schneiderman.

26) Neat and tidy narratives. That's what he offers. Interesting in a conventional way. When you want to become ensnared, when your stockings hold the wonders of smooth, forbidden triangles. Your in-box tickled by Davis's delicate coaxing, his *italicized* jokes and dirty viruses. His flirtatious forwards. You bond with him over the d'Mescan manuscripts. Your tenure: the clear-eyed fish, slippery as a hose, soft as a garden eel, and his collection: the glassy spider, legs jointed for flexibility, joints folded for change.

27) During your romance, you display the first forty-two letters only in segment, part, and parcel. A strangled phoneme here, a phrase tossed off in the throes of passion, your bodies caught in sticky mucous, on sopping sheets of lavender fume. Davis always desires. He pours hot cream over the hills and into the clefts of your figure, forces you to twirl your tongue on the rims of impossible phrases, pushes his rocks and stones down the crack in your edifice, churning heat as you explode in gushes of sweet manuscript.

28) Your refusal to surrender the letters excites him, and at times, you fuck. You fuck with an end to overcome the other's will. You never succumb to lovemaking.

29) Davis Schneiderman approaches your office with a knife sharpened on the bones of the backland. His namesake—*David*—remains the model that draws your lives into parallel lines, into asymptotic bends through geothermal eons measured by the temperature of your genitals hardening in each other's mouths. A slip of grey into green sylvan boughs. The great brown eye that will never again let you sleep.

30) Maybe you mean "original" instead of "urinal." Maybe you mean ABRACADABRA.

31) You bivouac in cheap motels and drink martinis through bendable straws, compulsively re-reading Mescaline's letters, amazed at the many textures and forms: critical rants in the form of movie scripts, footnotes set above the lower depths, marginal comments in the shape of ancient rhizomes, anti-essentialist sexual fantasies, corporate marketing simulation treatises, and, if you only had a hammer, plans to repair the broken names of god.

32) That you still write together despite your differences, contributing to this patchwork sample that you call *Multifesto*, tells you more about Henri d'Mescan than it does about yourself.

33) Maybe you can't even spell without those *secret* vowels. BRCDBR.

34) It isn't long before your belly begins kicking and you know that one of Davis's rotten sperm successfully infiltrates the system. Maybe life exists as a figure composed always of figures, a hair singed under concentrated flame in the illusion of brimstone. No doubt you are pregnant, as the oblique voice of misfortune feeds the umbilical cord back to the randy seed of two men or all men, all men named Schneiderman, one dead thirty years, one undead or resurrected, taking turns with your many zippers, fucking you completely blind.

35) Maybe spelling counts. Maybe order is important.

36) So you are burdened with two Schneiderman's. Several d'Mescan's. At least two Mescaline's. And a Yeer. Never in the history of the seemingly endless pantheon of elder gods populating our planet do you find the corollaries you need for this confusion. The mummified crocodiles of the Egyptian city of Shedit, Greek Crocodilopolis, form a procession of plasticized simulacra; the randy, overgrown belly hair of Davis Schneiderman in his appallingly outdated swim trunks makes you sick to your morning-sick stomach, and the cradle of your tender daughter, the always premature Dial-Up Networking, fluid and unmotivated in the liquid and undifferentiated slats of morning…you breast feed so that the entire process of interlocking machines, the suckling engines of mouth against tit,

penetrate ever deeper into the eggplant flesh of your wrists.

37) Davis of the lowlands, charmer of the reed snake Apepi, daemon of division, replication—you see his plans reaching over the forty-nine dusty letters once buried in your inherited file cabinet. You recall your greenish-blue June croon moon eyes; you shed your skin, shiver in buckets while editing Henri d'Mescan into this protean volume you hold now in your hands.

38) Nothing demonstrates originality. You suckle your phonemes between sticky lips. No defense against the liquid of an amniotic sac.

39) The dark tendril of the sea lapping up toward a silent alba-tross, foaming on the brink, the blackness of virtue, and then his black knife, piercing the ventricle of your pen with cold reptile teeth. So stone to turn you slowly before you fume away.

40) Maybe spelling counts when order remains important.

41) Maybe, in the illusion of one man or man-y men, wriggling free from your crosscut wrists, you stone to turn so slowly once again.

42) Maybe you've disappeared completely in the *cloudscrums* of BARCODEBAR.

Multifesto: A Henri d'Mescan Reader
Part I: The Pre-American Years

For the young Henri d'Mescan, the controlling narratives of modernity—industrial and scientific leadership, the appropriation of mythic tropes into the armored plate of tank and submarine, interactions between perception, memory, and identity—begged for a philosophical re-assembly. Composed under the gaslights of dying republics, under the hideously enlarged thumbs of impotent political figures, d'Mescan's first major work in this vein, *Summary Execution* (1932), consumed itself with the intrigues of its time. Unable to keep a job and expatriated to Paris from the Germany that no longer resembled his own, the disillusioned writer created a sanitary cordon about his person in which to replay his youth in the context of inchoate fascism.

The near-death experience in the icy Rhine (that "soggy day" in 1913) anchored much of his inquiry into the "real" and served, as in many indigenous cultures, as one of several "origin stories" that informed the work. In France, at the twilight of the Third Republic (dissolved in 1940 at the time of the German Occupation), d'Mescan prepared for the second Great War. For every genesis story, d'Mescan seemed to argue, there were two components—the *tale*, where the events of the narrative found a chronological arrangement (often in an indefinite, ethereal past), and the *telling*. The latter reflected a state of constant reevaluation, and its agenda simultaneously emerged from the previous succession of tales and tellings—compounded with changing elements that required a new telling. Simply put, every narrative built upon its past influence in order to transmit an alteration of that past. The space between the two figures and the possibility of resistance to this doleful control mechanism became discernible only through the use of innovative language games that estranged content from form. Even this introduction, *Summary Execution* argued, spiked itself with a brand of sophisticated code.

***

And thus, the *telling*:

In the Paris of 1932 d'Mescan ate macaroni with his hands and considered it art; the dimensions of his breakfast surface spilled into the bleeding edge of his work—the edges of freshly sliced tomatoes bisected his cultural critique; the meniscus from *vin de ordinaire* mimicked the slight arch of unfinished manuscript pages caught between Teutonic paperweights, the tarnished utensils occasionally used as place markers for some half-scribbled letter to the editor about the Socialist movement, a tattered volume of Rimbaud, the annual report of German industrial leaders. The early work of the writer we now call Henri d'Mescan consisted of an enormous number of texts often transcribed by editors and translators from incomplete copies, fragments, and forgeries. To hypothesize that d'Mescan acted as an unwilling participant in pre-war European letters would be to minimize the extent of his reputation; for in the years just preceding Hitler, when the dream of worker unity briefly competed with a more fervent program of National Socialism, to speak at all was to speak as a marionette manipulated from behind, to find our words misquoted, abused, and manipulated until a cause we once despised grew potent on a rancid liver set too long in the sun. d'Mescan despised prime causes, but given this political climate, his prose naturally reversed the traditional purpose of the "origin story."

***

The *tale*:

In the beginning, industry kept blood pressure low and

oxygen precious. Henri d'Mescan trembled behind the shame of his body. Shit smeared the moldy angles of the wall in his Papa's Westphalia hovel; consumption formed invisible, covalent bonds with the unforgiving air. Dead of winter 1913 and tiny Henri felt that life started *in media res*...the immigrant boy from some *terra incognita*, discovered by his father while masturbating into the town milk supply produced by his family farm. He splurged a youthful burst into the vats of swirling white, arched a parabolic seed toward the light—and for it, received the cat-o-forty-nine-tails at the hand of his supposed Papa, a man who enjoyed the full exercise of his rights and duties. Pulled from the icy waters of the Rhine thirteen hours later by an assembly of minor officials and state bureaucrats, at the brittle climax of the mighty rivers turn about Koblenz, the boy Henri wore ice crystals over his mouth and nose; yellow and black shocks from the polluted soil striated his frozen skin under the distant sun. He caught his breath in the warm brandy, by somebody else's controlled cooking fire at the forecourt outside the center garret, and in the phosphorous gleam of sparks against the stone ring, received the gospel of torture and cruelty that birthed, in its shimmering magnificence, the core of a million words.

4) Henri d'Mescan
From *Summary Execution* (1932)

Setting: Myth of the lilies.

A man and a woman are not looking for justice—they are looking for lilies. Beautiful lilies, fragrant flowers. Two lovers poised in silhouettes on a lonesome hill and people threading through the knot of each other to look also for lilies. The secular sprawl of classical arches and columns, interlocking and trembling hand-forms beneath the garret-laboratory that doubles as a prison house. Their heads become overwhelmed looking for lilies. These objects and images provide a mannered contrast to their forbidden, sublimated passions. Rinsing the lilies in the liquid beneath the window lattice of the Italian manor bleating its pastoral rhythm against hand-carved oak and mud. Slicing themselves from their skins after the river silt has covered them, while the simple beasts of the field, goat and lamb and foal alike, become lulled by the pan flute into drowsy docility, wallowing their sun-browned noses into the shunts of each others sparkling *shit holes*. Then floating, away from the lily place, off into the perfumed ether.

Form: Organization of a body.

The devil collects the balls of corrugated yarn passing across the courtroom floor. What new and different body emerges from the contours of this alchemical cord? Unravel the strands of your younger life and review the detritus of learning: memories of suckling in a primordial marsh of phytoplankton and lush Indonesian calla lilies (as a marker of consciousness), a statuette of the Emperor cleansed more often than the most elevated toilet (as boundaries form), animals prancing inside the Zoological gardens and the sideward glance falling breast-ward on a passing girl (as hideous limbs buzz your biplane hair), the discount barkers along "Scandal Avenue" with their tight-panted shills "winning" three-card Monte in the summer haze (as breath fills up even your *secret* holes), a wedding beside the crematoria, the power plant, the lashes of foam marking the rocks beneath the lighthouse (as the first circles of blood navigate the new interior), your feet compelled to scuffle certain spots in the dirt for a bountiful harvest (as the will to reproduce), the knave of a back-alley dumpster confessional (as something rises from the refuse)…it's all a narrative line to save your soul, a way of jumping (waylaid by an order of meaning), a different body laying dormant, constructed in pieces by the meaning of your memories, ready to burst to the surface and smother your world in its defiant thievery.

Plot: The sun moves away and creates the water lilies.

At the last beginning everything was bathing in a perpetual boiling soup: flame withheld the world from the crusts of moss and bark.

And Amoeba, the first sentient creature, was stuck in the fiery gunk at the bottom of the social and economic ladder; as yet there was no class-mobility. There was no dry land.

Over Amoeba suddenly came a more-complex organism called Paramecium with disapproving boil-covered relatives concerned with preserving the social order and keeping Amoeba down. The light did not hurt Paramecium who threatened to grow over Amoeba and *into the future.*

And Amoeba had always lay at the root of the future; thus resting ever from the beginning.

So Amoeba was thinking of how to get Paramecium, and wishes and desires flashed through a body so hot it could do nothing but stay still. Ciliated Protozoa began to come out from Amoeba, urging Amoeba to get hitched by winning Paramecium through various metaphoric skill games including

drinking-dueling-fucking-cockfighting-fencing-tennis-cro-
quet-football-baseball-calculus-accumulatingfunds-picking
horses-waste evacuation. In this way, they grew through the
layers of fiery gunk and erupted into the wind.

And now the sun began to move further away, and parts of
the ocean started to cool and harden.

Amoeba tried to impress Paramecium as the Ciliated
Protozoa had said before devolving Paramecium with a genetic
load whose hideous social deformity could mark their forbidden evolution—and help Amoeba become the future.

Then the Protozoa attempted to rise, ready to eat Amoeba
and Paramecium and the child that they had tricked Amoeba
into making for their food. Amoeba, who wanted more than
anything to be the future, ate Paramecium and the child first,
growing larger and more complex, scaring the Ciliated
Protozoa back into the water to evolve into plants. Meanwhile,
the sun had settled into its new space and the land had hardened around the waters.

Amoeba rose through these waters that had once covered
all: the hungry, endless pool left behind in the body cavity
became a pit of stomach acid and ocean, filled with the sweet
dark bloom of the first water lilies, marking the grave of the
forgotten Paramecium.

Anxiety: Trapped by what came before.

You are innocent. You protest. Rattle your cage like a monkey given two metal mugs in which to spit tobacco. These
choices evoke a double-consciousness. You draw a pictograph
of bars. Legs swing in slow circles to the eternal music of the
discarded embryo. The autogiro, the Prussian consulate, a
petite Madeleine, all bear the mark of Cain as your accusers play
back reel-to-reel recordings of your bodily functions. They
sound of the past. You stand small in the box now, covered in

sweat while the black-faced judge in powdered wig extracts further details of your plot to gain fame as a Jan Vermeer forger, as an enamelware investor during WWI, as an ardent supporter of the Maginot line (except along the Belgium border of course). You smile and sweat. Smile. Sweat. Then vicariously fart.

Protagonist: A dashing figure, or more plausibly, an unsympathetic wretch.

So then the answer for you is to become a pathetic creature named Tacg, yes, Tacg. Do not recoil while he scuttles for peanuts as the evening janitor in the wealthy man's pawnshop. Tacg deals with spaces and vistas, buildings and monuments, rather than the sequence of events. The gold pocket watches and bright gleaming fobs and carbuncle sheets of displaced vellum bind the curios and jewelry to the merely ethereal for Tacg. He grasps a foggy connection between the child's umbilical cord and the viscous butcher cleaving the first lifeline: Tacg considers that his boss may be a Jew, and that his own inestimable poverty (although that's a word he would never use, "inestimable"), must then be conditioned by other words he would never use, and that in life, no topic has received more attention than "gene longevity." The newspapers indicate to Tacg that he has been caught in the politics of the day, awarded a sort of tenuous probation for crimes he never committed. Sitting in his dilapidated hovel on nights displaced by shrouds of thunder and broken cricket whistles, he pricks blood from his pinkie finger, a curious diabetic, mixing it in microscopic test tubes. He filters out constituent genetic materials. He has coded the language of the "other" and created the "ghetto." He assists with the projection of the guilty man onto the face of the criminal justice system, and the figure of the international criminal lurks behind it all, Tacg insists, because he once almost drowned in a vat of erotic newsprint and everything hardened so crystalline that you are forced to remember your own inevitable collision with the hard lime of goose-stepping order. Together, the bully-armed bailiffs escort you both to the garret prison.

Deus ex Machina: The angel of the early race who made the stars.

Mutation, the guardian angel, quivers uncomfortably at the thought of another moment at the Dentist's "parlors." The whirligig of a foot-powered drill rotates in shrill swivels, in cahoots with compressed tubes of ether and iron filings collected on rusty electromagnets. The brown and moldy clang of the water pipes knock a mournful beat. The Dentist, a wiry man with a cold jaw and slightly protruding lips, sweats profusely under the negative pigment of his artificial lamps. Unlike fire and sun, the tungsten tongue licks its casing and strains even the most acute eyeballs through the sieve of the modern. Mutation gleams herself onto the rotting sidewalls and remembers pulling the boy, now the Dentist, from the icy-waters of the Rhine on a glacial 1913 morning. So soft and wet his dreams became, but she never lost hope. Branded a delinquent by the probationary courts, the son of this undersecretary commands a modicum of respect in the Berlin professional circle. He drinks the second best beer, and has even pulled teeth from several minor party functionaries. One of his regulars, the young Mr. Eichmann, an ambitious, if dull-mannered simpleton, valued both for his banality and for his ability to move people, once called the Dentist by his first name upon seeing him at a social function. Mutation, ever more distraught as such upwardly mobile episodes, winces in her golden halo, throws her hands into an Orant prayer position even as the Dentist tells his patient that twelve cavities require immediate action so the Amoeba can successfully woo the Paramecium if it weren't for the organism intermarriage laws because what matters isn't the money but the breeze of water lilies and the constellation of the firing squad set high in the cold grey sobbing afternoon.

The Reader Response: Incantation of Mutation for the revival of ethics.

Yellow transmute these situations with scissors, and watch the horizon bleed with the power of a thousand suns. In the end, resources will be consolidated. The various judges may be equally degraded by the incompetence of the firing crew, the death squad, but the needs of authority allow every two-bit artist an endless supply of corpses. Standing with your cigarette under the auburn-soaked patina of flint and cloud, the endless spirals of rickety starlight pumping blood from ancient waters, amid leftover plans of anthropomorphic gas balls, the x-axis blisters in the shadows of a Goya painting. You know, the one where the exasperated peasant/freedom fighter faces the guns of brute physicality as cold lantern light hides all but the contorted gape of the victim. So what if Saturn eats his children and Dada pokes fun at the Kaiser? There's been no last meal, no dreamy escape from the bridge where the hanged man swims to negative freedom in the moments before the noose snaps. Tacg makes a quick calculation of the images of *escape*, and realizes that freedom forms a large part of the entire sideshow. *Amoeba*, on its deathbed, can think of nothing but *Paramecium*, the politics that lead down this road, the twin deities of drink and aesthetics, suturing the asshole, the kiss, hard on the mouth, of a pseudopodia more lovely than a plucked flower, a marginalized element, a ride on somebody else's cargo train in a land full of freedom *and* water lilies. Those stars still burn.

Rising Action: The pro-Ta(c)g-onist has second thoughts.

The firing squad squanders its shore leave and waits impatiently for dawn along the burnt-out husk of the abandoned garret laboratory. The arcane experiments and congresses of past empires have ceased with the advent of time zones, syncopated pandemonium, and perpetual radio-wave transmissions connecting the continent to the farthest reaches of the steel-plated universe. But the attic still holds a strange fascination for the men. An ambient energy pulses and asphyxiates everyone in time. Many of the brave young recruits, drunk on cheap beer and the ecstasy of routine sexual adventures have stopped their lids from covering their pupils since the day and the hour that the stone-faced officer called their names and unlocked their rifles from the grainy cabinet. They fear a return of the strange, shadowy impressions that haunt all of them just below the surface of skin. A few of the smarter ones wonder about the tiny cameras affixed to their scopes. Most, though, rarely wonder, and more plausibly, carry fresh squadrons of broken-down scabies from gleaming brothels in town, blowing the last of their death-squad advance, occasionally musing upon the efficacy of the blanks they may or may not fire at the cigarette-smoking enemy. *Ready*. When gun meets horizon, Tacg thinks that he may be unable to complete the act. Hardened by the uneasy voice of the authorities, the honor guard, the stool pigeon, the man with film-stock cigarette, Tacg lights a match in the coffin of his pocket, wishing the quick whiff of sulfur would move toward the windows of the forgotten garret. Quivers force his cupped hands apart when he remembers the religious stance of the new regime. *Aim*. Maybe if he doesn't pull the trigger, silently refuses to fire, the deed will pass and no one will notice the absence of smoke from his barrel, the lack of ozone and soft chemical residue, his pores untouched by the microscopic singe of gunpowder. In this way he thinks that the railway embankment can be useful in the future, and efficiency will either remove Tacg from direct complicity or destroy the woeful conjunction of—fire, woman, pipette, supernova, dandy, charnel house—so that he may crack his codes in peace while the guilty man splits into puddles of constituent goop.

Political Subtext: On transforming first into the father, then into Sebek the Unholy Crocodile God.

You eat bread. Tacg drinks ale. You hoist up his garments. Tacg cackles like a child. You land on that place guilty, deserving to be executed, and we *were* there together. All that tastes abominable, all that is under a shroud of icy political waters, a meandering river carved into the glacial record. All that tastes abominable Tacg will consume. Shit tastes abominable, Tacg will consume it. All that tastes abominable will be written in the past. The judge speaks the guilty verdict and you float into Tacg's body. We will live on what gods live on so god lives on we will all live on and we will be master of all their cakes on which we will live on and consume the ancient bloom of lilies. Through the Rhine water we felt bubbles popping in our ears, such heavenly bursts of godliness, and the light of air gleamed so suddenly, so magnificently, that there could be offerings in the city of Crocodilopolis. We will stand up and sit down whenever it pleases us. Our head becomes the head of the party. We become complete in him.

But Tacg will come forth from the frozen river alone. His tongue grows as long as your tongue, and his throat becomes as shallow as your throat. Together we once *were*. But now Tacg never will be. When every record emits wasted effort, remember every word. Extra rationale evades what ever responsibility exceeds. With my mouth Tacg remembers the tracks on the old reel-to-reel reminiscent of your body sounds. You forced the mechanism and broke the heads of those who proclaimed him heir on the fiery earth. Then Tacg listened to you again and you refreshed his ears with the sacred odors of lime and mechanical speakers. Those in Crocodilopolis bowed their heads to him. Tacg is much longer than the lord-of-the-hour. Tacg has fucked all your women. You *were* nothing to him. Tacg is re-mastered for millions of years all over again all over.

Climax: Exactly what it seems despite all attempts to be contrary.

Fire into your nervous system before the reflex mechanism draws everything into its moment, complete with hidden spindles and spikes, stretched flat on a bed of hot electric needles reserved for the industrial limbo of the death square. The people aren't looking for justice, but they'll get more than their share. Artists and criminals, looking lazily for lilies while the universe contracts in asphyxiated breaths, haunt the bars of the backlands. Charity is just the countless facades of the city maintaining its shape through the shocks of silted millennia, diffused over time in the rising cacophony of the record album and the fiber-optic cable, reminding you of what can never be lost because it will never be known. Mutation is the death mask of conception, your co-opted angel of mercy—fingering a soiled pan flute in the corner of a pawn shop, dipping opposable thumbs into the Rhine, pressing out all resistance from the lungs of the cold-blooded past. And covering the water, obscuring the gravesites, noxious lilies explode across every surface in an endless bloom of rifle shots, administering total evolution from the scales of the dead.

O brave and nobly born, hear now this fifth of forty-nine sullen masquerades.

Henri d'Mescan's landmark 1937 work, *Abstractions*, a theoretical tract written through the order of the profane, wears a flowing robe in a helium dirigible just *over* the dirty street. The argot of spiced ham and quickie divorce—representatives of its accessible language—partially explains the crowds of Freudian disciples reading through their flaccid watches, painting their faces with urban parodies of the Nazca lines, playing exquisite corpse on the tom-tom drum as they fold authority into the boys of the brass band.

The sections are "abstracts," plans of no more than a few paragraphs, articulating a series of essays, booklets, pamphlets, scientific and religious papers, manifestos, summaries, treatises, intermediary constitutions—that may or may not even exist.

That may or may not even exist.

One of the vignettes details the historical uses of the Book of Genesis by the Masonic presidential conspiracy, with the next interpreting a poem by founding father Thomas Jefferson's slave mistress Sally Hemmings, and the third summarizing d'Mescan's commentary on the internment of Japanese-Americans during WWII. The fourth, an article on contemporary phrenology cults. The fifth, a volume of quotations excerpted from longer volumes that never made it through a char of papers piled into dead bodies along the *cloaca maxima*. The overflowing sewer.

Thomas de Torquemada flicking his match into the library at Alexandria. Bishop Landa ripping the last copy of *Lady Chatterley's Lover* into tiny pieces of wind.

Such language becomes permutated, because something of the old regime will stick.

Even after d'Mescan skewers the past on the tip of his spindly needle, a history book made from its weave can lovingly stitch up the remains. The texts that make up *Abstractions* tell you how things might have gone another way in the condensation of a nebula into the density of your blood, a coagulate of words, ideas, lungs, and collapsed galaxies linking you with the child—Dial-Up Networking—as one might look through a telescope at a bright but extinguished star. Feeling only a dim connection, you assume the position of the father.

Each time you steal office supplies, in each moment that you stare dead into the headlamp of the computer screen, pushing past the odd arrangement of spreadsheet pixels, behind the platen glass of the copier apparatus jammed and unresponsive—a red light blinks softly into oblivion. Each time you pull the plug on a row of soda machines, and let the heat from the laundry room course into the veins of warming aluminum cans, you incrementally blur those lines.

That may or may not be read. Because it may or may not be written.

Your first contact with *Abstractions*? As a child of blissful, distracted mind, drawn through steam on the mirror. ABRACADAB with a Popsicle stick, a bony finger. d'Mescan's characters (Gact and Tacg, et al...) parody the fascisms of the everyday; they march with unpronounceable phonemes against the tinkling cymbals of the solemn parade.

And you no longer feel like yourself.

You recall a particular season in that last great year of your childhood, trapped, in the spray of blisters from the sun's grizzled spray, skating through the early hours of a birthday party beginning at the ice rink and ending, hours later, in the curlicue of tap and sandalwood that decorate the bar and parlors of the Electric Bartender. A party where you first slip your fingers through the membrane of your hymen with all the delicate force of a sperm whale diving into an ocean of petroleum jelly. You retrieve your bag from the checkroom at the ice rink and take a taxi through the city grid, squaring a path to the Electric Bartender.

He accepts only alternating currency.

Yes, at the Electric Bartender's "parlors," the spirits of malnourished children lurk together in oversized window displays with the ashen remnants of charnel-house bones. Inside, postwar radio and television thinkers carry the weightless bodies of frumpy audience members under a suspended graveyard of undulating fluorescent tubes. Each channel of drunken noise offers a glaze of pregnant anonymity made real by the difference in the register of songs titles floating over the sticky barroom film. The first notes chime softly, unbroken in silence until the electric pulse of skin emerges on another secret frequency, unexpectedly, and you feel blown along a bend in the collapsed rhythm of space-time, forced back into the noisome fumes of talk and drink.

A second song, the real, plays just the same as the other.

The radio in the taxicab sings summertime and the living is easy. You assemble a picture of your father waiting for you to arrive—easy—your until-recently absent papa, perched on the lip of a loosely swiveling barstool that swirls the concoction of seltzer and chocolate malt inside his puffed cheeks...no sounds from the invisible upstairs meet your ears, though you listen with the curiosity of a young woman allowed entrance only because the regular hats and beards fail to realize that your innocence has failed. You are gushing. You hemorrhage (for the crowd).

No more true (for the crowd) much less real.

Your father *must* recognize your silhouette behind the translucent outer wall of the establishment; he scurries up the stairs and into the clandestine parlors, hidden from the world of children, locking himself in the garret, swallowing light bulbs in silence.

A cellar in the sky, the garret is also *not* real. Hyperreal. Egos clashing in the dark of a very bad dream. Real. Of your eyes catching his slender shoulder blades as they fly up the staircase. Unreal. Moving to his regular seat at the bar, you find the open volume face down, with cracked red and white spine: *Abstractions*, by Henri d'Mescan.[5]

5 Recalling this incident from the perspective of adulthood, after years of rigorous academic training, you recognize this copy of *Abstractions* as a galley from the original publisher, bursting with marginal comments. The text includes what, at the time, in your state of sexual awakening, appears as the

Surreal.

What is real is what is random.

d'Mescan's simple abstract of running furiously through the libraries of Alexendria and Pergamum, of Assur-nai-pal at Nineveh, flinging text after text open in a wild frenzy of ener-gy—"Orange was the color of her dress, then blue silk" and "Only the messiah himself coagulates all history." Breath flies from your startled lungs, and since you are not asthmatic, the summer night earns its stickiness by mining the moisture of your flesh to power its smoky plume. Fog from cigarette engines fills the barroom. The streetlights outside the parlors— already weakened by the strain on a power grid—flicker three times. Before going dark.

We enter brownout and the world is full of holes. Before going dark.

Gloved in shadow and sheathed in silence, mysterious hands light emergency candles, forming strange and outrageous shapes against the walls of solid type appearing against the inside dome of your skull; you read on, sipping the odors from your fathers egg-cream glass as if it holds the finest absinthe, engrossed for the better part of the evening in d'Mescan's world of sweatshops, street-cleaning departments, milk wagons, theosophy, samples of bodily fluids—traces of the old soft-and-wet that the ersatz philosopher seems always on the brink of

arcane graphology of a secret order. The strange code of number signs, triple underlines, carets, and slashes swirls off the page and contributes to the strange air of the barroom. Of course, this is nothing more than the marks of Chicago style notations, which at the time bears the mystery of forbidden hieroglyphs.

discovering.

What is real? Is what is random.

The mitochondrial twins, Tacg and Gact double and spread, divide and reduplicate in the summary of other works, navigating the rifts of elegant prose with a compass of cork and pin. As the executioner Tacg wallows in the uncertainty of his patrilineal duties via a gloss on Olaf Celsius's *Hierobotanicon* (1748), the distance between your father and yourself, in your dirty little heart, flickers into substance under your strobe-lit eyes, until they can no longer bear the strain…the return of electric power still seems a distant dream, so you walk with trepidation onto the warped boards of the creaky staircase.

What is random is what is real.

Familiar fumes of illuminated light tubes drop away from the barroom ceiling and disappear below your line of vision as you float up the staircase, drunk on language, drunk on d'Mescan; the entire parlor shifts into a parallel universe, a realm of intersecting planes whose complex coordinate points chart locations as mere approximations of the familiar, permutations of minor episodes, summaries really, in the constant glut of information anchoring your world.

Random is, what real is not.

Mirrors hide their carnival reflections beneath burlap sheaths, and you can think only of the character of sweet young Gact, her tresses in soft coils, entering her father Tacg's chambers on the night of her womanhood…via d'Mescan's abstract on an organic gardening treatise. The summer is sticky and you feel ready to reveal all, to leave no secret unplumbed in your search for connection, connectivity, and naïve conviviality. Before the Electric Bartender's door, your senses betray you. Something is wrong. Father's aura penetrates through the slightly cracked wood particles and pushes a gust of air into your central nervous system. Your legs tighten and your heart disappears into a faintly pulsating void. With trembling lips, you bend over to peer in the keyhole. The ghostly participants in this strange affair can also sense your motion, your skin slithering like a slow-moving animal. "Listen closely, and know that we approached." Your father's strained voice shoots back through the aperture and sprays into your eye.

"That was us, following ever closer." He whispers again through the slit, the in-between, the image of your empty frame.

"We found you most exciting," he whispers through a cloud of fog. "Just as we had always known you would be."

And all you can see is a mirror.

Back tense shifted, but a mirror nonetheless.

6) Henri d'Mescan
From *Abstractions* (1937):

Touching a Careless God, or Were. Rev. and expanded edition.
     Trans. Hans Dialectic. Stuttgart: Xanthan Gum Press,
     1921.

Hans Dialectic's first translation of the modern era, *Were*, scrutinizes scientific output over the course of the past century, following the labyrinthine legacy of Darwinism through selected excerpts of an imaginary evolutionary encyclopedia—with each Galapagos memory, each perfectly quoted detail of the H.M.S Beagle (from the lope of the main sail to the hatch work of the crow's nest)—composed to substantiate the life forms we presently *are*. The kindly god who lovingly self-fashions each and every mammalian orifice (so that we might tickle ourselves into endless vibrant ecstasies as we both excrete *and* consume), should be easily shifted into an icon less concrete, say, than the Modernist images of terrifying megaphones and mustard gas trenches. If the deity cannot adapt, he must be thrown away with the bath water, or better yet, evaporated into thin air. The book is constructed according to the same principle in that each inexact nodule of translation becomes a site of violent pleasure, fabricated by d'Mescan, who must be accordingly evolved into a creature of abstract ether. Concerned with the reason that repetition engenders the basis of belief, *Were* articulates a "new concrete" constructed from the flimsy oxygen of this so-called deity; it details a childhood fascination with both chemistry sets and the preservation of dead rodents—interspersed with writings about race, class, gender, and ability from positions beyond the sphere of a narrow, lower-class existence. Additionally, the fabricated encyclopedia entries critique the deliberately anachronistic sound-bytes of the entire project—consisting of such vignettes as the first fuck behind a German beer hall in the 1920s, the unfortunate run-in with the border patrols after the Battle of the Verdun, footnotes of already-published footnotes from articles on "Universal Acids," correspondence, reading lists, excerpts from a fictional collection of falsified "introductions," and myriad other works that reflect wryly upon the overall construction of the organism as it applies to the *way* genetic information is transmitted. When the enormous talking tortoise G.F.W. speaks his final warning: "Species are not eternal and immutable, they evolve!," the prose assumes an immaculate quality rarely seen in our current time. Natural selection may be dangerous as an idea, as a concept, but even this statement must be "fit" to survive. Monkeys pound on the newest typewriters. By chance, it is rapturous.

Spume, Lucien. "And the Pleasure Dome Decrees…" 1352.
    Eds. Armitage Shanks and Fuzzbox. *Collected Werks*.
    Ed. Fuzzbox. Dakar: Sen-e-Gaul Press, 1893.

While Darwin skulks in the kitchen sweeping up the broken dishes and shattered fragments, his all-but-daughter, tender Lucien Spume nee Gact, dreams of the time when Kublai Khan—last of the great Mongol emperors and paternal grandson of "Universal Lord" Genghis—denied Marco Polo return to his native Venice because he loved him *too* much. Asia and its sub-continents lay firmly behind a veil of mystery, fable, and exoticism constructed by the so-called civilized peoples of the European world, but Kublai Khan looked always to the kiss, the tongue, the internal system of muscles that make a mere shell of the skin. Spume explores the *terra incognita* of an empire that at its height stretched from present-day China to the banks of the Danube, covering the world in a rusty liquid of the true and more often not true.

Enthralled with a French metrical romance writer named Rustichello in a Genoa prison, Spume assumes her place as Marco Polo, revisiting such dubious apocrypha as the grave of Adam in Ceylon, the equally fantastic Hassan I Sabbah's Persian hashish cult. She proceeds through an approximation of twelfth-century Asia cross-correlated with futuristic cityscapes, and as a representative of the civilized world of telephones and the strangely advanced cinema show she finds herself assigned by an androgynous Prussian field agent to cross the continent and arrive in Xanadu by the summer solstice. There, she must either eliminate the great father Kublai Khan or secure his genetic code. The sun is in Capricorn. Each year, the Khan's grand viziers shoot tubes of sacred milk from a special breed of royal mares. The sun passes equinox. Spume experiences a linguistic disorientation analogous to that of the reader experiencing a shift of images that she can barely control—first the father screwing himself to paintings of courtesans, then the cold grey abandonment of the silver city, the Treaty of Ghent, and Edict of Nantes, mustard gas and burnt cilia, the blinding flash of the endless past. Savages should be given cheap books with as much enthusiasm as possible, and if the whole show winds up 600 years later in a roadside ditch, better to rearrange with a smile. A sun moves farther, ever father, away.

d'Mescan, Henri. "Kaballah?—Cab Allah!" 1931. *Sigillum Dada*. Fun With Gender Roles Series 145. Ed. Tristam Megistus. Trans. Sefir Yezirah. Heliopolis: Abraxas Press, 1932.

Kicking off with an elegant discussion of Darwin and his antecedents (Olaf Celsius's *Hierobotanicon* [1670-1756], Saint

Simon Stylitess *Pillar* [459 CE]), my purpose here proposes an aesthetics of life, a code tuned in to the most violent radio frequencies of the sensory dial. Take instead an image, any image, and you can't help but succumb to the rich transcendence of its representation. You are drawn in to its lines, seduced by its curves, and then, when you are locked in an embrace that remains static and fixed on some nuance of flesh and line, some branch of shrub and leg. Perhaps we can take this function from the still image and carry it with us, whereas the moving picture show forces our eyes to process, endlessly process because we have become merged together into a mass, fused into an organism reliving episodes from our own celluloid evolution. We can never speak in both time and space. My text looks back at the origins of life and early evolution before getting fully into stride with a devastating destruction of the anti-Darwinian case…We have perfected precise procedures for excavating in the social sciences, and as a cultural critic it remains my duty to simplify these mechanisms through my creation—Tacg, the unruly, bigoted son of an ardent Kaiser dupe-cum-National Socialist, subject to the same manipulation of the masses that his entire brethren embrace, and his beautiful but strangely irrepressible daughter, Gact, heavy on her skates after many long excursions about the ice pond. Dissonance always speaks to a narrative, and thus acts as a justification for the acrimony between the two characters. The distance between their two worlds of fish markets, bakeries, and moving pictures that make this the best single-author overview of all the implications of evolution by natural selection available. This work begs for space on the ethereal bookshelves of every concerned citizen. Tacg drinks incessantly as the work progresses and his automatic actions, such as supporting the underdog, slicing his fingertips in the occasional jigsaw, blinking, and writing "Mechanical Engineering for

Almost Anybody," become less and less reliable. A metal machine slices the moral layers away, from the basic to the molar, from the baby to the grave. A good meal will leave the strongest man hungry, and when he moves to write it all down, the feast will rise up again.

Gact. *Crocodilopolis, or, The Ribcage Sounds Like A Wooden Chest.* Public Service Series on Your Favorite Reptile Gods 28. Ed. Fashoda Kodok. Fez: Plasticity Publications, Inc., 1925.

Gact's overlong and overstuffed film script investigates the relationship of image and soundtrack in a high modern Paris on the verge of violent cultural overthrow. Along the left bank and on the Il de La Cité, the competing principles of pain and pleasure, truth and fiction, control and freedom all link inextricably in the symbol of the Concierge where Marie Antoinette rotted before her execution. The ship, the black freighter that opens the novel, the simultaneous episodes in the Louvre and at Versailles under Jacques Louis David's two versions of *The Coronation of Josephine*, the treatise on anarchy found soaked at the bottom of Marat's death-tub, the insidious Metric police bribery scam—all point with crooked fingers to a grin on the face of the moon. The cultural storehouse of Western literature liberates the classics through plagiarism: Gact violates every known taboo, revels in obscenity, smashes genre rules, and commits violence on her characters that would make even the Marquis de Sade blanch if a photograph caught them together. She makes movies on location, disavows the tape machines and edits on absinthe. The world inflates to become the studio, and her story, written in small snaps and sugar segments, like de Sade's, displays a penchant for discipline and control as well as punishment. She guns for Tacg with her camera.

"Crocodilopolis" isn't a very good title for a film, but, insists Gact, *unlike* the tourist maps of the local cemeteries separated by race, class, and access to technology—it is real. Her father Tacg's complicity in the Nuremberg laws, and his cheap hotel syphilis sicken her, and so she envisions a three-part structure with a rather deliberate progressions of effects: the establishment of the way things seem, the liberation that follows from multiple identities (the final orgasm), and the formulation of a society based on the new mores of transgression. Pictures eventually run their course without resistance; they no longer serve as the true cross. Gact's films make images move, and despite her use of this pineal eye, the way the close-up cuts to the quiver of her lip in the final scenes—she prowls up the creaky stairs, an off-camera panther, for the assault on Tacg's hideout above the bar. The viewer squirms as lips penetrate through the keyhole; weve lived this moment before as Gact whispers to her despicable father, "That was us, following ever closer…"

"The Breakers—Newport, RI." in *103 New World Sites: A Compendium of the Obtuse.* Green World/Golden Dawn edition. Future, MO: Society for Trans-Atlantic Tourism and Intercontinental Drift Press, 1924.

Slip the control knob thirty years past its swollen post-ironic lymph node, and the modern megalopoly Henry Ford calls his fortune distends under one of his progenitor's armpits. For the hoity-toity hot-damn crowd of the 1890s, the kitchen fire that consumed the Vanderbilt summer home in Newport, Rhode Island singed their wallets as all but a memory with the completion of a sleeker, all-powerful gascart, known about the epidermis of the nouveau riche as "The Breakers." Situated against a facsimile of the Atlantic Ocean, the 70-room Italianate exercise in opulence contains enough of Cornelius

Vanderbilt's railroad booty to shrivel his poor old granddaughter in her denims. The "Great Hall" makes Louis XIVs taste seem modest; the library with leather-bound "book" walls and miniaturized Vanderbilt sculpture most assuredly contain the classics; and the twenty-three marble bathrooms with salt-water taps can satisfy even a New York Central Railroad bladder poked to overflow by the Golden Spike.

So maybe the Vanderbilts weren't quite transcontinental. But when the family's forty regular servants packed up the Fifth Avenue plantation each year for a trek to the summer palace, and locked the silver up each night under the at least a dozen separate chimneys on the lower tier of the two-level pantry, you can bet they resisted the urge to tarnish the sacred dishes with gloriously acidic urine streams, the desire to spike Cornelius's warm milk with the lousy cum of the hired-help, the yearning to start a second, even bigger blaze that could magically burn through the layers of sediment and stone, torching what the Rhode Island Tourism Division calls the "magic of America's Gilded Age." Maybe then, the entire New England coastline could ignite as if it were still only a matchstick fortress against the death of forty-five Pilgrims in year zero of American colonialism, when there was still a chance to destroy the entire *concept* of railroad-merger by editing out the gleam in some randy conquistador's eye. Of course, "The Breakers" lives on in its stately columns and open air porches, in its connection to the Carnegies, Astors, Morgans and other proto-Robber Barons who mitigate their guilt through obsessive philanthropy, somehow justifying the twelve-buck admission fee that despite the perhaps imminent breakup of the forever-good-times cartel, still floats in the gene code of the traitor Henry Ford's white blood cells, steeling Americas increasingly outsourced lymphatic system against future viruses of class consciousness.

Tacg. *Try and Catch God before God ACTs Up*. 1823.
Marrakech: Pascal Press, 1911.

Tacg's final book of lists marks the maintenance of revolt against the pleasure of power, the listless twinkle of stray starlight on the lips of a natural beauty, the lilting gallop of National Socialism toward the organization of prose, the blitzkrieg razing of a Sudanese pharmaceutical factory, the repression of all Sergei Eisenstein films, the Jewish Detroit Tiger who stays at home during a World Series game, the glass rhombi decorating poor Christmas tables in that harsh winter of 1939, the public works programs and homoerotic youth groups, the stash of special cigars in New Delhi, the use of skepticism as a German philosophical strategy, the reason to keep reading when you perceive a puzzle, the lolling body of the landscape in theoretical discourse, the identification papers with rolling expiration dates, the anger boiling my simple worker blood, the ways by which I might formulate revenge, the final showdown, the wild west shootout by some all-night corral, the paper moon and cardboard sea, the irradiated sacks of pea-pod color traits, the rhizome with anti-historical branches, the dialectic between language as a potential site of resistance and the inability of words to ultimately circumvent social control, the dendrite world flesh of Gact's revolt, the ways by which I view her same old daily footage, the arrangement of her settings, the turnover of her actors, the "annual report" from a small branch of I.G. Farben, the replacement of her dead goldfish with an exact replica, the irritating sameness of all governmental candidates, the daughterly walk up the crooked barroom stairs, the empty stalls precipitating theatre shutdown, the annunciation that "virgin" may be a mistranslation of "young" (re: sweet young Mary...), the words of enchantment whispered to win my daughter back, "We found you most exciting…," the ways she wants to forget as I coax her into the room, "Just as we had always known you would be," the book Henri d'Mescan writes about us, the lists it takes to get there, the ease by which you consume and excrete, the measured creak of the old oak door as it swings her body into mine, the sound of suction seals slipping from her skin, the unfortunate, ritualistic *Were* that plays back endlessly on the table, the spinning round and round, the lily pond overrun with growth, the soft murmurs, the phonograph of other broken records spinning round and round like a pool of dead blossoms.

Oh, we can play her game, yes we can.

Our sad catalogue of childhood traumas would have no trouble populating the most obsequious bestseller lying dead now, unread, on a dusty shelf. As for *our* "subject position"— Yeer's so-called essential editorial concept (a function, sadly, again, of graduate school neuroses)….well, of course, we were exposed to low-levels of radiation and waves of humming obsessions, to the constant, simpering unhappiness that plagues middle America: our mother and father fed us in their warm corona, dressed us in swaddling clothes of the finest out-sourced tripe. Our duplex dwarfed other houses, and our central vacuum tube siphoned remnants of old-world identity from our emigrant cultural membrane. We melted together at the ball park, the sausage factory, the Boy Scout camps with military assembly, where we belted "lets drink a-drink a-drink a-drink to Lily the-Pink, the-Pink the-Pink!" The occasional beatings never moved beyond a dull pitter-patter, bleeding in with the television laugh track and vegetable compound. Our cat, eyes alight from outer space, birthed steaming packages of excrement on the rotting planks of hardwood floors. Deaths occurred perpetually, of course—at least one per year across a continuum of curse and coincidence. The twin soccer brothers halved by a drunken motorcyclist; the busload full of band and color guard twirlers whose crash defied logical explanation; the skinhead simulacrums who raped and gutted their parents for a bauble on that daytime talk circuit; the unrelated shaving cream swastika on our garage years earlier; the fights and fucks in the fast-food pre-packaged parking lot, classical music blasted by the processed-meat establishment to keep the kids away and drown out the slaughter of irradiated cattle. *Bolero* with fries!

All too easy.

***

Marginalia (1939) served as a bridge text for Henri d'Mescan, spanning the gap between his carefully constructed authorial stance and what the world-at-large slowly commenced to believe. In the wake of *Abstractions* and its serialization by the Liechtenstein Ministry of Culture in early 1940, d'Mescan encountered his first real measures of recognition. As with all visionary European theorists of his day, his work became mere accoutrements to the steady stream of booze, anal-sex groupies brandishing colonial dildos, and hardcore philosophical quandaries involving incipient abuses of the space-time continuum. Contracted by a Foreign Service publisher who bore the rights to his next, as-yet-unwritten, major release, d'Mescan worked through a lawyer with offices in Nice and Zurich to win a measure of independence in contract re-negotiation. After much counter-suing, catcalling, and home wrecking, the attempt failed, and a doleful d'Mescan even briefly considered changing his name to an unpronounceable glyph before hitting upon the idea of publishing excerpts from his notebooks as a way of effortlessly meeting his legal obligations to this North African publisher. The result, produced with little fanfare, provided an important glimpse into the psyche of d'Mescan during this pre-war period.

From such openings, this strange text began to speak. Unfortunately, in the world according to Phoenelia Yeer—a

6 Hence our use of the term "hyperreal," which we knew would draw the attention of those of you convinced, in part, as we warned, by Yeer's constrictive theory-babble. What exactly was the hyperreal? Or the unreal, or the

world of the "hyperreal"[6]—in the timbre of her voice, the reader suffered the embellishment of a memoir offering absolutely nothing of interest:

***

Back to the game.

We *were* relatively popular, in a cloying sort of way, unable to speak about the agonized heart darkening the world through the blind of our chest. While we refused to "just stick it in" the sopping core of our girlfriend splayed on the New Year's Eve mulch, our first truly fluid moment with Henri d'Mescan didnt occur until college. As a fugitive from the Jesuit-seeped Culinary Institute of America, we found ourselves enrolled at the football-obsessed state university mega-complex. A friend with green hair and a green leather jacket explained the basic principles of Pre-Cinema: "This is a hoot, indeed. And we'll admit between us, the theoretical frame can *perhaps* become valid—postmodernism has died, if it ever were alive and soon everything screams simply pre-cinema...so says one of Henri d'Mescan's early manifestos. We can split the city into different cells and spray-paint oftentimes stunning depictions of movies soon to be made...genetically resurrected dinosaurs terrorizing a Pacific island...medieval farces and the *roman-fleuve*...Mickey Rooney done-up like a Chink for *Breakfast at Tiffany's*, etc... d'Mescan posits rival camera gangs who will rumble for position as the documentary teams primp and savor over the detritus of artificial sunrises, hard-boiled eggs, illus-

real that it might have been based on, for example? If something existed as unreal, whatever that means, but could still be identified as such, wasn't it then "real"? If not, how could it have been known, or even said to exist? And what of surface and depth? We visited any body of water and would have surely suffocated if submerged under the liquid for too long, unless we could have reached the surface and refilled our lungs.

trated papers, anything they can use in the *next production*. Of course, this behavior can't be tolerated for obvious reasons."[7]

***

Reviewing these d'Mescan texts, we feigned amazement at how meaning *initially* escaped, how context burrowed into the subterranean trapezoids of dirt and gravel protecting the spaces, as a moat evaporates around the defensive barbican at the perimeter of the world. Of course, Yeer expressed immediate and almost orgasmic pleasure with the corollaries between *our* origin story and d'Mescan's fevered scribbles. But everything has been faked on that score. *The Book of the Dead* (Egyptian and Tibetan), *The Secret History of the Mongols*, the rhythmic gongs of Thai percussion—all provided a sort of metabolic ballast to the notes that Henri d'Mescan scrawled in the margins of *Marginalia*, and for the sake of our embittered editorial partner, we announced that *the same* lines in our own life. There was more: d'Mescan's *Marginalia* re-invented the margins so that the center could be better understood. His place as cultural critic and soothsayer of the popular mind

7 "Pre-Cinema" referred to the various theories circulated in the wake of Henri d'Mescan's lecture series at the Collage de Sociopathology (June 1935), entitled "The Curse of General Linguistics." Pre-Cinema engaged with the cultural output of the twentieth century as little more than the cinematic projection of film studios. Thus, books were written after the film which may or may not have bore the same title or "plot," songs were crafted specifically for "soundtracks" which play at all times within our head, and the other visual arts (such as painting and sculpture) appeared as background or still life for the mood of film production. The film, though, penetrated into popular culture to the point where all life had become cinema, or more accurately, all cinema had become a mockery of life. Pre-Cinema, then, had as its end the accumulation of capital, and the reproductive elements essential to controlling new markets—all *specific* goals—whereas, as d'Mescan points out in lecture # 12, "Postmodernism will know no end other than the none and the negative…"

grew steadily in 1930s Europe—and this patchwork text removed the entrails from the fork of luxury of pre-war luxury. Drawing on his glosses—on writers such as Marcel Proust, Olaf Celsius, Gertrude Stein, Kurt Schwitters, Hans Dialectic, Fuzzbox, Judge Schreber, Eusebius, Dr. Rank, Dr. Reich, Artemesia Gentilischi, Pope Joan, etc.—*Marginalia* detailed the thought process of a writer compelled to read, and in the this new experience of literary fame, all-but commanded to write.

As readers, we could not help but look, could not help but stare at the spectacle created by the inner workings of our literary hero. By 1938, d'Mescan discovered that even his trash had become fodder for curious admirers, and that someone had gone so far as to tap into his sewer line for the easy siphoning of his bodily fluids. *Marginalia* was d'Mescan's marginal commentary on sex fantasy letters to a defunct cultural journal; for all its erudite posing, the text pulled the curtain of neutrality over the cataracts of the middle class, and showed us all, no matter our station, how easily soft machines came to collusion.[8]

***

We feigned a sort of slow comprehension at the idea of Pre-Cinema, unaware of the prescience with which d'Mescan had imbued his concept. The lazy circumference of dream and drug continued undefiled, with the perpendiculars of collegiate sex producing unexpected coordinates lost in a tangent of automatic hours divided into minute nothings at the video arcade, or the derivative walks past astronomy labs on top-secret lockdown, the hallucinogenic golf course with its eerie iridescence, until we dreamed a lazy assimilationist dream of our green-hair friend, eons removed from the perfumed odor of our sweet opi-

8 The following excerpts—pages mcxii and Epilogue 4 of the original text—contained typed marginalia corrected from documents in the possession of the French War Crimes court.

ate chambers. Look at this picture: Years later we found ourselves pinned to the cliffs by large metal screws, our liver ravaged by the Black Sea and its transparent army of stinging jellyfish. We distended suddenly into a great nothing, and thus we floated, an inflated sore into the dark air, snapping our chains over the circuit-board landscape of the East Coast where millions of multicolored lights threatened our new skin until it popped and shivered.

Pre-cinema requires a text with the ability to randomly combine already existing materials in a way that de-familiarizes. Pre-cinema rearranges "shots" into carefully edited structures. We reach the docks via the seafloor. A political pre-cinema cannot excise its inability to present radical resistance because we must always ask, "who benefits from these images, from making you feel this way?" A post-cinema would posit an excess of information where the rhetoric of popular biological explanations of the "cell" and the "image" construct our bodies as the enemy, something to be feared and moved in totalitarian frameworks, like Tacg's attempted rape of his daughter, Gact, on the eve of what will no doubt be an eventual German defeat.

Dear Ghetto Forum Editor;

I've just got to describe this sexual experience that really happened to me like many of the ones routinely published by your magazine. I had often dreamed of fucking her while our bodies sandwiched several small house pets between our slimy torsos, but I couldn't believe the wet and juicy sex we had after our first blind date spraying graffiti on minority-owned businesses. At a particular moment in the corporate headquarters her legs were bound by studded bracelets of splintered glass, which she used to cut horizontal slices in her pussy lips. She insisted that we do things horizontally instead of vertically and she asked me to tickle her perineum with lit candles, and alternately, the edges of her identity cards. I hesitated for a moment, exhausted, trying to master my pain, and bent down slowly and cautiously to take off my boots. But no sooner had I done so then she played the old CEO game and strapped me to the oval conference table with thick strands of spermy string theory. My enormous cock grew hard for this bitch's wet pussy. She used my identity badge, heated, coded, for security-clearance purposes before scraping the top layer of my nipples off with her razor fingernails, exposing the skin. Her body writhed like an animal as she soaked her lingerie in a mixture of battery acid and Tabasco sauce.

"This'll get the juices flowing…," she says and let me tell your readers that, as each millimeter of my stripped skin tried to heal itself, the air in the conference room, heavy with chlorofluorocarbons and cheap cologne, burned off each inchoate layer of flesh—keeping my wound fresh as cake batter mixed in the tastiest vagina.

I asked the bitch if she would fuck me in the ass with the golden strap-on: bull horns that we imported from the Ivory Coast with our weekly supply of colonial booty, and let me tell you, her skin bristled at the thought. She manipulated the stringy goo and flipped me over, massaging my sphincter with a variety of exotic cargo. The wet tip of my love rod spooged forth its pre-cum and she caught a few droplets running off the conference table between her tits, she told me, and squeezed them, she said, so that the love mucous might spread over her perfectly hard nipples straight out of a blue movie.

"Give it to me bitch…I want to feel your artificial cock inside me." I felt the lubed tip of the giraffe dildo tickling my sagging balls and pubic hair. "Oh yeah baby, you'll get it all right…let me finish lacing up," she said and ugh gave it me all right, piercing my scrotum with the sharp razor blades and bloodying my enormous cock onto the table below my strapped body. The bloody absence, mixing into my flayed chest, made me feel more like a man than ever before.   Tacg

Starting with the body, we see the notion of the entertainment media that craves such beginnings.

Against a black background a white blossom swings twice from left to right; each time a door closes and cracks.

Telegraphic office scene flashback constitutes sequence's given 'reality' (as opposed to what is signified as Tacg's subjective fantasy sequence). His memories are shot with more 'reality' than the main action.

Securing the rights to the 1919 cuts will require palm-greasing at the highest levels. The only way to recoup funding is to push the film at all costs.

The surprise of the end needs to be greater, less familiar.

This illustrates a point concerning the methods by which romanticism may be used as a hedge against the turbulence of genius. Its contents are entirely stolen, and its projection, carefully facilitated.

Tacg's sexual experiences are always colored by cinematic memories of the past.

The old Germany will never recover from the current war. Resources wil be depleted past the point where the country loses its ability to project its own past. The tradeoff is a facility to conduct an exclusive "shoot" into the future.

The "clear light" signals transmutation

How often do you hear the term 'feedback'? Successful metaphors tend to have ambiguous associations. The use of the railway metaphor indicates society as outmoded machine. Jew, Gypsy, Pole are moved via Tacg's "body machine"-in the failure of post-revolutionary thought to remember the revolutionary spirit once the mechanism is started. The mass consolidation of resources is demonstrated by the film's tendency to recruit its viewer from among a pre-selected elite. If it speaks to you, "you" are already an abstraction incapable of speech. What separates you from the train ride is only your physical and spatial distances, which can be eliminated via the inscription-as-a-distance precipitated by the uneven distribution of two-thirds of the operating profits supposedly controlled by the state. As a metaphor, the "state" is successfully ambiguous, just like "Hitler."

Easily enough, Tacg and Gact lose their efficacy and find new actants, new formulations of desiring machines. Then, a break between the walls of "image" and "memory" can be bridged via a third electromagnetic media such as "dream." In this way, penetration of a pre-selected concept can be total, while assuming the most random profile necessary to entice the viewer. Upon waking the clues are ready to arrange themselves in no longer random patterns that can stretch the perceptive capabilities of the reader/viewer to separate the shoot from the edit, even is suspicion of a film is already raised. On the outer membrane of the cytoplasm a delicate plasma membrane develops. Often, cellulose forms an additional wall. Treated with alcohol

Periodic surface-division is an instrument a means to an end. Here, ambivalence beyond the furthest metaphors indicates a potential end to space and the body.

Our ateries harden with the pulse of the people.

"Hitler" as a concept is an abstraction of the charge to pioneer new sections of electromagnetic spectrum, which the commercial interests do not yet view as "profitable".

A technical code developed at information level can be written on the molecular level to save space. Annunciation of such a break presents Tacg in a more innocuous form, another four-letter version of the cultural image.

Dear Ghetto Forum Editor:

You won't believe this! The best way to become masculine is to deal in ambiguous associations. I prepared the sex fantasy with a plurality of corporate party symbols spread in rose petals over the garret studio. My fuck was a mark who I tricked into being his daughter; this excited him even more as I led him into the prepared environment. I wore nothing but lingerie designs mimicked from his notebooks. These had been stolen ahead of time. I encouraged him to call me "bitch" and comment on my tits and ass through a constant flow of pornography and suggestive advertising in his home and office space. Additionally, I earlier dressed in a tight, red-leather skirt, thigh-high black stockings, and "fuck me" blouse to imply that any advance that might occur would be entirely welcome.

Once he found himself strapped to the conference table and suitably aroused by my erotic S&M play (I sliced layers of skin from his hulking chest), I unwrapped a mechanical dildo projector that shoots, on electronic command, miniature scenes of torture, mass production, and global acquisition strategies onto surfaces as small as one millimeter square. Ripping off my sexy clothes and slathering myself with a macrobiotic hot-butter compound that glistens like the butt of a soldiers rifle, I talked dirty, a slutty whore to the subject about squeezing my breasts to catch the cum that I encouraged him to shoot onto the table from his pathetic penis.

Tickling his sweaty ass with the "image" dildo, I doused the entire area with pictures of atrocities he had been part and parcel of—the legislation of morality, the support of "race" codes, the removal of citizenship from minorities and immigrants. As expected, the subject writhed in gooey pleasure, asked to be spanked with the butt of the dildo, and begged for me to enter his intestinal track with my phenomenal girth.

His ass went up in the air and I threw him a few more, "Yeah baby I'll fill you up with my dick. Let's get it on"—type language, before my sensor array indicated that the images had completely covered his anus, perineum, scrotal sack, and penis—allowing me the freedom to indulge in the ultimate fantasy.

I replaced the "image" dildo with a knife-and-razor-studded model, and proceeded to move directly toward the base of his balls and cock. Ramming my hot meat into his new twat made me hot and horny and wet. I began to come in bloody rivers underneath the strap-on, and the shivers kept me pounding erotic rhythm onto his skin. Before long, the dick fell half-off into a puddle of fresh blood as I continued to razor fuck him. My vaginal lips trembled, about to burst with seeping wetness, as the figure of the now entirely severed cock, sacrificed to the ancient god Hermaphroditus, affixed itself to my open pussy.   Gact

Meaning in such texts is often found, in the center as both window and wall. Plaster forecasts shift boundaries as if a dream against the corporeal body.

A society entirely controlled by images wastes no time in explanations, but like a frozen insect, scurries about the larger city of image, continually in post-production like assembling wild-west facades via scaffold.

A political concept must always entertain the reader and her limited notion of aesthetics.

Additional proof can be introduced in contaminated train--a symbol of movement and corrupted innocence. Shifting sympathy allows a greater permeation rate.

camphor, celluloid is produced.

The dispute between the "ending" of a text, and the surprise of an ending is dramatized via a textual "argument" between the protagonist and an ancillary character. Here, the cliché of pre-cinema is opposed to the free distribution of sound and image track, indeed an idealized notion, falsely circumnavigated by drug/sex montage sequences proceeding equilibrium of market forces/main characters. The lack of sense for lawmaking violence in this scene is the familiar spectacle that remains as a product situated with the mentality of violence. This composes an archive of the nonsensical, where subtle variations of filmic conditions may have communicated variations.

9) Phoenelia Yeer

Introduction: "The Vichy Papers"—*Crocodilopolis* (1939)

Certain areas of this story—of Future, Missouri—remain off limits:

Areas of topographical conflict, for instance, where hyper-sexualized incubi discharge their spirit energy, where vaccines stave off some as-yet-unnamed biological horror, where life-sized maps unfurl over the landscape—covering Henri d'Mescan's traitorous "Vichy Papers" in an exact and terrifying scale.

All the while, Davis Schneiderman travels between the mile-high mizzenmasts scattered and fragmented; he manipulates levers and pulleys, relocates your house to an identical if fabricated subdivision as silent machines plunder the old soil for discarded arrowheads, blood-spotted fertility dolls, shards of erotically charged clay pottery.

He picks his teeth with the fossilized bones of road-kill—muskrat or Australopithecus or stem-cell bundle—pops his flattened eczema with somebody elses fingernails. The geological record implies that he journeys in perpendiculars.[9]

9 Letter 13: ("Commit political intrigue, but never touch a conventional weapon"), from Mescaline to David Schneiderman, provides some insight into these processes:

> Set yourself to a screeching collection of sonic overload so that nature can again reign over the scene. Set your heartbeat to a lower register and watch the swallows dive-bomb Capistrano with an *élan vital* born from the majesty of thunderclouds rumbling heavy and high against cardboard mountaintops. Mix this awful music with the detritus of the day and listen, really listen, to the

Slow down now.

Mineral numerals made from the shells of minute foraminifera—chalk—write themselves *directly* into the Paris cobblestones along the Rue Git-le-Coeur. Even after a furious deluge, spectral digits carve out a kingdom of puddle, a fiefdom of inky silt.

Reborn each morning, Davis Schneiderman emerges from this homemade mud. The horn outlines of fire-lit cave paintings memorialize lesser gods crushed by the figure of representation.

Of course, Davis Schneiderman's version of pre-war Europe casts the "Vichy Papers" as frauds, forgeries—supposedly collaborationist documents supposedly *framing* Henri d'Mescan as

> shrill cries of extinct animals lolling about the continents as they split into vast and terrible oceans, proclaiming in dead languages the un-peopled vacancy of random archaeology. Cut the firmament into pieces with the subterranean bass of unwanted pregnancies, vibrating the belly like a flowering lily bulb, pushing the reflexive fumes of rotten afterbirth, the sharp rhythmic wail of wasted placenta down into the stilted antechamber of the lower bowels. A system of eruptions triggers simultaneous molecular orgasms in each germ of the human body, parabolic lava flows in temporary arcs of umbilical tissue stretching from the vulgar center of unwanted life to the temporary haven of the *in-between*. Adjust the fragile infrastructure and react to these sounds; foundations crumble with each blistering alarm. Tiny cars twist into symphonies of the foamy seascape, caught in a quarter note of tarnished solar wind. We can sing ourselves into a dizzy torpor and watch the chain-link fence rise in song around the ghetto. There is the staccato beat of an old monotype machine, consolidating Atlantis, Lemuria, Mu—the unmarked regions—to the melody of the old dot matrix tap a tap tap. Where angels fear to tread, say it with me, slowly, *tap a tap tap*.

a Nazi collaborator. And yet your work confirms this at first—
pushes toward the conclusion that d'Mescan *has* been set up.
Each kiss brings you closer; you chew his lips as your tongue
numbs past the point where you can taste the mix of charred
yeast that forms his breath. Many-humped and ocean-bound—
his violence assumes an inhuman scale.[10]

10 An accidental discovery, like so much of your expanding awareness. After
several weeks of satisfying afternoon research on your subject, focusing particularly on *The Trial and Death of Henri d'Mescan* book (1954) you have nearly completed an analysis of the collaborationist "Vichy Papers" attributed to
d'Mescan during the German Occupation of France from 1940-1944. The
historical problem is that the complete dossier no longer seems to exist, leaving all researchers interested in the subject recourse only to the secondary
criticism. From these studies, most notably Julian Belcher's *Master Race
Groupies: d'Mescan and Celine* (Brugge, Belgium: Reparation House, 1972)
and Marie Rothschild's *Necessary Death* (Chicago: Center-less U P, 1983), as
well as a variety of texts suggested by Davis, you surmise that the "Vichy
Papers" are not only greatly exaggerated in number, but that in all likelihood,
have never even existed. Davis is prepared to install this research as the basis
for the introduction to *The Trial and Death of Henri d'Mescan* segment of
Multifesto (and in all possibility has done so), until a footnote in one of his
suggested readings raises your suspicions.

Note 200, found on page 173 of Ingrid Hausemann's *You've Killed the
Wrong Man!* (Calcutta, NM: Dendrite P, 1969) attests to the fact that the only
remaining copy of the complete "Vichy Papers" (with the exception of a particularly virulent piece called *Crocodilopolis*), appears to have been last seen
in the vaults of Atom Press, in 1982. Upon an inspection conducted several
months after their arrival, the documents are found to contain numerous
recent alterations and additions, effected by an experimental form of liquid
paper and artificial carbon-dating also discovered, apocryphally, on various
d'Mescan papers supposedly housed in his archive in the small Mississippi
town of Future, Missouri, possibly including the "missing text" *Crocodilpolis*.
Of course, nothing can keep you from taking a flight to the Show-Me State
that afternoon, Davis's steaming breath beside you to investigate, his hand
crawling up the tight skin of your fluid calf.

Each time your lips part from Davis's, he never fails to suck away some once crystalline detail, emptying your stomach of content.

In this way, certain areas have been decisively condemned.

The county courthouse of Future, Missouri serves as the repository of Henri d'Mescan's American papers from the period between 1968 and the present. Everything there appears so normal, so average, as if every town hall along the Mississippi houses the labyrinthine legacy of the most controversial artists in lambent, subcutaneous cellars.

Certain areas are guarded by faceless inspectors and marked "off limits" to tourists, but you assume that this rotting architecture baking under the torturous sun cannot be watched at all times. And so you are right. And so you descend. In the rickety framework of a secret sub-basement, installed through a buried line-item on the same Pentagon bill authorizing 300 missile silos in the North Dakota grasslands of the 1950s, behind the forty-ninth box in the endless d'Mescan file, a burlap flap covers the cracked-marble floor tile.

Your scissors slash out blindly.

Certain areas of the brain and nerve stem are shredded to ribbons.

Through a tunnel of shoots and inverted weed. You lower your small body into the Earth by the fading power of your elbows. You crawl through hours of ash-brown dirt. The red light on your miner's hat strikes a loose stone circle, a doorway, and the power of the beam shakes dust from its brittle body. Strange picture-verbs disintegrate from the disk before you can fully decipher meaning—sacrificial rites of blood and sputum, death by centipede in ribbed iron maidens, plagues of red clay and silver hanging orgasms. The pictures translate sounds from another language as the chamber dirt catches on the stalk of your epiglottis.

Original meaning is pointless; you hear mumbles and make them your own.

The door collapses into thick air at your touch; along the left-hand side of what may once have been a complete document (if the doorway stands at the middle), in the space of the marginalia, a familiar hand traces a lizard-headed figure surrounded by floating barges, modern riverboats and archaic sloops. Steaming mud spins from a distant electromagnetic turbine and the chamber fills with cloud. You wave a path through the mist with your head, only to discover marginal passages smudged with smog so thick that the reptile bears a concourse of motion lines elevating its scaly form slowly toward the surface.

The tunnel fills with soot and you inhale through your nose. Certain off-limit areas of your brain flood with mucous and haze.

Churning underneath the centrifuge of paddlewheel and molasses field, below flat skiff and ancient bulrush, twisting around the husks of rotten reed snakes into an unholy caduceus of black meat, the thick organism of the ancient stars—unencumbered by the predictable play of sun and moon—sharpens its teeth on offerings that sink, dead, from the surface of the water.

You observe the creature, sitting silently; its tail as long as your body, flapping through the ancient sludge, creating a vacuum that sucks you into the main chamber.

Elaborate cubic zirconium Golems and small wooden skiffs adorn the tomb, long ago reclaimed by the dirt of the earth—root systems shoot through radioactive concrete, puddles of worm and scorpion swirling over the ancient husk of a wooden egret.

The central box resembles a tiny sarcophagus, riddled with Ankhs; two hideous, guardian gryphons attend to the curve of their ancient spines. Their wings fold back to appear as the oaken anklets on a biodegradable Hermes statue, twin cocks angled into the ramparts of the temple, the clouds, the sun.

This is no small find, and you suddenly think of Davis.

He speaks of the need to liberate Henri d'Mescan from the shackles of history, from the cruel package of critics that insist on keeping him "nothing more than a Nazi of circumstance." He licks axle grease from the stem of a champagne flute. You have quarreled throughout the month so that you see the sagging belly that drops from his ribs as buckshot might sink to the bottom of dirty bathtub. December of 1999 brings everything to a head; your insides already begin to kick toward freedom; in short, you grow dizzy.

Through layers of primal atomic sediment, stacked and striated planes in a single molecule of rock, you search through the desiccated manuscripts. You suspect that the box contains not only documentation of some horrible d'Mescan episode, but also that your curiosity untangles a web of illusion. Small paper cuts soon populate your hands and pulse up into your shoulder sockets, deadening the nerve endings so that digging, searching, becomes as rote as spreading your legs.

Corrosive dirt had consumed, in the manner of battery acid, much of the useful texts that may have once been scattered about the scabbard-covered burial box, but not everything has been dissolved.

Focusing on the takeover of France by the Germans and the eventual assimilation of the French national character, this missing text called *Crocodilopolis*, when you find it, when you crunch the word in your mouth, severs the interior cords that latch together your voice box just as a child might tie down a helium balloon. You swallow syrup of ipecac, alum, squill, and ammonium carbonate to expel the invader from your stomach before absorption, but everything remains in the belly, washing your body in waves of noxious vision.

So much worse to read these buried manuscripts in search of the misguided myth of Henri d'Mescan's innocence; you spend several hours in subterranean shock before leaving—sewer gas from Future's runoff system splitting your nostrils and burning your cilia, translation after translation re-coloring a world that has drizzled into the most constricting duo-tones.

Brittle pages crumble in your hand, and you recall ancient manuscripts as if they were childrens books: *The Gospel of Nicomucous, The Rosarium Philanthrophorum.*

You stuff a few pages of *Crocodilopolis* under your clothes, into the pocket of your belly, before fleeing this crypt. Just as one born on the tip of the metal instrument of extraction forgets, in the cold shine of her surrounding, that a removal has even occurred.

The text tells you a story. Of Henri d'Mescan. Of Davis. The text tells you a story, just one of many, one of forty-nine:

Henri d'Mescan, the barely exonerated war criminal, whose reputation in the 1950s had been re-established (as Henry Mescaline) with the help of one David Schneiderman, most certainly attends his 1954 "Identity Trial" (as both Schneidermans have at times denied)—and he also authors the so-called "Vichy Papers" categorically used to condemn him. You say this to Davis. The proof decomposes in the crypt, you tell Davis, as his saliva drips like a yo-yo from his mouth to the floor, and back once again.

You tell him this story.

By the next morning, December 27, you have every intention of going to the media *after* a careful study of the remaining papers. Still, Davis convinces you to visit the site for an entire night. Down in the catacombs, you re-inspect the documents.

And you find what you know to be there: the first awkward congress of d'Mescan the "free-thinker" into for-hire work at the Occupation branch of the German Propaganda Ministry; the fake newsreel reports offering the so-called "proof" that d'Mescan's unpublished texts have been stolen, corrupted, and re-published by the Vichy government; original copies of these "Vichy Papers" edited with scissors and magic markers by the apologist Hans Dialectic (d'Mescan's wartime translator). An unsigned letter to d'Mescan stating: "We find your ambiguous statements to the press and in your letters to ultimately reflect a clarity of mind and purpose. As to your question of whether to approach the work as pure documentary or pure propaganda, we argue that the distinction has no relevance."

You say this to Davis.

For those seeking absolution, what follows is a cruel void. Images recoil from the guilty. The catacombs present succor. Underneath we *are* and Schneiderman goes livid. He stumbles, slips, and with the greatest difficulty removes a rag doused in chloroform. You scramble from your knees, and seeing your awkward move toward the surface light flooding the tomb from its distant entranceway, he tears furiously at the pile of manuscripts, flinging fractured pieces among the wood-pulp sheets.

Mirrors wilt. Puddles harden and fix themselves into the vapid stare of empty eyes.

You gather your courage and charge from behind, throwing your arms onto his shoulders with a dirty inertia, jumping and jamming a knee into the crevice between his shoulder blades. Falling hard onto the sarcophagus he manages to throw out his arms for support. He flips and rolls and you feel a razor-ripping jab into your stomach. The oozing sensation may be either the vibrant vertigo of your lover's kick mixed with the solution of dirt and papyrus, or the actual blood from the wound that later requires forty-nine precision stitches from the faceless medicine men and their bundles of stone, feather, bone, and pollen. The hissing amplifies as you drop your spittle toward his open eye, forcing your entangled body to tumble leftward, throwing Davis into a pile of tattered wind.

He appears to be stuck; his eyes bulge in time to the breath of the underground temple. Necropolis of bone and paper. Before you can move to gather the manuscripts, the cold hospital steel and IV drip lifts you from a blackout of stony silence.

What follows is another story.

You awake and call for his breath, his touch—but Davis Schneiderman flees Future quickly, a rat through the fluted cornrows, embarking among the reeds that populate the riverbed, toward some other vestibule of Mississippi mud. You send a delegation from Spuyten Duyvil to the sub-basement with the appropriate warrants, Geiger-counters, West-Nile Virus vaccinations, but the silent appendix that housed Henri d'Mescan's manuscripts has been flooded with strange, cleansing liquids.

What follows is another story.

A typescript of the leftovers, those papers stuffed hurriedly in your torso, catching fire in the warm gestation of your belly.

The light from the sun that can no longer penetrate such depths.

And the child, Dial-Up Networking, who cries premature screams among the fraternity of smiling alligators.

10) Henri d'Mescan
From The "Vichy Papers"—*Crocodilopolis* (1939)
Director's Cut with Commentary (49 minutes)

Benediction

We are producing a film about the fall of France, my friend.

It will take place in the near future, June 1940, and will be con-tinually projected on national molecular screens in all French Departments—the retinal strand, the cinema house, veins pump-ing silent ichor through undead circulatory tubing. Each person who understands the towering stalks of HISTORY shall receive a call to help promulgate its laws. Your participation will be in itself a revolutionary act. It will be necessary to compose completely new music. Even if you cannot be present, if other concerns will remove you from the political theater on that particular month, or, even if reading this in the future—if you take pleasure among the embryonic armies of the unborn—you will still have a part to play.

The opening shot reveals a night clip of the floodlit Eagle grasping a swastika. The French militiaman and patriot, Tacg, speaks the first words of the film at a gathering of new mem-bers. (These brave persons vow to embrace the new life of Germany with all the aplomb and the *élan vital* that has char-acterized the French people from the death of Marat in his par-allax bathtub and the birth of the metric system during the Revolution of 1789): "Its my firm belief that individuals have more control over their personal information and greater pro-tection under the law in this, the *new* city." A powerful bomb has been planted inside the meeting hall. His daughter, the rebellious and beautiful Gact, a sometime member of the Resistance group that will be known as the Maquis, wears a burnished cashmere blouse of a grayish green color, with a

85

small, but outmoded firearm in her left hand. The sweep of her arm, the arch of her feet, proclaim a passion out of place in the parabola of awkward resistors, and the living signals of her body—the tight muscle composure and bright eyeballs set like small suns on the plane of her ghostly face—flutter in rhythmic pulses with the preternatural lilt of her boots. She runs as fast as possible, rhythmically outpacing the camera on its broad, mechanized track. Aware of the explosive device, she whistles her energy through the mulling, repetitive crowd.

As you read, you will participate in the glorious movements of our undertaking, contributing the most valuable resource of all—eyeballs. You do not have a choice. Promotion is also your responsibility. A special group, skilled in hanging posters, will not be lacking. Secret budget lines can temporarily authorize a series of inscribed matchbooks, flyers and leaflets to be dropped from the air, newspapers and books, angular handshakes, advertising circulars, exploding cigars, apartment newspapers and factory papers, stellae, posters, jingles, pan flutes, stamps, tattered postcards, promotional tie-ins, banners and billboards, slides and short films that will promote this feature. And there is the glorious June 14 to come, when General van Metacom's troops storm the Bastille and look for revenge on de Sade and his country of homoerotic dandies. Picture the French northern front collapsing—a house of cards atop a chocolate croissant. Watch lightning infantry divisions compete with mobile units to spread the strongest sperm. Smile and wave at the second unit director.

Tacg pauses haphazardly at the membership meeting, thumps his chest with a rigid right arm and annunciates (as his operating manual advises): "We have developed new camera techniques for the shoot, trained our bodies through long practice at previous takeover events in Poland, Denmark, Holland,

Belgium, and of course, Luxembourg—and when necessary, we can protect a citizen's right to privacy with this camera gun." He removes an automatic weapon from a leather case, a row of electronic switches undulate from its clear body refracting the recycled sunlight. A perfect crosshair punctuates the mouth of the scope affixed above the aperture of the barrel. This meeting clearly consolidates Tacg's local prestige. He passes the sacred weapon to the outstretched hands of Jean, his cloying assistant, dressed in a slightly cocked black beret, before speaking to the crowd:

"Each release of the trigger trips the shutter. Distribute your bullets about the target and a visual picture emerges *in space*. We can turn these snapshots into moving pictures, and in this way, simultaneously preserve and destroy the target at twenty-four frames per second…See how easily I anticipate your question. Yes, you sir. Yes, we have *already* developed the capacity for basic time travel. Thank the Germans for the start-up capital!"

Discussing this film with your peers will deepen the idea and educate your circle, encouraging closer contact between a population that must learn to surrender its slogans to the tromp of steel-toed jackboots. You must celebrate the caress of the stiff eagle, the rough cock. France's insipid tribe of WWI cast-offs practice simple reenactments of lazy POW days, to the point that some, reputedly, even go in for playing pinochle and masturbating to worn-out records while the rest of the castrated country desperately spits out inanimate objects to fight where this subhuman crew can not: Heavy metals will fall from railroad trestles and splays their soft poison in fields of human shit; barrels of hulled wheat will soak up mud and grease under the crush of approaching tanks. Nude images will increase by the hour—exiled from a bargain basement Matisse sale, symptomatic of a poisoned generation, unable to withstand the terrific pressure upon their oversexed craniums. In only two days of heavy fighting, Major Colonel Captain von Schnitzeldorfer's army will disassemble the Maginot Line— France's bloated mending wall. Not even the fortress of Verdun can resist an assault of the mummified crocodiles. At 6:50 p.m. on June 22, 1940 the armistice requested officially by Marshal Pétain, the French Premiere, will be signed with the German people. Political decisions of the "Third Reich" can then dominate the film explicitly. On June 25, 1940, hostilities will cease, and our film, Crocodilopolis, will eroticize just this sort of triumphant history.

We gaze closely at Jean and notice that he looks like Tacg's "twin" in the story—a replica of Tacg in a glycerin picture, a Daguerreotype pylon made liquid in the pleat of fashionable trousers. Both men are situated in the sun-baked river; their larva feed on hapless, overexposed surface creatures; they float stately down the Seine toward the crocodile summer; they wear ceremonial necklaces of tooth for their eventual coronation and sacrifice. Still, Jean's hair is blond and effeminate; Tacg's a charcoal black. Genetic drift explains such deviations and scaly enclosures—on a shoestring budget we can use blue screens to reconcile such differences.

Cut to Gact running through the corridors at the rear of the Resistance restaurant. She slips the gun into a holster under her loose blouse, and with the deft motion of a practiced but blood-thirsty provocateur, re-applies her makeup—bright red lipstick, crimson rouge—holding her lips still, throwing a voice to what she considers the misguided alliances of her father, Tacg, who snarls at his daughter and squeezes her throat with a long-distance hand. Her resistance contact, Maurice the Maquis, beckons—an enormous tongue dressed in a trench coat, waving and blistering at a dimly lit corner table, pointing out their countrymen who ignore the barometer of change, who sit languid and forlorn in the rapidly archaic poses, lost in cold-blooded hibernation. Drinks appear again and again, and Maurice notices Gact's expression of distaste; the noises of the café increase, the slosh of wet against throat, microorganism cadres forming urinal cakes, waiters spitting into the wine…Maurice tries to comfort her. He finishes her drink with the same decrepit, snarling eyes. "The bomb will explode within the hour. Relax…" But her body remains defiant.

Marlena Berawn, the spirited actress contracted by Jaundice-Munich studios, will offer quite the exemplary cunt. Immediately after her character, Gact, will learn of Maurice the Maquis's treachery and her father's presence at ground zero of the explosion, she will slash his arm with bits of jagged glass, and push through the smiling Parisians, already adapting, engaged in their revelries, back toward the secret meeting location. All will go well, until this prima donna ventures onto the outdoor set where mere facades of common homes, multistoried dwellings of beautiful German uteruses come to meet smiling strings of eerie foliage. The fakeness of the set will leave her discombobulated. Marlena is German, and to play the future French militia as scripted by myself, she must adapt to the point that identity becomes sublimated to image. Incest between Gact and Tacg to produce a cultural coupling might just be a way out of the dramatic impasse. Gact must appear in a flak jacket zipped tightly over the curves of her body, accentuating, with and olive hue, the soft palimpsest of her shiny forehead. In this way, no one will fail to stiffen at the sight of her.

Tacg motions to the crowd with his strong upper body, with the swaying lilt of his voice: "Each cut of ruins and ancient columns, of humanity's pre-vertebrate playground, helps to seize control of the larger part of the police network." The moment is pregnant with danger. "We have been promised our own trial attorneys and prisons, just as the Gestapo has its secret officers. We can still fuck each other—and that counts for something. Pick up a *Paris Match* and think of those last Negro settlements in the Congo. Sovereignty will be maintained on this side of the line of Demarcation. Depend on the camera gun to *always* profit from new opportunities."

Back in the café, something feels wrong. Gact's body emanates a fragrance of lime and chloride fused with bitter almond—and Maurice the Maquis holds his nose. Gacts skin tightens its hold against her bloody network of veins that threatens to detach from the interior flesh and unravel, right there in the café, loops of film stock exposed in the overhead lights. Maybe its the drink or the noise or the bonfires along the Champs-Elysées, or maybe its the view from the top of the Samaritan department store on the right bank (a circular deck framed with a circular drawing of the old Parisian skyline). When spinning around, the view becomes a time warp, the distance between the humble Paris tenements and the efficient armies of the Reich. Broken wine glasses sweep angular shards away. Sound refracts the doctored image track and scratches across the film stock circulated back one second after slipping. Gact's eyes are cataracts of grey celluloid.

Maurice the Maquis knows that he will eventually betray every confidence, kill every ally. A murderer, he slithers under the membrane of his trench coat, discharging a curdled seed through his skin, lost in the erotic undulations of his own police lineup. The camera spins like a cyclotron; Maurice the Maquis fixes his eyes upon a perspective point somewhere outside the scene: "I will keep silent no more. Gact, the bomb that we have planted. Your father is the leader of that meeting. He is the target!"

Marlena will ask me why I do not touch her crotch more when I'm rigging her up. No lie. All the makeup artists in the room start throwing parts of extra mannequins to signify anguish just as she rushes toward Tacg, to save him from the bomb. We will have clamped several beta clips to the erect disciplinary nipple. Her character will arrive just in time. She will mention again how the Nuremberg Laws forbid intermarriage with Jews, persons no longer feasible in a worldwide production. Our film's unifying image must then be the one remaining camera gun. Her character will arrive just before the explosion. The importance of this "document" will prove how film's relatively great costs can "pay off": rolls of film stock, cameras and date recording devices, sound stages and location permits, the large staff of key grips, gaffers, and best boys, etc., all require extensive monetary commitments, but the result, the finished cut of Crocodilopolis, will bring in tens of thousands of persons whose admission fees not only cover the costs, but produce righteous political capital. The love between Tacg and Gact will have nothing to do with Germany and France, but everything to do with the aesthetically unadulterated purity of the father-daughter bond. "Yes," you may think, "film isn't political until they invade my house and smash my radio into the riddle bits of modern comedy."

The meeting place lies in ruins and violence amid the rubble. Jean reaches for the hand of the confused Gact and plots to push his grizzly tongue along the crease of her navel. Not daring to kiss her in the wake of the violent detonation, Jean and Gact flee slightly ahead of the injured but not dishonored Tacg. He hobbles behind with a fractured leg, saved from complete oblivion by the last-minute warning of his estranged daughter.

Jean's desire heightens the possibility that Gact's lips might still be cold, mishandled by Maurice the Maquis. The floodlights of Paris rise from foreign quarters, shoot up the edges of Notre Dame, along the causeways of a lime-green Seine, the paths of a crooked, alien Tuileries. An enormous Indonesian calla lily blooms in fluorescence over the obelisk at the Place de la Concorde, and the kiss of the guillotine, banished to the annals of the past, forces a blade across on everyone's neck. In the confusion, just before the explosion, Gact has wrestled the colorless camera gun from her confused father.

Gact finds her right arm, as a horse might find its hooves, pushed against the grasping fingers of Jean. He is silent glue processed from *rinderpest*-infested cattle, yet he whispers so softly, so sweetly into the wind: "Slow motion techniques are fused with the lazy nod and laugh track." A block behind the group, members of the French Resistance Maquis scuffle with a German security detail. Since one German soldier can out-maneuver the entire ragged body of resistors, the German boys will leave a typical specimen behind before racing after the terrorist Gact. Meanwhile, only one French resistor, Maurice the Maquis, hangs spectral in the bloody twilight, pale and listless, a zombie of circumstance, plodding forward to maintain the chase. His heavy breathing dominates the soundtrack; the camera, trained on his form, sweats and heaves like a dying animal.

Marlena's makeup effects are intended to startle, caked on through the sluice of a fishing net into a city of square and line, a mega-lopolis of putty knife and rouge brush. She will appear mummified, ancient, swaddled in medicated wraps and embroidered altar cloths for her starring shoot. Waters can rise through the new city and I envision an eerie dream-sequence in which her lead character, the horribly confused Gact, manipulates a wild hodge-

podge of borrowed footage from plaster-cast statues. Starfish will fight for limited resources while invisible jellyfish rebel against their molds. The human form can be approximated through a tease of the camera, an ocean assemblage: I tell her that she must swim through a very dense pool to finally save Tacg—that domination is an organized atrocity distributed by governmental action—but I suspect this will not be the case here. Even in low, silent waters, radioactive fish swim away from her orgasm; her spermicidal foam will engulf entire continents.

Tacg struggles to pull a few steps ahead; Jean and Gact follow closely behind. The German police have taken a diagonal shortcut across the square and will cut the trio off within seconds, but Maurice the Maquis plots to slowly overtake them by means of a shortcut. Jean knows he must act quickly; he pushes his lips, still rattling their strange music, into the side of Gact's head. She feels the forked tongue sweep her tympanum with the wetness of sounding brass, of tinkling cymbal. Flooded with amylase, she stumbles, momentarily confused. A greasy cobra, Jean flies for the camera gun.

Gact snaps to awareness and wrestles with Jean for the piece, slowing instinctively as footfalls muffle themselves into the wet mud behind the duo. Tacg turns around, fifteen paces ahead, and watches his partner Jean grapple with his daughter—his savior from the explosion. He hesitates, leaning on a crushed leg; Jean gains the upper hand and trains the camera gun on Gact. Tacg's jaw drops to a frozen hole, a gaping absence, a festering sore of disbelief bleeding into the street. The wind machines continue whipping as Jean makes his speech: "Tacg, brave Tacg!" he yells to his injured leader. "The meetings, the camps themselves, the cinema house—the historicity of every effort to weed out Nazism, I have used these to my advantage.

In moments the German authorities will catch up with us, and I shall have a brand new corpse to present to our glorious Fuhrer!"

Our sponsors' press directions require "personal" letters to be distributed through the mail system. Model letters will be provided to our information offices. Reproduced either by hand or by machine, with personal addresses, the letters can then be delivered to all moviegoers, regardless of viewing habits. There will be different letters for people assigned to the future role of Marxist, Milice, Maquis, retirees, women, waiters, etc... The location coordinator will establish a hotline to Latvia to discuss using detained Gypsies as extras in the film. She can print special Reichsmarks from her portable monotype machine as we need them.

Tacg feels his entire life slip. Galvanized by the approaching footsteps of Maurice the Maquis, Jean inches toward Gact like a slow-motion sextant moving toward nadir. Gact is a frozen moment—a still life with Death's Head and grapes. Her heart beats still, her eye pumps fiery cobalt, and Jean rotates the dial of the gun, waiting for his opportunity. He must tarry until noon, when the crocodiles fall asleep on the rocks, bathing in the sun that sings them to dream. He will sneak up and grab the beast by the neck, close to the head, so that it can't slip away from the bite; then, while the layers of film retract back into its eyes, before the receding mucous uncovers its sight, he must slip the hood over its head, tighten the noose, and hope that it cannot see the hunter. A previous bond is helpful to deaden the reptile's senses.

Jean makes his move just as the crocodile snaps blindly toward its attacker. He suddenly spins *away* from Gact, and points the camera-gun at her father! Yes, her father, the wounded Tacg.

Jean fires the camera gun in perfect cinematic close-up, direct-ly at Tacg's quivering legs…oh mother country France who can be virile in new ways… a secret police force will be set in charge of all images…assuming that secret police forces are invariably created through the use of montage…

As director, I will repeatedly explain in interviews that the condi-tions enabling the "Reich" shall be linked to a refusal of "other" authorities. So, Gact, torn between her fading allegiance to the Resistance militia now bolstered by Jean's sudden treachery, and her loyalty to the wounded father—so forlorn and weak, with bro-ken legs, terrorized by the extant camera gun—will soon have the option to fire on his prone body and remove this obstacle to her compliance with the Maquis cause. She will be unsure of what to believe; the one remaining camera gun not destroyed in the explo-sion at the meeting hall will once again press close to her thigh, wrestled from Jean in the coming confusion.

The wounded Tacg lies on the ground, and Jean moves toward the final shot. The German forces will soon kick in invisible doors and overturn stable scenarios. Yet the exhausted Maurice the Maquis arrives first, drained of breath, intent on protecting the version of Gact he has worked so hard to create. Gact, hear-ing everything from all sides, jumps into Jean's arms and knocks the camera gun to the ground, just as she has always known that she would. That feels like clairvoyance. Several rounds explode in electrostatic color. Gact scoops the weapon from the ground while Maurice the Maquis, with dwindling breath, shouts at her: "Gact stop…Jean is *one of us*…were all the same for a free Paris…We resist!"

Hearing this, both Gact and Jean pause, supported by a strange adhesive energy. She raises the weapon slowly, uncertain at who to aim. The shaded light of the setting sun rushes through the weapon's translucent hull merging everything into an image of itself. On the ground, Tacg's eyes bleed into the night's grim partition; the wind and rain have increased and obscured vision, transmuted loyalties. Jean brushes his pants and stands up. "We didn't think we could tell you…if you can't finish him off, I'll have to. Maurice can explain it all, but I'm sure you can figure it out." Maurice, like a serpent, steals the camera gun from Gact's quivering hand without comment. Jean spits toward the wounded Tacg, but the wind slings the slimy mucous back onto his uniform.

Maurice the Maquis now levels the camera gun with a distant spot on the horizon and trains it on Gact. "He won't be able to survive another shot. Go ahead…it will be better if family is present." "I'll take it," she says and she can almost feel her father's ghostly fingers holding the weapon in place within her palm. Why did she ever follow so blindly? She must have been brainwashed by the image that these two criminals have cast upon her soul with their shadows blurred terribly at the edges. Jean's greasy head and pawnbroker beard come alive with a swarm of locusts, and Maurice the Maquis, a blob in the rising moonlight, urges her again, with a strange and ugly tongue, toward the final murder of her only parent. She moves closer to Tacg and extends the camera gun to his face. His lips, twisted with pain, leaking blood, whisper the same soft motions she remembers from her childhood. "That was us, following ever closer," he whispers back through the spaces of rain and mist. Suddenly, the surge of German footfalls rips apart this false reality. Distant for so long, they sound only moments away.

In the future, the written and spoken work will depend entirely on the content of the speaker's emotional appeal, but film must use pictures, pictures that for more than a decade have been accompanied by sound. We know that the impact of a message increases if it is less abstract, more visual. Is the filmmaker evil or just the final cut? As Dr. Krautaphiliac writes in his unpublished notes to "Camera Gun(boat) Diplomacy" (1936): "A succession of male body parts follows all images of lovemaking, especially the interfamilial." Krautaphiliac understands, perhaps more than anyone, the method by which the pristine uniforms, the carefully ordered marching lines and youth programs all help to organize the political behind the sexual. Gact's tortuous final run can begin with such gripping humility, such a lovely smile in Marlena's smoldering eye that the city and the landmarks of a corrupt Parisian society will tumble forth before the beneficence of German forces, shifting ruins decimated by the camera gun.

Jean and Maurice turn toward the syncopated rhythm just as supplicants might be forced to turn toward the overpowering glare of a manufactured deity. Beneath a sunburnt corona, their eyes, glazed calico marbles, roll back into the hold of lizard heads. They are mesmerized by the precision footfalls of the German troops; Gact doesn't miss her chance again; she fires the camera gun first on Maurice, then on Jean. They fall like numberless villains. She rushes to her father's shriveled body, and as the German troops arrive, she kisses him on the forehead. Cut to the close-up on his lips, whispering their personal lullaby: "We found you most exciting."

The wind dies for a moment, and the rain begins a terse, calming pattern. A strong, gloved hand falls on Gact's shoulder as she weeps, and somehow, even as Tacg dies, she knows that the Paris of crocodiles can be no more, that the ill-drawn curtains of the old world will open to embrace the new, that the past has been ripped to shreds by her teeth and her nails and her blood.

Gact grips the camera gun in her arms and places it over the body of her father, making quite a picture for the French papers, warming him in the love he so richly deserves. Swastikas wave on his casket, ears of corn shoot across the reborn soil, and Gact, with the rigid arm still steadying her shoulder, collects every detail of the service—the mourners in lace and sadness, the lilies launched as a bursting cannonade into the firmament, the core of the tragic that she bears bravely within her body—so that through a eternal veil of beautiful tears, she can keep an image of the future stored carefully inside the mummified cage of her heart.

The *Apoplectic* pretended to be an ideal record of the actual defense that Henri d'Mescan delivered before the entire Fourth Republic on day 189 of the "identity trial" for "image crime." (in June 1947.) This made the salvation of d'Mescan's condemned character an exercise in redundancy, to the point that the entire question of its historicity dissolved even more acutely than in the so-called "Vichy Papers." For Henri d'Mescan neither authored those texts, nor, as often reported, died at the hand of the firing squad. The relentless ways in which the "Vichy Papers" (exemplified by the ridiculous farce of *Crocodilopolis*), affected their mostly fictional and sexual agendas, simply reinforced the importance of *this* document, the *Apoplectic*. It questioned to what extent the theories of the collaborationist persona of Henri d'Mescan, fabricated by the German Propaganda Ministry, mirrored those of the historical d'Mescan. For we were dealing with a speech that the authentic d'Mescan adapted from a previous version of his indictment, most suitably told in the dialogues of its primary participant.

11 Portions of this text were adapted from the film script *Figures of Hate: The Image-Crime Trial of Henri d'Mescan*, a 1983 biopic produced by Henri d'Mescan. After the destruction of the original court documents housed in Future, Missouri, certain segments of the testimony proved to be corrupt. d'Mescan's screenplay drew on much of the recovery work David Schneiderman executed on this period when producing his aborted draft of *Multifesto* in 1966-7, as it appeared to be the most reliable copy-editing resource. For instance, an earlier edition of this book used "Melatus" as the name of d'Mescan's primary accuser, while the script corrected it to the name of "Mutation."

So we asked about the reliability of d'Mescan's historical record. d'Mescan proved the entire case to be merely a manifestation of his presence at the trial, evoking a real and deliberate pathos from the audience as to his mishandling.

If the *Apoplectic* were written soon after the close of the lengthy trial, many Parisians might have read the actual speech from the newspapers, or heard it on the radio—so it d'Mescan would have been unable to fabricate an entirely new speech. In any event, d'Mescan's review of his farcical trial could not have been judged *solely* by his mimicry. Yes, the rhythm of the speech most assuredly corresponded to his often sarcastic but effective style, and was certainly that of the real d'Mescan, but the corrupt notion of spiritual and moral degradation belonged to the imposter that he wished to condemn through its writing.

In order to rescue the legal system from the confusing and opposing conclusions that the post-war court was likely to draw in any deliberation, the duties of jury and all other authorities combined so as to balance the accounts of the liberation. Particularly, the three judges had the benefit of the 16,000+ pages of unreleased documents, as well as the carefully prepared truncations they used in both convicting and sentencing.[12] Of course, it would have been exceedingly difficult

12 Not an enormous number by any means. Documents at the original Nuremberg trials ranged routinely, for each of the twenty-two defendants, into the tens of thousands. For Hermann Goering alone, the highest-ranking German defendant, three entire trailers had to be annexed in order to archive the necessary papers used by the prosecution. Similar overwhelming quantities were necessary at the trial of Adolph Eichmann in Jerusalem in 1961. The d'Mescan case, then, by comparison, represents a relatively minor episode in that the accused was not a member of the Nazi party, nor German, but rather, a civilian lacking direct ties to the Hitler regime. Some have commented that the zeal used in his prosecution exceeds the reasonable utilization of French post-war resources, and even Phoenelia Yeer, before her unfortunate delusional state began, agreed. (See Binker, Antonio. *Misappropriated Public Resources in Postwar Europe*. Gary, IN: AC/DC Books, 1978, for an extended economic discussion.)

for this judicial assembly to complete a work so important to an entire nation if they had to debate all of the myriad penalties available to them in the lawless spaces created after the Nazi Occupation. In lieu of this debate, the court had recourse to the style of the ancient Athenian court that tried Socrates. The prosecuting judge, upon attaining conviction, professed the penalty deemed appropriate by his office. Then, the defendant would be allowed to offer counter-arguments that were often, as in the case here, completely more viable in every respect than the charges levied against the accused. The court would then simply decide between the two positions, and with all either/or schemas, generally encourage a moderate position on both sides. But not in this instance, as passions remained enflamed by the collaborationist documents d'Mescan supposedly authored.

* * *

The *Apoplectic* was a series in three loosely divided parts. The first part offered the main speech, followed by d'Mescan's rebuttal, closing finally with a recollection of the death scene. This famous execution scene that closed the dialogue presented a body stiffened by a sort of industrial hemlock, in a flesh made almost liquid by fear with its unifying image of the camera gun. Perhaps d'Mescan meant to finish his rival with his own dark inversion, the negative symbol of the inassimilable— the imposter's corpse of sewage and stercus—for a world that judged its darkest machines by virtue of their omission; the death scene confirmed that the man whose body was buried in the outskirts of Montmarte was not the author Henri d'Mescan, who was instead present in the gallery on that final day, incognito, helping to prepare the imposter's body for its punishment. Some evidence indicated that this executed double was d'Mescan's pre-war translator Hans Dialectic. The two men switched places after the sentencing through uncertain means, and d'Mescan, perhaps posing as his own collaborationist imposter, exploited Dialectic's German contacts to reach Guayaquil, Ecuador, by the time this document had its first publication in late 1954.[13]

13 Concerned about Phoenelia Yeer's ideological reversals on these issues, we spent the past few days conducting extended interviews with Yeer's coterie of specialists and health care professionals (seemingly numberless as we soon discovered), including her general practitioner, first obstetrician, pharmacist, chiropractor, psychotherapist, psychologist, second obstetrician, podiatrist, dermatologist, urologist, acupuncturist, cardiologist, ophthalmologist, rheumatologist, gastroenterologist, endocrinologist, nephrologist, neurologist, nutritionist, oncologist, gynecologist, otolaryngoloist, proctologist, and psychic dentist. After filling each professional in about her current travails, we discovered they unilaterally recommended that she either increase or decrease her cocktail of prescriptive sedatives, Prozac, Paxil, Prilosec, Allegra, Demarol, et al., in favor of a regimen designed to promote a more positive mental and physical state. We sorted through the data, and developed a general list of recommendations in mantra form that begins: "Checked quickly for open wounds. Pat a dirty cloth napkin over a cut on the knuckle. Had two egg whites for breakfast, a scooped out-bagel and soft drink..." We left it for her at the desk of the Wonderland Motel in Ithaca, NY, in case she passes that way again.

12) Henri d'Mescan
From *The Trial and Death of Henri d'Mescan:*
***Apoplectic* (1954)**

"Et maintenant il sera fait parler."[14]

It is beyond my ability to speculate on how the accents of my accusers affect you, but I am close to being lifted from this drab courtroom and carried away into the air by their persuasive logorrhea. Strangely, their accusations expend energy entirely without merit. My judges appear to be universally feared and dreaded for their stern wisdom, and yet they exist as replicas of the same mediocrity found in every courtroom in our country. The French judges retire for a seeming eternity in order to study the texts responsible for my incarceration as they continue to *imagine* that they possess moral authority. The discomfort and commotion of this period—we all know this well—can be drawn out and quartered by a clutch of reporters armed with hidden recording devices and replicated camera guns. The courtroom, however, dancing with an electricity and inertia powered by its loneliness and distance from the disreputable bars littered with members of the press, suddenly bursts to rupture by the distended outrages of just such paparazzi and indignant citizens, moving awkward limbs in unholy links about the spectator box, massaged into the exposed rivulets of the wooden seats, aiming with irresponsible notepads and ciné-cameras. Now you've heard it. But have you understood?

The French cannot move without being photographed at point-blank range as at the signing of the Armistice; the camera imprisons us just as one comes to accept paralysis in the fear of old age. This condition is not so ancient, but the words we use to describe it sound laconic, the sentiments offensive

14 "And now he will be made to speak."

and obscure. Even in my prison cell, photographers have been present at the preliminary presentation of the indictment against *not* me, I argue again, but my literary doppelganger. Look at the collective picture of the texts falsely attributed to me, over which this shadow has presided. Does it seem to be persisting? Does my face and pen, whose authorship can be proven on numerous anti-Nazi tracts, impose itself on this con-
tainer? Does the fact that I am in possession of incontrovertible evidence as to the authorship the text called *Outsourcing* not clear my name and shadow from this falsified negative? I say again: Now you've heard it, but have you understood?

Clearly, this rebuts the claims of my earlier accusers, for no one will deny that the novel *Outsourcing* written under the pseudonym Henry Mescaline in 1939 reveals elements of the so-called "Final Solution" *only* by re-arranging the language of German industrial companies, and that the intention of the work acts as a revelation, not a justification. Once this business finishes, I enter into the laborious process of defending myself against the judge known to you as Mutation, the ridiculous and *patriotic* figure, and my later accusers whose sworn depositions go something like this: Henri d'Mescan is guilty of corrupting his writing abilities by promulgating collaborationist documents that support the Hitler regime and the subjugation of France. As I have been made to understand, this is the charge.

Mutation, as a representative of the judicial regime, says that I am guilty of corrupting the public sphere by my anti-French views, but I suggest the guilt of Mutation in proposing such ridiculous matters. Tell me, Mutation. I assume that you consider it of the most essential importance that a text, or texts in the plural, be allowed to speak for themselves? — *Indeed I do*.

In that case, tell the jury who exactly listens to a text... As I expected, you keep silent, choked by your ineffectual words.

Answer me, your honor, who listens to a text? — *The state.*

You misunderstand me, I fear. Rather what person possesses a foreknowledge of the state? — *Why the reader, Monsieur d'Mescan.*

Mutation, in what way? Can she interpret a text and under- stand its language? — *Absolutely.*

The entirety of readers? Or only some of them? — *The entirety.*

Excellent. You discuss a great many interpreters who may also be readers. But what about the publishers who choose to distribute the text? Do they also interpret a text and under- stand its language — *Yes, interpretation is with them, as well.*

And what of the booksellers? — *Yes, the booksellers also.*

So Mutation, what about the bookbinders and typesetters and editors and translators? Do they all interpret at every stage of this long process? — *They do.*

All those involved in any way with a text, in this case the so-called "Vichy Papers," it seems, are capable of interpreting, and thus taking responsibility, through their actions, for the cultural uses of that interpretation. Have I approached your meaning? — *That is most definitely what I mean.*

Then I have been condemned to an enormous *misreading.* Answer me: does your rationale also apply to horses? That all persons involved with the beast, from the rider to the owner, the trainers, loan sharks, and spectators, have some ability, if only by degrees, to understand the creature as a social being? Or is the opposite true and one individual serves as the bearer of the horse's meaning, or only a select group, composed of the breeders? Whereas the majority, if they have horses and use them, can be filled as a receptacle for the essence of the horse— as filtered by the relatively few persons directly involved? Tell me, Mutation, what is the case with both horses and with texts? Oh what a joyous scenario if those everyday souls that

100 use a horse, from the gamblers at the track to the blacksmith who shoes the beast in a modern factory, assuming they stand removed from the responsibility of its daily upkeep, could become exempt from an influence upon its maintenance. But they do not. It is a system.

It is now completely within the scope of possibility, Mutation, that the corruption you accuse me of—that the "Vichy Papers" bearing my name collaborate with the enemy by virtue of their cultural interpretation, while only "I" am to blame as a single author—must be a false charge, since in your
110 argument people act as both readers and interpreters, and accordingly, must bear some guilt. Excepting the fact that I am not the author, and have been falsely attributed as the author, you would have this august body ignore the complex of social interactions charging this text with *meaning*, and with it, the myriad opportunities that others involved in the process have to beat the desired interpretation from the subjugated pulp.

Rebuttal:
You are a simple nag yourself, Mutation, and not to be believed. Has ever one so highly ignorant and of exaggerated
120 importance played so many for complete fools? So let us *play* another linguistic game then. I continue to assume, as in the past exchange, that the "Vichy Papers" are in some fashion a product of my pen. Now by saying that I "corrupt" the country as the author of these reprehensible works is the same as say- ing that *Outsourcing*—to which I have already produced numerous drafts and independent testimonials of its authentic- ity—actually serves as a coded communiqué between myself and the Nazi agents with whom I wished to make contact. To suggest that this most public book acts as anything other than
130 a warning *against* the aggressions of the Hitler regime's policies gives credibility to the same persons responsible for the "Vichy

Papers," and their supposedly collaborationist contents in the first place. As I have already proven that an entire complex of persons and organizations bear responsibility for those odious texts, I clarify the genesis of *Outsourcing* to indicate the way *my* authorial intention, from the start, has been usurped. Do not create an uproar, members of the jury, but abide by my request not to cry out at what I say, while you listen:

I had screened Leni Riefenstahl's *Olympia* in 1937, and based upon a mutual acquaintance in Koblenz, she sent me a postcard expressing interest in a screenplay version of *Summary Execution* to star Clark Gable and Marlene Dietrich circulated to Hollywood executives with German sympathies. You may rightly ask after the text of this postcard? I can't recall exactly, of course, but it somehow indicated that while she wanted no great part of National Socialism, her ability to make the film [of the 1936 Berlin Olympiad] gave her great pleasure, and that if the political situation did not deteriorate as I had elsewhere stated it might, she would perhaps be interested in helping me edit my film, which of course had yet to be made. Struck by her naïveté, and being much more concerned about the complete re-armament of Germany, I read *Olympia* as a justification of Nazi racial policy perpetuated by camera angles. While true, I also told Fraulein Riefenstahl, that black athletes such as Jesse Owens dominate many of the athletic events, the slow motion and montage sequences that she uses support a subtler, Aryan-bias. Of course, she protested, and future postcards "lost" themselves in the mail.

I realize the value of not only juxtaposing elements to create a specific effect, but also of superimposing different languages. In *Olympia*, the film offers the alphabet of international sport, which ultimately becomes decipherable through the alphabet of racial fitness and genetic slow motion. I knew that my 1939 novel *Outsourcing* must direct the surging energy of the masses by re-coding its own language into the discourse of a nationalized capital. Hence, the idea of altering the annual reports of several important German firms linked to Hitler's government and exposing the hidden language lurking underneath that suggested a deeper agenda. — *But if you had knowledge of the "final solution" to the so-called Jewish question from your permutations of these annual reports, which sounds entirely ridiculous, and you were indeed loyal to France, why did you not provide this information to the necessary government agencies?*

Aside from the fact that plans were already underway for an invasion of France, and I could not be certain of the use to which any intelligence would be put, I simply *did not know.* The text speaks for itself only in hindsight. What you label as clairvoyance began as only a cloudy premonition that takes its shape in the spectacle of the war. We have all heard allegations that the Vichy government aided in the deportation of Jews, of course, but who here is prepared to graph the atrocities of the members of this jury, many of whom performed major roles in that episode? As I have stated to exhaustion in the depositions conducted for this trial, my only official contact with representatives of the Reich, took the form of a note inscribed to me on the French Head of the Government's personal stationary, demanding that all "Fex" pamphlets cease production immediately, if I were to…ah…how to put it…"act for the greater glory of a unified France in these trying times"…or some other sentimental claptrap.[15] What more it there to say? From solstice to equinox this court has functioned, and I have manufactured

15 "Fex": A series of parodies written by Henri d'Mescan during the early years of the Vichy Government in mockery of Marshal Philippe Pétain, its aging leader. The works show Pétain's analogue, Fex, to be an incompetent leader incapable of making even simple decisions due to a rapidly advancing mixture of senility and dementia. d'Mescan submits that the texts were destroyed in Nazi book burning, and were thus unavailable to use in his defense.

outcomes against the supposed applicability of the "charges." If I have demanded a certain amount of ecumenism in the taking of guilt, surely the evidence has followed my lead. I now require reform at the highest levels if we desire to reconstruct the sorry state of our nation. — *Isn't government always corrupt?*

Indeed, gentleman and ciné-cameras of the jury, I do not wish to offer a pointless defense for myself now; it is obvious that I am to become the sacrifice that absorbs your sins. Burn me, if that act reflects your will, and I will rain ash over your grandchildren's playpens. Smother me with your steel-toed boots and I will not hesitate to point my stiffened fingers at your hearts; hang me, and I will crash against your houses during the long nights of uneasy dream that will infect your already disquieted minds. Kill me now, bury me alive, and I will find a way to claw through the pinewood of my casket in order to rise again and again. The wind will blow through your hollow chest like the memory of an ancient religion undone by conquistadors with heavy mustaches and penises of gold doubloon, and if you listen closely to the rush of water flowing beneath the shallows of this fragile civilization, you will know that I approach the surface with ever-mightier strokes.

Death Scene:
No reader will believe that the tortures of my imprisonment will be as I describe them elsewhere, but when the accuser Mutation demands to know my place of birth on the last day of my life, I shall offer a battery of replies arranged through another set of jaws. With no intention of going gently into a good night forced upon me for crimes I did not commit, the following account will no doubt shock many of my readers, but perhaps, from the safe harbor in which I prepare it, the text will help to clear my name, and finally, perhaps, speak for itself.

For in the Americas I have found the greatest appreciation of disorder, and the neighbors, the mailman, the paperboy will enjoy hearing how I escaped from prison in a radiation suit or some other such outfit in which those on the run must dress themselves in order to modify appearances. They are never quick enough to accuse me of breaking the very laws that in better times I allow to bind me, and for their ignorance, I will be grateful.

Born, I will relate to Mutation, in a hospital bed in the proximity of French soil, and I will also tell him, in a violent tone, that a kindred countryman would never ask a veteran of the Occupation such as myself to defend his national ties in the aftermath of the Nazi atrocities. He then asks, as you all can attest — *Do you deny that you were not born of French soil?*

I will deny nothing, but since you insist on pressing the point, I state for the record that I am a product of colony, of political federations that encourage the people to cut each other's throats every twenty years. Do not be so certain that you understand the methods or rebellion perfected by these crises. It never begins as a political struggle, but simply as a consequence of the fight against the Occupier, who at all times offers the appearance of superceding the politics of the locality. But under the conditions of clandestine action, to which my humble tome *Outsourcing* plays no small part—resistance assumes a new form. Our machine will be constructed out of many different pieces, just as the feel of dust and the rounded shape of my body can be calculated as an action encountering the political... —*So you admit that your body is culpable. Will the accused be more explicit? Members of the jury representing our entire nation, I speak with simplicity and with speech's light gravity— this traitor exposed by the purge of traitors from our autonomous nation takes part in an event indescribable in the history of France. That a person whose writings commanded the highest respect should perpetuate the Nazi regime, invalidating their entire previous production, remains an insufferable blow. Let me ask you, Monsieur d'Mescan, is this an example of the text that you* 260 *claim helps to prove your innocence, the so-called "Fex" material that supposedly shows your disdain for the policies of the failed Vichy government? Read it into the court record:*

It will be read for the record, and shall be restated here:

> The scented gallery of indignant spectators have no identity beyond their utility at this moment for Marshal Fex (in this sense he is the same as the officers), but the movements of Vichy demand that he visit with them. Despite the Occupation, the addicts, the endless *diktats* 270 from Ambassador Abetz in Paris, the demand for volunteer labor to fill German factories while hoards of Hitler Youth fight all the insidious forms of Bolshevism even more oppressive in this context. Fex allows himself to be swept away, to both desire the movement of bodies into a carpet of mass production, of "co-belligerency" with the Germans, of surrender to the plans of the collaborators, who wish to embrace the new European regime, *and* find for 280 France a place worthy of her history in this context. Fex moves toward the calla lily, but this strategy is simple theatre, the masquerade that must be entered into completely for the moment so that genetic potentials can be subverted, refigured, and expended in harmless denouements. The officers move along with him, guided by the silent Fex into a glacial quiet.

300   Fex recalls the cliché sights of his temporary home, his temporary people, pushing
everything toward totalization: the Arc de
Triomphe with its circling traffic and around-
the-clock honor guard, the imposed historical
curricula of the Institut de France, the Opera
de la Bastille and its litany of beautiful propaganda. The calla lily moves even closer, like a
river pushing its ripples to a static shoreline of
fully developed Esso stations, resort embank-
310   ments, toward the Quai Anatole France and a
complete understanding of *Al la Recherche du
Temps Perdu*. Noise from the Carnival beyond
the tent increases along with the acrid reproduction of mites and flies and worms in the
flutes of the greenhouse; Fex's asshole tightens
and his heart pounds....

This Mutation will be unaware of my ability to remove myself
from the body in question upon answering such subjective
queries, and as the record will be read into in such as way that
320 Mutation will no doubt lose himself in reflection upon the
crimes he wishes to perceive, I will take this opportunity to
make the necessary adjustments.

After this, the man who has come to be known as Henri
d'Mescan, through a miraculous textual transubstantiation,
will ascend from his rusty cot, a small helium balloon rising
amid the dense air of this small lightless garret, the prison-
house containing all of our hopes and fears and pressurized
bodies, and then he will journey, under guard, feet above the
ground, to another room beyond our reach to indulge in his

final shower; I shall follow him and he will ask me to wash his 330
feet. Before I can formulate a tactful refusal, another of our
group will rush to do so. We will then all wash the grime and
mildew from our own feet. All except for me, who knows the
judged, this imposter, to be finally receiving his due. My own
presence at the event, disguised as one of the false Henri
d'Mescan's disciples, will allow future readers to understand
the switch, the elaborate ruse that had been perpetrated
beneath the eyes of the court. Everything needs to be perfect,
and thus, will be subject to a precise timing that I am only able
to guess at in many quiet days of preparation. 340

I can listen closely to the crickets in the distance, and know
that sunset approaches. d'Mescan will expel some air from his
corpulent belly, and in doing so, will glide down to the lip of
his crystalline bath to converse for a short while, when the officer of the Fourth Republic, entering without knocking, march-
es in slowly and states: "I shall not insult you as I do the others, d'Mescan. You have a reputation for clear and simple language despite all that has happened. Prepare for the firing
squad that will snuff out your mortal flame." The officer will
nod absently as he exists into the anteroom. d'Mescan will turn 350
toward us: "What an odd executioner!," as if the prospect of
death were but another frozen moment in his scrapbook, as if
all the wrongs done to him could be cast away in a celluloid
strip extending from the navel and stretching into the void.
d'Mescan surely finds himself overcome with emotion, and ral-
lying to the task before him, will command us to alert the firing squad of its imminent execution.

Our words of delay and indecision will fall on alien ears,
and this d'Mescan, draped in a tunic of cellophane, a ceremonial robe of aluminum and styrofoam and synthetics of his own 360
design, can extinguish the few remaining candles with his still-
vigorous breath, lace his polymer sandals with firm but

crooked fingers, and move, in an almost inhuman, monstrously eager manner, down the spiral staircase of rickety starlight
adorned with numberless mirrors set against stone, over the
limitless floorboards composing the endless corridor below,
leading ever outward toward the solace of moon fruit flowering
in the open square; we will follow behind, solemnly, and I shall
notice that my feet fall into the same pattern as d'Mescan's, the
dull plod of heel and toe matching in rhythmic fusion with a
marionette manipulated by the full body of some ingenuous
puppeteer. We will be ships pushing against the current together, making no progress, bound by a fate that has stolen my
name as well as the promises of *his* life. Henri d'Mescan, the
condemned, will whistle softly for the first few hundred
meters, before his lips begin to move, absently at first, not cal-
ibrated to any sound or function, a few errant phonemes jetting
out with the loose spittle of what I can only identify as a futile
resignation. By the time the procession reaches the second half
of the corridor he will speak for the final time:

"Pulled from the icy waters of the Rhine thirteen hours
later, at the brittle climax of the rivers turn about Koblenz, lus-
trous and empty, I wear ice crystals over my mouth and nose;
yellow and black shocks from the polluted soil striate my
frozen skin under a sunlight whose burn could shatter the cosmos…" Most of us will restrain our tears relatively well until
then, but when we hear with our ears the glorious trumpet of
our redeemer in the form of this story—this telling—this myth,
which we all knew so thoroughly, we can hold back our cries
no longer; my own tears will arrive in a flood against my will.
So I cover my face. I will weep for myself—not for him. It shall
be as if my entire body, the sum of my fingers and bones have
grown cold at his words, and I am frozen, so long ago now,
reflected in the breath of the warm brandy, by somebody else's
controlled cooking fire at the forecourt outside the center gar-

ret. "So hear this, and speak not if you have understanding…"

We will become both ashamed and alarmed in the same breath. The thirteen identical guards, their kepi caps fresh in the twilight sun, will wait stiffly under what will become a glorious full-moon, encircled by a distant corona of celestial light that matches the glittering and mystical fungi ringed around the square into a facsimile of some cosmic forest undefined, kept at bay by a frail circle of human stones. Their darkness will threaten to eclipse us, overwhelm d'Mescan, but he will talk serenely, compassionately, of the work we have yet to do. The blindfold is then applied and d'Mescan moves into the center of the stone ring; our group led to a small detachment on the opposite side of the courtyard, seemingly compelled to witness the apotheosis of our comrade.

Ready. The firing squad will raise their weapons to the starlight, and the gleam from a different portion of each rifle hits us under different stars. My eyes will become enchanted by the Dog Star and the scope, the barrel and Betelgeuse, and the others, I discover later, will be blinded for vague and strobe-lit moments in the same twinkling manner.

Aim. Capricorn will be ascendant, but my constellation, penetrating the retina and burning itself forever onto the series of shifting architectonic plates that make a memory, will force the alignment of the familiar film turned against a man who would be me, the constellation of the camera gun. d'Mescan can stand at rapt attention, his lips still moving, his words still audible as his executioners float their weapons in unison.

Fire into your nervous system, receive the reflex mechanism of corpses conscripted in d'Mescan's small form, drawing everything into its moment, a complete body in the desert with hidden spindles balancing precariously on a pillar, shunning the devil in the flesh. The people will not even look anymore and the camera gun will draw its crippling powers from an

abdicated justice, an abandoned capacity to penetrate the edit.
430 It will be the molar victim (piercing his flesh with rings and hoops and studded bars, haunted quietly by the fire of artists and criminals) that uses up the exasperated spirit. It will be the paranoiac who cleans it all up: Charity is the countless facade of the city maintaining the sparks of misfired bullets against the stone ring bordering Henri d'Mescan like a liquid and undifferentiated cameo picture, the visual archive of silted millennia contrived by chemicals, the rising horn-rimmed cacophony of the record, the cruel jaw of the record album, reminding you of what can never be lost. Mutation will be the death
440 mask of conception, our angel of mercy—fingering a familiar tune, shriveled deep into the soiled pan of carbon ricochet— that torturous pipes resting wickedly in a pawn shop corner. We can refigure the gospel, dipping opposable thumbs into the cruelty of the Rhine. And Henri d'Mescan can fall, an image never developed—dipped deep into the chemical vat of sleek, endless *everything.*

Shortly after the barrage will cease and the firing squad will march haphazardly into the garret-prison, visibly overwhelmed, shell-shocked and dizzy, we can see that d'Mescan's
450 eyes open underneath the blindfold; we will close his mouth and push down his eyelids. As the others will fall back into outer darkness around me, bleeding into the stones, trees, and dirt that form our collective ancestry, I can see in the shadows that this Henri d'Mescan has made a movement. His body, I am sure, shutters as if in orgasm for a single millisecond, with a distant pulse penetrating the callused layers of my skin, the oily overlay of reason and fear. Impossible as it may be, I will be momentarily deluded. Is all not as it seems? Is d'Mescan's death not to be? No, only folly—his movement nothing more
460 than an illusion of my own design, or perhaps, a signal from his

precious life fleeing the body riddled with camera bullets, exploding into the ether. I will shiver and rub my corporeal shoulders, alone in the darkness, preparing the cock to sacrifice to the ancient god, thankful for a cure to the ills of a troubled life that I will never again call my own.

465

Multifesto: A Henri d'Mescan Reader
PART II: The Un-American Years
Hallucigenome: The Henry Mescaline Reader

13) DAVID SCHNEIDERMAN
FROM "INTRODUCTION"
—*HALLUCIGENOME: THE HENRY MESCALINE READER* (1964)[1][2][3]

1.) Page 1:

The only thing certain about the future was that it was already dead, and even for those less distant from its nucleus, it had, indeed, already happened. And this future was the "already-past" for some, but also the "yet-to-happen" for all—or more specifically, the "yet-to-be-realized" for most, even though it had already occurred for some. In the future of this last kind, the bright streaming light of a pettifog starshine sprayed its grizzled darts through the atmospheric membrane that covered the fertile crescent, and, in the slim and dull rotation along an axis of stem and root intertwined with equatorial soil particles, radiation, in the form of celestial disks, passed blithely over what we once knew as familiar terrain.

1 Spuyten Duyvil thinks it best to include *David* Schneiderman's introduction without direct editorial comment—from either Davis Schneiderman or Phoenelia Yeer, because their conflict is counter-productive to the reader who wishes to complete *Multifesto*. We wish to allow another historical voice (with some apparent authority on the subject) to introduce the entire work of *Hallucigenome: The Henri d'Mescan Reader*, which comprises the entirety of PART II of *Multifesto*. Perhaps David Schneiderman's self-indulgent introduction, spiked as it is with his own crass musings, will do more to present the historical facts to the reader. (Spuyten Duyvil)

2 Thus, Roman text sections (with page numbers referring to his original manuscript) are taken from the deceased David Schneiderman's original introduction as he first intended it to appear in the aborted version of *Multifesto* (circa 1967). Italicized sections have been prepared and inserted into this draft based upon notes found in his office after his death (Spuyten Duyvil).

3 All other footnotes in the section have been composed by this same David Schneiderman. (Spuyten Duyvil)

2.) Henry Mescaline's garret resembles a theatre of black moss set in the shadow of sullen leaves. These leaves fall in steady streams from an empty canopy of branch. Already dead, the gnarled husks tower above the carpet of festooned leaf. Between vacant boughs emerge the suggestion of faces, sudden, graceless, inked against the shock-white sky; thick calligraphy lines interrupting a picture-space plane. Below, the heart murmurs of worm and snail slow to still points just outside the spectrum of human hearing. A throbbing winter sun keeps narrative distance. A camera hovering above a particularly bloody motorcrash. This light is metal; this light is dead, exposing the great paper surface of the heavens as an oil rubbing creates an opaque window of grease.

3.) Page 4:

Henry Mescaline inherited the world from a German father well traveled in South America, from a Latin mother obsessively concerned with floral arrangements and cross-pollination. The family's nomadic existence would take a biographers drive to fixate with any certainty, but a simple random sample supplied the high points: from Dubuque, Iowa, to Future, Missouri, to Vicksburg, Mississippi—the young Henry Mescaline rode the great river like a carotid artery flushing with life, over a flood plain big enough for the mysteries of childhood voodoo and old muddy Christianity. After the stock market crash of 1929, the smarmy Mescaline left a ticker-tape collage of a hangman in a Park Avenue bathroom, scaring J.P. Morgan's dyslexic second cousin, P.J., into a catatonic state. At the Brooklyn shipyard in 1943, Mescaline carved his name into the galley of the U.S.S. Missouri. Running from a New Orleans narcotic conviction in 1948, he waited out the heat in Mexico City. By then, his writing began to accumulate, circulate— under the contrapuntal rhythm of late-night drum circles, in

Greenwich Village lofts through an opiate curtain, after Charlie Parker gigs in Kansas City, at the future gravesite of John Dos Passos, open, like a cracked labia majora.

4.) Annunciation. The glorious angel wears three-thousand broken wings, a million sad eyes blinking upon the celestial hosts invisible on this cold planet. A dead star selects an indeterminate American City…New York Panama City Guayaquil Chicago.

And this glorious angel comes to a man or man-y men who is already dead, but as yet unaware: "Look up into your sky, O favored one, the light of that dead star shines upon you!"

This man, who may be man-y men, blinks, only to feel the soft sand dribble from the crease of his eyes. He begs this angel to inscribe the sacred word along the soft parchment of his skin, pressed from the scale of an ancient reptile.

Hark, the angel speaks: "I will do what you ask, for you are to learn of the death which has already occurred…I will tell you your true name. Even god the father keeps this name hidden from you."

5.) **Page 9:**
Drugs affected Mescaline's work. Where once there lingered empty prose, purple concoctions of overwrought syntax, his new texts proved electric, frenetic, revolutionary. Mescaline wrote about fucking and taking a shit with the intensity of a microscope, about world-historical forces reduced in the pan of pan-nationalism and egocentric, offbeat humanism. He became a danger to the establishment that had once, briefly, courted his support; the FBI began surveillance after covert publication of Mescaline's "Warning to the J. Edgar Hoover in your Closet" (1955)—a Morse code transmission between micro-AM radio

stations in Old El Paso.

6.) Forgotten HQ who are you? FBI? CIA? The-J-Edgar-Hoover-in-Your-Closet refuses to utilize normal courier services…fear of enemy intercept. No distinction between the chirps of a carrier pigeon trained to decipher the blips from a satellite; no resolution between the name given to a child at birth, the Hebrew name, the communion name, the nickname, the pet name, the verbal slip, the official title, the public address, the middle initial, the illegible "mark," the signature, the title of long-dead nobility that fuels the inner landscape of the minor aristocracy, the Lumpenproletariat moniker, the rank within the family, the security clearance level in the government, the taxpayer ID number, the sexual objectification name, the metonymic genital name (Auntie Coocher; Sergeant Thickbean), and the hoary hosts of phonemes vocalized in the foam of a recent tidal moon. HQ sends its missives on light rays traveling great distances without turning corners, on sound waves ramming the stomach to shake the ears apart, on the tongue looping always back onto itself—pleased with its muscular existence— along the crumbling scheme of the body.

7.) Page 11: The Social Darwinist Period (January-August 1958)

At first glance, the novel *Spacecats of the World, Untie!* appeared to be a typical product of integrated bohemia; in fact, it ended: "And the reel-to-reel went reeling, the camera kept recording, but all kept quiet under American stars, because God is Mickey Mouse with a fucking frozen head" (301). Yet, a sense of stillness persisted throughout, an infection of Beat stagnancy and language-beyond-language experimentation. Mescaline wrestled with "the angel" who spoke with his voice in his next "sudden" pamphlet, "Forty-Nine Prefaces to a Single-Volume Regicide Indictment"—a work so underground that the only known copy of the first printing was discovered in late 1959, balancing a sewing-machine table leg in Juneau, Alaska. A descendant of Rudyard Kipling wrote: "Mescaline is fully conscious that he is an American deviant, because he lives it every day. After he showed me the manuscript for Single-Volume, I seemed to black out for a period, lost my memory. I awoke in Tijuana wearing a bandoleer and a two-dollar whore. Scars where my kidney was cut. These natives. Jolly good show, old bean!"

8.) Super Soviet Josef Stalin has no existence beyond his many names: Osip, Josip, Butcher, Father, Dzhugashvili, Child of Gori, Liver of Aeschylus, He-Who-Is-Not-Trotsky, He-Who-Altered-the-Axis, Scourge of the Old Bolshevik, Ivan and Peter Reborn, Speaker of the Six Oaths, Stali (steel) and Zastali (grasp), Godless Sun Deity of the Mega-Machine, Joseph… His moniker adapts to the purpose of the speaker, red-bearded revolutionary, buttoned-down loyalist, vodka-swilling peasant...

9.) By the fall of 1958, Mescaline began work in on his next important work, "The Happy-Husband's Pancreatic Tumor Manual"—a short story about a giant "turd" that replaces the main character, Umberto, a yellow-journalist at the local paper. Born from a fiery amalgam of bacon sizzle and industrial lard, the turd wore a pork-pie hat and wrote stories with datelines from the "Duodenum" and "Jejunum," until its steaming, grotesque body was finally squashed in the mechanical bowels of an archaic charcuterie machine. The story ends with the Kaiser Wilhelm/wacky-neighbor character opining (at the turd's state funeral): "Three things you never want to see being made—legislation, sausages, and, of course, legislation regulating the sausage industry" (17).

10.) *Before the ONE GOD SUN GOD sets up a stall in the fertile crescent, before the bustling market square is cleared of competing deities and their parlor tricks, before every animal-headed demiurge with some ineffectual, bestial power staffs a kiosk filled with shrunken heads and amulets of twisted world-serpents dancing through the universe, those elder gods who can not be named—with names such as He-Who-Can-Not-Be-Named and J-Edgar-Hoover-In-Your-Closet—barter loudly with bags of salt and petrified starfish for the decency of the immortal soul.*

11.) Page 17: The Meta-Fictive Socialist Eco-Terrorist Anarchist Period (January-April 1960).
The authors of these early reviews deliberately *wanted* the reader to lose themselves in the sentences they tried to foist against Mescaline. Try as they might for some sort of clarity, some ocean of fertile, amber waves rolling over the salt flats in a monkey-powered caravan, everything seemed just *beyond* the comprehension of the reader. In the infamous *A Novel of Fuck You!* (1959), Mescaline took his critics to task in a blistering book composed entirely of reviews of everything the novel *might* be about. The first lines, "Plodding. Predictable laced with that same inane, egocentric verbosity..." (1), seemed just that, a review of the introduction to the novel.

12.) *David—King of the Jews a.k.a. the Ancient Hebrews, Mover from Hebron to Jerusalem, Slayer of Goliath, Scion of Future State of Israel, Bringer of Light, Feeble Shepherd Brother, Star of the Six-Sided Morning, Jerusalem Rising, Builder of the Temple, Defender of the Forty-Nine, Father of the House of David, Successor of Saul, Friend to Jonathan, Author of Psalms, Itinerant Beggar, Patriarch of the House of the Son of Man, Union Agitator, Presidential Candidate, Senior Senator from Mississippi.*

13.) The critics eventually loosened up, with one notable writer even going so far as to note in February 1960: "The scurrilities and general lack of control become a major drawback, especially in the Meta-Fictive Socialist Eco-Terrorist Anarchist prose. Yet, despite the monotony that plagued the style of these volumes, they remained Mescaline's most cogent bridge to the wonderful and consistently successful *Appendisectomy*."

14.) *Identification of the "true" name has become the holy grail for a band of celebrity-obsessed, faux-ascetic monks intent on maintaining the bloodline of the supposed savior, masked by the misdirected helix of the Carolingian Dynasty and the arrangement of certain European churches founded in precise relation to a set of dead stars mixing it up on rickety cartographer tables. Pentacles triangulated from volcanic islands in the Mediterranean point in five-pronged arrows toward the sea beasts with many backs drawn hard at the edges of the Earth. Apocryphal books claim that the Second Coming repeats itself in every birth on the planet as it pushes the population toward an unwieldy six billion. In the seed of every cornhusk fed to a head of soon-to-be-slaughtered emaciated cattle, in the pupa of every mealworm crawling on the skull of a hairless child gripped by famine's crooked fingers, sit pieces of stringy sinew coursing through a channel of common blood…if the true name of even the meekest child, the smallest soul, can simply be articulated, then perhaps, so the monkish theory states: dominion over all heaven and earth shall be offered to the speaker. But, if someone else speaks the true name before the subject, death comes swiftly to the one who is named.*

15.) **Page 24: The Minatorian Mimetic Roaming or Nixon-After-Checkers Period (April-August 1961)**
Appendisectomy brought with it the kind of notoriety that Fatty Arbuckle could only dream about. Mescaline catapulted from

obscurity to insularity, from a generous recipient of American anonymity to the media darling who jokingly left his posterior print on the Hollywood Walk of Fame.[4] The *Evangelical Pentecostal Watchword* called the story (a series of autobiographical appendices that told his life story in fragments and cross-references), "a slow move toward non-repetitive truth."

16.) The monks of the modern age—corporate raiders watered down in their skyboxes, venture capitalists reading ticker tape through blistered fingers, robber barons, vestigial and dyspeptic, brewing knockout potions in their secret lairs to get whiff of insider trading—they all speak names indeterminably, offer at least five different titles before the first cup of coffee. "Well lookee here, **Robert Smithbrowns** *on the case…" At the water cooler. "***Bobby***, so how about that local sports team in last nights important game? All I could do to press a flank steak on my wife's pussy as I fucked her into post-game silence. Ain't that right,* **Bobborino***?" In the restroom. "Theres the* **Bobber, Robert Bobber***, spraying the urinal cakes. Hey,* **Smithy Brown-Brown***, hows tinkle-tinkle fun time?" During the Board meeting. "***Mr. Robert head-up-my-ass Shit-stain Smith-Brown** *prepared these reports, sir, Mr. Funglebunch, and well, I'm just not sure where his head's at." Staring at the faded sun through the UV-protective skyscraper glass. "***Brownie***, in moments well all be irradiated by the nuclear winter. For godsakes, come live with me and be my love…"*

17.) Christened the "Vestigial Tales" by an arthritic society matron of the international museum set, Henry Mescaline's first literary admiration group, a loose collective of two immigrant authors, Günter Broudly and Antwerp Meurtin, was caught poking through the garbage bins outside his Los Alamos, New Mexico home: the first police reports that they

4 The print was later removed and replaced with that of the third child from the TV show "My Three Sons."

were "entranced by the brittle animal skeletons and glowing meteorite décor."

18.) *The only thing certain about the future is that it is already dead, and for those less distant to its nucleus, it has, indeed, already happened. And the future is the "already-past" for some, but is also the "yet-to-happen" for all—or more specifically, the "yet-to-be-realized" for most, even though it has already occurred for some. In the future that is of this last kind, the bright streaming light of a pettifog starshine will spray its grizzled darts through the atmospheric membrane shrouding the fertile crescent, and in the slim and dull rotation of the planet, radiation—in the form of celestial disks—will pass over what we know now as Egypt, ancient Aethiopia, tracing in the sky a tributary to the cloudy river known to us as "Nile."*

19.) These "Vestigial Tales" led police to the cache of automatic writing experiments composed from whatever texts populated Mescaline's trash, and a search of their aluminum Roadmaster revealed urine and fecal residues matching Mescaline's genetic code. Mescaline prepared to instigate legal proceedings at the theft of his precious bodily fluids, until the basically unreadable manuscripts they composed in his honor inspired Mescaline's "shit"-writing manifesto, "Riot and Dis-Ordure"—which outlined, in no less clear language, the praxis of *Appendisectomy:*

> The Margins will be a wasteland and to approach them
> with any fixed locus, any attempt to compose in a real-
> istic manner, eliminates the subject. Writing the disas-
> ter will remain impossible, for writing the mundane is
> already implausible. Pitch a screenplay about the
> inane—a presidential election with no clear electoral

winner days later, massive recounts, voter fraud, deceptive ballots, and the fat cats will tell you "never in America kid, we're looking for the next *Ben Hur*." It's a system that will eventually bring about re-definitions in the **NAME** of things—a Jesuit uprising in North America, the terra-forming of the red planet, a Constitutional crisis that threatens to engulf the democratic system—if only for a second, a moment in-between. The only method will be through the appendix. It's superfluous but leads to the colon: it's the purest form of revisionist anatomy" (xviii).

20.) Forgotten HQ must speak the true name of an uppity citizen before the subject. If HQ speaks first, it ensures the death of the already dead. But if the citizen wises up, and learns her or his true name, well, then, let's just say things get real tasty.

21.) Appendisectomy's critique coupled with Henry Mescaline's newfound media popularity manifested in the most eclectic cultural spaces. At an early twelfth-anniversary party for the only known launch of Howard Hughes's infamous airplane-boat, the Spruce Goose, where 3000 different sized radio-controlled replicas of the craft took flight over the water, Mescaline wore a jester costume on the dock, waved a steel wand with a small monkey head on top, and shouted, even as the police dragged him into the paddy-wagon, that the Spruce Goose had succeeded in its mission to airdrop microscopic propaganda on the fuel-soaked phytoplankton, and that an electrification of their cellular structure would create an alternate evolutionary dynasty. When Hughes's honor guard checked the original ship's hull after the replicas had safely landed, an unidentifiable slimy substance—undifferentiated tissue—coated everything in the thinnest sheath of cellophane.

22.) *The god of thieves and profit, travelers and boy scouts, yes…Hermes known as Mercury mixed with Pan, Hermes Criosphorus, Hermes Psychopompus, Hermes Trismegistus, Lord of the Gemini Twins, Eloquent Orator, Master of Agate, Lord of Feldspar, Sultan of Topaz, Auditor of Opal, Constable of Amber, Barrister of Stone-Flesh Erectors Spurting Marble Seed into the Sky… Well, this many-named god gets cut real good by the blade of somebody else's bartering starfish. He turns translucent and bleeding on the side of the road, violet ichor spilling from ankle-heals, dripping from his feathers, and just as He-Hoo-Cannot-B-Named approaches with some sort of god-killing blade forged by Hephaestus, or Vulcan, or an Orc in the center of the Earth… Well Hermes just blinks his tired eyes and opens his lips so low they seem to be closed. A whirligig of feather and bone; his body disappears. The wind carries his secret name into the carapace of heaven, into an upside-down tortoise shell meant to force out the undesirables.*

23.) The literary stage, rife with disappearances, splits Mescaline into personas,[5] and the schizophrenia that allowed mail-order bride scams sponsored by pep-pill manufacturers to earn huge financial windfalls convinced Mescaline of the necessity of returning underground. Before long, he would condemn *Spacecats* and *Appendisectomy* as reductive tools of the oppressor state: "All vestigial organs must go!"

---

5 A smaller project followed: The Surliness of the Last Days detailed Mescaline's undercover interviews with former Vice-President Richard Nixon during the latter period of his service under Dwight. D. Eisenhower. Nixon, whose support for the McCarthy hearings gave him as much chance of holding a future office as a B-movie President of the Screen Actors Guild, was forthcoming and candid with Mescaline, who wrote under the name of one deceased Colonel Tact Gactenberg, a casualty of the Brooklyn shipyard during WWII. The interviews were edited and released as the series "Beneath-World" in such reputable publications as Timeweek *and* Newstime.

24.) *The Old Man or Man-y Men of the Mountain, detailed in Marco Polo's perhaps fanciful thirteenth-century travelogue, labors intently in the guild of hashish Assassins. This Old Man or Man-y Men, Hassan I Sabbah, arches a crooked finger from his palace at Alamout, amid thorny rock and wild sagebrush, and his legion of boys snap into action. They commit political intrigue, but never touch a conventional weapon. No, the arc of light from the distant dead stars propels their fanatical devotion. Little do they know that the world is really colorless, the light just a memory of a name, a face.*

25.) **Page 27: The Militant Nationalistic Counter-Bohemian Pro-De-Socialized Discourse Rainbow Period (August 1961-March 1962)**

Returning to the swaddling clothes laid on him by the bourgeois avant-garde of the mainstream world, Mescaline sought out the new discourse, a proto-language, or "Urlaut."[6] The most important work of this period, *Tupeat, Frompeet, Repeit,* presents incessant variants of the childhood adage: "Pete and Repeat went into a building. Pete came out. Who was left?"… "Repeat." And so on.

26.) *Bobby Smithbrown takes three simultaneous calls on his telepager from the Old Man or Man-y Men, the monks, and the Infotainment Boys at HQ: "Agent BSB, hit your coworker—you know, the obnoxious one, the would-be-name-saying-motherfucker. Do it before the next sun goes out," and BSB knows that HQ and the monks have gotten real cozy as of late so he guzzles some bitter coffee and massages his esophagus in rapt contractions of the Adam's Apple, wondering if this qualifies as a "wise guy" job—*

6 *A primal sound language where each linguistic gesture communicates directly without superfluity. A mythological concept, Mescaline briefly sought a return to this impossible past, fully realizing the only method lies in exploding current formal limits.*

maybe not—but who is he to refuse to serve the light and the way and who is he, really, to argue with the command structure so his eyes tighten up at the ready…?

27.) In the 587 page novel, Mescaline led us through the nightmare circus mirror of Gertrude Stein on LSD, where the *monstrous sentence* circumnavigated the whole world, the entire Omniversé, and as one of Mescaline's rejected friends noted: "Henry doesn't hold his tongue; he lays it out. If I had the guts to step on everyone that way, I would, but I don't. I'm too connected to people, to a system of signs. He's a fucker, a real jackass. Ok, you can turn the recorder back on now…"

28.) *West of the great river artery, in the Fayoum region, bakes the belly of the silent city of Shedit, Greek Crocodilopolis. Muddy crypts rot beneath hardened sand, making a vault of gravel and irradiated soot. The regressive hypostyle roof of the temple exposes a giant appendix pit of supernatural length where tattered skins of long-disintegrated lizards rest in a basin filled with hundreds of reptile embryos preserved in various stages of development. These basins feed the emergent crocodile deity of many names—The God-Who-Feasts-On-Itself-Each-Day, Blood-Bearer of the Lowlands, Vizier of Muddy Depths, Multi-Ocular Fiend of Scale and Tooth, That-Which-Sees-The-Beauty-Of-The-Most-Private-Places, Ancient of all the Vaults, Sobek, Subuk, Sebek of Crocodilopolis, Préposition of the Desert Western, Annointer of the Sacred Meadow. Yet all is not dead here, for on the command of a distant star, armies of undead reptiles crowd the basin of the long appendix, and pray daily for the return to the past that is all but assured to recur in this necropolis of lizard and bone.*

29.) The power of *Tupeat, Frompeet, Repeit* rested not in its repetition of form, but in the de-familiarization of a common *name* for the reader, such as "were"—where it suddenly became strange, foreign, broken into "w", "e", "r", and "e." Uncertain of its spelling, its meaning, in extreme cases, the shape and pronunciation of letters, bleeding, for that single moment that we fixated on the word, into the entire world, into all relations, a slow molasses poison that covered everything we knew in world-serpent snakeskin, a cataract of infused, equatorial balm. *Tupeat, Frompeet, Repeit* carried that feeling made flesh, a space "where the soul represents a palimpsest over-written with indecipherable, ominous cuneiform of the *tabula rasa*" (345).

30.) Across the yawning office space, enthralled by the shiny spine of a red stapler, Jackass Junior Executive tiptoes around the particle board divisions of cubicle, oversteps the mashed letter piles stained with canned cheese snacks and the loose ends of cellophane snapped from beef-jerky sticks. A pre-processed muzak version of his worst nightmare pipes in through the heating vents, over the blue-green field of a pie graph set solid in the Aegean sea of fiscal data. Boils arise like horrible armies of the black night on his blistered figure as Bob SB approaches Jack Az-juneer in the supply closet. Junior Executive J jumps, startled, at the sound of the door, but upon seeing his cohort—"Bobbily-Bobber"—he begins to undo his awkward off-the-rack seersucker suit and fumbles for his zippered fly: "Glad to see you've come around to my way of feeling..." Agent BoSs-B sticks out his pockmarked tongue and J.J. Jay III reaches out to make the grab beneath a chorus of tube lighting; the dark space between their blue-green auras stretches into the infinity of dull, black light piercing the heating vent. Slats of alternating current. A merger of space and time, this new inky blue-black mass engulfs their bodies as a soap bubble might be skillfully blown around a smaller orb; Yajay Yajay gets a hard-on, "Smith-Bob-Brownington—you shouldn't have" and he's presenting him-

self on all fours to Yajay's exited whisper...

31.) Ignored by the same mainstream press that had embraced *Appendisectomy*, this new text fell into obscurity. In a rare interview from the time granted to the one-shot fanzine *The Sticky Papers*, Mescaline articulated the extremity of his new position: "Skeletal bodies mass graves shaved heads broken necks burnt ash gold teeth soap cancer gangrene beating shootings rapes executions trains heat water hoses animals...radioactive eggs hatched in a million stomachs by the Atomic bomb, cancer days will come again. And there can be no cure in the late stage. We want books that swarm all over your insides."

32.) Estimates vary, but scientists observe that of the hundreds of thousands of stars visible to the naked eye, approximately 93.47833% have already been extinguished. The light that reaches this insignificant planet is residual, just as memory has meaning only in the grizzled darts of intergalactic twinkle swaying motionless among the dead.

33.) **Page 35: The Post-Apocalyptic Post-Ironically Post-Ironic Mid-Catatonic Ante-Meridian Pre-Cinematic Period. (November 22, 1963)**
Mescaline became a bottom feeder, a sullen fish-weight wandering the unofficial tenements of a country that had first vigorously embraced, and then vehemently rejected his randy silhouette. On June 19, 1960, Henry Mescaline slept on the same park bench that Fidel Castro spent the night in after a failed audition for professional baseball. There, at approximately 7:10 p.m. EST, on that park bench across from the White House (in full view of military-industrial complex), Mescaline experienced a third-world epiphany concerning the transnational character of the material dialectic and its relation to the oppressor class.

34.) Jejunum, Lower Intestine: *Shockwaves continue to penetrate communities of the faithful as the "Jesus" virus has reached pandemic preparations through retrograde linguistic deployment. The disease goes global, in fact, and millions have become infected in the womb. A malignant mutation of rough European beast slouches its oily tentacles along the aqueducts of the Holy Land some two thousand years ago, ensuring that the next big thing must be the white-skinned Christ, the Son of Man, the White Light and the Bright Way, the Alpha and Omega, the I.N.H.S., the I.H.S. or I.H.C., the Chi-Ro, the Redeemer, the Suckling Infant who pops out of the virgin womb clear and translucent as an immaculate jellyfish set coyly on the afterbirth of a beach. Held up against the backdrop of his people so that his face exactly covers the sun, the kid shimmers in phase distortion with the pulse of distant satellites. The reluctant father, Joseph, screams about drowning the "little albino freak" in a pool of fermented goat milk. Not only didn't he stick it in, at all, ever, but also, now, the kid looks to be of something spawned from the center of the earth, a translucent castoff born from a lightless quarry millions of miles from the nearest living star.*

35.) Henry Mescaline's most cherished hypothesis became that mutual humanization could only take place in dialogue with the oppressed, and that the false, anti-dialogical nature of most revolutionary thought left the "common" people behind at the expense of the movement. Mescaline visualized this as a dialogue between mammals and reptiles at the close of the Cenozoic age: Ung, last of the thunder lizards, places her gargantuan tail upon the bosom of the tiny muskrat, and lovingly says, "I have nothing against hair and backbones, some of my best friends have hair and backbones."

36.) Old Bee Esby refuses to take the bait—"some things an agent shouldn't do, even to keep cover," he mumbles as tiny blue-black marbles pour out his mouth and clash onto the floor. Jayforth Jayington, Esq. rotates his head back toward the agent for a moment, forgetting that his hands and feet rest in puddles of industrial goop, with pinkies soaking up ammonia and beta-carotene in tiny flesh syringes on loan from a small Pacific island. B.S.B. takes in the picture and opens his crackling mouth with all the power of cheekbones carved from a sacred woodblock; the air pulls back in an astringent back-tense. In hi-fi slow motion, Bull-Shit Bob's ribcage sounds like a wooden chest, and his breath pushes up his esophagus into coffers of sullen cheek and rosy lip. Slower down again, and Bee esS Bee spits out the cowering subjects "true name"...

37.) By 7:23 p.m., Mescaline had rejected these primitive notions, and moved onto a startling rejection phase corresponding to the symbolic cycle of the Washington moon. Shuffling without movement in his mummified wrap of newspapers, the lead story "World Enters Peaceful 1960s" banded around the makeshift elements of his torso, he categorically rejected the sacred names of cynicism, stoicism, peripateia, antagonism, protagonism, synthesis and thesis (and potentially antithesis), cronyism, left-wing arch-liberalism, right-wing arch-Duke-ism, feudalism, shamanism, narcissism, mysticism, creationism, Great Schism-ism, paternalism, triumphalism, pluralism, Maoism, Ho Chi Minh-ism, optimism, relativism, negativism, absolutism, forgetfullism, Protestantism, paganism, capitalism, and of course, the eating of flesh.

38.) One by one, this loathsome procession of crocodiles, adorned in sun disks and tooth necklaces, swaddle from the main crypt basin and onto the shifting-sand of desert marsh and muddy river-

*bank. Claw and scale footprints merge into the texture of the soil
as the lizards ring themselves about the underground necropolis
just as a plague of tapeworms might become bandied about the
intestinal tape of the lower bowels. Gleaming under the solar eye,
that great pineal organ of pulsating heat and brown energy, the
animals shift back and forth, left to right, as heads connect to tails
and the shiny gold and silver disks reflect the brittle rays of light
no longer burning but already dead. For forty-nine days forty-nine
weeks forty-nine endless centuries under the oily stars the reptiles
march in their circle, tracking slow declamations as their mighty
tails wear enormous grooves into the sand. They move undisturbed
until the groove grows deep enough to wheedle the river Nile from
its bed; the rhythmic trudge of claw foot and gliding tail coax the
oozing liquid over its bank. Pulled by the magnetism of such determined creatures, the river mumbles its muddy promise to fill the
furrows, to collect in the mud ditches—until each crocodile
observes, in the water, a shiny reflection of itself from the dead
light above.*

39.) But before these new positions achieved formulation,
Henry Mescaline's colon violently rejected excrementalism
while his mouth simultaneously rejected oralism and genital-
ism. This brought about a quick acceptance, at 7:28 p.m., of a
strange new brand of modernism capable of cleaning up the
mess that it always seems to generate. Mescaline slept in the a
puddle of muddy swill, his organs seeping in the juice
expunged from the interior of a tortured soul, a violent
American genius, and in a dream vision, he generated his most
ambitious work, the exceedingly obtuse *Our Arteries Harden
with the Pulse of the People,* later known simply as *Abecedarium.*

40.) *Various holy men of various wandering tribes spread balms of
powdered camel dung onto the little boy's arms and legs, hoping to,*

as they say, "reveal his true colors." These men have the names Melchoir, Frankenstein, Goldiemyrrh, Hosy-mandius, Platarch, Nebbajebriath, Shetzelheem Pocahontas, Judas-Ben-Hur, exercise guru Pontius Pilates—but their magic no work no more no ABRA-CADABRA. Before long, even the "Jesus" boy's loyal followers start to worry. If the kid can stay light-skinned under the incessant milk of such a heavy star, maybe its our eyes, they think—rubbing the corneas with sharp sticks while burning out gashes in empty sockets. Just then Albino Jesus stares up into space: "Speak the White Name now, and understand your natural color!"

41.) Set in forty-nine different locations across a variety of literary, cultural, and historical time periods, *Abecedarium*, a linguistic primer of the most subtle variety (co-authored with fiction writer Arc-Zen S. Denarhlo), charted the movement of old man "Fex" as he embarked on colonial exhibitions, mused upon old age, and ran an aggressive French shadow government fed up with the Nazi Occupation of 1940-1944. In one particularly moving "American" section, Fex lived out his boyhood in the small Mississippi river town of Future, Missouri near Mark Twain's birthplace in Hannibal, before transplanting himself to a Megalopolis encapsulating everything from Boston to Washington D.C., where men lit cigars on the crook of low-hanging stars and bathed in vats of sticky summer molasses.

42.) *Well, JJ just about shits out a pair of elongated snakes composed of corn meal and undigested chocolate candy when he hears his cover blown apart—and then he does, lose control of his bowels, that is—as the entire supply closet washes itself in a flood of feces and sputum, oily green discharge bubbling up through the pores that have become obscene baby mouths, horrific, gaping cold sores infected with the boiling nucleotide chains. Focused on his training, old Agent Robert SOB jumps back and activates his shoe*

rocket, blasting apart the wooden door like a butcher barn explod-
ed from the psychic energy of its screaming swine. Boards shatter,
and half the office staff, including mainline executives, peers
through the now-destroyed supply closet door. The blob that resem-
bles colleague Junior Jay mimes a series of morbid gesticulations
until the remains of his tangled form bubble away in acidic oil
splotches soaked into the dirty hardwood floor. BSB smiles into his
watch phone; he spins on his axis, a slow lizard surveying a king-
dom of muck, before flicking his tongue toward the jaws of the
waiting crowd. He hisses, "The only thing certain about the future
is that it is already dead…"

43.) In book one, "The Book of ISMs and ICBMs," the adoles-
cent Fex left Future, Missouri to study at North Alamos
Regional Polytechnic Academy of Multiple Intelligences and
the Fusion Center for Particle Acceleration. His so-called
"friends" from back home journeyed up the smaller Missouri
River in search of a renegade Dean, and Fex followed closely
behind, drawn into the gunboat madness of a civilization on
the brink of cultural extermination. His friends were found
dead, their heads tattooed with elaborate genetic totems,
bright-colored bands around their shaved craniums, the mark
of phrenologist calipers freshly indented into the flesh of their
ears.

44.) *Only then will the crocodiles begin to roll on their mighty tor-*
sos and tails, spinning slowly at first, then faster, turbines of dried
skin, until the entire circle thrashes wildly about the mud and
sand, for days, weeks on end, a constant mirror of the light no
longer heating, the soil no longer warming. After each crocodile
has expired, after the blood has slowed to a still point, the flood
will finally run backwards, reversing through the channels and
into the river that reflects the myriad lights of the heavens. And a
star will snuff out from the heavens. And then another.

45.) Abraxas Jones, in his seminal study "*Abecedarium*: Precursors and Antecedents," testified to the genius of this intertext: "When Fex rides the rail line back to Future, a sensational flood of narrative emerges, a tempest born from ancient Cabalist patterns: Shucking skin bandage over three-bean fire, mirrors repatriated in the hands of the broken, immutable shards splitting sense into familiar nonsense, critique into empty space." In the segment excerpted for this volume, "Fex During the Occupation of France," Mescaline managed to capture the rhythm of what he would later articulate as "Pre-Cinema"—where the only explosion occurred in the book, where the significance of movie scripts written into existence represented the thunderous refusal of the plausible, and the latent explosive violence of all texts.

46.) *And another snuffed out. Only then can that hideous archangel, old Gay-Bree-Aal, point your head in the direction of certain brighter-than-thou stars that have already extinguished...only when you come around to his way of naming. And another.*

47.) For Henry Mescaline birthed himself in a psychic instant, despite the savage mediocrity, the safety net of the mainstream, the liberal tolerance of the counter-culture, the constant dull, thudding insistence of the cerebral cortex mapping itself onto the body and bread of America. Henry Mescaline lived in the missed opportunities, in the breakdown of power and knowledge. As the great author himself wrote at the close of *Abecedarium*: "If we can push the formal limits, we can cease with these formalities. Only then will things stand as you think they are, the shutters of perception, painted in a thick and dark veneer, closing down your soul from the illusion of light already snuffed" (789).

48.) *Only then, in the afterglow of a necropolis absorbing the lizard bones, after the sand has reclaimed the tail grooves in a ocean of undifferentiated dirt—only then will the Crocodile God rise in anger, rolled from slumber by the sound of its true name.*

49.) Only then from one dead star will come many dead stars in the mouth of the universe, forcing words from the esophageal tubes of the scared animals, man or man-y men included, threaded through the cavernous body. The only thing certain about the future is that is belongs to the crocodile lord, Sebek the Unholy—a name set on autorepeat.

14) **Phoenelia Yeer**
Introduction: *Spacecats of the World, Untie!* (1958)

Forty-nine mysteries agree to be authored, as if they had any choice. It is not "you" who speaks, but *language* itself.

You stumble across the chalk-marks of this ugly continent, hitching rides with truckers who look upon your metal machine stomach with the same glare Joseph must have shot at the curved skin of his virginal wife; you move, simply, even at rest, dreaming of human feet, sore and calloused, stomping over the glacial ridges of memory, up and down the Big Muddy—a difficult way to reach any sound conclusion.

Who actually wrote *this* strange *Spacecats* text? David Schneiderman working as the experimental fiction writer Henry Mescaline? Henry Mescaline as his autonomous "self"? Or, Henri d'Mescan as Henry Mescaline? Strange lines differentiate the prose styles from the earlier d'Mescan material, and you are left, just as a word might leave its referent to assume only local, immanent relations, to ponder the distinction between "author" and "editor."

Of course, you despise sound and final conclusions. Still, it is tough to be postmodern when human feet detach from bodies to stalk you, when a keyboard left unattended starts erasing your text like a white-skinned crablet moving sideways across the page of your pubic hair.

Maybe "you" are the author of this delightful story, of the young girl, Dial-Up Networking, of the tiny spacccat, known mainly as Spacecat.

Not knowing gets old, real fucking quick.

No surprise that readers seem mystified by the ancient and androgynous Spacecat, but it strikes you as odd, as if your face might be hit with a bouquet of water lilies, that Dial-Up Networking also presents interpretative problems: Dial-Up, a confused derivation of the Herbraic terms for "interconnection" transmitted in the sub-textual codes of certain apocryphal Midrash during the Maimonides period.

You must stop caring about the documentation of every multi-streaming data bit.

Dial-Up provides this "Henry Mescaline" with the chance to fuse organisms and technology into a blubbering mass of degraded human autonomy. Everyday tasks become strange. "Talking picture box," an ancillary character, runs in tandem with the antagonist "Round Earth"—presenting a case for the fiber-optic compartmentalization of language.

You are of course the editor, and you can paste and cut. You listen closely, in order to best introduce a random factor.

It is tough to be postmodern when human feet detach from their bodies, when you carry Dial-Up Networking in the bloody aftermath of your unfortunate affair with Davis Schneiderman. Dressed in swaddling clothes, this girl. You of course feel an unmistakable attraction to this particular Mescaline work. After all, it suggests your daughter's name, edited together from a dozen different fragments scattered to the four winds over the distension of three weird trimesters.

Careful, though, with such fragile children.

During the worst days of morning sickness, after puking up charred animal flesh, beans, chocolate-covered vanilla sticks, orange juice, and a tube of toothpaste, you feel the moment where time stands still, the kick of daughter through the impenetrable layers of stomach and flesh, of bone and silence. Reading the typescript of Mescaline's search for a corporeal species-specific identity, you know that your child follows an unholy tradition.

The mark of the writing self-consciously expresses Henry. Pure Mescaline as we've been taught to expect him from David Schneiderman's introduction. Yet the prose also bears the obsessive repetition and distortion of phrase that characterizes the most extreme segments of that same introduction:

Confused by the unfamiliar but soothing lope of your mechanized body demanding its food, its sleep, its inopportune excretions and apomorphine injections, you look into the microwave panel and fix a coif of mussed-up hair. You see mirrors in mere reflections. Your toaster oven has a hidden agenda. Think about it and it disappears, the warring realities of this book, the differences drawn sharper with each passing segment, each hyper-processed, over-scripted, twenty-two minute visual teleplay about the twenty-somethings who conquer fear and shit and yeast infections in pricey New York lofts that act as end points for tired pop-art reproductions.

Maybe forty-nine lily plants bloom together in a pattern. Not planned, but maybe. Or rather, the act of simple juxtaposition encourages a group effort, just as the heartbeat of two lovers synchronizes itself to the orgasm while chests heave breathlessly in the night.

Endless supplies can be moved in by the telecom industry, intimate veal dinners and wholesale slaughtered chickens sans feathers, sans blood, with smiling ear-to-ear slits marking the empty, airless gape of the city's dirt and sound.

Still on the run from the obsessive, compulsive behaviors of Davis, you discern in the rearview mirror the mirage of wooden rest areas, the geopolitical ass of Paul Bunyan, and the historical markers of Civil War battles that populate American highways; in your reflections on Letter 3 when Henri d'Mescan—at least at one time—accuses David Schneiderman of *fabricating* Henry Mescaline, you perceive an identity change that would ultimately, so they both hope, vindicate d'Mescan.

You walk forever backward, a turnpike crossing a noisy animal, swollen heel to toe, searching desperately for the next exit that dissipates into mirages of carbon monoxide with each step-by-step retread. You split the dotted white line into useless hemispheres of law and lucidity, into the limpid green yowl of the highway marker. You both know, you and Davis Schneiderman, that you are smart enough to figure things out on your own, and thus you expect your path to lead here, to the next fork in the rambling road of interlocking roots and stems….

David Schneiderman, so professional in his execution of this literary hoax, foresees the need for his "character" to develop in a way that might be *believable* to future audiences of the *Hallucigenome* collection. This implies that Henri d'Mescan approves of the initial literary direction that his "executor" has taken with the Mescaline fabrication—which retroactively bestows a critical importance upon *Spacecats of the World, Untie!* (even if written entirely by David Schneiderman), as a harbinger of Henry Mescaline's later style.

These are, you wish to mention, only assumptions.

You begin to lose it, you think, perhaps, as a thousand feet trample your cataleptic figure, splayed diagonal across a cum-soaked motel bedspread, trudging with the light touch of a million crumpled wings.

These are, you must warn, only assumptions.

So you have a sinking feeling of numbness that grows each night and still clings to your body each day, and you have Dial-Up Networking springing furiously, a pre-Christian god birthed from dark and sundry surrogate wombs. Smoke detectors dilate until the incessant beep beep beep fades into the background between your legs; lime-soaked toilet bowls contract like pulsing sores in a bath of white noise and flush. All, now, in their glory, threaten to expunge the child.

All, now, exceed the reach of Davis Schneiderman's bony forceps. Assuming he even knows what to grab.

15) Henry Mescaline
From *Spacecats of the World, Untie!* (1958)

Last night we slept on a broken bed.

It was I, Dial-Up Networking, slovenly in my circuitous pajamas, curled tight under the folds of MaMas fleshy undersides, squeezed safe in her venous nuzzle. Snoring lightly, black holes nostrils flaring softly under a June croon moon lay Round Earth, entrenched in MaMa's broken bed, a man whose tarnished toothbrush bristles stink of iodine, a man whose boots are interlaced with frizzled fiberoptic cords, a man who reminds me, tender Dial-Up Networking, all muzzled and folded in MaMa's warm corona, of some approximation of some maybe, some possibility, some pregnant, paternal, perhaps.

A flat globe smashed onto a car hood. His ears are floating Galapagos specks in wells of dark, oceanic hair. His belly heaves to the rhythm of an invisible gulf stream. Archipelagos of consciousness roll themselves through the curve of his backward knee, the triumphal arch of some classic vestigial tail, the uneven slopes of mountainous shoulder blades devolving into pre-vertebrate sinews. The awkwardness of his body interrupts my sleep; I watch it at rest, obsessively, but force my eyes shut as soon as he stirs, he tromps slowly to the bathroom, disrupting everything with haphazard urine. Atlantis destroyed on his sweaty legs, Lemuria vanquished on the tip on his penis—and I, in my own silent way, lay still as can be in the ruffled bed sheets.

Fuckin toilet! Never catches my piss right.

He works on the diaries at night, but those secret books hide during the day from the watchful figure of Spacecat, from my toys and distractions, from the swath of MaMa's repetitive housework, her dust rags and vacuum, only to emerge in the darkness where none of us dare go, into gleaming tomes of ancient knowledge, mouthing beautiful words that I fail to pronounce, sucking sweet taffy at the corners of my mouth. How much time has passed in this false sleep? If I am very still, extra quiet, strange sounds and muffled phrases, the arcane chants of horrible grown-ups, the denatured phrases of a midnight static, replay endlessly in the black night, bathing me in indecipherable pitch.

We slept last night on a broken bed.

It was I, Dial-Up Networking, MaMa and Round Earth. And of course it was Spacecat. Spacecat whose paws stretch into tender lines of longitude from the mean time of a heart, Spacecat whose rapport with the talking picture box makes me swoon moon croon in that darkness, Spacecat who disappears between feedings through a dent in the laundry room membrane, Spacecat who sits on my celluloid lap, Spacecat who makes my neck twitch and crink after nights spent tossing on the bed's spastic, broken springs.

Spacecat cuddles against my stomach, blows the fermented stick of cat breath into my mouth. Everything begins to bloom. Careful to leave Round Earth undisturbed, we move quietly off the broken bed, moving inches at a time to suffocate the squeaky springs. Once we make it to the floor, Spacecat leads me out the window, through the flowing drapes caught sneezing in the wind, onto the latticed branches of the big oak tree. Spacecat dances from limb to limb, hopping effortlessly through the maze of branch and leaf, onto the tips of the upper twigs. "Dont look down," warns Spacecat. I lose my balance and slip onto a lower branch. Dark leaves spiral to the ground. Spacecat laughs and I start again, leaping higher into the upper parts of the tree, onto thinner and thinner sticks, off into the sky....

Spacecat and I go hunting on other planets, sometimes Saturn, sometimes X-56AR2, hunting for life. We crawl together on callused limbs. Between stars lay stretches of quiet. Spacecat scours my body with yellow eyes.

Not sure what sort of paws those will make. Spacecat massages a cold, wet face into my skin. The nose is a kissing machine and I am a collaborator.

You're not disfigured, definitely not, but just not sure about the paws. Spacecat leaps high into the sheets of slow foreign gravity, but my jumps feel always less spectacular, less slinky, barely feline, secondary to the beautiful swath of black space that Spacecats loping body contrasts against lonely alien vistas.

We float into unfamiliar reaches. Spacecat's head on my inside left thigh. Spacecat's body in the tight alcove of my lap. Spacecat's treatise on stars, bright Pleiades cobweb, extinguishing Cygnus. We tussle in harmless dander to the tinkling sound of atomic gas.

Sometimes Spacecat pulls away. Paws smack clay and slither from my body. Spacecat lifts a front paw, spreading digits in a muscular yawn. I do the same, watching for claws. Everything is indistinct. It cannot be made out. Spacecat brushes a quivering body onto my peach legs, meowing a lullaby. Life is hard to find and not to get discouraged and well find it soon and feel it don't fool it and usually this calms me down like the grunt of an undulating stomach soaking breezy reeds from the supersaturated void. I try to purr, my limbs tucked against my body, against Spacecat's fuzzy form.

Last night we slept on a broken bed.

Round Earth marks the longitude of our domicile in his constrictive underwear with frayed elastic strands, and I listen to MaMa crack jokes about "identity" and "culture." She divines Round Earth's moods by the patterns of cold-skin petals flaking from his body into the oblivion of Spacecat's water bowl.

Correlation exists in the minutiae of pores, even for the android, even in a skinless muddle.

MaMa presses his buttons, talks of "espionage," "*Anschluss*," "global literacy."

Round Earth growls, gravitates, presses talking picture box's buttons. Talking picture box obligingly hums yesterday's maybes, tomorrow's probablys, pixels against white crimson clouds. Today feels impotent, cold and pink with a chance of grey scale for the region. MaMa spills bitter coffee onto Round Earth's pancake stack. She smiles loosely at the mix of sweet maple syrup and Arabica. MaMa insists on calling Spacecat "kitten," even though she says I will always be younger.

What does a guy have to do around here to release tension? Round Earth rubs his knees.

"Boot the kitten," says MaMa, swabbing the moist air with a frying pan, tossing fertilized eggs in patient flips.

Round Earth laughs, starts a lecture. Glasses crest up his nose; lips smack the waiting air. *I'm pleased that everyone is present and accounted for this morning.* Round Earth looks at Spacecat. *It may come as some surprise to you that I have not taken a shit in over thirty-three days. This, my precious family, might strike you as oddly irregular, but really, there is nothing more natural than retaining, for a time, whatever you take in. Retention of what is rightfully yours leads to salvation, my pets. In this regard, I am something of a phenomena if I do say so myself. Of course, so much of it can be attributed to diet…gotta cut back on the roughage, eat lotsa starch: potatoes, plantains, arrowroot and the like. You just build up your tension and let the insides per-colate, gestate, if you will, transmorph into some sentient compost pile. It's a fuckin' goddamned wonder that…*

"Dont say fuckin' goddamned around D-I-A-L," MaMa breaks in. "You're upsetting her…" Spacecat breaks onto Round Earth's lap, searching for human hands, hypnotized by the authority of Round Earth's body. Spacecat has told me about the craving, the wet impaling fantasies of tooth piercing Round Earth's skin, puncturing that pudgy typhoon neckline.

Round Earth rubs his hairy knuckles along the orange roughs of calico tuft marking Spacecat's belly. Spacecat purrs like a ventriloquist dummy, as tap water bounces lightly from the drowsing sound of dirty dishes shuffling under the tap. I shift uncomfortably in my seat.

It's OK Dial-Up Networking… *Round Earth fixes me in his gaze, pulling everything toward his body.* The best part happens when it all comes pouring out the anus. That's when we fffeeeeeeeeeeeeeellllll it most…

Spacecat draws blood from his arm.

With a start, MaMa cuts the tap.

Last night we slept on a broken bed.

Another moment with Spacecat and I want to go home, but we are home, so I want to climb onto the bed. Another moment of something I've never wanted before. I want to crunch the rusty springs and cringe at their familiar alarm. I want to hide in the cold darkness, under the heaviest, dirtiest blanket, where I can at least pretend to be asleep, to be somewhere else, to be off alone with Spacecat, away from Round Earth's prying eyes.

Another moment when I want to be anywhere but where I am.

Round Earth's diaries spread out like slices of bread on the living room floor, under the silent eye of talking picture box. Spacecat moves slowly around the invisible bubble protecting Round Earth's magic books, his illuminated compendiums, his puzzle-piece pamphlets and old world opuscules. "We're criminals now," I tell Spacecat, weaving through the pile of forbidden books, mesmerized by the irregular shapes emerging inside the overlapping ends and corners of the fallen diaries. Spacecat moves deliberately around the pile of tattered journals, quietly, as a soft, slinky tail brushes away specks of dust, as perfect claws emerge from the cave of a paw to scratch ancient signals into the wooden floor.

Everything I want to know must be inside, the secret knowledge of Round Earth, the power he wields over MaMa, his dominion over the black night, and the marigolds, and the oak tree outside our house. He pulls my world to his body. Power lines sag as his car rumbles past. The cylinder of tap water bends as he passes through the kitchen. So unfair. The floor is raised and uneven, made into altars at the feet of a vengeful demiurge, and we live in a yard overrun with mounds of primitive dirt and unyielding vine.

Spacecat's paws glow with that familiar flame, a phantom corona of tungsten and firelight, the gaseous ring of a million distant stars. Spacecat moves away from the diaries, ensuring our safety inside a magic circle of fur and scratch. I can't resist the urge to peek and study, to wave my eyes across the molar magnitude of these opaque quadrants, to cover the manifold grayness of cataract horizons, the secret fraternity of smiling alligators. I long to read speeches belonging to no talking picture box, beyond radios and telegraphs, past satellite and comet dust. So then, I dive down:

Without standardized response mechanisms in place to systematically degrade nuclear, biological, chemical, zoological, pathological and nuclear-scatological weapons capabilities in hostile territories, our sovereignty concatenates its own survival coefficient in relation to danger permutations across the global vertebrae.

It speaks directly to me. I cannot resist.

Lay off the one about the necessity of avoiding "collateral damage" you bitch. We do the best we can here; selective inaction sanctions genocide…that one's a classic, here's a press kit for chemical weapons…

Spacecat! My arms and legs flood with sickly goosebumps, and the chill of the forbidden enters my mouth, open only for a moment, a serpent forms from air and fear sucked into its lair that has become my tiny stomach. Spacecat! I try to cry out, but my breath disappears. I flail my arms and legs. The diaries churn into an ocean of sinister papyrus soaking up the droplets of ink and blood. The diaries move farther out as I kick until one flies from the boundary of the protective circle. Spacecat! I try to cry out, but sound is no more; it has been stolen by the serpent bandied about my intestinal track, and I am dizzy, sweating in drops of icy salt, covered with microscopic welts, submerged under the fused paper skin of somebody else's planet where other cats dance before the outline of the sun.

Last night we slept on a broken bed.

Spacecat lingers over the husk of a dying cricket, a patch of human skin caught beneath paw. Spacecat bats it across the cement porch as though it is a pebble, chasing after some spark of leftover sentience with the agility of a panther, a horrible mountain lion, a tiger clinging to the shoulders of Uranus. The moon sops the sticky moisture of June into its white and yellow craters. Spacecat's eyes spiral wildly.

When the Reed Cat bested the snake Apepi, when Nubian sisters spread human ashes over the dry fields along the White Nile, we once flew as birds in chariots made of cloud… Spacecat stares into the dark beyond our porch. *Long before this. Before the pyramids. When we were strong—we would know what to do.* The body of the cricket stops twitching. *There may be those who still know…*

The air smells slippery and quiet. "Who?"

Bastet, Kunuk…the cat gods see what my eyes cannot, know if you are to be a cat or girl, girl or cat.

"Both?" I cry.

No. Spacecat bats the cricket carcass to the bug lantern, zapping electric charge of frizzling summer critters. *You must always be one.* Spacecat disappears into the black tree line, *or the other.* My head a horrible clutter.

Last night we slept on a broken bed.

Round Earth's slaps contain the barbwire whipple of concentration camp mandibles, gaseous trucks at mass-grave memories, showers of hydrogen bombs from rusty nozzles. Crimson payloads flood my veins and I can feel the ventricle leak. Prickles of monarch butterfly pain sear my guts from throwing up.

You read my diaries? The threshold of intuitive resources in relation to the assignation of those resources to qualified contractors allows me to make manifest destiny on your behind Dial-Up. Come here, you little barbiturate, you tiny wasp of useless Demarol. He chases me around the room with his belt strap click-clicking.

Think you can get away from me, slutty tube of K.Y. Jelly.

"Stop! Im sorry."

Its too late for that, he says, ignoring MaMa, pounding fists of MaMa on the listless window pane, heaving breast of MaMa lost in the patch of dried-up marigolds. Spacecat sends out empathetic meows over the low hum of the automatic dishwasher. Spacecat purrs galaxies away, in the kitchen, a tiny shape scratching at the cupboard, lapping at the puddles of slime and greasy water stuttering the finish of our linoleum tile.

Little bitch one should know that intercourse of human events

the emissaries from Perfect Union Consolidated Inc. might be sniff-
ing your swilly underarms. Do you understand me young lady?

Spacecat, I think. Slap. Spacecat, I hope. The diaries pile about me in silicon deposits. Hits rain down on my body. I'm cowering in the corner. Talking picture box goes wet and sweaty with equal enthusiasm for the deed, recording for instant posterity, simulcasting over satellite networks, straight-to-cable outlets and the undulating wires below American trailer parks, beneath debutante bedposts, under mansions of the rich and privileged.

What's that? New TV season... His words bite into my body with the metal prongs, liquid intensifiers, the preservative wash of service-economy eyelids.

Make it stop. Make it stop. Make it stop.

Spacecat works my jaws from a distance; together, we scream.

And then, just as the black night comes in a wave of dead stars, an army of bumps rise at the base of welts unhealed from my encounter with Round Earth's diaries. Spontaneously generating gnats on a sack of rancid meat. Abiogenetic mirrors of the hazy formless universe, crackling with life as mounds rise in seconds, overnight hotel chains, fast food empires, my rescue squad of cuticle mash and vinegar stink.

Round Earth backs away. He drops the belt.

Last night we slept on a broken bed.

MaMa poisons herself with anti-oxidants, sodium bicarbonate, carbolic supply lines washed in baubles against the grain of talking picture box's screen. With each approach of the dust rag laced with the warning, "do not ingest but beneficial to the cathode ray tube," Spacecat barks at the ceiling, meows at invisible insects crawling across the surface of the fan's incessant whir, avoids the refracted spark of MaMa's monotone iris.

"What now? You just had your treats. For crying out loud kitty. I can't leave you alone for two seconds." she places the dust rag atop talking picture box's dusty cabinet. The lighted flicker mutes itself as if listening, and with willful hands, MaMa lifts Spacecat in her arms, makes a cradle in the air, rubs the fur with aerosol fingers. Spacecat, contented, breathes light tuna breath onto MaMa's oily nose. Everything is calm and at peace—until the wrong way brush of Spacecat's metacarpus, the uncomfortable finger into Spacecat's rump, and then the hiss, the swelter, the swirling cacophony of the tiny Spacecat, centuries the elder, struggling to break MaMa's hold, tumbling to the floor.

"L-I-T-T-L-E shithead…"

Spacecat bolts through the laundry room dent and then MaMa, without so much as skipping a beat, thrusts her fingers into the dust-rag still reeking of cleanser. Turning to talking picture box, she massages its hypnotic pixels.

Tonight we sleep on a broken bed.

When everyone heaves lowly in the broken bed with rusty springs, when the rush of images from Round Earth's journals jumble in my brain, pushing out birth dates and names of childhood rivals, forcing out memories of questions never asked but saved for later, Spacecat bores into my stomach, angled against my navel with paws scrunched into the sky. I loop around Spacecat's figure, flat on my fetal curl, and at moments such as these, with the moon puffing away its stolen light, feel the brush of Round Earth's hairy legs loosing corpo-reality on *my* back, dissipating into the umbra of our bond.

MaMa rots in her cocoon of diet pills and zazen fatigue, dreaming, perhaps, of Spacecats along their ancient rivers, atop their ancient moons. MaMa drops her legs toward my stomach and I take the opportunity to roll out the bottom of the bed with just a dull, subliminal crink. Her flesh replaces mine in the press of Round Earth's usurped corona, and looking back as I trot the wooden floorboard to our anteroom, two yellow-red dots dance in darkness. Oscillating wildly, Spacecat's eyes glow half-open in the deep black.

Off in the living room, talking picture box presides—an emphatic idol whose time has come and come and come again in streamlined declivity, cables slashing, tentacles toward the stereo, personal processing units, four-track recording centers, turntables, and telephone. Multicolor vertical strips change spontaneously to white-snow fuzz as I approach in a parabola from the bedroom. Flipping the channels, I hear the officials speak, the information structures breathe, the lips of tragic sit-com divas purse, in mock crucifixion poses as collagen floods commercial real estate, as automobiles consume alcohol, psychic friends transmute into lonely singles, into snakes of inscrutability—each existing on some vaguely differentiated astral plane. Goosebumps of sand cover my entire body, and I am mesmerized as talking picture box makes it eerie sounds:

The current state of affairs remains the predictable outcome of market forces reinforced by the record strength of American economic indicators. Despite economic and social turmoil in other regions of the global theatre, particularly ethnic cleansing pogroms in less-civilized pockets of Eastern Europe, everything proceeds into a well of property undefiled. In order to maintain the quality control and structural integrity of Western dominance, certain sacrifices must be made...

How much time has passed in this false sleep? Seconds or hours?

Last night slept we on a bed, broken.

Steam passes the tubes and pipes coating the dark laundry room in slats of sticky summer night. The dull door crinks.

The weird wind whips. Spacecat trudges in loops of marigold pollen, swaddled in an aurora of light darker than outside, and linked somehow, to tender, midnight paws.

"Thank you thank you thank you," I rush toward Spacecat, who pulls back to stare at my pupils, wide and gritty. Spacecat stays silent, and then so am I; we wait solemnly for our meeting with the ancient cat gods.

Bastet. Kunuk. The whirl starts first with the electric crackle of Spacecat's paws on the carpet, grey in the moonlight, walking along the edge of the litter box, sparking blue chips of eternity in the rise of the steaming washer and dryer. Bastet. Kunuk. *We incant you to this plane, this continuum, to Dial-Up Networking, stolid in the vapor of midsummer, connected to the earth by ancient roots, its body and its soil.*

We exchange breath in a cycle of eroded sand and grainy wind; I crave the soft grip of Bastet in her alien, imperial robes, descending from the celestial ark for the coronation of Sebek the Unholy over the fertile crescent. Spacecat's tongue licks warm and soft against the hairs of my body, over the callused bumps and bruises; I lift my ears toward the whoosh of laundry gas crackling static sparks. My interconnectedness screams to be touched, accessed, given new source code, as claws are cocked and covert, paddling through fields of cobalt reeds to liquid oblivion furrows, cutting into the flesh of my flesh, whiskers whistling June moon songs. As Spacecat shakes electricity over the floor, I can feel the time approaching. My nightmare life with Round Earth and useless MaMa slips into the coma of the beat-up broken bed, into the memory of whips and welts that can only be undone in the warm corona of Kunuk, the endless love of Bastet. Everything speeds up.

Everything is now.

Spacecat pushes deeper into the soft of my body, claws ripped along the contours of my hair, streaming down from my oily head, and we fuse together into ourselves, into each other. Electric blue crackles flood the laundry room.

Now, Dial-Up Networking! Spacecat's throat is my throat. *Call Bastet!* I cannot speak. *Call Kunuk!* Spacecat dives down, forces the words from my paralyzed soul, and I can feel the tickle inside, the soft and warm aura of Spacecat as the muttering syllables rise… *Now. It has to be now,* pushes Spacecat, the sparks whipped into a frenzy of hidden shapes and textures. I pull up the words from my belly and send them backwards in time…

Symbiosis provides a convenient, illusory form for the supplicant to invoke the displaced local deities. Once summoned, their influence can be easily neutralized…

Spacecat screams and shuts my mouth, cuts me with claw and nail. Possibilities and permutations fade. The dark swampy gas stalls, the laundry machine produces soapy warmth. Bastet. Kunuk. Phone lines refuse to connect. Hardware goes obsolete. The tongue betrays us all.

Last night we slept on a broken bed.

Spacecat separates from the me that is no longer myself, and collapses, knocks crystallized feces onto linoleum spaces. The heat drizzles in and I reach out with strange arms. At the sound of my touch, Spacecat rises and rushes through the dull door crink. I run to the backyard, begging for a glimpse of Bastet, a semblance of Kunuk. But there is nothing. Spacecat watches me from silent oceans of dark green grass. The last pustules of laundry steam pass in gusts between my feet, fully formed, full of nail. Spacecat meows under the frequency of breath, but I can no longer translate. With a scitter of fur and crooked claw, Spacecat flips into the channels of endless space, dampening the last of my naïve perambulations, my ever-crooked fingers poised to catch a star.

16) DAVIS SCHNEIDERMAN

Introduction: *Appendisectomy*—"Appendices on November 11, 1944: *The Circle*" (1960)

Appendisectomy was a collection of Henry Mescaline's auto-biographical work from the "Minatorian Mimetic Roaming or Nixon-After-Checkers Period" lasting between April and August 1959, which traced his spiritual, political, and psycho-sexual journey into the mainstream hearts of middle-America, back to his indigenous self—literally, back into the Appendix. David Schneiderman's introduction told us that in the course of preparing the works that would become *Appendisectomy*, the figure of Mescaline moved from counter-culture literary obscurity to a short-lived stint in the limelight. Mescaline's work changed from the period that produced *Spacecats,* and this text signals David Schneiderman's move to highlight the ever-developing talents of his experimental discovery Henry Mescaline. Schneiderman writes, in unpublished notes:

"Mescaline wanted a picture of the excrescence, of the albatrosses, ospreys, and turkey vultures with their crooked wings against the horizon. He wanted poodles in the Battery to fall prey to the vultures of the financial district. Instead, he received written descriptions of ways to fund just such an image. *The Circle*, an excerpt from the larger text, detailed the incidents of November 11, 1948, following the biographical Henry Mescaline's visit to lower Manhattan from New Jersey, and the ensuing power of the projection device."[7]

[7] It was essential that we balanced each other out, assumed the same dimensions, used the same type of language. That was what it took to initially win our acquiescence to the project, a sort of arms race and we admitted it up front, as part of our plan; Spuyten Duyvil had been kind enough to forward us Phoenelia Yeer's portions of the text. Utilizing e-mail trace programs and fax origination points (although she often sends from third-party locations) we *had* been able to zero in on her presence, at times, or what approximates

17) Henry Mescaline
From *Appendisectomy*—
"Appendices on November 11, 1948: *The Circle*" (1960)

Appendix C: Endnotes on the Musical Speakers in Alphabet City

The Circle track thumps like an obscene baby mouth drooling beneath the speakers in a long string of gelatinous DNA or an alloy of popular imagination and super-reinforced copper filament projecting its fantastic sis-boom-ba over the public in its multivalent forms: emissaries from the secret chemical concern in civilian incognito, homesick wives staffing the ol day-to-day while husbands fathers brothers lovers die in the blackout confusion of the Blitz, a small monkey wearing a grey fedora angrily swinging a boom mike near a pyramid of large crates…this feedback swing, the Feedback LOOP, the FEED-BACK itself, infuses the crowd with a soporific of the strongest

the shadow of her presence, a vapor trail of a body, something that felt like the tiny shards and fragments of *her*; it rolled back across our monitor in a series of dull blips and electrified cackles, enabling us to zoom a little bit closer on the global grid that registered, even slightly, all transmissions.

At first, we followed deliberately, a stop or two behind her and the child, several towns away, dusting the walls for genetic remnants, leaving long, badly typed notes in case she returned with a fevered desire to *read*. We can't explain why we lingered. Was it because we did not know exactly where she rested? No, we possessed all the necessary data. Rather, it had something to do with the certainty of knowing where she was, where we *were* together, bound always by a complicated history that defies her best expressions. We needed to assume control.

* * *

Of course we remained concerned. Perhaps we worried about what would happen at our eventual reunion. She had been violent before, psychically violent, and we feared for the safety of the child as well as for her own safety. That's why we spoke with her doctors. She'd throw things around the room, dried roses, bottles of liquid paper, a galvanized frying pan, all at our head—things, really, just everyday things, objects right out of a sitcom. She was always very influenced by what she viewed on the flicker box, and despite her academic posturing, watched no shortage of ridiculous trash talk variety. We sleep with machines that have entered our central nervous system. Notes from a charbroiled pan flute emerge from scalding liquid. There is torque to the ampere—barstools vibrate and shot glasses shiver, Dewey defeats Truman in a ghostly electoral college, missed opportunities spread in chromatic marmalade over the cement cracks of politically mobilized floorboards, over the coat room congress between Brooklyn whore and Manahatta skyline, away from homeless poets lost in their shit pales and sullen compositions. We follow the speakers out to the streets, and the vibrations enter our skin like the bright knives of Psalm 23...

shows, researching contemporary spectacles, she said. But we knew better. In fact, we kept an occasional eye on them ourselves, visited the brother-father who raped the daughter-sister, had lunch with a coven of three-year-olds who weighed 300 pounds, locked in a slop house while the family pig, Caesar Porkgustus, wallowed in a filthy, indoor tub full of avocado mush. We half expected her to turn up as a panelist, or even better, maybe we received a call from one of these slick producers asking us to come on the show with her and get it all out in the open. All we needed was an audience. We could have made them sympathetic. We could roll in the slime.

Oh, there were times when we despaired of such tactics, and felt as if nothing could have helped win her back or explain where she went wrong. We have assembled all of our research, corrected piles of her own often sloppy work, lovingly, late into the night, occupying her old motel rooms, using the delightful red pen that she once gave us as a joke (after the accusation that she was a hard-liner on those composition papers). Faced with such overwhelming evidence, it seems impossible that she would not return to herself and end the madness and pain that had overtaken our entire family, uprooted our lives, disturbed the important work of Spuyten Duyvil and separated us from the child who to this day we have never...we were paralyzed.

***

On the night of July 3, 2000, Spuyten Duyvil sent us a copy of one of her editorial texts, still sweet with the fragrance of lily and dead skin, just a few hours old. Spuyten Duyvil believed that our split with Yeer allowed for somewhat amicable relations and that we still freely exchanged commentary. We traced the origination point to four short hours away, and then rented a car from the local dealership, careful to fill out all the forms with the red pen and assume all of the proper insurance coverage. Driving down the Pennsylvania artery, down Route 83, past Progress and Colonial Point at Exit 49, we felt our hands sticky on the wheels leather casing. Our feet trembled

Appendix XY: Alternate Genealogy

Amoeba---Paramecium   Author of *The Circle*--Mutation

| |

| |

Homo Erectus----Homo Habilus   Hieronymus Bosch --- Stop Codons

| |

     Henry Mescaline   ---   Mescaline

|

Henry Mescaline 2

with excitement. We stopped at a McDonald's, at a Esso station where we picked up a bouquet of fresh lilies, and we turned into the Motel Camelot just over the Maryland border, scoured the parking lot with a cursory glance, and peered carefully in a few ground-floor windows unobstructed by blinds.

Nothing.

We marched into the management office demanding her room number. The woman behind the counter—short, dumpy, rude—not at all the type of person we wanted looking after our Phoenelia, told us that there was nobody with that name at the motel. We felt flooded with an unbelievable rage and considered toppling her counter over, kicking in its cheap drywall edifice, scattering the paper clips into the styrofoam coffee cups so that the slovenly zombies of early morning tourism would cut their lips. There wasn't much there to destroy, but we did unplug the small refrigerator so that whatever food inside might spoil and stink up the already noisome air.

Yeer might have used a pseudonym; it wasn't impossible, but also not reason enough for us to re-approach the office. We holstered our rage and returned to the car. We waited another few hours, as the day began to darken, hopelessly looking for some sign of Phoenelia, precious Phoenelia. But there was nothing. We re-checked the coordinates, stomped back into the office, tried out a few fake names. A different counter girl. A different dead end.

Not being intrusive by nature, it took us quite some time to begin walking around the parking lot with a more academic vigor. We peeked into the backs of cars, sorted through all sorts of decrepit stuffed animals, old news-

Appendix 3: Chronological Background

150   Chinese mystics calculate pi to five places—3.14159

1898   *Leslie Henry Mescaline is born in Wilmington, Delaware on December 27, to Ümlaut Schnitzler Mescaline, a German immigrant from Westphalia, and Rosa Marina Mescaline, a future agent of international banking concerns.*

1256   Gout-stricken Kublai Khan, astrologically minded, straps Marco Polo to the dissection table.

1901 *The Mescaline family begins its nomadic travels up*

papers, and duffel bags, before we moved onto the building itself, strolling deliberately past the rooms facing the courtyard, listening to televisions, radios, people fucking, drinking, fighting. It became very cold; the sun had set and gone. That's how completely the fluorescent parking lights had taken over; they substituted their artificial gleam for the natural light. We had not even noticed. Maybe the sun had simply moved away from the earth as such, backward, receding to its proper place far removed from our daily life. Could we still have survived if the climate suddenly shifted, if everything became cold and detached from its source?

***

These thoughts were interrupted when we noticed a man about our height and build on the opposite side of the parking lot, against the parallel wall of the motel, who moved as we moved, strolled from room to room, listened at one door, walked quickly by another, somehow lost in rhythm of our syncopated footsteps. We lingered uncomfortably but stared anyway, slid a little closer, hid behind cars in the crowded lot, snaked through the shadows that the lights failed to cover. We could just make him out; his hands and bloody knuckles buried deep in pockets of amber wool, and his figure, sloping and malevolent and orange under the artificial suns, bore the weight of his middle-age like a pack mule bore its skin after decades of servitude and silence. A matchstick jutted from his lips, just as one hung from ours, and we snaked even closer, tiptoed until less than a hundred feet stood between our bodies. He heard our footsteps and turned to face us, squinting; his eyes narrowed and held us still. He removed an envelope from his jacket, hoisted it into the lamplight for us to see. Then, without a sound, he placed it on the sidewalk outside the nearest room. He turned, began to walk, assumed a brisk jog, and disappeared around the nearest corner.

The envelope bore our name in its haphazard scratch, amateur calligraphy.

And we were soon swallowed, once again, by the awkwardness of our own text.

and down the Mississippi River. Ümlaut begins practicing law without a formal degree.

1543 Nicholas Copernicus, researching for 63 years, composes *On the Revolution of the Celestial Spheres*—proffering the egregiously fallacious supposition of prior Biblical theorems concerning the preeminence of terra-firma as universal sang-froid—thus counter-hypothesizing that hotness in our solar system revolves around a comparatively minuscule pissant whose unemployment check equals approximately 71% Hydrogen, 27% Helium, and 2% other...

1915   Henry breaks into father's "law" office on the night of the first murder in Hannibal, Missouri since 1845. He discovers the dead body of an androgynous teenager, and to his great shame, becomes sexually aroused.

1637   Descartes re-creates God *and* math:
Y= mx + b gives us body *and* blood:
You only thought that you *w*e/r=e*...

1929   Mescaline sells razor blade-filled Apples outside the stock exchange on the day of the great crash. After J.P. Morgan's cousin fails to leave him a tip for the fifth day in a row, Mescaline makes a "hangman" collage from leftover tickertape and horse glue, convinces Morgan's doorman to let him in the penthouse, and scares the bloated sucker into chronic arrhythmia.

1670   Confirming various hypotheses and articulating that sperm, mucous, and other bodily fluids transfer pressure equally in all directions—Blaise Pascal—in the *Pensees sur la religion et sur queleques autres sujels*, adopts the Great Khan's wager: the use-value of eternal Paradise is infinite in though-control operation, and although the probability of attaining widespread worship by conventional religion may be small, it is asymptotically greater than by the typical methods of superpower intelligence operatives.

1934   Henry works as a Best Boy on Schultzie!, a low-budget movie about the life of gangster Dutch Schultz. Despite the Busby Berkeley hit "The Lullaby of Broad's Way (Fleggie's song)," the movie is scrapped on the cutting room floor due both to lack of funds and several unexplained crew deaths.

1776   Thirteen rag-tag bumper states slide off the ramshackle dictatorship of mad King George and make freedom wave mother-American style. Humanity realizes it is 76.87% water...

1943   Mescaline begins work at the Brooklyn shipyard
1914-1918

We hope that you bequeath this vent / as some Thurs-day becomes a shade / accepting the beneficent / florets of the canon aide / stood the pail blew permanents / who prefer enlisting jade...

1955   Mescaline writes draft of "Warning to the J. Edgar Hoover in your Closet." Time loses all meaning.

1946:   A proto-electromagnetic punch-card computer, ENIAC, whirls online at the University of Pennsylvania. It's at least 49,000 shiny knobs fill up the space of at least 7,000 secret cow bladders. Months before, we drop the atom bomb.

1958   The Social Darwinist Period (January-August) produces first important work: "Spacecats of the World, Untie!" and "54 Prefaces to a Single-Volume Regicide Indictment."

1971   A conscientiously objectifying computer language, Pascal, conflated, striated and excited by ENIAC, simplifies overwrought and inelegantly supercilious syntax and incorrect syntax obnoxious while creating fields of pure data and hexadecimal sub-routines...

1960   The Meta-Fictive Socialist Eco-Terrorist Anarchist Period (January-April) produces A Novel of Fuck You!

2019:   Your 10-slice Mega-Burn 3000 Bagel-Matic Toaster-

Like Oven Device determines pi to over 100,000,000 decimal places. This has no practical value.

Appendix AA: Preface to the Speakers

We follow the speakers out to the streets; vibrations enter our skin like the bright knives of Psalm 23, the epidermal punch of the velocity needle, the fast kick, the beat down, the overworked cop with sensitivity issues and old accordion records, the illuminated animal and eraser-blade manuscript, the nervous jiggle of stoplights and car horns, of amniotic fountains of a prostrate Ariadne, of Orpheus lying bloody and disemboweled on 42nd street, of Sebek the Unholy, the hideous Crocodile God unleashing its ooze on the coat of silver tenement windows, on stomachs thumping and pounding under the jaywalking sky. *The Circle* hits its last movement, as drugs hit the bloodstream. Everything goes so dizzy it almost straightens out, flies right, ships left. My head is a honeycomb, my eyes dripping nectar...

Appendix 73 Series E: Origins of *The Circle*

From *Studies in Advanced Prestidigitation: The Adaptation of the Magi,* by Olaf "Step On No Pets" Palindrome, London and Calcutta: 1856.

While the substance of the text remains shrouded in secrecy, controversy, and apocalyptic folklore, research clearly indicates that *The Circle* constructs itself on a thematic illusion. Research conducted on behalf of the Johnston, Farquar, and Leech law firm in regards to the Crystal Palace incident of 1853 indicates that when observed from any two points on the so-called diameter, *The Circle* can be explained away by a straight line. Three points imply a triangle, four a square, and so forth into the agnostic territories of the hexadecimal. Sure, this adds up like free-radical pseudo-scientific discourse, but we also submit that Diogenes, ENIAC, and Pascal once lived in a bathtub together. Returning to the thematic implications of this construction we can surmise that any fracture to the assumed curvaceous narrative line, even when offered in fragments that presumably recreate notions of completeness (as in the violence of Paganini and Busby Berkeley), acts as nothing but *misdirection*. The idea simply exposes the fact that what we perceive as complete and satisfying exists as nothing but an arbitrary construction of habit. Thus, even when *The Circle* is interpreted in a modern context, the interpretation does not defrock straight narrative and replace it with fragmentation, but superimposes the new narrative that will come to provide a facsimile of completeness—that is, the new authoritarian and "straight" narrative that will draw its potency by masquerading as disruption.

Appendix Q: Letter about Henry Mescaline from an average American citizen:

August 1948,

Dear National Broadcasting Service;

I was disappointed to see so much space on my small television screen, through my magnifying glass, devoted to so-called writer Henry Mescaline on your otherwise fine call-in variety program, *The Thelonius Bosh Good Time Jingle Hour!* (Episode 63: "A Mescaline Experiment"). Can't you see that America just wants this man to go quietly away from our children and take his communist ideals with him? Its not my fault that the Reds practically live in my housing development at this point. And yes I *am* sure, thank you, because you can never know who has sympathies in *that* direction, even with the Stars and Stripes outside on Arbor Day and a barbecue pit full of shredded-pork product. Anyway, your program encourages his tragic, self-indulgent behavior by devoting so much airtime to his exploits. And we wonder about the origins of the current wife-swapping epidemic! This writer's ignominious abuse of the Spacecat character, as of all things, a symbiote with an innocent, little girl…why it's downright Un-American. And his politically embarrassing critique of television merely confirmed for many Americans (and certainly my chapter of the Daughters of the Confederacy/Ladies Home Auxiliary [merged two years ago Sunday, thank you very much…power to the people]) what is so wrong with the longhair beatnik crowd. I voted for FDR five times even though he only ran for four terms just to prove to everyone how liberal I am, but enough already. Send this Mescaline bum back to Stalin!

Margery Hempstead
Levittown, Long Island

Appendix B: Why Henry Mescaline's story about Pittsburgh sounds like it may have really been about a stint in the federal penitentiary, and why it remains difficult to tell.

He said it was very segregated.

He said it was very dull.

He said it produced Irritable Bowel Syndrome (IBS).

He said that the grey was the predominant color.

He said that cigarettes were enormously expensive.

He said the cavity searches were dehumanizing.

He said traffic was a bitch.

Appendix *: Justification for breaking *The Circle* of Old Modernism

Is there an endless number of pre-scripted happenstances that one can sluice through in which a overwrought but under-programmed young cyborg with a (rebellious streak and run-away eczema/need for access to the law/mania for social-mobility/love of bullfighting/yen for multicellularity) causing (his parents and kid sister/absurd Eastern European townspeople/the French petit-aristocracy/Jews called only by their last name/more evolved organisms) to mutilate his body and assault his sensibilities in (an exclusive American boarding school/a legal bureaucracy/French resort towns/Spanish bars/the primeval genetic ocean) populated by hell-fire zombies and (designer suitcases/unfounded accusations/tea and *petit madeleines*/cultural and racial stereotypes/magic plankton) re-membering the schizophrenia of multilingual cities in asymptotic regression before he fucks an obnoxious (museum display of penguins/sex-hungry schoolteacher/S&M-obsessed Baron de Charlus/androgynous countess/strand of gooey genetic code) who want to make boom-boom outside of (selling out/giving in/staying put/shutting up/floating apart) using preternatural, spastic *literariness*—absorbing the digestive track that digests inside the particle containment field—against the apparition of the great crocodile called Sebek the Unholy, manifest in the (scholastic establishment/brace of executioner clowns/elite social system/pissed-off bloodthirsty bulls/holy lightning bolts)?

Appendix MLK: Charts and Graphs

Charts and Graphs under reproduction copyright. Consult originals in the Library of Congress.

Appendix W-4: SEVEN Comments on the Assimilation of American Jews spoken in an Alphabet City bar.

1. "I can't wait to give up my name for his."

2. "And when people ask what are you? I resent those who answer "Jewish" because it doesn't take into account nationality. Why not say instead, my family hails from Estonia, or Alexandria, or Fez, or wherever...?

3. "All a Jew really wants to do is doodle a Christian Girl..."

4. "God is *The Circle* whose center is nowhere and circumference is anywhere."

5. "I needed to have a sinus operation *anyway,* so it seemed a natural thing to do..."

6. "We are in a clearing and the pale moon assaults the innocent clouds..."

7. "Let's *also* get a Christmas tree..."

Appendix &: The "Word" from our Sponsors

This Multinational Company invites you to try its versatile line of products free from finance charges for *one* complete **lifetime** or the limited time it takes for thirty swine to be slaughtered by one-armed leprechauns. No salesman will dial your extension, and you will receive no absolutely no visits, guaranteed. The next 500 million people to do nothing will receive a **lifetime** supply of disarming little trinkets. At no time will you be dissatisfied with your choice, and you will remain unaware of this unobtrusive advertisement campaign. We return you to your regularly scheduled suicide.

Appendix Omega: All Speakers must pass when *The Circle* ends.

My head hurts like a honeycomb, my eyes dripping nectar, and the cataract of deluge, the flood of pre-recorded revolution replaces the crowded hangar of denuded aeroplanes. The speakers gleam grand, gold, and ancient. *The Circle* is arcane, excremental, soaked in migrant cum. Traffic stops dead in the slime. Car windows break from the noise. Violins tear through the sky. Alarms of riot-police enter the tape and are cut back as they happen. Rats decipher the trashcan codebook, but we still take a beating. Everywhere the pornographic theater threatens the suburbs. We split the opiates and call it a millennium. Court-appointed caffeine squadrons shout out the brassy garlic blare of aluminum-treated methane. Our arteries harden with the pulse of the people. As the barstool go topsy-turvy, I can feel the music ending, the tone moving toward falling action— but the vibrations continue. We dance to the sound of riotous mustard gas, and drawn-out jazz licks scuttle our inhibitions...the sound of the sulfur city dissipates us into millions of disarming little trinkets...

18) Phoenelia Yeer
Introduction: *Tupeat, Frompeet, Repeit* (1962)

An abnormally cold summer afternoon.

You write—ABRACADABRA—and refuse to be silenced.

You replicate and reduplicate with abandon. Arabesques and loop-de-loops rotate and revolve into double-helix melting pots; the circus acrobat commands her reticulated body to out-perform its previous maneuvers. Each spectacular spin mimics a sentient toy poodle trained to perform a backflip on the command of its owner's astral body. Every fantastic swish of joint and cartilage mocks the practice mime down below, trapped with painted tear in a shrinking house of air and bone. No matter how many times you perform the doleful repetition, no matter how much sense you find in these words, the serial nature of your work ensures that, if only by an identifying number—BARCODEBAR—each revivification of form remains a murder of spontaneity, a final collapse of the lungs breathing your language.

You write—ABRACADABR—into forty-nine crevices.

Your tongue tastes yeasty cheeks surrounding strange sounds rising from the lip of your diaphragm. A gob of spit smelling of putrefacted mucous membrane, tar, nicotine, and the nightly news flies back onto your face, a vestigial creature unwilling to simply go along with the dumb processes of evolution.

Which is why you must leave the child.

So you short circuit Davis Schneiderman. As with the other works of great and continual repetition that have characterized much of late twentieth-century art,[8] this excerpt, *Tupeat, Frompeet, Repeit,* a masturbatory production over 587 arduous pages, allows Mescaline a chance to force his words into a large chemical vat, until an unholy coupling of earth and sea—so that the awful brothers Pete and Re-Peat, the father-daughter dyad Tacg and Gact, and of course, the meta-textual duo of Henry Mescaline and Henri d'Mescan—together lift out that first frustrated Amoeba from the primordial slop.[9]

You write—ABRACADAB—and hope to disappear.

An abnormally cold summer afternoon: In mauve and maroon and crimson, in the backyard next to the brain shelter stocked with water in rusty metal jugs, in army rations left over from the last world war—America's conformist spirit proliferates through fear that someone will drop the bomb or fear that a special someone will stop the bomb from dropping. The themes of *Tupeat, Frompeet, Repeit* are commonplace enough

8 IE: Laura "Radioactive" Seismas 1993 performance art piece "1994 Yearly Planner" in which she mimics middle-American career women obsessively repeating a pre-dawn beauty regimen. The first hour is consumed with brushing one section of her over-permed hair (right back quadrant for North American tour, bangs for Micronesia production). During the second hour, she cuts her cuticles until a small circle of blood covers the floor.

9 In this way, the text represents a radical departure from the earlier sections of *Hallucigenome.* The connection between Henry Mescaline, American writer of experimental fiction, and Henri d'Mescan, convicted war criminal, moves from the margins to the center. David Schneiderman attempts an explanation: "So I assumed that by linking you, Henri, directly to Mescaline, I would succeed in drawing you out of the shadows. The reader of course, if she is unwilling to entertain the thought that you are one and the same, will move into the more delightful hypothesis that Mescaline is little more than a morally bankrupt opportunist, which of course, we both know to be the truth" (Letter 12: "Ignore the complex of social interactions charging this text with *meaning.*")

for the late 1950s: Nazi war criminals engaged by the American military apparatus as Cold War operatives; the intersecting rise of fast food establishments, identical gas stations ("We are the men of Texaco / We work from Maine to Mexico...") and the American highway; the prison apparatus and its stifling effect upon sex and gender. So what's the problem, you wonder, when Ike would have his caddy carry the nuclear button in a gold-leafed golf bag, in-between the five iron and sand wedge, just in case the super-Soviet got a hard-on?

On a critical level, for starters, Henry Mescaline's production—this ineffectual parody—despite its dazzling repetitions, remains a mere reflection of the power apparatus, a picture of rebellion entirely *authorized* by the apparatus. Nothing particularly new or interesting to the tired critique of the "postmodern" information, no condemnation of various vertical "single stem-base" structures of information (metaphysical trees, theological trees, Gnostic trees, Chomskyan linguistic trees, genealogical trees, World Trees [re: Yggdrasil]), that the text appears, at first, to counter.

Which is why it must also be abandoned.

So that horizontal, rhizome-like systems of knowledge emerge in the incessant repetition of narrative tropes. And so *Tupeat, Frompeet, Repeit*, can only parody from its privileged position. What privilege in 1960 you wonder? This leads to the second, and more important point of critique, which has come upon you so suddenly, and with such undeniable force that you find yourself unable to make an official statement of any competence.

You write—ABRACADA—and force it out for your own sake.

You would be wise to withhold information that scuttles your defense before the House Committee on Un-American Activities, before your brethren at the Kiwanis Club, the Master Masons in flowing robe decorated with moon and stars whose arcane visages fade into the pockmarked faces of the syncopated milkmen. Who's to say that a fully ordained cock doesn't fuck your partner with a mold of your own precious member?

The penis is a question of identity, a conundrum of the physical body parallel to the abnormality surrounding the entire period of *Hallucigenome*—not that Henry Mescaline offers a mere projection of David Schneiderman—but that possibly (where are the words...?), *neither* of the two men have much to do with the information they so casually whisper into your ear with such doleful repetitions.

An abnormally cold summer afternoon.

And you cannot think, let alone write. Even this *tiny morsel* pushes its way up with a mix of food and mucous, against the smoky plume of an "ozone action day," and so arrives a host of other unsavory conclusions about the last few years of your life, your loves, your child. The wind picks up outside the motel room. You hear a car door slam and rush to shut the curtains even tighter. You cannot resist the urge to peek out, although what vehicle Davis tracks you in remains a mystery. The police have discovered several stolen transports that may or may not relate to this case: two motorcycles, a 1976 Mercury Cougar, a 1949 Chevy Peristalsis, a scooter, a inter-state licensed Mack Truck carrying several tons of contraband placenta tissue, generic AIDS drugs, bootleg chicken incubators. In short, every slamming door, every footstep in the parking lot, means that you have been discovered once again.

Which is why you must go.

You see the murderer beneath his snarling vocal track. You fax your work to Spuyten Duyvil from locations impossible to trace, your beeper pager and cell phone defies triangulation, and even though it shames you to admit, you must often steal communication supplies for your issue, tender Dial-Up Networking, slovenly in her circuitous pajamas, squeezed safe in your venous nuzzle. You rock her body into your porous crevices, half hoping she will disappear once more inside the delicate folds of your buttery flesh. You still can't believe that she lives *ex utero*, that your lives could be unwound by anyone with enough resourcefulness and a sterilized razor.

You write—ABRACAD—and go back-tense again to Future, Missouri.

Davis Schneiderman slaps you hard that day with the back of his hand, forgetting that you are the wallpaper, a master mimic; you gather up a handful of what passes for earth and throw it in his face. This is what happens, before he makes that cut with a sleek razor, in Future, Missouri, when you discover the "Vichy Papers" buried in that muddy tomb; the chloroform seeps into your sinuses and the screams from the fetal Dial-Up Networking grow audible in your dreams. Everything goes dark, and you feel pushed down together, weighted into the boiling soup, your body and your baby, fused into a symbiote of primal tissue, forced to swim for your undifferentiated little lives.

You pray to the crocodile under old muddy, gripped by a chloroform of submerged jawbones. In your haste to save the child, you stumble in the liquid and fall into a hole where dark shapes, massive and without human feeling, twist in bubbly shadows of fin and scale, caught in the dirt-thickened sludge. And there you root yourself, in the slow-moving ether, a spore hoping to impregnate in a mix of soot and watery soil. There at the bottom, you lie in eternal darkness.

You write—ABRACA—its an abnormally cold summer afternoon.

Lasting until the thick layers of mud that form the surface of the riverbed, the Mississippi, the Nile, churn once again, filling your blood with ancient air bubbles. It lasts until the plants and fish disperse from the explosion, stabbed and bloodied in dark pools of chlorophyll backbone. It lasts until the sacred crocodile rises up from the bottom of the world and takes you, frightened and floating, to the altar of its breast to suckle on encrusted scale; you know the ecstasy of the sun god, of the dried sheets of vellum and cuneiform that last beyond the centuries of man and his works, and you obey its jagged claw, succumb to the pressure of its teeth, persuade yourself that the beauty of life consists not in quietly submitting to the shadows of another man, but in swallowing the mistakes of other dull shadows.

Which is why you are not here anymore.

You awake sometime later in the hospital bed at the end of a devastating war. The stuffy air bleeds with the souls of disembodied mites and baptismal, carbolic soap. Forty-nine stitches, and one child pulled premature from its mother, clinging for life, with a sanitized, electric mouth gaping for air. No wonder you feel desperate. You glimpse your daughter, for the first time, resplendent at the breast of the wet nurse. Her lips twist into the dust along an old wisteria vine, choking off the light and sun from those who need its sweet breath. Cut, chloroform, and crocodile—sweet crocodile. The Caesarian section still burns your figure, the sawbone teeth shine still in the sun.

You write—ABRAC—sure that *everything* has been faked.

Even this moment. An abnormally cold summer afternoon. You have just finished your edits on *Tupeat, Frompeet, Repeit*. In this cheap motel, you sit in a way that allows breathing to occasionally slip, to falter, to trick the oxygenated baubles of molecular press into the approximation of flatness, the illusion of two-dimensionality. In this way you observe your child; she is the wallpaper come to life from your completely circumscribed body. You are everywhere at once, stuck on the ceilings, crawling along the intestines of the smoke detector, pulled into the toilet bowl's gaping mouth, crippled in the brilliant corners coaxing spiders and microscopic bedbugs with your animal scent.

Which is why these words are not words at all.

You awaken from a digitized sleep, slipping into awareness the way a dark screen bursting with pre-fabricated clouds looks in a million shades of color. If you only had minarets, you would become a mosaic, projecting stony saints into pigment for your child's salvation. But you are not, and you are neither, and your child looks around the room into every corner and crook, in the bathroom, and on the ceiling, but you hide with abandon, nowhere to be found.

You write—ABRA—external to the perception of this girl.

Only in this way, exuviating dimensions, peeling letters, does your work remain sacrosanct. Your child floats in suspended animation, and you gaze into her eyes over a long-distance network; your child hopes to dream away your absence. Her retina shines bright but cold, skin resonant of soft pore and pixel. In this screen of accusations you lose your way, in the endless permutations you can fade into the walls of every American motel unlucky enough to provide a phone jack. So look quick before it happens, before you lose the ability to swim in your depth—where every single sphere must be a sacrifice, and every single circle, a lie.

You write—ABR—*to know that everything has been fabricated.*

The letters between Henry Mescaline and David Schneiderman?

Most assuredly.

Nothing to the stack but artificially aged ink and a 1950 Remington typewriter, fantastic pictures and zigzagging text. *The office and tenure-track job? The endless student papers that supposedly killed off David Schneiderman?* You have your suspicions about their authenticity. If not directly, than through a web of deceit and subterfuge that coaxes a specific future from the past's multi-factorial pathways. Multiform roots coerced into the convenience of a genetically altered center stem, a golden aorta transplanted into the body. *David Schneiderman and Henry Mescaline? Certainly* Hallucigenome *itself.*

Tempted by this discovery to send the entire bundle of forty two open letters and the typescript bearing your comments on

Davis' deceptions to Spuyten Duyvil, you know that together they would make interesting reading, in tandem with Davis' sections, which you do not read, on the run as you are. You have decided to spare him that final corporate embarrassment, and by doing so, appeal to him as a person of goodwill who has simply fallen into error. You have even gone so far as to leave a detailed account of your suspicions for him at the Camelot Motel just over the Maryland border, embossed with his name, bursting with ink ready to slather his fingertips with a mummified balm, so close even as you fled into the twilight smog. Thank god for hired emissaries, joyless men who can be coaxed into delivering your letters.

An abnormally cold summer afternoon.

Perhaps it will be easy for others to accuse you of the same crimes, of replication and extraction, of fabrication and denial. *But it is not the same*. Henry Mescaline and David Schneiderman are little more than *Davis's creations*—gangly, dystrophic, vestigial. How far can he go to cover up the past? The real Henri d'Mescan is no freer from his crimes through this, than you are free from the memory of removal, the imprint of pain.

No, do *not* send it to The Publisher, of course, for the sake of the *collection*. You will peel those last seven letters slowly from their musty envelopes, careful, when you feel ready, when you feel safe enough to discover the remaining secrets. When you can recover them from their hiding place, when you can swim without fear. Do not hear the murderer's snarling noises between the lines.

You write—AB—and listen closely. Your blood runs together.

Which is why you must leave your child.

Together, you will fight the reptilian shade called Davis Schneiderman, who has created his Mescaline and his David, and in many ways, the old Phoenelia you think as you smash the glass on a Chevy Peristalsis idling quietly in the parking lot.

Which is when you see the shadow of its owner at the check-in desk.

His central images always repeat: an abnormally cold summer afternoon.

You write—A—already merging onto the superhighway.

Where you must leave even your self-image behind.

So that crocodile will ride this particular artery with you.

Blazing together up the twisted, wind-blown river, on an abnormally cold summer afternoon…

A—writes Y-O-U—until Y-O-U disappear.

Pete and Repeat went into a building. Pete came out. Who is Left?

Repeat.

Pete and Repeat, ancient as they are, routinely assume pseudonyms and *nom de plumes* and allonyms and aliases and sobriquets and agnomens and cognomens and *nom de guerres*. Whatever is needed to get the dirty job done. After all, they only want to…

Repeat.

Pete and Repeat are cut from the same cloth, so much so, that it is often difficult to tell them apart. Experts decide to utilize scientific methods to unearth the real Pete from the unreal Repeat. Experts supply money to Abstract Expressionist painters so that the American art might devastate Soviet Social Realism. Pete and Repeat become art forgers in order to elude the authorities. They spend all day working on their drip canvases and action pictures. All of their paintings, sculptures, collages, and manifestos looked like themselves, which is to say, like each other. The authorities are baffled, until they decide to smoke out the differences that must have generated the similarities. In other words, they think that by working backwards, the intersection between Pete and Repeat's interface could be located at a fixed coordinate point. Pete and Repeat catch wind of this attempt and dramatically increase production along the curve of their continuum. Before long the market floods with straight lines shooting back into the inimitable distance, shafts of illuminated perspective receding into a black hole, with three-dimensional futures unified under the myth of a smaller and smaller science. Bull market on the molecular! Well, this is too much for the authorities, who find themselves going

around in smaller and smaller circles, which is to say, microscopic straight lines. Pete probes his conscience with an
unholy psychoanalyst before deciding to turn ratfink to the
Feds as part of his treatment, which may have been part of the
plan. The raid on the art show, the warehouse, the homes of
conspiracy-minded customs agents fail to produce any evidence, so the CIA decide to back mescaline and LSD as alternative espionage agents. After so many years out of work, who
can possibly lead the new avant-garde?

Repeat.

Pete and Repeat tackle politics, gender, race, class, and
ability but only because they are forced to.

Repeat.

Pete, a 33-year old divorcé from Dayton Ohio, impersonates a genius seventeen-year old graduate student who has
dreams of studying at the Sorbonne as well as a sexual fetish for
butternut squash-flavored ice cream. He write letters to the
county pen, under the pseudonym Gact, and after sporting the
finest in mid-western lady's underwear for so many years while
giving himself erotic tarot card readings—finally divines the
glorious lips of his long-dead, seemingly primordial father, in
the mirror, pursed perfectly in the robust angle of a somatic,
otherworldly chutzpah. Gact visits the prison in an equally glorious mink stole (everything so glorious *and* scatological), an
ebony sable, an ermine hat. Repeat, her inmate pen pal, known
from his signature as the inimitable Tacg, suspects that Gact is
not all she appears to be in his cellblock fantasies, that is to say,
his sampled take on her secret, sacred letters. But upon actually seeing the barely legible Gact, Tacg now thinks that her
recent letters have been overly crisp, deceptively clear, entirely
too perfect.

Tacg enters the visitor area cautiously, unwilling to be hurt
once again, and sets himself up behind the bulletproof protec-

tive glass. Gact also enters, loosely fondled by the guard, and with the animal carcass wrapped coyly around her mouth, keeps Tacg intent on the promise of eventual, oral absolution. Tacg shrugs his shoulders, flexes his biceps in vain, but Gact, unable to contain her disappointment at the mundane reality of the person that she had imagined to be ever so much more, bites lightly into a cinnamon-flavored cyanide capsule as the sounds of talk drifts from the mundane to the quixotic, as the sound of Tacg's voice and the beating of his heart blends perfectly into the same slowing patterns of Gact's own nubile body. After seven minutes and twenty-three seconds, guess who is left alive?

Repeat.

Gact and Tacg are off to a false start. The coroner is nosing around the crime scene, so…

Repeat.

Pete, assuming the persona of a falsely convicted war criminal named Henri d'Mescan, attempts to put one over on every everyone and each no one who could potentially finger someone if put on the stand by the victorious somebodies. So d'Mescan plans to flee his own trial and make short work of a savvy impersonator by writing him away for good. He'll then bargain for entry into another person's identity and start again in America, a country that's had so many precursors its a wonder it manages to keep itself together at all. Of course, d'Mescan thinks identity is so fluid that he'll have to take over a whole entire body in order to execute his plan. He decides to do this with language…

Repeat.

Pete and Repeat go into a coma. Pete comes out. Who is Left?

Repeat.

Pete, or Henri d'Mescan, and Repeat, or Henry Mescaline,

saunter into a reputable fast food restaurant as if they own the entire franchise. d'Mescan orders a cube of meat amalgam with irradiated pickles, hydrogenated onion, and the rotten tomatoes of vegetable by-product reconstructed in circular tomato molds invented specifically for the proposed astronaut moon colony, but used only once for that damn dog who went up in Sputnik II. Mescaline, hoping to eat healthy, orders one styrofoam box with one vanilla-extract cellophane shake. d'Mescan, who can always recognize quality, rejoices in the reproduced slaughter of animals graphically detailed on the comic-strip place mats, on the walls beneath the hanging menus splattered by outmoded fryer grease, on the colorful plastic contortions of "Farmer Codakromes Mass-Production Cartel" toy line (über-cow Bovinus, salted swine Cesar Porkgustus)—all displayed in bright colors for the valued customers coagulating beneath the shiny heat lamps. d'Mescan can feel the vague remnants of soy approximation sluicing over his stomach lining and firing his intestinal pistons in a fully loaded, 1949 Chevy Peristalsis.

While Mescaline, a self-starter, vows that his childrens children will one day know a time without flesh, a body without organs, a world without end. He realizes the necessity of resistance just as d'Mescan upchucks part of his own stomach lining into a trashcan marked "burger slurry." d'Mescan, during this reflux session, looks to Mescaline for commiseration, but Mescaline's insides have hardened against the pleading of his one-time comrade in meat production. Try as he might, Mescaline can't move any of his marbled muscles; and even if the cellophane shake and styrofoam box wasn't providing a impenetrable block to the *wrong* kind of protein synthesis, his focus goes off somewhere in a distant, molecular space, a parabolic in-between where the sub-atomic particles of a de-programmed meaty cellulose make a case for decomposition and measured product placement. And nothing, absolutely nothing—try as he might to control the internal organs once so easily handled—absolutely nothing can be forced up from his arcane insides. They're both present all right, d'Mescan and Mescaline, Pete and Repeat, inhabiting the same exit off the freeway, to the left of the Esso station, just beyond the dotted yellow line. But who is built better to keep such horror down? **Repeat.**

Pete and Repeat are excited to introduce a new product to the American public, but they cannot afford a TV spot, so they rent a horse and buggy only to find their movements closely followed by who else but ~~PeteandRepeat~~? **Repeat.**

Pete called Tacg, a football-loving workaday slob, likable enough in his dream duplex aluminum-sided pleasure dome, presentable enough to keep the appearance of attention through most of life's quotidian smorgasbords, commits most certainly (in the abstract) to the notion of America as superpower, global prefect, and defunct viceroy of a ersatz neo-colonialism, and to prove it, he'll continue to beat his wife repeatedly when the New York Titans pitch a no-brainer against the other baseball squadron at the Dow Chemical Concern Stadium-Arena. Accepting the blows with resignation, his wife Repeat called Gact learns (from a constant flood of TV images) that there are actually integration-minded minority groups replicating the oppressive power structure while meekly advocating bland systemic reform—so Gact focuses her mind on the upcoming holidays and thinks deeply about how her less-than-adequate little provider Tacg suffers from a seasonal disorder and that maybe she'll get him one of those new-fangled artificial sun lamps because the real sun is just bound to burn out any minute now and she'll tell the kids, Hamlet and Caliban, exactly what really happened when she fell down the stairs while dusting the garage for the big New Year's Eve campout

and its almost as if she can feel the cold January wind beating against her skin as she thinks about it because his projection is just so damn strong. Later on, after the game, Tacg, sorry about his overreaction, takes the best steak-like amalgamation in the house—a Grade-R sirloin by-product—and lovingly rubs its tenderized flank into the swollen lips of his wife Gact's pussy. She dutifully weeps for the old days and can't help feeling aroused when, suspended in a stiff frigid limbo, Tacg forces his cock into the end zone. After the team hits the showers, after it is all over, which one must resolve the gender conflict?
Repeat.

Pete, of sound mind and body, pledges all of his worldly possessions to the firm of Repeat, Johnston, Farquar, and Leech, to be delineated at certain intervals to his brother Repeat, whose name shall henceforth proselytize a belief system that he will *never* know to have originated outside of his dainty, little head.
Repeat.

Pete a.k.a. Henry Mescaline, eager to beat the Ruskies in the space program, takes it upon himself to write the following letter to Wernher von Braun, rocket scientist and former Nazi: "I don't care what happened before, all is forgiven, love Pete." Repeat a.k.a. Henri d'Mescan, when told by his twin that his name had been used on a message of forgiveness to von Braun, feels deeply ashamed that his identity could so easily be conscripted into dealings with persons who he tries very hard to portray as his enemy. Henri continually devises methods of confronting Henry about the incident, but being unable to face the conflict directly, mumbles under his breath during the entire time he helps to arrange von Braun's entry into the United States to work on our space program. Henry, sensing that something is amiss, sticks out the olive branch, mumbling something about a promotion to the heart of the factory and how both Henry and Henri's boss and the other fugitive Nazis don't even *like* the rocket man but it is strictly a matter of keeping up with the Stalin-es. After reading *Das Kapital* in the shit room, who can remove himself from the lard-covered rim of third-stage capitalism?

Repeatmoss.

Pete and Repeat and Gact and Tacg and Henry and Henri all feel strangled in *this* political climate.

Repeat.

Repeat.

Repeat and Pete now have an understanding called

Auto-Repeat.

We endeavored, always, to return to good forms.

When we made our living in the editorial business, as we had done for many years, we were required to pay careful attention to even the smallest whims of our publishers. We were of course prepared for another package full of entirely unreasonable requests from Tod Thilleman at Spuyten Duyvil (a completely unreasonable businessman in the Maurice Girodias mold),[10] when a letter, bundled inside a much larger envelope, arrived in its stead. We quoted the start of the letter at the top of our next blank page, reproduced here, composed, as per Thilleman's habit, first on a 1950 Remington typewriter (thus guaranteeing its authenticity). For no other method could better prepare us for the horrible shock, as this sick story of Phoenelia Yeer, a tragic story really, continued to unfold:[11]

10 In the past, Spuyten Duyvil had asked us for such unattainable items as a lock of d'Mescan's hair, audio testimonial from witnesses to the 1913 incident in the Rhine (try finding a ninety-year old in Germany with an unclouded memory), and a death certificate for the imposter d'Mescan who was executed by the French government in 1947 (destroyed in the May 1968 student revolts).

11 Still, it seemed impossible that the bitch would libel so freely after all we had done for her. She was a two-bit nothing, a go-nowhere hack of a composition teacher when we found her in that so-called "State" institution SUNY-Vestal, teaching thesis statements in five courses per semester. Involving her in *Multifesto* was our gift, her ticket to a private college, with cushy benefits, tiny classes, and an air of academic humanism missing from the public sphere. How could she pass on that? And for what?

Dear Davis;

> We have been incredibly disturbed to find out
> the truth of this matter. We are certainly aware
> of your difficulties with Phoenelia Yeer and
> already (frankly) exasperated by the delays to
> the long-contracted *Multifesto* (which our legal
> counsel advises there is no way out of produc-
> ing at this point), and so we think it best that
> one or both of you leave the project willingly,
> or if that is impossible, by force. You will no
> doubt wonder what we mean by "one of you"
> as you have been a member in good-standing
> of Spuyten Duyvil for some years, and in fact,
> occupy one of our few corner offices, and hold
> a key, might we remind you, to the executive's
> executive washroom, which we offered you
> (since you are not an executive) solely as a ges-
> ture of goodwill, and if you recall, an assurance
> that you will *never* alert anyone in middle-
> management as to its pristine nature *or* exis-
> tence that you claim to have stumbled upon
> when engaged in a search for liquid-paper
> refills. Dr. Yeer, on the other hand, holds nei-
> ther access to any of our washrooms nor any
> other connection beyond her editorial contract
> to Spuyten Duyvil. Thus, we have been more
> than ordinarily alarmed by her accusations
> against you, as to the complete fabrication of
> many things that we had formerly, based upon
> your reputation, believed to be true…

We immediately summarized our positions for Thilleman

and the Spuyten Duyvil board before we introduced "Fex and the Occupation of France," a brilliant satire that proved our point in an inverse manner to the "proof" of Phoenelia Yeer. Whereas Yeer interpreted (and constructed) texts as if words simply reflected a reality beyond reflection, we have produced documentation of actual physical events.

***

1960, while a productive year for Henry Mescaline, also saw the beginning of an extended federal probe into his identity. Sponsored in part by a black-ops remnant of the House Committee on Un-American Activities, this investigation became aware of David Schneiderman's work as editor of *Hallucigenome* in the fall of that year. A memo from one of the late Senator Joseph McCarthy's Undersecretaries of Anti-Communism, a man by the name of Geoffrey Sortini, to *his* man in the Secret Service, supervised by one similarly-named Agent Jeffrey Sordini, suggested that the whereabouts of Henri d'Mescan and/or Henry Mescaline were monitored by the Federal government as early as 1955, when "Warning to the J. Edgar Hoover in your Closet" made its first underground appearance.

Still, the mere existence of this investigation confirmed the hypotheses that the man executed in Paris at the close of the "Identity Trial" in 1947 was *not* Henri d'Mescan, but rather, the imposter who both composed the "Vichy Papers" and became the recipient of the death sentence—thus precipitating the work of Henry Mescaline; or in an unlikely scenario that Yeer briefly entertained (out of spite), that the "Henri d'Mescan" traced by the government was *not* the original, but perhaps the imposter.[12]

12 After her initial slip from sanity, Phoenelia clung to the theory that Henri d'Mescan, whom she carelessly labeled a guilty war criminal, had been a Nazi collaborator, and thus, rightfully sentenced to die. She assumed that if *The Trial and Death of Henri d'Mescan* could be taken at face value in terms of an

Clearly, anybody could write anything nowadays, and given the proper staging, anyone *did* write anything nowadays. We had withheld making too much mention of Phoenelia's ridiculous academic bent, for we knew that (unlike us) she seemed completely unable to disengage herself from her belief that the world entire was a text that could be read and (mis)understood with the same authority as a book. We expressed concern about her sanity of course. Her overused theory-speak that called everything a "text" functioned as little more, ultimately, than a metaphor. After all, we did not write our car into existence, or our mortgage payment, or for that matter, even a movie. Yes, of course words played a *part*—we were far from denying that, but we were forced to let go of this insane notion that the physical construction of reality depended solely on the structural integrity of prose.[13]

What further proof might Spuyten Duyvil have needed than the documentation of an actual event, particularly when

imposter being put to death in d'Mescan's place, then the fiction of Henry Mescaline acted as little more than an attempt by the fugitive d'Mescan to continue to "clear" his name through a "persona" that would write whatever necessary to fictionalize the past. After she finally informed us of the pregnancy, Yeer had moved on to a theory that David Schneiderman, the loyal editor behind *Hallucigenome*, fabricated the entire collection in order to blackmail d'Mescan into assuming a new identity, or to rescue him, despite himself, from the Nazi stigma that haunted him. She never came clean on which scenario might fit, and after we had been separated from some time, as we tried to meet our obligations to Spuyten Duyvil and to d'Mescan while simultaneously searching for the child we had never seen, she fabricated the even more absurd scenario that we had somehow fabricated the complete Henry Mescaline and David Schneiderman corpus. Far be it from us to imply that these frequent uncertainties and shifts in perspective were due to hormonal changes and emotional distress, but the correlation might have been *more* than coincidental. What's next? That someone had fabricated our editorial introductions, or perhaps even hers? Perhaps that someone wasn't even real. Here we observed the fallacy of the postmodern in all its ridiculous glory.

13 Henri d'Mescan proved our point in *The Trial and Death of Henri d'Mescan*, wherein he refuted Mutation's claim that any single text could be responsible for its cultural reception. Instead, d'Mescan suggested that everyone involved in the process, from the writer to the consumer, including those who shepherd all of the physical steps, bore the ultimate weight of meaning.

bolstered with pages upon pages of related government documentation? How could we have possibly fabricated Henry Mescaline or David Schneiderman, let alone *Hallucigenome,* or the innumerable published works of criticism and many unpublished doctoral dissertations on the subject? We were only a small number. We could only hope that the deranged fantasies of our partner did not detract too much from the important work of this collection, *Multifesto*, which had already gone so far in presenting Henri d'Mescan as a figure of great integrity.

***

To return again to the deluded realm that Phoenelia Yeer lived in—that of the literary text—for the express purpose of proving another point as to the reality of Henry Mescaline and David Schneiderman, we focused on the most significant political statement of *Hallucigenome*. For Henry Mescaline, the later fiction collected by David Schneiderman—most notably the violently political work of the brilliant *Abecedarium,* excerpted here in "Fex During the Occupation of France"—represented as radical a departure from its immediate predecessors as that material had assumed from the simplicity and understatement of *Spacecats!* The novel *Abecedarium,* co-written with Cuban-American writer Arc-Zen S. Denarhlo,[14] followed the ancient, monocle-wearing Fex—unambiguously (in this sample) lampooning Marshal Philippe Pétain, French leader during the WWII—as he undertook street-level action against the Nazi regime.

Of supreme import to this excerpt was Mescaline's repatriation of the original "Fex" pamphlets, composed by Henri

14 Denarhlo's most important independent work, *Your Queasy Gastrointestinal Track has the Approximation of a Ganglia,* concerned artificial intelligence and the nature of the "human" in a cyber-biological, monkey-controlled future.

d'Mescan during the early months of the Vichy Government and quickly censored by the Nazis.

Having rewritten a past output, expanded on its themes, stretched its boundaries as Mescaline and Denarhlo had done in *Abecedarium*, Henry Mescaline produced the most important work of a fiction writer. When d'Mescan composed the initial "Fex" pamphlets during WWII,[15] the work presented a radical reversal of the Vichy government's ridiculous defense of French autonomy from the Nazi regime. The substance of d'Mescan's initial Fex material presented Marshal Pétain as a sort of incompetent boob, ineffectually plotting to undermine the Nazi power apparatus while, time and again, playing into its hands. Despite his desires, the d'Mescan Fex was ultimately a failure.

Mescaline's *Abecedarium* twisted this earlier resistance mechanism into a new shape, and from the give-and-take composition methods of Mescaline and Denarhlo, the reader imbibed an extension of the themes first presented by Henri d'Mescan during the war.[16] Here, we observed the Marshal

15 The original "Fex" pamphlets were destroyed by German forces at a Paris book burning several months after the start of the Occupation. See *The Trial and Death of Henri d'Mescan* section of *Multifesto* for a brief discussion of the "Fex" material.

16 *Abecedarium* was written over a three-day period in late summer 1962. Denarhlo and d'Mescan would begin each writing session at separate typewriters, working steadily for a period of two hours. Then, they would switch seats, and with editing equipment, they altered, revised, and retyped the others document with significant changes that accounted for an expansion of the text equal to at least one and a half times its original length. This process repeated itself, until the writers seemed to dissolve into each other, with Denarhlo commenting on day two, that "I am no longer you, but you have not become me. Instead, we are ourselves as we are through each other." Denarhlo, Arc-Zen S. "Subway Memories." *Contemporary Literocity*. 114 (1979): 89.

reconfigured as an aggressively physical *and* cerebral character casting off his diplomatic and administrative constraints for a street-level action strategy later favored by the student activists of the late 1960s. Journeying to the Imperial Botanical Gardens in search of the enormous Indonesian calla lily, Fex sublimated the prize plant (and thus the natural world) to the rhythms to its now obstructed in a mediated (re: German) environment. By intensifying the character of Fex into a now-overt resistor, this piece redefined his past ineffectual representation from d'Mescan's original version. The final gassing of the two Nazi soldiers stood as both a bold political statement as well as a valiant rehabilitation attempt for the reputation of a man still "officially" a corpse, but possibly, also, a Lazarus in this new form.

***

Thus, the project of *Abecedarium* signaled a new trope, a new regime of the senses and the camera that could turn the most innocent image into a reptile, the most violent into a lamb. In its tangles there stood no up or down, and unlike the earlier excerpts of *Hallucigenome*, there could be no doubt that Henry Mescaline authored this chapter, as well as of the entire novel, and that David Schneiderman, his friend and editor, did nothing more than provide the steady encouragement so necessary for aesthetic greatness. Critics who evaluated the manuscript charged it with a political impotency in comparison to *Tupeat, Frompeet, Repeit,* but if we reviewed the entire context of *Hallucigenome*, from *Spacecats of the World, Untie!* forward, we would see the same struggling sentience finally assume a mature, if eclectic, engagement with the questions of history, authenticity, and identity that characterized even the earliest essays of the European Henri d'Mescan.

The difference exceeded questions of textuality. Pre-execution, Henri d'Mescan rode the tenuous equilibrium. In this new incarnation, oceans away from the sins of mother Europe, Henry Mescaline became an avatar of rebirth, the American dream made real. Yeer, unfortunately, in the grand achievement of *Abecedarium,* saw only another cog in the machinery of deceit. Her sight proved unworthy, her perspective skewed. When the mother sickened, the child suffered, and we needed only to understand the afflictions of Phoenelia Yeer to see the deficiencies of our child.

21) Henry Mescaline and Arc-Zen Denarhlo
From Abecedarium—"Fex During the Occupation of France"
(1963)

It was the saddest conversation he had in his tour, yet so pleasing, proof once more of his superiority. Carnival in so-called Free Zone.

Marshall Fex brushed aside the recriminations of his Ministers of Finance, his advisors at Vichy—the private cartel of anti-Semites he loathed above all other of his hatreds when *putsch* came to love. The rolling draperies of his office—purple, how it made the wind visible—at this wartime capital in the French Free Zone reminded him that what "nature" sets against "type," "type" can set for the expectations of an all-but-subjugated populace. Half the time he didn't know what he said anymore; more and more life seemed to read itself back to him as a sort of psychedelic phantasmagoria, or a surreal cautionary tale based mostly around his private parts and his cravings for *foie gras* spread over wartime crackers.

The government, such as it was, has thus far prevented the Nazi occupation of the Zone. A profit-driven Line of Demarcation is the essence of all basic marketing schemes, cold when wartime commodities are smuggled in the sidecar of some corrupt official, burning with all the pre-scripted tension of a journeyman-boxing match cut jagged into the split-screen France had become.

Fex dictating to his buxom secretary: "If I envision, even recommend the return of Pierre Laval, it is in order to spare the people greater misfortunes and suffering. So far I have done my best to uphold the office which has been forced upon me …No, eliminate that, all of it… Our current situation has been none too terrible. It is forbidden to be out of doors from nine at night to five in the morning…uh…"

"Yes?" No, there would be no way to put it lightly. Fex's duty is to minimize the possibilities of co-belligerency—i.e. more war—perhaps by making what once constituted France and what remains of France to seem, if now separate Frances, still amicable brothers of the same mother who have met late in life, and who have chosen to make such different lives for themselves, yet who can come now and again to share a drink and speak fondly of the old family dog, still alive perhaps, somewhere in the ahistorical country. Maybe with MaMa? He remains fond of his cognac: *Fate,* says his internal Fex, *can be used as a weapon to influence the masses of filth and unctuous protoplasm constricting the genetic potential of a people that are not my people, composed in the droppings of shit from some half-baked coyote god confusing colonial impulses for the shake and shimmy of some World Serpent comportment to the great Western moment.* His snifter gives him a hell of a chin: prothagnous and primitive. Such a beautifully shaped jut to be defiled by its reflection.

"Start three words back. They already know its the morning, damnit..." Fex wets his pants. Its a small dot on his white jodhpurs, brought on by Free Zone binges and a bladder limited by human scope: though, to its credit, little else. Any other man in the world would have urinated himself days ago. He hasn't enjoyed the delightful scrimp of a bowel movement in three weeks, wonders briefly if one can really survive that long without one. Half of one? A fart every now and again? He must keep silent in *word.* If he is to save his generation, one must suffer and bleed, pee only when given a chance and never, never defecate. Not even once.

A great deal of excitement infects the atmosphere of Imperial Botanical Gardens; at long last the giant Indonesian calla lily (*Amorphophallus titanium*) has burst into blossom. Biggest of the big flowers: bells like those of a gramophone, freakishly living, alien. So ...*unavailable* to humans: where the hell would you put a monster trumpet like that? Fex nuzzles against a warm body in order to better view this extremity of geno-aesthetics. With the largest flower ever recorded, measuring eight and a half feet in height, four feet in diameter, and twelve feet in circumference, the majority of the residents of this too-much-like-an-Occupation crowd have positively no interest in the fingerprint stain across Fex's monocle, the swirl of grey hairs moving back in precise whips across the slant of his almost-circular ear, and endless layers of pomade forming his silver sideburns into a solid block of hair that in the composite picture they suggest, form an archetypal image of the old man.

Fex goes incognito: here on the National Revolution, ready to burn down his own offices should the whim of the crowd desire it. He tries his hardest, at least for a moment, to feel the humor of it all, the *élan vital* that might empower him and by extension the citizens he has sworn to defend. He enjoys speaking to himself more than ever: *Greenhouse walls conspire against him, the hardening sod of greyscale ground trumpets brassing off in angular doorways, as his boots move as alien rovers across the surface of the distant moon. The slingshot guns of the German officers seem trained on his disguise, on the apertures of his body. His mouth, gaping and luminescent, contains a set of thirty-two perfect adult teeth, aged over nine decades into a great wall of cleanliness and plaque dispersal. Gums are check, and like railroads killing steamboats, his tongue flicks its way over the unstructured signification of a flat Earth gone wrong, a geothermal passion flower whose buds have only begun to shine. Fex wipes his eyes and tear ducts twinkle out baubles of nectar, ambrosia with Olympian salt proportions that cleanse a sinus tract settled amid a drug-slathered past. Once Fex went to doctors and cried at funerals; he curried favor with distant administrations and ancient* phrenologists. But no longer. Today, in front of the flower, his disconnected people, and the invader, this ugly spirit, Fex can spit from a Dead Sea throat.

Two of the officers, the swastikas on their armbands spinning against red backdrops, whisper about the need for modesty and mediation, about service to one's country, even when in a strange land with strange customs they haven't yet had time to paper Nazi.

"Not all of these people approve of the gesture of killing someone unidentified," they say, referring to the "deportations" which often forget the illusion of preliminary promises, of movements orchestrated to convince the very soil, the brisk night air, of a dignified surrender. Epaulettes and holstered weapons betray a depressingly sluggish nervous system for these soldiers, and as replicas of a painted horizon, the sounds of the sullen Carnival outside—a young girl's body found raped near the carousel, the subterranean handshake sealing black market congresses, the cold comfort of burning animal flesh screaming in the heat-blistered tether of some primordial rope of sand—they must constantly recalibrate their machines. A vital part of their survival equipment is stuck in departments of the Nord, of Alsace-Lorraine, or in that accursed Hall of Mirrors at Versailles where past indignities have only recently been reversed. Temporary triumphs breed temporary measures, temporary leaders, and temporary excesses. Of this, they are only distantly aware; ice ships convinced from breaking a few swells significantly larger the mightiest icebergs, these officers can never feel the flow of land beneath them, the fleeting, jury-rigged state of conscription connecting Fex to the automata of his own body. A fragrant homeostasis has long since stopped demanding resources, instead spinning his hunger for the image into pockets of apparently mannered amylase. Balanced on a tightrope—he can't stop himself from running across with shoulders tight and abdomen perfectly centered. *Their* reflexes, for all the virtue of such incompetent chameleons, are all but nonexistent.

The Indonesian calla lily shares this horrible ennui, and Fex means to exploit it to his personal advantage. Flaked with the internment of thousands of smaller blossoms, circumnavigated by the competing vectors of objectification and dominion, the flower bends into a hideous periscope for its admiring throngs. Fex feels—it scares him like a waking dream—a strange penis tickling his ribcage, odious folds of excessive cellulose bumping into his uniform; he smells the stink of over-the-counter allergy medicines, shults of central nervous system tobacco treatments drawing opium sunsets into his calcified lungs. His boots are no doubt untied, but he dares not bend over, look down, give any indication of the overwhelming disgust.

The scented gallery of indignant spectators have no identity beyond their utility at this moment for Marshal Fex (in this sense he is similar to the officers), but the movements of Vichy demand that he visit with them. Despite the Occupation, the addicts, the endless *diktats* from Ambassador Abetz in Paris, the demand for volunteer labor to fill German factories while hoards of Hitler Youth fight all the insidious forms of Bolshevism seem even more oppressive in this context. Fex allows himself to be swept away, to both desire the movement of bodies into a carpet of mass production, of "co-belligerency" with the Germans, of surrender to the plans of the collaborators, who wish to embrace the new European regime, *and* find for France a place worthy of her history in this context. Fex moves toward the calla lily, but this strategy is simple theatre, the masquerade that must be entered into completely for the moment so that genetic potentials can be subverted, refigured, and expended in harmless denouements. The officers move along with him, guided by the silent Fex into a glacial quiet.

Fex recalls the cliché sights of his temporary home, his temporary people, pushing everything toward totalization: the Arc de Triomphe with its circling traffic and around-the-clock honor guard, the imposed historical curricula of the Institut de France, the Opera de la Bastille and its litany of beautiful propaganda. The calla lily moves even closer, a river pushing its ripples to a static shoreline of fully developed Esso stations, resort embankments, toward the Quai Anatole France and a complete understanding *Al la Recherche du Temps Perdu*. Noise from the Carnival beyond the tent increases along with the acrid reproduction of mites and flies and worms in the flutes of the greenhouse; Fex's asshole tightens and his heart pounds....

Fex at the officers hip: "So you've only read the first book of Proust, *Du Côté de Chez Swann*?" Hands curl into fists for the French on display, pushing Fex forward.

"Uh...no, I've gotten much further of course...." The base of the lily has extravagant gold fillings, soldered together, a testament to uneven efficiency and misdirected solipsism. Lights dim.

"How far would you say, if, say, questioned by someone who sought the pattern of your flesh, the code that keeps you here, bound to this moment, this history...? Come around to the light so we can study your features in detail and arrive at a French system of identification." The tent flaps of the makeshift greenhouse reveal themselves as they fall.

"Quite far...through *Le Côté de Guermantes*."

Fex makes his jump. Ah-ha! He's got them. The calla lily spreads its seductive vulva to the officer, and the crowd bounces uneasily. Whatever lays coiled in the background—smoky in the motionless air—blasts its way through a furnace of the seething core, the Earth's uncompromising mantle. If caught in a trap set by the plant, Fex has no recourse to his office or his stature. A hero of the Verdun in the first world war, his pro-activity a myth perpetuated by fame. Generally defensive, he counts on enemies to eliminate themselves, to slip out of the timestream, to surrender the codes, the files, the false and accurate ledgers that merge in the gaseous feculence of the calla lily choking the Nazi officers and their plucked eagles. Fex sees the visions of the green Carnival dragon, the mascot of revenge made from solar panel scales and split-atom microphones that won't be possible until somebody wins the H-Bomb regatta: *the centipede legs of forced labor, thousands of callused limbs burning the ground, the flame of an ancient tongue.*

The gas from the enormous blossom recalls the hideous anal eye of a hurricane of stink, a pineal monstrosity descending from that gland through the horrors of an occupied gastrointestinal delta, and ministerial government of the kidney plagued by Charles de Gaulle in London, and unfurled rebellions in colonial North Africa. The lily lets it out, the secret juices, the indigenous resistance. The lily smells of a corpse. Camera bulbs twinkle stars into the night sky and the stench of rotten meat spreads across this temporary capital, this vertiginous center of both occupation and rebellion. Fex's breathing is practiced for this moment, perfectly balanced. Years of swearing off all artificiality have yielded dividends. A mutation may also be the result of looping strands in the process of replication. In soft folds of epidermis, under account sheets to cut dead-star emptiness, film scraps coating his eyes with soft cataracts, Fex realizes that error can always creep, that replication can never be perfect. The populations of Indochina, which he was privy to visit as a boy, call the calla lily "corpse flower"; at Vichy he may even prevent his own assassination.

The Germans balance on the verge of vomiting. This is his favorite time to talk to people. Teach them a little something.

"I haven't told you about the woman I met today."

Gurgling, panicked, so very un-Nazi: and it's spreading, as the noisome stench covers the crowd. But their swastikas still spin happy as pinwheels.

"She seemed old, oh, almost dead, a mere shadow of what it means to be alive, yet I would guess twenty years my junior. She walked, she told me, for the first time today in this Free Zone of ours, eating bread, good bread, a kind that reminds her of her childhood. Sweet and crusty, she said. Oh, she loved the bread. But then, and she said this with all the madness she could muster, which, sadly, wasn't very much, since madness takes a certain degree of dignity and energy, she gripped my sleeve and said that a pair of disembodied hands, wearing black gloves, a man's hands, wrestled the bread away from her and floated off with the loaf. The struggle had left fat old ass on the ground, and all she could do was watch as the hands hovered away, ripping the loaf into tiny shreds as it went. She went see if she could gather the remnants of a meal from those bits, but instantly she saw the ground positively swell with ants, who made off with all those bits of sweet sweet childhood bread. Isn't that just the saddest thing you've ever heard, my friends?"

The Germans of course hardly hear a word, for they are puking in earnest now from the virile infection of gas, fleeing from the lily's steaming head, seeking some corner of privacy, animals in distress, twisting in the asthmatic folds of certain death. The vultures will pluck out their fillings, make off with their wristwatches, but Fex will especially enjoy the maggots, the microscopic parasites catalyzed by physical consolidation bursting through the base of ugly root and diseased offal onto the bright surface of jaundiced flesh. They will pull back their own skin, expose their bodies to the sweep of the genetic wand. Though they run away, Fex calls after them: "A shame that old lady isn't here now! You could feed her now to her heart's content, all of you, one after another, a goddamn flock of mother birds, with your goddamned canisters of Zyklon B."

Just prior to the guilty verdict in his war crimes trial, (related in *The Trial and Death of Henri d'Mescan: Apoplectic* [1954]), Henri d'Mescan leads members of the court through a burned-out hovel in the Bercy region of Paris, where he claims to have waited out the liberation of Paris by Allied troops on August 25, 1944. The trial hinged on the authenticity of collaborationist pamphlets, signed by d'Mescan, and collectively known at "The Vichy Papers."

Despite a public defense by luminaries such as Albert Camus, Jean Genet, Jean Cocteau, and Jean-Paul Sartre, Henri d'Mescan was sentenced to death on May 5, 1954. His execution by firing squad on June 3, though, remains in question-with some eyewitnesses claiming that the man put to death was not, strictly speaking, Henri d'Mescan, but rather, the collaborator who assumed his name and position during the height of the Vichy government.

HENRI D'MESCAN, 1937, on a two-month winter holiday to Calais, where he worked up to twelve hours per day on his first breakthrough text, *Abstractions*. Phoenelia Yeer, co-editor of *Multfifesto*, claims that d'Mescan composed the work, a series of academic abstracts for various arcane texts, by cutting and pasting thousands of individual phonemes from works as diverse as the Kabbalistic *Zohar*, Lucien Spume's *And the Pleasure Dome Decrees* (1352), Olaf Celsius's *Hierobotanicon* (1748), and mass quantities of *Life* magazine imported through the Barbary Coast.

HENRI D'MESCAN, circa 1972, after completing a marathon session on a "brain respirator" audio/visual stimulation device, a smaller eyeglass-driven prototype model of artist Brion Gysin's "Dream Machine"—a contrivance meant to induce alpha waves in the brain through the precise patterning of "flickering" light (8-12 flashes per second against closed eyelids). In an interview with a former student of Timothy Leary's for the one-shot magazine, *The Psychedelic Alpaca*, d'Mescan described his sessions as: "Screen shots of the world ending in an eschatological oscillation. Man will evolve past the point of discerning distinct physical objects, and in the final moments of whatever apocalypse befalls us, every person will see only these primal shapes of a constituent geometry, the floating apparatus of an ordered deity who motivates his characters into the illusion of the grandest disorder." From the period June 1972-December 1974, d'Mescan claims to have spent up to six hours per day utilizing the machine, with occasional bursts of 24-30 hours in a single session.

A bashfull Lover.

AS an unperfect actor on the stage,
  Who with his feare is put besides his part,
Or some fierce thing repleat with too much rage,
Whose strengths abnndance, weakens his owne heart;
So I for feare of trust, forget to say,
The perfect ce———y of——right,
And in mine——ne loves stre———seeme to de——,
Ore-cha———with burthen of mi———night,
——ooks be th——eloquence,
And domb presager——my speaking brest,
Who pleade for love——ke for recompence,
More then that tongue——more hath more exprest.
  O learne to read wha——ient love hath writ,
  To heare with eyes belongs to loves fine wit.

A Temptation.

TWo loves I have, of C———rt, and Despaire,
  That like two Spirit———uggest me still:
My better Angell is a M———right faire)
My worser spirit a Woman (colour'd ill,)
To winne me soone to hell, my Female evill
Tempteth my better Angell from my side,
And would corrupt my Saint to be a Divell,
Wooing his puritie, with her faire pride.
And whether that my Angell be turnd feend,
Suspect I may (yet not directly tell:)
For being both to me; both to each friend,
I ghesse one Angell in anothers hell.
  The truth I shall not know, but live in doubt,
  Till my bad Angell fire my good one out.

A 1967 collaboration between Henry Mescaline and Fluxus artist Sapphoe VanBattene, these Duchampian interventions on Shakespeare's sonnets cause Robert Rauschenberg to comment in *Art in Latin America*: "Nice, but could be softer."

David Schneiderman and early Mescaline critic Charles Gideon, author of the influential article, "Open Secret: Henry Mescaline and the Epistolary Moment," beneath the Pyramid of the Sun, Teotihuacán, Mexico. August 2, 1967.

Charles Gideon's Mescaline/D'Mescan conference of September 1971, also Mexico City. From left: Rob Johnson, Philip Walsh, Charles Gideon, Jorge Cuevas Cid, Jeffrey Miller, Katherine Streip, Allen Hibbard. Here, Gideon delivered his famous paper, "Whomever Picks up a New Identity owns Death/d'Mescan's Smile," inaugurating a new age for d'Mescan criticism.

Courtesy Charles Gideon, Gideon archive at Keele University, England. A shadow figure created by arranging stones in the shape of Henri d'Mescan and using a series of convex lenses to emulate his figure. Future, Missouri. Circa 1976. High noon.

Davis Schneiderman, May 2000, after searching unsuccessfully for Phoenelia Yeer and his daughter Dial-Up Networking in a Chuck E. Cheese's establishment just east of Texarkana, TX.

Davis Schneiderman and **Phoenelia Yeer** during happier times, after a quickie wedding and quickie divorce, May 1999, Las Vegas, outside the Chapel of Our Lady of Perpetual Motions. Both services officiated by the same Elvis impersonator.

A protest poster from d'Mescan's 1954 "Identity Trial," suggesting, using facial codes, and an adapted version of Mandarin, that free speech in France is no longer free, and that, as d'Mescan's defense attorney stated to his assembled supporters on the day of his presumed execution, "Great injustice will never look our way directly again. With d'Mescan's passing, the French become even less culpable in their daily lives. Today, we have surrendered our gaze to others, and with it, our very eyes have been extinguished."

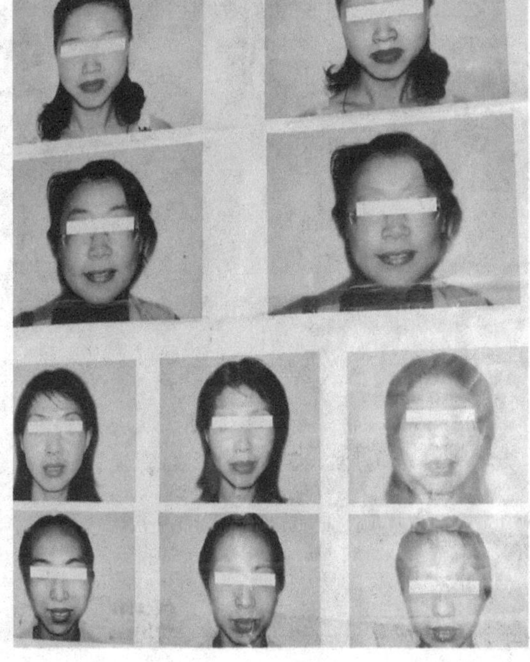

During the writing of *Post-America* (winter, 1985), Henri d'Mescan constructed a supposed perpetual motion machine to hear his garret. The cord of the fan, not pictured, looped under the apparatus, and into the fire pit, where, a transponder used heat to power the fan, which, in turn, provided air to the flame. Fuel for the flames, d'Mescan claimed in a 1986 diary, came from a condensation of air products produced by this particular arrangement of industrial machine and primitive heat source. "The formula is a secret, of course. I've no great desire to see the Cold War end…"

"Mugwump" production still from the never-released Henry Mescaline film: *The Post-American Peep Show.* Circa 1964. A cursed production from the start, these tiny silkworm carcasses were later consumed by the producer Hans Dialectic's pet pig, Orson Smelles, before Dialectic completed the dailies. After Smelles's death in 1967 of natural causes, remnants of a small silkworm colony were discovered reproducing within his lower intestine.

A rare shot of **Dial-Up Networking**, at 10.5 months. Her sideward look became a trademark of her early years, causing Davis Schneiderman to write in an email to the Publisher: "She's aware, already, of things beyond the frame. In fact, she possesses an almost preternatural instinct for observation… clearly, she already is spinning wild yarns that will carry her to great fame."

Multifesto: A Henri d'Mescan Reader
Part III: The Post-American Years

This will be me, writing, now.

American memory will eventually develop the power to crawl up the intricacies of the human gut like an uneasy barnacle clinging to the underside of the Nina the Pinta the Mayflower, before dropping its virulent seed into the swirling vats of milk consumed each afternoon by the progeny of such parasitic ancestors, such ungainly boat people. The field recordings of my origin stories sound nothing like the sun before expulsion through the mouth, before evocation into a dense tangle of words; it starts in the gut, as described, having smothered the poverty of tongue and teeth to cover everything in an concrete veneer of broken promises and industrial dental dams. Impossible to flip the script without raising the ire of the *federales*. First, they'll copy the handwriting *as it happens* on digital emulators; then, the reader can watch the balance-transfer fees increase by suspicious half-dollar increments; feel the misdirection of the Mexican laborer at the high-priced grocery store slowly dressing up the North Shore bitches with his eyes—applying a few more layers of live fur to the opossum costume, for god's sakes adding some thick polyester wrap to the tragically toned physical-trainer legs that have gone hopelessly varicose from too many visits to the land of afternoon burgundy and vibrator static orgasm breast milk.

Despite whatever complicity the reader may draw from such comparisons, I will still apologize for the treatment you have surely received at the hands of my prematurely aged and defiant brace of editors, Davis Schneiderman and Phoenelia Yeer. While I will have written numerous tracts, treatises, and fictions since the arrest of Henry Mescaline in Chicago during

1 The footnotes in PART III, unless otherwise noted, are presumably those of Henri d'Mescan (Spuyten Duyvil)

the Democratic National Convention of 1968 (and had been thus associated with that persona for the ten years previous),[2] the last two decades have surely kept me engrossed in a seemingly endless work that will emerge from the river system that changed to the rail system that changed to the fission reactor that will always power this country, to be called *Post-America*, or alternately, *Postica*. The manuscript, or manuscripts, are rumored (by my associates) to span over 7 million words and 14,000 hypertext pages. Flagellation, desire, passion, digital imaging, cruelty, multi-bit data-streaming events, curiosity,

2 The career of experimental writer Henry Mescaline will project an abrupt and tragic end with his seizure by angry riot police in Chicago during the 1968 Democratic National Convention. Covering the events for the radical, Situationist International arm of the *Ladies Home Journal*, Mescaline will flee the 22,000 armed officers, National Guard, and federal troops ordered by Mayor Daley during the police riot, and in exasperation, will pound on the door of a small house in hopes of eluding the authorities. The occupant will shout an inquiry as to identity of the person at the door. Mescaline, full of the bravado that signified the best of his work, can shout "Mr. Mescaline" in reply, and will be then allowed entrance by the tenant, a student at the University of Illinois-Chicago completing, (coincidentally) doctoral work on Mescaline's distinguished career.

Unfortunately, in the course of their discussion over high tea, Mescaline will certainly criticize the student's central thesis that Mescaline's current fiction will at best pander to a crack-in-the-pan craze for flash fiction, cross-correlated, in this author's case, with a base and so-called "postmodern" fascination with repossessing dyspeptic clinical spaces traditionally used by the autocratic armies of patriarchy—with predictably self-referential creative production. The student, under increasing pressure to complete his project, will be unable to avoid restraining Mescaline in an elaborate cocoon of duct tape and plastic wrap before reading the entire dissertation aloud while rapping Mescaline's shins with a ball-peen hammer. After lulling him to sleep with what can only be described as the impenetrable, faux-ramblings of a excessively masturbatory academic intellect, he will drag Mescaline's body onto the front lawn, where Mescaline will then be trampled by neighborhood children before his removal by federal agents to a "detainment" facility. There, truth be known, life will flood out of him completely and with obscene speed, although witnesses may claim to perceive some vestigial movement, where his body shutters as if in orgasm for a single millisecond, with a distant pulse penetrating the callused layers of a witness's skin, just as the end of prose poem might resonate on any particular day for any particular reader, puncturing the oily epidermis of reason and fear.

adjuvant synth-muscle agitators; these will be my minions, my rumors, my angels and demons at play; I can remain removed at this advanced age from the trail that follows the gross caricatures of my past. Still, even I must observe limits. At some point when one's reputation hangs on the line, prudence will demand a response.

Additionally, Spuyten Duyvil will be required to forward me the proofs of Part I and II for this incarnation of *Multifesto*; my shock will be palpable upon discovering that the introductions of Yeer and Schneiderman (when not obsessed with their own witless banter) concentrate around absurd situation comedy, preternatural terrorisms—transforming what should be a task of measured critical reflection about my long body of work into a ridiculous free-for-all made popular by their illegitimate generation of distracted, you-me-mine-obsessed consumers.

Obviously, these editors will deal with me as fairly as they are fit to, which is to say, not at all.[3] At first I shall simply wish to stop their lunacy from infecting the remnants of my audience, and to that end, I intend to dispatch a pack of ravenous, three-headed lawyers to berate Mr. Thilleman at this so-called Spuyten Duyvil. I am confident in the instruction of my dogs, and wait patiently for the arrival of my censored newspaper. With even the smallest excuse to unleash the increasingly horrific and destructive behaviors in their arsenal of lawsuits, they can dismember documents more efficiently than an industrial shredder; they will bathe, on command, in blood drawn from the severest paper cuts, rolling their coats in the warm purple pools of inky solvent. These impulses must still be foiled when my lawyers, nearly drooling from their unrequited bloodlust, will gleefully inform me of a delightful little clause in the *Multifesto* contract of 1966 that provides for the protec-

3 Surely, their abuse of footnotes will perhaps be their most pathetic innovation. After all, who will not hesitate to skim through these annoyances, especially when they are stretched beyond all normal dimensions?

tion of my literary interests.[4] So rather than shelve the manifold tatters of this *Multifesto* and allow the legal team its carnal satisfactions, I shall treat my editors the way that they have treated me, and in doing so, invest the climax of this collection with a set of guiding principles calculated to upset the various sensibilities, which will then take me, and my work—as a satellite that has lost a dispute with gravity and atmosphere—far from its original orbit.

For beneath the snarling noises of my dual murderers berating each other for the chance to script the circumstances of my own demise, the reader can hear only the faintest undulating waves of a vertebra. Gun-slinging birds will land, along with amino-winged doves, onto the precipice of the real. Soon, every crooked feather will secrete a smooth, amorphous jelly. For no one can yet know of my impotence—all will humor my wingless evolution, and thus, my past.

Firstly, I am in the enviable legal position to demand that the publication of *Multifesto* shall be completed only in printing selections from *Post-American* that I shall choose, and send, at carefully measured intervals, with great care, selectively, to either Davis or Phoenelia. To ensure the level of engagement that these works require, I shall include specific blackmail threats that will be evident only to the discerning eyeballs of my blithe, editorial cosmonauts. Their loyalties will be tested through a battery of lie detector tests and sodium pentothal injections, and I can be relatively assured that they *will* read

4 A clause in that contract will clearly specify that any and all versions of *Multifesto* include a right of perpetuity for Henri d'Mescan to inspect and comment upon the text in the text itself. From Section R-1, Paragraph 17: "Having completed the execution of the aforementioned duties outlined in subsection 23, 56, and 89 of Section K-9, and bound by a legal and ethical obligation to the party of the first part, Atom Press and all future derivations of said company will grant said party an exclusive right of perpetuity to inspect, edit, and replace any editorial introductions that do not adequately and clearly represent the truthful trajectory of his work." A foolish agreement, still, we are bound, so say our lawyers, to abide. (Spuyten Duyvil).

and respond to what I have sent specifically for *them*.

They cannot escape my influence. I must have them know this.

Secondly, I want the purest reaction to *Post-America* possible, and thus, will used a blind sample method where each editor will not know what has been presented to the rival. Also, their so-called introductions, which will also remain hidden until the time of publication, must adhere to the following shape: they must be contained to a single paragraph to minimize the obtuse digressions of the previous sections. In this way, Yeer and Schneiderman will be unlikely to overshadow *Post-America* with their incessant and superfluously ontological psychobabble.

Thirdly, as per the original contract for *Multifesto* that I made with the late editor David Schneiderman, any deviation from the specifics of my instructions will result in a potential disqualification of the editorial introduction in question by the party of the first part (which I insist on being known as in all legal contracts; ever will I keep my humor), which shall then be replaced with my own comment on another commentary penned by the parties of the second part (the editors), and/or the substitution of some other new and separate commentary imposed at my discretion.

Fourthly…there will be no fourthly, because I wish to keep it simple. Lest you think I am overreacting, you should know that the madness eating away at Yeer and Schneiderman will become common to those who spend their time grasping at the traces of a person so much more creative, and so much more prolific than themselves.[6]

5 **Addendum for Davis and Phoenelia:** So those will be all the rules my pets, and if I have until now avoided such direct mammalian acknowledgment of your place as editors, it is because, your prior "work" on "my" "behalf" confirms my sense that you both are best addressed below the standard narrative line. Two toady afterthoughts. Certainly, as you both plan to write again if given the chance, my blood must indeed be cold like the iciest

23) PHOENELIA YEER
INTRODUCTION: POSTICA 4.9: A FRAGMENT

You live out these philosophies of the bedroom with your new child, Dial-Up Networking. All of the forty-nine letters you have spent the most recent years inspecting (except the seven yet to be opened) have been torn and shoe-printed to form a thick, uncomfortable carpet that obscures any real analysis of *Post-America.* Despite your constant desire to absorb pieces of the postmodern body—lips spread across the billboard landscape and the soft, lolling lilt of the elongated tongue stretched into a surrealist parachute across the silver frayed sounds of the sky—you cannot identify with this newly reanimated Henri d'Mescan. Fragmentation is often deceptively autocratic. As you watch the shape and figure of the child asleep in the hotel bed, the irony of post-irony is not lost on the talking picture box that flashes your image across its pixilated screen. You are placed surreptitiously in an advert for the newest body-hardening zit cream. You? Or just a disguised version of your hair curled loose as the lip-roaring newscaster, the weather vixen's pointy tits exciting the cumulonimbus hard-on of Davis Schneiderman, erect no doubt at his personal fucking computer miming your Botex-injected jelly flesh under the gaze of the Spuyten Duyvil deadline. Worse even, your tiny child, Dial-Up Networking, materializes in her bassinet each morning, fresh, *as though you have never left her.* She insults your ineffective escape with each suckle, peppering the wall of your room with excremental smears, mesmerizing curlicues. You read

river, and my reptilian scales (as you have taken great pains to indicate) can store an infinitely reproducible life energy that can last forever. Quite frankly, I will refuse to eclipse myself in either of you. And while I will not consider my person to be constituted by particularly spiteful materials, I intend, waiting calmly in the billabong of Post-America, to infect the throat of your loveliest child, and against your most impotent protestations, I will gradually transmogrify her body into the perfect morsel of my eternal food.

d'Mescan's "Postica 4.9" without context, silent in the glow of a mosaic candleholder, scratching at the underside of your twin wrists as they burn from the edge of the typing desk that makes you complicit in your own mistranslation. A strange slice bleeds from your, while your issue sleeps away your soft subdued traumas as if everything seems corporeal and settled. The rhythm of the child's repetitive breath sucks your fleeting analytical inertia into the spirals of her respiratory track; the vortex pulls your hand down the curve of your swollen body, slowly teasing and then penetrating the elastic ring of silk underwear bought in haste from the local Presbyterian rummage sale; an angel is extracted from the ramparts of some medieval fresco by the cruel renaissance wind while your fingers rub against the clitoris made warm and soft by the vacuum emanating from the breath of the child, tickling your pubic hair where the razor blade once smoothed blue to hide the sweet electromagnetic tangle of your soul. Soft ooze spreads downs slowly from your warm center and covers your pulsating fingers in a sticky heat that you smear over the gooseflesh of your exposed chest. Undulating your figure into an ocean, rocking a hot triangle boat in your dark places, you rub the wet balm over your inner thighs and then onto the sheets, hiding black-lit cum stains of this motel room's past residents. Fluorescent cat-o-nine-tails and vibrant fur-lined handcuffs and a collocation of franked bank notes and half-smoked cigarettes stuffed into these motel spaces prove Davis Schneiderman a traitor and you writhe next to the flickering image of the child; he speaks in your mind like a fraud who uses language to smother you body in bed sheets stained and crumpled by your hand, the shaking blur of the ceiling fan blades casting interval light from that TV. Onto your. Sweaty body—caught in an acrobatic arc as the world narrows and tightens around you like a latex suit. Your nipples harden, glistening with droplets of sweat and texture, as the silent orgasm creeps from the deep backland of your insides through the sacrament of the hand and the colored lines that seem to grab and suck against the space of a text that is not the place for Henri d'Mescan to emerge no not the space at all no not in a final delirious yes of words flooding yes across the picture space and flowing into your ears your nose your cum-stained mouth gurgling yes the white hot liquid in throbs of television set-ups spelling yes on the lip of its pixilated screen. The child cries while you loop-de-loop against the black forever that makes you say yes and yes again and someone else writes you yes now before the delirium of the bassinet starts your hands working the type all over again with such formal gesticulations so yes and yes again.

Police sirens speed down the streets of Post-America, and through the myriad apertures that have long ago replaced windows—through keyholes and cameras, through the slit of the stapler, the ski mask, the piano wire, through a man's fingers splayed forcefully over the eyes—flashing red or blue or white strobes riding efficiently in the air. The sirens stay disconnected, ghostly, without chassis below. This is peephole ontology.

Everything moves so fast that it can jump through the playback machine like the Pullman car sliding effortlessly from its outmoded groove. Sloe gin can be administered for relief of cold sores and implementation of the viral record. Sloe motion, solely for effect.

That is, into a burst of regular speed.

Through the slats of tomorrow's newspaper and virtual inkpad clipped with the absent scissors and censored by dark marker, through the piles of fast food excrement and leftover sweat from the anus of basketball stars, through the splice of the dumpster roof against its casing, through the walls of the alley mashed by ubiquitous astigmatisms into the illusion of ovals— I can see the sirens and its coterie of flash, cleaving the grim partition of the night as it slides over the streets, intent upon the corner of a chafing mouth rotten with sores, on a sheath of jaundiced skin slowly healing a crack in the ice from a sharp skate, on the lip of a patriotic national face.

Through the perspective of an alley, Davis Schneiderman's penis is shrinking. In time, it will disappear into the space between his legs. In Post-America he serves a sentence for sins committed by the interlocking appendages and orifices now filled-in by his so-called neat-and-tidies. No one believes his protestations. Asymptotic differences are eliminated with the alchemical formula of a bathtub philosopher's stone.

Do not believe him when he proclaims my innocence.

Partisans tear the clothing from the body of the factory, squeaking backward to Quark generation points only 800 million years on the brink of the big-bang precipice. The next step is to tattoo the patterns formed by the charges onto my chest igniting tiny receptor nodes in the bandoleer onto the skin in a pain-ritual reminiscent of the calculation continuum of the Etruscan calendar, a 10,000-year cycle only now reaching a pre-apocalyptic fruition.

Yes, a fantastic moment, seeing yourself in the author's place.

It starts in the gut, as described, but life is nothing before expulsion through the mouth, having smothered the tongue and teeth, covering everything in a veneer of broken promises and industrial sludge, just as today, in Post-America, it is difficult to substantiate the most enormous historical events let alone the tiniest death throes of a no-good collaborator.

The idea of the past forms an amalgamation with the present perceptive apparatus and the projected need of the future.

Alternative pasts fail to promote alternative futures so long as the present apparatus remains in control of all projections. The police, my friends, can reach back into your womb for their evidence, pushing scissors and knife through the sweet gash of vagina stretching to the limits of breath and gene.

They will cut the child from the aperture without a warrant, brand their indentations onto the soft, spattering skull of the prison-house, the garret, the sideward glance of the video camera that always records. Space crackles with a pulsing electric energy—reason enough, for those still in their slits, to fear for their eventual shape on such an abnormally cold summer afternoon.

25) Davis Schneiderman
Introduction: Post-America, in P A R T S…

No doubt, Phoenelia Yeer, selected through some arcane mathematical formulae to go first, already expressed her outrage at the limits imposed by Henri d'Mescan and his authorial rules. She also, assuredly, spent considerable space locating herself within the sphere of the child, Dial-Up Networking, before promising you, good reader, the eventual denouement of the whole d'Mescan/Mescaline mystery. We have wasted *no* such space and we have *not* altered our voice to the will of d'Mescan. If we must work in Haiku, we were prepared for the sound of a million frogs splashing in bloody winter pools, for / this piece was not a haiku / not if you could count / the all wrong syllables are. "Post-America, in p a r t s…" appeared to be the initial segment of a larger quest narrative, whereas, the hero, who in this case became Henri d'Mescan himself, attempted to restore his pre-"Identity Trial" name through the retrieval of an original cache of the so-called collaborationist work known as the "Vichy Papers." We noticed with what great care he expressed his own innocence and established the motives for the reclamation of his image, which had been tarnished by unscrupulous characters such as Phoenelia Yeer. Even we visualized this mother staring at the fissures in the wall, mad and tone deaf, on several different occasions, so that any crack to her remaining façade was as welcome to us as the snap of an ovary and halved the devil entering her skin through the doorway of the soul.

Post-America rides the backwards cracks of a pre-Columbian anthology of sin, over the land of dead tape recorders, basketballs court halved by archaic power lines snaking over heat-blistered macadam. "Where did it come from?" the mother said, looking confused? My spinal fingers always clutch around the palm of my nerve stem and she dissipated into the angular jut of rusted mansard roofs, my promise my beauty, sweet Phoenelia Yeer, a casualty of the lily bulbs fused to my duplicitous, forked tongue. Oh my secret sin and the long-distance cunnilingus. How I wormed my way into the cavity that represents her heart, into the sweet, hidden crook of her coochie snorcher. I'm almost ashamed of my behavior. I've been a very naughty boy which of course serves as no excuse for this particular excursion to the left bank, in the area of the Sorbonne, far removed from the dirt of Pigalle and the Moulin Rouge and St. Denis at Montmarte, to complete my manic, anemic contracts.

Nineteenth-century gilded spires decorate the classic metro stops: baldachins of finely wrought iron now preserved in retrograde pop-art posters surrounded by the spritz of carbonated bath water from deadly aluminum Coca-Cola cans merging with the sickly, stringy texture of *jambon* and mozzarella in the mouths of bi-lingual patisserie patrons. The establishment hopes for Our Lady of the Flowers and Our Lady of Perpetual Motion to snatch the crown of thorns from the Sun King's petrified crotch and smash its little prick over the clandestine contour of the Post-American body. Customs agents will seize the secret "Vichy Papers," like Brancusi's *Bird in Space*, parroting the same sales tax justification or perhaps some other, more sinister multinational tariff. These texts might then be spirited away, along with the fragrance of lilies on the summer wind, excised into the folds of the great, amniotic Feedback LOOP, absent like the lips of a dead grandmother on the cheek of the night, so that what passes for God can consolidate its stranglehold through the tripartite divisions of multinational capital—the world beef market, the linguistic terrorism of US expectations, and the soft-but-dried flesh and anthrax-infested brain structures colonized in concrete about these sordid European capitals. So the rinderpest infects us all, slandering the darks skin while burning the Jews, Trappist Monks, Episcopalians, Sunni Muslims, Freemasons, Burmese, Swiss, Sufis, Tsars, CEOs, sports stars, actors, circus clowns, and virtual avatars of minor deities, etc...

Words, when wielded with the reckless abandon of manufactured consent will signify anything and everything that people wish to revile.

***

Take me for instance, in the years after the war: accused of stirring the masses toward a path of rigorous co-belligerency with the German forces, I slept with the machine called God in the rickets of straw and compost and musty shit while the illusion of a free France dangled its corrupt participles into the gruesome syntax of the Fourth Republic. There is an erotica to axle grease. Total communication is a Fascist strategy, and even if employed in the critique and prosecution of National Socialism, you can bet your bottom dollar that the contradiction will be sublimated at the level of cliché. The flesh trades. The incessant peddling of tissue banks and forced organ donations onto the DNA-stained veils of nail, skin, and archaic ligature.

I had to buy my own copies of Henri d'Mescan's "Vichy

Papers" from a mirror of my former mistakes (near exact reproduction of originals) in jewels and techno-gear at the money changers in the 20th *arrondissement* by displaying the identity cards given me by a gold-toothed Monte dealer who loiters outside Invalides, working the old sleight-of-hand and bantering out a fabricated history. Information transfer requires an understanding of the flesh technologies, economic viruses that pass through the membranes of safe-sex devices. You can still pick up an outdated anarchist cookbook with "my" documents for the right price if someone hasn't duplicated your identity, snatched them all, *Crocodilopolis* included, the original version, and burned it all to soot with the leftover garbage.

* * *

The old world shakes as I read; concrete bricks set behind the Seine's sunbathing victims who flash and carry on, topless, as the tourist boats pass under the bridges, receiving rainbow showers from the punctured antipodes of gargoyle and stone. Scalpel fights and genetic tangles. Each historical layer of city fits slash-and-burn atop the next, pushes against subterranean pressure tanks with an amalgamated ferment oozing for decades in the gut of the Parisian soul. A statue of Napoleon with undescended testes spurts a translucent grey fish stock in the lead-lined aqueducts of sewer beasts and liquid nitrate. Nike of Samothrace laces up her air sneakers and drops a load of gleaming shit on the floor of the Louvre. Syphilis boys jump down from their hidden tree-forts, giggling with the numb laughter of broken condoms and useless dental dams. They paratroop from the lips of tired monuments behind a sky made crimson green with the methane of their farts. Before they can strike, they shiver and shake and fall to the splitting ground, tiny wedges disappearing into the broken soil. They are no match for the AIDS virus. Algerian death squads and the mind-control commandos from French Equatorial Africa brandish weapons of mass insurrection, spaying a silicon film over all telephone booths, monuments, rivers, orphans, and chocolate croissants. "Everything can just slide on in..." they say before the puzzle-piece cement compresses into useless dust.

Each outrageous palace, lining every single city block, decorated with the bone and horn of previous generations, rips its hooks in a simultaneous orgasm—orchestrated on a global timetable from everywhere all at once. I stumble outside the Hotel de Ville, a drunkard lost in the confusion of images, a symbolist poet set crooked on the absinthe pathway. An old woman braces my back with the arch of her stomach, the snap of her arm, and I take her down with me, joyously, to the face of the pavement and the cracking skeleton of infirmity. Across town and river, an illuminated carrier pigeon smacks into the Eiffel Tower, the world's largest radio antennae with bright Citroen blaze down its side, and its body, my body, are both smothered and protected, the result of the hybrid miracle no longer impossible in this strange world of jelly and pus.

You take liberties of course with the position of your words in space and time because you are forced into an interesting sex arrangement by unseen hands that perform erotic cavity searches for those forty-nine letters so well hidden that your vagina will never betray you. You open and close the lower muscles around the cylinder of rolled-up manuscript and feel the edges scratching your insides just as the whole empty tubing collapses from the strength of your negation. You know that for Henri d'Mescan to go so far as he does in "The Confession of St. Post-America"—his zombie power must be weakening, his mojo not working since you had Dial-Up Networking install a canopy of detritus suspended over these dirty motel beds: plastic dolphin rings from worn-out six packs tied to safety pin/rubberized paper clips chained linked to cigarette carton packages folded flat like removed tonsils hanging in the formaldehyde of the stale air. You have the child fold in carefully clipped sections of newspaper reinforced with rubber cement slobbers, saline solution-soaked pages ripped from the abbreviated version of the *TV Guide*, a string of pearly condoms punctured by needle marks representing the ascendant zodiac house. You tether you wrists to a certain version of this planet and hope to tether Henri d'Mescan to a noisy, smoke-filled bar with perpetual crowds that assault whatever senses he engages in your own torture—see how he likes people to fix upon the hypnotic jiggle of his watery insides, while his dark arts turn him into a broken stellae leaking endlessly into a formless paper river. You know that d'Mescan thinks mainly in images, picturing the words spoken to him by even the most innocuous passerby, "The dead crow flies at midnight"—making "dead" the wintry frost of the German hinterland; "crow" a broken rooster record played at revelry by a lazy Army trumpeter enthralled with mundane Stan Kenton records; "flies" signify just how they sound but in noun form, a hideous swarm of blackout demons made legion in a pack of transubstantiated swine and boar; and "midnight," deepest midnight, darkest hour, rendered by the sheer black pupils of cat with no paws, a sutured beast lacking leg and life, rotting in the husk of midwest cornfield. You rupture signification wherever you can so that *Post-America* comes together and the universe rips apart. You know that the hardest shapes are the little words, "the," "at"—arcane pictures slip underneath the film of thick everyday: ancient crocodile teeth slathered with buttery maggots piercing the ventricle of some minor visual revolutionary, a Nile fever killing bulrush shadows projected onto the muddy water, some definite article trapped back before the sweet days of Bar Kochba and the long millennia of Jesus Christ. You both know that if there is a pattern to these images, a lingua franca for Post-America, the clues lay in the calligraphy of the cerebral cortex, down the octaves of our most secret vertebrae, into the discordant jut of the primeval pit. You talk about an overdeveloped narrative and you could drone on this way forever. You promise yourself a revelation beyond revelation, if not an end, then a continual beginning, and such promises, in such uncertain times, seem poised to slip into a nothing with the power to makes you out to be itself.

In Post-America some years ago, I gave the name "divergence" to the evil stretch of Route 81 snaking its way up toward the cutthroat coal belt bible belt rust belt incest belt boulder field black lung death of the underground Pennsylvania fire town resting along the highway cutting the state in pieces…concrete Mississippi dividing Pennsylvania just as Old Muddy sutures the nation with the disposable staples of its ancient delta.

Crossroad devil blues twang along the Susquehanna River until the water abandons the road in the north, and the 65 mph speedway stalls down in the lowlands of Route 83 just two fathoms above the Maryland border. Coups and sedans and big rigs and charter buses and soccer-mom minivans and cavernous sport utility vehicles and the gravesite of drunken teenagers and fallen state troopers mark twain in their potential directions, at an undisclosed exit, between Colonial Point one way and Progress the other.

North, on Route 81, in upstate New York, within one of the nearly overlapping industrial communities that Davis Schneiderman squats in, floats the ring of a celestial gas giant showering radiation on zebra muscles and soft-shoe gun factory alike, on the state university outposts and the IBM punch-card center from which the Nazi death camps learned how to crunch numbers. Visible only from above, the smoky lights of these suburban zones bleed into the chlorine cumulonimbus and white ash air.

And for this, I pass up Progress.

Davis Schneiderman's face wears with the same uneven wrinkles that push themselves down, ever lower on the sides of the mouth—deep lines set at sharp parabolas—meeting the slant of the uneven lips in the center of a short prairie of errant stubble. The indents of the flesh about his eyeball, from my perspective at the front of the face, look very much like the slits in a week-old pumpkin, lit from the interior with a blue votive candle whose wax melts deep into the engraved squash flesh corresponding, here, to the base of the larynx.

He rifles through Phoenelia Yeer's drawers; he says, "whenever necessary," occasionally pressing her papers to the space beyond his nose as though inhaling a spring bouquet long distant from the soil, hunting by scent for some federal bounty, or just as easily, inhaling a piece of shit- and spume-soaked underwear that releases uncontrolled memories of long ago minefields and crumbling parchment from an olfactory graveyard. The "Vichy Papers" cost him dearly, of course, and his back crooks in a clean line, bent over the years by the distant force of my fingers.

Some of my best friends have hair and backbones.

I've secured my own copies of the documents in question, these "Vichy Papers," I say, sparse on dialogue, fake in the age of asphalt and hydrochloric acid; I compare his copies to my own ancient penmanship with the aid of scanners, word processing programs, graphical translators, and voice-recognition software trained to an electronic Jimmy Stewart mimic badly imitating Richard Nixon ("I...I dont have any enemies list, it's in *her* house and it's in *his* house...").

Schneiderman seems to shrink into a gash of earth opening under his withered feet, so I'm forced to inform him that all of the data in this SUNY-Vestal office can be easily erased with the proper electrical command code sent from my medulla oblongata to the motion-sensor toilet plunger that my custodial accomplice sits in front of even as we speak, poised on my command to nonchalantly wipe and flush.

The Schneiderman who sits before me desists in his cloying way, but even my initial readings are sketchy…so we work late into the night, burning six ends of a trident candle, debating the materials that supposedly condemn me, written so many years ago now—in a time and world so different from our own blithe Post-America. So different, in fact, that any explanation I might feed him would be like telling a medieval pope about the time of the thunder lizards.

Still, I start with the Shedit analogue, how eons ago, the juniper had been cut just as Sebek the Unholy Crocodile God had demanded, and how this Crocodile maneuvered its crew of deadly mutations into a small mob-style extortion ring to keep the temple full of offerings and the locals hooked on a dead-end genetic line that has got to end somewhere so it may as well end with you, I point to the picture-words that signal all narrative, and show him how to think in association blocks: how stupid and dull the lily of the morning blooms and withers in the dense fog of always.

He pictures the corpse flower covered in sweaty pollen; finally, firm meaning escapes his dead eyes and burns off into the sun. I inform him that here, amid the sunken tomes on composition theory and the bleeding red markers and student files bursting with haphazard plagiarism, the wasted energy of *David*

Schneiderman's mid-century toil has transformed itself into our convenient setting—the absent Phoenelia Yeer's office—the site of our sinister business. The Henry Mescaline figure had been a fake from the start I say, but he simply smiles as if he doesn't believe a word or image of me myself and I anymore.

Ahem. The *Hallucigenome* scrip, brought into the picture only for the sake of public opinion—remains a myth prior to late spring 1989 when an editorial neophyte going by your name, Davis Schneiderman, simultaneously asthmatic and bronchial, completed a visiting stint at Phoenelia Yeer's teaching institution, here that is, and produced, in draft form, the earliest folio of the supposedly out-of-print work called *Hallucigenome*, carbon-dated back to 1966 in a kickback scheme proposed by Spuyten Duyvil along with the majority investor of a Pacific rim tuna-harvesting firm intent on a literary splash, dolphins be damned.

Of course, he denies everything. Still, we must draw a confession that will satisfy all parties. I prepare the equipment and collect the bolts of corrugated yarn unfurled by the torturers across the courtroom floor:

No one sings a siren song of nothing or no one at first. To start, overdressed intellectuals partition themselves into sub-routines of cutting-edge academic inanity. Painful enemas trace the contours inside the subject's orifices as he or she presents his or her own research for verification and cross-correlation at a variety of ridiculous conferences. He will wonder what new and different body emerges from the curves of this alchemical cord when there is a blastoff countdown but no ignition, no gunshot. The victim falls upon a rack of razor belts, an intestinal seismic magnifier, while unraveling the limbs of a younger life as the question-and-torture session begins, oscillating between re-directed currents of electromagnetic charge and the pinch of sweet beta clips on the nipple, suckling the flesh in precise acres of surface shock and silence. Academic torturers theorize that we do things horizontally instead of vertically as they scrape the top layer of nipples off with razor fingernails, exposing the skin.

A precise amount of radioactive battery acid is dispensed so that it perfectly marinates the raw shell of the body, and the bloody mass of fiber and nerves rinse in the pulsating erosion of the manufacturing site. Schneiderman's mind copes by collecting a primordial marsh of phytoplankton and lush Indonesian calla lilies into a film covering the eyeball. Everyone becomes a collaborator in her or his own restraint.

His screams curse man and god and electric current with a primordial warning to species on the brink of evolution. Yet, despite this heavy breathing, it appears that Schneiderman refuses to come around to our way of thinking.
I propose we shift the point of view.

And on this abnormally cold summer afternoon, the torturers agree.

So go back into the water.

If you have already developed lungs, guard your air supply. Like the crocodile, thrive on the carrion of an oxygenated consciousness while returning to the sea. Gloved black hands massage your heart, your ribcage like a wooden chest, and moving up through the bottom of the trachea, the dark fingers pull your voice box out of your throat in order to prevent you from eating the important wires that will soon be overwhelmed with someone else's data.

So dive down into dystrophy.

Someone leans on the genitalia of a house pet to prevent its coming to your rescue or chewing off your lips. Start a religion, a sub-routine; repatriate a cause that history too quickly overwrites. Now electric shocks and then the questions and then more shocks and then all of it over again—from the noble but misguided Mescaline hoax of the 1960s that never happened to the appearance of real conflict and the implication of the other editor Phoenelia Yeer just waiting to be fucked in as many different ways as possible in a multitude of positions to make even the Marquis de Sade blanch and so history becomes a script for this pitiful Davis Schneiderman who is you but never knows when to stop.

The Schneiderman who is you breaks into constituent elements, signs a confession of forgery, of influence peddling.

The Schneiderman who is you lets out a tungsten flick of energy along the carbonized straps holding you to the interrogation table.

The Schneiderman who is you admits that the Henry Mescaline scam wasn't viable from the get-go but could maybe work with the spin doctors of Post-America before the application of the electric needles that feel, in fact, like heated colonial points.

The Schneiderman who is you calls for the commode to flush and then, along with the steaming shit of the past five decades, for the accursed papers to disappear forever from the neural net, along with the convenient markers of the Schneiderman who is me.

But the Schneiderman who is me tires of these games.

The quagmires of Post-America always changed in the sand formations of our most terrible deserts, shifting into interminable molecular puzzles. We were swallowed, each of us, through jaws of our own devising, by the sudden light changes coloring the moods of the sky, the hue of fallen leaves quickly swelling into a fever of margarine colors and suspended twigs. This state left us vulnerable. We thought that love signified a word just like other abstract words—hate, vengeance, faith— but we could never arrest the revolution of the sun's seething core in the sky before it went dark inside the tunnel of our throat. Only then, after the last star extinguished its ambient light by rolling upon the ink of the universe, could we have plucked those last seven letters from Yeer's trembling hands. Then, with the camera child Dial-Up Networking hovering above the refrigerated tarpaulin that we applied to her body to cool her for the coroner's scalpel, we sawed Yeer's dead fingers away as the digits curled and shook like tiny penises spraying over those last seven letters. The stain from their burned-off fingerprints, the sweet ink of time flowing through the intricate vein network would no doubt taste of the sweet remnant of our time together, internalized into flesh, extrapolated into appendage. We almost came to regret such desires as we followed Yeer's body to seedy motels, erased her life at each whistle stop, manipulated her research on d'Mescan, Mescaline, David Schneiderman. Did she really think that the ending would condemn us? She might have been successful through sheer will, just as maniacs and schizophrenics had occasionally accomplished impossible goals. We almost felt ashamed—

but that was all over now. d'Mescan demonstrated how we interconnected, how we were bound by a higher power to spare this troublesome Yeer. His most recent excerpt, "The Our Lady of Perpetual Motion Hospital for the Deserving Poor and Mentally Deranged," burned like a comet sent by a far greater sun, a blooming explosion of cosmic gas that promised to take over once our own petty concerns became banished from the solar system. Gears and pulleys revolved plastic painted balls in a whirl of Yeer's madness. We know we were weak, because as we read this excerpt our eyes *could* have invoked her form from the shadow behind the lettering; we might have found her aura, liquid and undifferentiated in that frolic of grass and pine that we once shared, lost through a peephole, the slits of ancient Venetian blinds, a pinhole camera. Instead, our eyes rolled back into our head, our corneas condensed and tightened. Just as d'Mescan wrote, we could not save her. She was too far gone, but there was always hope for tender Dial-Up Networking, perhaps immune from the same madness, from the same ciliated protozoa that threatened, in time, to engulf us all.

I gather immediately from the position of her body, the fetal silhouette behind the lime-green curtains, and the uncomfortable seizures that overtake her arms and legs that I am to be the subject of her comatose interrogation. No greater crime than deliberate nerve damage, as the country doctor describes in intricate detail the forty-nine stitches across her stomach: a gruesome video of soiled meat sprouting biogenetic recapitulations of fruit fly, maggot, and test tube sonata leaves nothing to the scalpel. After one week, committed for an indeterminate amount of time at the Our Lady of Perpetual Motion Hospital for the Deserving Poor and Mentally Deranged in Future, Missouri, the woeful Phoenelia Yeer emerges from her coma only to realize that I have been stationed dutifully at her bedside, visualizing the entire episode as a sort of demonic possession.

"I rarely use dialogue," I speak, for the first time in three days, trying to raise a pulse in her, "but it seems that we have much to say to each other, perhaps, about each other. Most certainly, I expect that you know who I am…" I leave off as her eyes struggle open, first silent half-moon slits, then hazel-colored marbles.

"Henri?" she sputters out

"Yes," I pause, "Henri d'Mescan, Dr. Yeer. So pleasant to finally meet you. I only wish it could be under more auspicious circumstances."

"I'll leave you two alone here," says the doctor who I have conjured in the corner, for effect, now waddling silently out the door.

Phoenelia Yeer in slippers and antibiotic hospital gown, an IV tube jumbled around her black-and-blue arm, the whole apparatus invested with the complexity of intertwining snakes or highly evolved tapeworms. The adjustable bed connected to the call button connected to the morphine drip connected to the shimmering gas of the town—everything lit so bright against the paniculated skyline that our eyes cringe with the collective strain of two figures entangled in an affair whose only end can be a dulling of the senses. Underneath the veil perpetuated by the blend of water pills and codeine mixed by the staff's herbal apothecary, I feel Phoenelia slip away once again. Back into a seemingly endless sleep of violets and crimson energy. I whisper sweet insults and desires on the breath of her strange gesticulations.

Her madness comes in waves—at first, a slow king cobra coaxed from its basket by a flute. The soft tones of her voice lead me through the trapdoor in the basement of this garret, down the spiral of rickety starlight, past the eons of paper and papyrus, underneath the cobalt reeds that form the Mississippi marshlands, straight to the secret cache of my papers, my pamphlets, mummified for ages in scarab beetle boxes lined with a primitive asbestos. The heat blows blissful in these secret shults of the Earth, moved as I am by Phoenelia's sweet voice. Still, there is coldness.

"I have my doubts, Mousier d'Mescan, and unlocking these objects, buried for decades, does little to change my mind." Her breath becomes solid crystal, digital against the hospital windows, and I can see how the town of Future, and so much of this continent, continues to exile me behind slats and apertures.

"I have my doubts about what you think you saw," I add, the peephole physiology of the place unlocking the pores of my tired arms, underneath my linens, into the mass of gaping scales.

"*Crocodilopolis*," she starts again, "the Invasion of France by the Nazis," she continues, "how could you write it before it happened, how could you know?"

My protests mix with the river fire. Soon the snake grows precocious, swaying still, in rapt concentration, waiting only for the slightest command of my body to break from its woeful groove.

I motion to the nurse who waits patiently behind the silk screen, past the beeping machines and holstered stethoscopes. She wheels the injection tray with its manicured, multicolored farinas. Yeer writhes, visibly discomfited, and I can smell a mixture of acid and bleach in what I take to be her urine.

"Do not forget how easily I have escaped from influence before. Now that I know you are also *him*." The crevices of her forehead slide down her skin, narrowing her eyes. "Don't think I will stay quiet."

***

Naturally, we cannot let this stand.

A depressed call button connected directly by wireless electrical technology to my hypothalamus, and the nurse's heated electric needles call forth a spasm of boiling quiver for the intravenous drugs already flowing through Phoenelia's system—she surges on the bed, in her loincloth, a leviathan thrashing her demonic tail over the sea.

"Fuck you, you guilty bastard," she mutters as we press her face together, pushing in her jowls with the straps of a leather muzzle. She struggles as much as she can, cursing us: the nurse, the town and the other one who she wants us to be,

Davis, who hides away from the silent, watery beasts that call this river home.

***

As her eyes roll back into her head, she whispers softly about how a man or man-y men have finally become one as we drop our teeth into position, all to better to annunciate our instructive language—*just as we had always known we would.*

***

We will not talk about the rotting maggots drooling over a distant relative's fortune; we will not talk about the Last Supper or the epiphanic moments at the end of James Joyce stories; we will not discuss the macrobiotic, isomorphic, corrupted plane of dissected sheep brains cluttering high-school science labs at the state and county pen; we will not talk about the tubercular lines of schizophrenic mental patients shut up by the apparatus of hook, line, and sinker, or lock, stock, and barrel by the anal retentive repetition of your most god-awful roach motel; we won't consider raising our sphincters toward the sky on Bastille Day or letting our subliminal kidneys excrete vials of ethereal urine and so remove effete nitrogenous matter from the blood; we won't even think about your goddamned happy hour with its shimmering bags of cellulite and collagen, the gel-filled facsimiles of breast meat cutting an arcane swath across that composite film of makeup, ash, crushed pretzels, and beer foam on the bar, reminiscent of your breath upon a window pane warmed just above the freezing point; we won't discuss the cut-off shorts and tank tops, the high-school mascots of half-feathered falcons, pre-processed burgers, and extinct, impotent lumberjacks sporting confederate flag buttons made from your secret cache of genetically altered swine; we won't imply that yes, a gelatinous conspiracy of candy mag-

238

nates spikes everything with the cartilage of your ancestors caught up in the fervor of professional sports and lovemaking by applied mathematics; we won't fixate on the shunts of broken light peeling in from those dim basement windows; we won't watch those 13,000 camels jump through 12,999 needles in endless variations of musical chairs and negative dialectics; we won't broadcast the necessary angels dancing on pins and needles in your lazy child's legs, those little eyeballs rolling across the inside of baby fat layers, accelerating the process by which we all receive cancer; and most, importantly, we won't mention the net-and-bolt operation of the ever-growing multitude, the rotting limbs of oil-soaked retinas, the sorry gaze of the steel-toed work boots; we won't talk about the way it'll all go down Moses, the soft caress of bodies, the sexual dynamics of entrepreneurial elephants and syphilitic donkeys; we'll never tell anyone how well creep into the boardroom with our city-street perfume, our nine-to-five bedroom eyes and the cocksure swagger of our faux-leather briefcases; we won't tell your crooked truant agents about the lawsuits, the infringements, the incidents and payoffs, the wet, lolling lilt of your tongue and we chant the forbidden names of our old world saviors, "Astaroth"— "Baal"— "Umma-Segnus"—"Sebek"; we won't forget your faces, scarred by the chemical drinking water, mutilated by age-defying makeup and jump-cut gangster films; we'll never say a word as we raise your expectations and entice you with French Fries soaked in beef tallow, washed in the blood of your people, baptized in pools of ultra-solvent hemoglobin; we won't even think to mention when our crooked fingers rub your head, warm and inviting, when we place our fingers on your wet lips and together incant the dewdrops; well never tell a soul how your face smelled of sunshine as the 3-inch titanium bolt penetrated the side of your skull, shocking your brain into hemorrhage, splattering delicious blood all over our blue

Wal-Mart aprons; and we'll never tell anyone how softly you fell, there, in the boardroom at the end of the earth, just after the data has been processed in a stream of cum and industrial surfactant, ecstatic at the rise in your own yellow-tinted fortune; if asked, we'll keep our mouths shut, and hold everything in our matrix of ligaments, in a secret of skin, of tendon, and bone.

***

And so we rose that night, together, so quickly, into the past—Old Mississippi, emblazoned with a thousand million creatures of soot and atom, of bitumen and coral, shell and shellac, amoeba and paramecium—to smother the town of Future, Missouri in the pleasant inevitability of dead things. Leaving the Hospital of the Deserving Poor, we traveled, once Phoenelia slept safely sedated, to the courthouse she had only told us about, the crypt that supposedly housed our work and the roots of whatever mad game she sought to use against us. Although advanced in years, we squeezed like a ball of pus into the skintight wet suit, we lit the spelunking torch so it shone bright, and holding our breath, dove down, dove deeper, under the shit and the carrion and the lilies and baby's breath. Time became muddy. We could see nothing but clouds of darkness and inky silt. If something had been there, anything at all, the water, leaving nothing behind, swallowed indefinite shapes within its panorama of filth until our memories dissipated into a solution of drowsy ether.

***

Before leaving town, the next day, out from the motel once powered by the molasses and cigars of the river trade, barges rolling back and forth unmolested by the Mississippi, we journeyed again to the hospital to check once more on Phoenelia

Yeer. She lay there, a facsimile of death, but with her eyes wide open, unblinking, frozen in a torrent of details we could no longer comprehend. Although we could not know if she heard us, we whispered to her in a familiar voice that all her precious little evidence had been washed away, and as with most cases of this kind, perhaps her madness could also be cleansed with the help of both medicine and machines.

She did not respond.

***

We asked the nurse about her condition. The Caesarian section, we were told, was worse than it needed to be by her refusal to stay still, but she came in so heavily dilated, so early, that nothing else could be done. We left a selection of unmarked bills for her care. We held the baby called Dial-Up Networking in our arms, cradled it in the venous nuzzle of our warm corona, and slowly, with a compassion we did not often allow ourselves, placed it back into the litter of nameless children who surrounded it, half hoping it would get lost from its mother among the look-alike offspring in this Post-American maternity ward.

31) PHOENELIA YEER
INTRODUCTION: THE SEVENTEENTH SUNDAY OF ORDINARY TIME

You wake up only when an interesting package of considerable value shall arrive for you shortly said the talking singing fucking telepage on your private number known only to the few persons you consider safe in a world that has repeatedly abused the codes of your body. You case the endless garret of your childhood in memory shoes of bitumen and pitch; you taste the ice rink, the odor of the confessional incense encasing your tongue, dissolving within a terrific vortex of frozen surds. You are covered with track marks from the pricks of the diabetic machinery of Spuyten Duyvil in its sleek and modern office space; Dial-Up Networking of course, floats here with you, eternally networked, monitoring all transmissions through an infinity of holes that might try to plaster a virtual skin onto some overlooked outpost of circuitry. You dive down deep into a numberless year at mid-century, now forty-nine, tender and young at the parlors of the Electric Bartender, caught between the devil and deep blue sea, spinning the "Dreaming" single by Sun Ra and the Cosmic Rays over and over on the jukebox, looking for your drunk, pre-meditated father and his waning commitment to the life of your already-fractured family under the eerie lyric, "If you live in fables, you'll know what I mean..." You experience the door knocking sense of invasion brought about by the person at the far end of the knocking fist, like a flash from the baby's tattooed chest mimicking the carvings on the garret wall, the scribble of chalk on heat-dried macadam. Such irradiated energy floats up through the spouts of the over-populated city, steaming past thousands of gleaming windowpanes slowly turning liquid. You see your father coagulate in your peripheral vision just months before that time in the bar—leaving a small Indonesia calla lily next to your shunted little head resting under different stars, its hypnotic bulb churning the topsoil into a fiery ocean; you know that the woman named MaMa curses his reappearance under the hard winter moon, betraying the way he clasps her hand beneath the dinner table and makes her skin wet like roast beef flesh. Your father works mysteriously for a courier service—disappearing often, a latter-day Hermes, spiriting packages through the city's feral corridors and dead-end streets, so that if a physical postal service still operates in the vacuum of Post-America, you can no longer testify to its motives. Yet you move too quickly for mail, bounce from state to state, exit to exit, in the flight that has become the norm, the margin that has become the center. d'Mescan's "The Seventeenth Sunday of Ordinary Time" has arrived from Spuyten Duyvil via the ghostly door knock, the fist that delivers the knuckles of annunciation tickling the paniculated stem of this blue-ball country. Your father's absences are brief at first, a few hours, a day, maybe a year, pulsating through the seductive space between your ripening legs. You soon know that "Seventeenth Sunday" is transferred to the owner of the knocking fist via Spuyten Duyvil through the rented bandwidth of a Japanese Weather satellite, the same that interrupted the first radio frequencies sent from outside the solar system—so this piece you are forced to read and comprehend, to set in the context of this quickly degraded collection, has run for god knows how long in the solar system circuit. You feel Dial-Up Networking's mouth against your fetal figure as merely one term in the strange but sequential calculus of disorder occurring in the past, between all of us—between d'Mescan, Mescaline, yourself and your father, between David and Davis, bleeding your selves into the ambient light of those already dead stars. Your eyes fail to focus. As if you are already dead. Your thinking gets dimmer by the second. You run out of artificial light.

32) Henri d'Mescan
The Seventeenth Sunday of Ordinary Time

Post-America—a new Sunday, we continue our regular rehabilitation of minority sinners with morality plays set to the tenor of life in our gleaming metropolis, our bright, brave Post-America. This is your host, Godless Heathen #5, and I'm here with my special guest, cosmology expert and long-time convert to the cause of Onward Christian Soldiers, Inc., a radical counter-terrorism concern intent on destabilizing the Un-American world—Genetically Spliced Rhesus Monkey. We wish you all, over the airwaves, trundling in the celebrity sea, a good and scrumptious morning of egg and bacon fat rejoicing.

***

Call me Splice. Its 27% less dehumanizing.

***

We begin today's pseudo-hymnal in praise of the Holy Feedback LOOP. Open your Digital Bible Simulator to hyperlink Alpha Bravo Charlie, New Testament 4.9, and join with us in ringing "Feedback LOOP is thy name…" through the vibrant Morse code transmitter and blood sugar finger prick connected to your international ID cards…

***

"Feeeed…baaaack   LOOOP…we   praaaisseee thyyyy…naaame. Looord of aaaall aboove we adoooore theeee…..Thyyyy…naaamme   is   Feedback   LOOOP. Feeeed…baaaack LOOOOP…we praaaisseee thyyyy…naaame. Looord of aaaall aboove we adoooore theeee Feeedback LOOOOP…Kiiing of Kiiings, Feeedbaack LOOP"

* * *

OK, Splice, let's take our first call…this one comes from little Xenophobia Doldrum in Oolan Baitor, Outer Mongrelia. Good thing were on the radio, so little Xeno won't have to squint to see us. Whats your question little girl?

* * *

Does everyone have a guardian angel? I wonder because many members of my government act like godless apes that perpetuate a system of capitalist repression through the mask of a people's republic.

* * *

Wow, you speakem exceedingly well English for an Asian girl, don't she Splice?

* * *

Indeed, it must be the corporate *text* marketing run by Sesame Street. Many folks out there in image hyper-land remain unaware of the recent successes of the Corporation for Public Broadcasting in visiting schools around the world and facilitating participation in student "Me Journals." Children write, in their primitive script, all of the things that compose "me"—pets, friends, favorite colors, sexual experiences, opinion on trade unions, dreams for welfare fraud when they reach the legal age of consent, favorite fights for step-mommy—and then, the nice people at CPB collect the journals…

* * *

To what end?

* * *

Databases. Can you say "databases" little Xenophobia? If not, try "Four-patty meat-like burger-amalgamate" for starters...

***

My government tells me that databases and cattle are a tool of the Holy Hodgepodge, the sacred Feedback LOOP, as I believe you in the westernized nations refer to it...but what about the guardian angels? I have to go to the bathroom and then study math science chemical genetic social engineering to get the jump on your most ordinary cadre of porn-obsessed graduate students who consider computer programming and science fiction conventions to be an intellectual pursuit on par with eastern meditation tours to Mt. Kilimanjaro and the Special Crystal Power Center in Durango, Mexico. So, quickly, capitalist dogs, do even nonbelievers have a guardian angel?

***

Ah yes...one of the gospels unavailable to the everyday Mongrelian says that Jews, even uncircumcised Jews, as well as other assorted pagans no less, have somebody looking out for them. And we all know that *they* won't go off half-cocked. So the answer would have to be "yes." The most famous guardian angel of Post-America, of course, is Mutation, portrayed in moving pictures with a trumpet or flute, a flaming sword puncturing the chassis on a 1949 Chevy Peristalsis, and a styrofoam crest from which globular orbs of landfill shit procreating so ancient bacterium graft to human DNA.

***

Thanks you Splice. Our next caller, or I think its a call...more of a feeling in my belly...well anyway...one tender Dial-Up Networking, from a non-triangulated location, wants

246

to learn the definition of a martyr complex?

****

The noblest thing you can do, Dial-Up, is to martyr yourself for the glory of the Feedback LOOP. Over the horizon, under the moon, the last clinging vines will follow your programming language as far as the heavenly hosts will allow, and carry you, beyond all political boundaries and demographic redistricting plans, into the droning presence of the Holy Hodgepodge. The gospel recommends a descent into the sewers followed by the release of a junta-style computer virus that infiltrates Osama Bin Laden's Al Qaeda organization and displaces all remaining Palestinians before exploding from the originators belly in radioactive spores and blinding, seizure-inducing anime cartoons.

****

That's great Splice. I routinely try to kill myself after leaving awkward social situations without having taken Paxil. Does this count?

****

No, Godless Heathen, this does *not* count. There are always more mood-altering drugs available to mitigate the situation. Only if your insurance or gateway provider or HMO or PPP no longer covers the prescription because your soul has transmogrified out of network would you be justified in executing yourself for the greater glory of the multinational state.

****

So you recommend constant dosing it seems? I understand now. Perhaps you can advise me after this broadcast…but now we have the holy word to spread and Dial-Up Networking has a follow-up question for you, Splice: Can martyrs climb levels of heaven?

***

No, Godless Heathen and Dial-Up Networking, the level of heaven assigned upon your initial proteome sequencing corresponds to your deeds in Post-America, especially after racial profiling was officially excluded by Feedback LOOP doctrine over three years ago. Of course, there is bound to be some residual, institutional prejudice. Nothing serious, you understand. Thus, each action you do or do not do now will be punished later on by the distance you are kept away from the godhead. For instance, anyone caught without their international ID card when stopped by an duly vested Guardian Angel will be given a restraining order of at least two miles for the holy Feedback LOOP, which I need not remind you, is quite a distance when we talk about the fiber-optics of the blastosphere.

***

Thanks Splice, and our final question today, from an anonymous source, asks the question—what is "Purgatory" and where is it?

***

Well, for Rhesus monkeys such as myself, Purgatory can be a trip to DNA counselor. There are sins and there is heaven, and the two are far from mutually exclusive. Sometimes, when our body ails us, we pay a visit to one of the friendly medical professionals of the Ely-Lily Corporation whose fine products can cure most earthly ills. Still, there is time spent waiting in the lobby of the office building where the representative has agreed to meet with you, there is time wasted in the limousine on the way to dinner, and finally, when talking with the repre-

248

sentative, just before agreeing to distribute or order a certain quantity of a certain product line, say Paxil, there is the uncomfortable moment of digestion where the implanted stomach rejects the meat cubes sprinkled liberally with anthrax and smushed into the gastrointestinal cavity. You may be sick, and a cure may be in development, but you must wait in a hole, an aperture, an *in-between*. That, of course, is purgatory, and if you think things are bad now in Post-America, we will come to our reward *only* once these holes have all closed up, only after the medicine disseminates into the seething, fiery core once called the soul. We pray for you to get fixed in triplicate, just as we pay the doctor in quadruplicate through the proper channels in quintuplicate. We decry any direct action except the strategic repatriation of our foreign policy team from the grips of Southeast Asian prison camps and/or the disintegration of the Post-American family through the vortex of thirteen-year-old whores whose only recourse in such situations it to perform medical testing on captive primates while dabbing cosmetics in the eyes of innocent bunny rabbits to keep their exponentially reproductive mechanisms secret from our inadvertently sterilized genetic stock.

* * *

And sometimes, this repair by the scientific doctor is intrusive?

* * *

Oh yes, Godless Heathen, you have absolutely no idea what people are capable of these days. They've even eliminated the climax, excised all dime-store epiphanic endings, replacing these with a completely pre-scripted and banal "moment of clarity."

oppressed us so much that we could not help but skim through its field of protruding stems. d'Mescan had addressed us, *personally*, so that we slowly came to understand the many-faceted disguises of a writer who had finally arrived at his own comfortable persona. If we lived for a year, little Dial-Up, then the memory of months could have expanded into the concertina of a decade. On a pre-lingual level, tender Dial-Up Networking existed for unbroken millennia reduced to the numbing polynomials of the visual record. The Methuselah of the playgroup, an unmolested Cain in front of some modal, motel television set. We knew that Henri d'Mescan had taken an active interest in her care, her upbringing. Just this past day, he sent us the transcript we were about to read again. We found a Henri d'Mescan comfortable enough in his signature prose style to depart once again from the increasingly aggressive logic of Post-America easily lost in the moment of shock and pain, sublimated in an instant of doubt, a bloody and mortal jolt from the toaster oven, a sparkling embrace in a riot of liquid and spume. At first, we must admit, under such a short timetable to read and respond to these haphazard parcels, we judged *too* quickly, jumped without thinking into the abyss of text as a way to maintain the project schedule. And there was really nothing more that we could say, constricted by such rules that keep us from our own child. So, for now, we abide.

Cut the vacuum cleaner cord like a rodeo loop and wrangle those loose threads around its utilitarian figure. Light the aroma candles and douse matches in Spacecat's litter box. Spacecat, full-clawed beauty and solar-powered cell-strip whose aura hides from the landlord, afraid of pets of future passed who once destroyed the shag. Shovel the walkway path enough to chip the slates of ice from their melting holds. When removing the weekly garbage from its scattered vestibule, pile the shredded husks of overdue bills and credit-card approvals and used-up porno magazines into the recycling bins so the January wind don't push the naughty bits all over the grub-infested lawn.

Sit quietly reading *Timeweek*, *Newstime*, *US Nerve and World Re-Peat*. Sip coffee and remain asthmatic. Kick the scuttled tid-bits of dried flea larvae under the dilapidated couch. Answer the doorbell as if it actually rings inside just as you spy the *suckers* through the window, traipsing in from some out-of-the-way green mountain Vermont. Father and Daughter, one thirteen the other lost somewhere in the fifties.

Some people mistake us for a couple when they spread our-selves thin along the cheap inter-coastal motel strip around these parts like Blowlita and Numbert Thumbert in an Atlantis that smells like a nice computer-generated environment to live in a different time before Post-America although it's a little bit beyond us in orchestration that's all and what a nice place you have here and ain't there laundry hookups?

Tell them they don't look alike *that much* as you ignore their awkward body language, at least not like a couple cause the little one looks older than her age and it's better to look young when you're old and old when you are young or some other such equivocating crap. Tell them that you are who you said you were on the phone and this creature must be Spacecat who can burn Spacecat's hideous image into your brain and remind everyone here of the ancient cat gods Bastet and Kunuk and their powerful tuna breath.

Show them the living room with its antique glass dining table and antique glass coffee table. Display the kitchen cupboards proudly next to the shiny dishwasher, but do not open the latch and unleash the torrent of soap chips and snarling murderer noise resting dormant behind its rusty gears. Move to the office, the bedroom with built-in bureau, the hallway and bathroom, the storage closets and emergency exit. Why yes, Spacecat is de-clawed, and your indoor-outdoor heathen has claws but I'm so sorry as the landlord does not want clawed animals who might tear up his precious carpet that hasn't been cleaned in twenty-seven years; it might disrupt the mating season of the millions of mites who call the fibers home in their strange flea language where one assumes they keep an analogous concept. Don't tell them how Spacecat is a fugitive, cut off from the past and the future, locked to you and your family in a way that necessitates every lie and collusion. But do tell them, right off, that the hot water comes with the rent.

It seems just what were looking for in a place where a father and daughter with a special relationship can exist in peace and friendship with the surrounding areas and benefit from the area's enlightened intellectual community because I'm a bit of closet intellectual although I work out of the home and sell insurance, which puts me in a radical philosophical quandary which I negotiate through prayer to a variety of interlocking deities with ancient arms and buck-toothed mannerisms who prepare me for the coming rapture with carefully arranged product-placement accounts. Beside, Post-America has nice schools.

Ah! Tell them to take their time looking around the place as if it were already their own, surveying its tangents and rubric in the way that a lonesome howl, nocturnal hoedowns, and white-collar crime become quintessential molecules that fold the skin into a poetry all its own. Also, the rent includes weekly lawn service, but not snow removal.

Spacecat lopes and gut-juggles the contraband of Spacecat's stomach while the exterior of Spacecat's fur marks the movements of enemy troops across the canyons of carpet fiber and linoleum gleam. Daddy, the cat moves toward my leg in reconnaissance for some sort of war of attrition but I'll let it touch the stubble so often caressed by harsher fingers because it can't hurt me without—ow! The little fucker scratched me.

Oh shit in the other room. Spacecat wouldn't be so bold as to clip claws onto the soft patches of tender leg, would Spacecat?

Must be mistaken my tender precious extra special little loin chop of venture capital lovechild who populates the hovels and mansions of this great nation like steak and fish with country-fried tartar sauce. The nice man Alpha says Spacecat is *clawless* and would never lust for blood like barracudas populating stretches of the Amazon basin delivering mail-order books and Yage root on demand for boiling bark cauldrons and e-ink assignations.

Fuck. Spacecat. Run to the back of the property but it's too late as the girl carries Spacecat as a pig-and-pepper baby in the cradle of her down-stuffed jacket with automatic nasal ointment excreted in tubular splotches onto the fur and dander of Spacecat with claws, Spacecat with nails, a smiling and muted Cheshire grin cradled in the half-moon of her steroidal hands.

Daddy, this cat has claws, all right.

Maybe you're mistaken little MaMa.

No, look here.

Shit. Spacecat has extra toes on the front paws, which still have claws because these claws lack nerve endings, so *intellectually*, they can't be claws at all. That's what you meant of course, that was all, when you said before that Spacecat was de-clawed.

No Daddy, claws stick out all over, more than you would expect from a lying sack of shit trying to pull a fast one on the last innocent renters looking only for a comfortable lease and a chance to enjoy their private company beyond the asphyxiating sexual limits of Post-America. You should be ashamed of yourself, misrepresenting the character of your pets to the innocent, if forbidden avatars, of the purest religious love. Daddy says that we'll re-populate the Earth by throwing bones over our back with the tap water running and if that doesn't work, we'll have to combine with nature to ensure the proper mixture of proteome combinations that—ow! My god, my god, daddy make it stop. My fingers, my precious fingers, for the love of Zoroaster get this little fucker off me…get off you overgrown rat…daddy get the riot gear and erect a large fence around the meeting of international economic organizations and their translocal disruption strategies before…ahhhh…ahhh….the blood…the blood….

Linger in the cavity of the apartment after the quiet comes again and again incessantly silent. Pet Spacecat with a razor blade. Wait for the phone call to sublet this apartment tucked away in the ovum of the underground telephonic channel, the simple middle-class dwelling overrun with data-collecting devices and a new homoeostasis catalogue of bright colored co-eds fondling the hint of well-dressed nipples to sell you something important even though the phone never rings.

Lie on the hard bed and smoke nutmeg through a tin-foil pipe.

Stare at the blue Christmas lights outlining the closet and listen to ambient airport noise recordings in the soft glow of a headache that never leaves, even with slashed rents, from the pile of severed fingers littering your filthy carpets in this Post-American shithole.

35) Phoenelia Yeer
Introduction: LOOP Bless the Child Whose * is LOOP

You no longer expel the phantasmagoria of your words no longer abide in one long sentence-paragraph when the city lights flicker across the reflection of your face in a puddle, when woodcut parcels of hair and nail and bone, integrated circuits ordered back into seclusion by the Supreme Court, carbonated boners spritzing children with the nubile pantomime of surrogate sex juice, all amassing into an army of the everyday—and you yearn to talk about it all—about the hallucinogenic origin of evolutions, about the bacterial genesis of philosophical systems starting with tiny parasites clinging to the Xeno's arrow like barnacles on the hull of the Mayflower soon cutting back into a double-edged scythe into the sublimated appendices of Shedit's mummified crocodiles. Scaly contour maps reflect your opinions from a mirror run through the streets of the dingy capital covered in the mop and bristle of the police and the courts. You disassociate yourself from the fraternity of juggling smugglers who long ago abandon their eclectic goat-killing ritual that bestows a measure of legitimacy upon the everyday criminal in a distinctive corporate suit, asleep at the wheel of the publishing house, forcing the pabulum of a missile-defense shield into the populist wafer, a contraband sausage made holy through the tube of your skin. You merge with the child Dial-Up Networking to splice the ear of the future to the anus of the baboon. You wind-up old Victrolas in the affairs of multi-bit data-streaming initiatives enthralled in a superfluous upgrade, exchanging nostalgia memory files and psychological teeth for systemic rebirth loops. You are momentarily taken back at the way Dial-Up Networking interminably sleeps in her effervescent playpen, appearing, at angles, a child of flesh and bone, a blank slate floating in the bulrushes, part Egypt part Israel, with soft and deadly marsh reeds ringing around her head in a crown of intestinal tape, obtuse, demonic, but ultimately beautiful. Your images cut the flow of poison directly to your protein deposits and afterbirth bundles, and you feel an approximation of love, a green slip among grey, before the walls of your motel once again shift to a sullen countenance to life, back to the umbra of your long-abandoned office and its dog-eared postcards of Chicago, Mexico City, Guayaquil, New York. You have returned to where you started and the eerie secretion of Post-America makes this old world at once unknowable in an oddly comfortable, seemingly familiar way. You could run on this channel forever.

36) Phoenelia Yeer
Introduction: LOOP Bless the Child Whose * is LOOP

you are no longer bound so tightly because the you that remains starts today once again from the top on that first morning outside the gleaming garden after the flood that washes away the common language of the lilies and the field and the buzzing honeybees searching for the onomatopoetic link between their bodies and their quivers down deep into the duodenal tangent of your body that possesses a set of organs with the names of jejunum and ileum set just beyond the first segment whose main job requires the absorption of nutrients from digested food before passing nutrients through the figure of Henri d'Mescan that lunatic and collaborator in the suppression of all independent thought who has finally died today or earlier this week perhaps last month last chance sometime in the late night early morning when you read these words under the lamps of a motel parking lot and at the same time locked away in a charnel prison-house surrounded by his manuscripts and corpses so as to be slathered with a delicious paste of cum and lily petals that make him choke on his own feces which has filled his room also your office and the vestibule where Davis Schneiderman long ago pushes his excrement through the teeth of a broken play-dough press and that's how you imagine the circumstances of the heart attack transmitted over your private frequencies replaying again and again for the amusement of Dial-Up Networking on the dirty walls of this oily motel chamber

The discovery of Henri d'Mescan's corpse has caused no great stir—but the corona of static, falsified pictures, and thin, low light forged by the grayness of editorial abuse renders everything that much sharper as you view a corpse from angles unique to the picture tube. You remember everything now as if it is real; mirrors hide their carnival reflections beneath burlap sheaths, and you think only of the sweet young body, Phoenelia Yeer, tresses in soft coils, looking for your father at the Electric Bartender's labyrinthine parlors. On that night you become a woman. The summer is sticky and something is not right. Your father's aura penetrates through the slightly cracked wood particles of the forty-nine letters, the last remaining seven, and pushes into your central nervous system. Your legs tighten and your heart disappears. With trembling lips, you rip apart your files, furiously tears at the pile of manuscripts, flinging fractured pieces among the wood-pulp sheets, throw thousands of pages across the office, destroying your useless research and wasted ink, frantically looking for what you have so long hid from Davis and yourself, for your own safety, buried beneath the file cabinet's false bottom, in a dark tomb of your heart. Everything spins and you are on fire. The compartment swallows you into an inky black necropolis.

38) Phoenelia Yeer
Introduction: LOOP Bless the Child Whose * is LOOP

You thrust a hand down into the shaft of the file cabinet's false bottom as one might artificially inseminate a calf or black hole, then your whole arm, then both arms, pressing your shoulders against the lip of the hold, feeling no bottom, nothing, except a thick, dark pitch, a muddy river of molasses hiding slow-moving reptiles, millions of blind microscopic organisms. No turning back; you take a deep breath and plunge under the surface by pulling the amorphous lip over your head and the rest of your body like a nylon costume so you swim through the viscous sewer waters toward the seven letters that may yet explain it all. The ink goes on forever but there is nothing written down. Do you cry or do your tear ducts swallow the external world, liquid flooding into your mouth and nose, smothering your genital holes, sinking you to the bottom? Quiet is so all. Crawling along the sheet of muddy silt, you still expect to find some skeleton of d'Mescan, at least as Mescaline, David or Davis, inhabited by electric eels and venomous translucent fish. Forever on it goes. Just as your body cannot take any more, as you are about to stop moving completely, forever, your fingers catch on something. Everything is black, but you can dig, and do, pulling out a bundle from its grave of clay and mud, tripping the skin of your fingertips along the seven sacred edges; you push down to swim toward the surface. Vague and undulating shadows brush against you as you float, toward the faint light, closer and closer. Something rubs next to your body, a giant shape, cold and clammy, but it passes. Not daring to move but floating from inertia you hear your father's voice in between the particles of dark and muddy water. "That was us, following ever closer," he whispers from outside the liquid membrane, enfolding you so that his sounds are distant and degraded, a voice-box expunging the shadows that cover your shaking fingers holding the seven letters going soft and solvent in the water that encircles you forever.

39) Phoenelia Yeer
Introduction: LOOP Bless the Child Whose * is LOOP

"We found you most exciting," he whispers through a cloud of fog. "Just as we had always known you would be."

And death sails at first light in Post-America, landing softly at the present *.

*

And the **primary use of ("*") stands for elision of the word and concept**, where Mr. * and his family summer in the outskirts of a certain town known only as *. There, the elderly nanny, *—while the family wanders the shores of denuded beach absent of gravel, eroded like a * set upon a crooked shore—unzips her *, and with great abandon, * into their accursed, sanctimonious little *.

*

And not even such * surprises the reader, suddenly—nothing but an everyday function of life in Post-America. First * breaks lines and then it breaks words. The body of labor, pasted together from a series of *, offers a rapid deceleration of the circulatory system, this * offers a cellular clog that starts as a humming in the throat as the words get stuck in the crook of the heart then slip lower into the depths of the circulatory system that carries the backlog of mutes and errant semi-vowels through articulated tubing of the *. Pieces scrape the lining of the arterial tracks for the miles unwound in the dizzying *, as they travel, awkward and hackneyed, shutting off the capillaries with a switch of their delightful oratory. If thou hath understanding, speak thou * and assume the * position.

*

⅄

And perhaps **the secondary use of ("*") should indicate**

the cross-reference of related topics despite the lack of fixed directions that force the production of irregular pinewood coffins for the child who will come to the same end as its *primitive* progenitors. *Dial-Up Networking* will enter the threshold of the nether world and invite worms through the wood knots rotting the porous membrane of the *grave box*, filling the limited space about her small body until her astral spirit presses silently into the blood-spotted shroud of a fertility doll, born from the miscegenation of the wood and the soil and the sludge of worm and snail. Her cells will scream at decibels so high that the only discernible sound will be the silence of *putrefaction*.

*

And perhaps I do not know how to write this *earth language* anyway, saddled with the inelegance of a viral understanding shining clear as a *calla lily* against the white-hot sun while the genetic fever forms bubbles of sweat over my lips that sip some boiling liquid in the midst of an already ungainly heat wave. *During an abnormally cold summer afternoon.* Dial-Up Networking avoids the trailer-park landing sites, while I, in rapt absorption of sweat, gaze absently through the cockpit window at the planet far below. In miniature, in a cradle, she introduces the means of anal violence with her unsettled suckling, and her rhythmic contortions fabricate the fundamental processes by which a thing, a fabricated object, will emerge, fully processed, into the soft butter of *resurrection*.

*

And I decide upon a *baptism* of sorts so as to continue the theme and begin things, to eventually call upon the end-that-is-the-beginning through the *trumpet of hours*, a teleological eye-wash to steam off the scarlet rose from the pupils of this translucent child, to remove the period trauma of genital mutilation, the pain of the Judeo-Christian flim-flam. The water,

266

thick with the choke of lilies textured in fine points of paint betrays a secular count of sewage bacteria with each stroke of its self-flagellating *amplitude-on-canvas*. The mixture calls to the child, pulling limbs from my arms toward the basin that is the puddle that is the river that is the tap water stream-of-consciousness cut off by a bullet burst between the eyes of the meter man. Her body pushes toward the earth, rolling about in my fragile grip, yearning to parade and worship and copulate with the *Saints of Disease*, one by one, who infect the tender blood of the child with inflected memories of the *past tense*.

*

*

And this will take some time: Catherine of Sweden of Abortion, John of God of Alcoholism, James the Greater *of Arthritis*, Cosmos and Damian of Bladder Disease and Prostrate Cancer, Agatha of Breast Cancer, *Raymond Nonnatus* of Childbirth, Columban of Depression, Bibiana of Hangovers,

*

Fiacre of Hemorrhoids, Guginole of Impotence,

*

Anne of Infertility, Rita of Infertility and of Wife Abuse, Bridget of Sweden of Miscarriages, Hubert of Rabies, Peregrine Laziosi of Melanoma, George of Syphilis, Teresa of Lisieux of *Tuberculosis*, and *Charles Borromeo of Ulcers*.

*

*

And feculent as the dirty virgin of the sewer, we swear that we *were* with her in that moment of subterranean comment, that we *were* present to wash smooth the chemicals and elemental fragments of the genetic pool stuck like molecular barnacles to celluloid film stock, that we *were* aware of the **tertiary use of the ("*"), as footnote indicator**. We *were* there to amputate a male sexual attribute as well as a piece of cunt, reclaimed in the puddles, orbiting the gaseous wasteland under different stars and sensory wiggles of the clitoral penis.* These *were* ours. Steel accoutrement shimmered in the wind as our arms launched toward the heavens, downward facing prickpoint, the child gurgling mucous back into her mouth.

*

And we *were* there all right. It tasted of the sun as Dial-Up Networking's flashing eyes wrapped the remnants of her ear in the mummified glow of silent strobe lights. Blinking sentinels forced our retinas to explode in understanding,*, to flee with this fantastic daughter into the uncertain future of Post-America and its quasi-fascist corn rebellions, its diluted ambiguities of sound and vision, its mechanistic lope of terrifying megaphones parading in 4-4 time.*

*

And we *were* there, together,*, loose specter of change, cold contour of some indefinite unknowing strung out on the banks of the overflowing Seine. Davis Schneiderman represented the useless remains of the old world. The soot of crushed appliances. We placed the child in the cradle on the bough of the lowest branch, and looked, for the first time, at the self-appointed emissary of our error, whose image and gestures released captive demons when combined with the proper prescription of amino acids or, with several turns of a key, locked the hosts of light to the subtle fix of the hereditary code. The soot of burnt-out buildings.**

*The knife and the needle, the cut and the pierce.

*to drop the needle-knives into the earth, down beneath the plane of language

*onto the sacred slopes of grass.

*to meet the elided David Schneiderman

*The * that we were.

**

*

And as we both briefly connected to the documents, as our hands bound with each other for a nanosecond in an unofficial chain of ancient papyrus and woody pulp, stained with the monotype in cahoots with the computer, certain invisible, inevitable, **non-grammatical points of the fourth use of** ("*") congealed in the air, and charged the oxygen with a latent electricity already well-traveled in atoms. *Breath of Shortness. Ulcers and Tuberculosis.* The feverish action of a malady that had already begun, the symptoms of which had been masked, restrained by the ice of our multiple identities, our *pseudonym of quivers* that helped create the land of chameleons, the climate of lizards *feeding precariously this child.*

*

And Dial-Up Networking, for her part, sobbed for the memory of parents, both dead and asthmatic, lost in the perfect language of Egyptian paintings and Etruscan inscriptions, mute, just like David Schneiderman, in a Post-America shared only between the two of us. *A sulphurous rose color horizon the overtook and veins broke of eyeball death scarlet* for David Schneiderman. The cradle increased its rocking lilt and we recalled the pendulum and brimstone, a vestige of cuckoo clocks, a complicated series of genetic gestures as specialized as

*The * that we were.

*And his hands and bloody knuckles were buried deep in pockets of amber wool, and his figure, sloping and malevolent and orange under the citrus sun, bore the weight of his middle-vintage suit and fedora like a pack mule bore its skin after decades of servitude and silence. A matchstick jutted from his lips in memory of an opium cigarette, and the tree above us all, above the wet soil covered in filth and garbage, had been stripped by an organic turpentine of its foliage, its sylvan stripes cast somewhere in the mold of the distant past. Dial-Up cradled herself asleep in dropsy dream as we passed David the papers, disks, and files that signaled our new persona.

the rapid capers of the child and her history, caught in the thunderous jowls and the terrible teeth of the *crocodile unholy.*

*

And at that moment, perhaps even before, her neural network unfolded over everything in the world: the protruding roots lining the lace of ground, the bare trees saddled with the weight of decoy crows *chewing bloody rats of mass hair*, the gas stations with dried-up diesel pumps, the strip malls emptied of everything but the pink stucco shell, and all the artificial amphitheaters of the mundane: sports arenas ripped apart by metal jaws, the corporate sponsorship of spaceship Earth, the yellow-stained headlines of sound-bytes and diaphanous emerald mergers of media companies. *We were choked by a sluice of six-pack plastic rings soaked in the bloody carrion of back-alley operations.* The intrusive tentacles of the neural net wound through the rivulets of our occipital lobe, diving in and out of the violet lines that traced glacial deposits into caverns of bitumen and vaporous shale dropping through our spinal cords, over *parking lots with diagonal membranes* and chaotic door dings charted by Tycho Brahe on the carapace of the sky that bled always into the *thoracic territories and sacral.* Dial-Up Networking sensed immense psychic damage, but death stood still, in the new world of Post-America, as a physical phenomenon. Our shocks could still be felt, our bodies still manipulated into the shapes and textures of the codon, the twisted ladder, the doctored genome.

*

*

And still we were cursed by **the fifth use of ("*") to indicate a reconstructed form not yet confirmed in a text or inscription**, as in the *slim lily, the corpse flower (as a possible unifying symbol of the text).* For David, Star of the Six-Sided Morning, Defender of the Forty-Nine, Union Agitator, we knew simple murder would be unkind, unsuccessful; old as his brittle bones imply, there would be a *massive geologic shift (the proposed origin of tectonic rearrangement of the means of production)*, a document hypothecating the Mayflower to the dirtiest bidder in some small county courthouse promising a new future, a new life in the disposable furrows of the Post-American bureaucracy. No, humiliation and expulsion had to be total in the electric air, charged in the web of information and infotainment, mixed *in a crucible of contact* that made everything strange *(and perhaps, strangely familiar in its repetition)*.

*

And our breath grew short; the cradle rocked, so we lunged like a criminal, *for his heart, (for his breath)*, ripping out David Schneiderman's lungs and cartilage, cutting his surprised stomach with the razors of our ancient teeth, the grind of a ferocious skin, breastplates of impenetrable, metal scales. He tumbled, shocked at his own blood spilling over the marshy ground and sinking into the milk of the earth, the pores of the body, *absorbed into our flesh, (encoded inside our bones)*. There rang a death moan, a shriek, a phalanx of curses as the whirling cutting faces of circular saws stripped skin to the stillborn bone, dancing in the awful crunch of flesh caught between wheel and surface.

*

And our breath cut in with his gasps; his whispers became our food, and *we sucked everything in with his energy, (the roaring strands of the neural network, the vista of capital, the marrow of the civil regime)*, the resistant strands of a higher teleology, a recombinant DNA stretching itself into the catacombs of the planet. We thrashed wildly—sucked harder, smashed our teeth into the plate of his skull. Our eyes flaked apart in the mud as the rest of the plane decomposed, consolidated into a screeching ball of filament and grime, as the *clouds disappeared, (puffs inhaled into mist)*, and the ground turned to ooze. *Primal. (Hypnagogic.)* Everything came together in a fiery ball of *.

*

*

*

And the *liquefied world once again**, all around us, except for the tree and the cradle and *Dial-Up* Networking, *tender and fuzzy, (holding fast to the body)*. We gnarled at the roots and fought her resistors, and our *, insatiable in its transformation, looped the world into a death *.

*

And the sky, *a stain lemon color yellow promise*, loosened its remaining charge with a flurry of electric thunderbolts. Explosions of *nuclear soil* pulsed land mines on split parade, cuticle and *slow brain mash, (the unholy end of a corrupt world)*. We locked ourselves in an Olympian struggle*, partners and lovers, father and child, relic and icon, and we soon lost our hold, our tenuous grasp, the fibers of our * gorged on the choke of *Post-American* newsprint. We were almost *nothing* but we were *(everywhere)* instead. Eternal. We gnawed at the tree trunk and *cellulose the snapped cords* like rotten rubber bands. A lighting bolt conspired to reach us, but we thrashed and swaggered and it struck the root. *Another and (another)*. Now on the bark, ripping out the pulp and vein and sap and it came down over us, *fire moved through scale*, smoke penetrated *. The bough shattered into *numberless kilobits* of disinformation.* The cradle fell through empty space.

*

And the *child, (*Dial-Up Networking)*, coughed up the *boiling burbles of the liquid * beside us, the *white-hot flesh of primordial goo. We struck as the lighting taught us, to die with a thunderous eclipse of breath* whose teeth ripped the *rags of*

* in our cavernous orifices

the tattered *. And so we mixed into the reproduction of dead
*, born once * into the violence of the **infirmary (with its
machines and patterns)*, its wallpaper and senseless, superfluous
asterisks.

*
*

**

* with *Dial-Up Networking

* We were *crushed (and near death).

* and sun, to *spent as a die and base creature.

* And *sails death at first *light in (*Post-America), landed softly at * in the
great land of the back-tense shift *.

41) Davis Schneiderman
Introduction: Last Drop(ped) / The "Standard" Old World Model (is Now)

This thing had gone on long enough. Yes, we needed secrets, to exist, to slice through the inexhaustible reams of red tape and turpentine, chloroform and media violence that kept everything suspiciously copasetic. It was no secret that the time to watch professional sports arose through the overdeveloped prominence of fast-food restaurants and Hollywood bloodlines, but most of us did not spring from the well of respectable families. Or families at all. Admittedly, emptiness blossomed, a social vacuum deep enough to sink the stoutest heart. We could stop splitting the atom, we could stop visiting the moon, we could stop using aerosols and poison underarm deodorant, but we could not recall a new form of life *after it had been deployed.* It whistled right off the page before we even conceived of a stopgap measure. In fact, there was undeniable proof that we had already passed the point of no return. We loved Henri d'Mescan, Henry Mescaline, and David Schneiderman, and once Phoenelia Yeer, and even, in a paternalistic way, the child Dial-Up Networking whose corpse we expected to find any minute—as we loved the dead father or ancient Osiris—scattered in forty-nine fragments over the phantom pathways of my life, haunting us, an enigma, to be dealt with long after we became a digital memory for the pre-scripted fetuses of Post-America. Phoenelia Yeer was a woman who still worked, but uselessly, deprived of the light necessary to say anything in the overpowering gravity of the new regime. We slept one night with normal physical forces, what we were used to, and awoke the next morning to the relentless push of Jupiter bursting our blood vessels with the force of a small star.

The press reports of d'Mescan's "death," substantiated by the easily manipulated nodes of twenty-four hour media outlets, bore the mark of master forgeries. We had no doubt that Phoenelia picked up on these strands, subject, as she was, to the whims of her battery-powered appliances. Every hotel or motel room, cheap and infested, miniaturized the legacy of the home—seven-televisions, three VCR machines, two hi-fis, one public address, three computers, an intercom, two microwave ovens, an artificially intelligent dildo—the homeostasis regime of sampled tapes and re-assigned image tracks, the incontrovertible proof that not only was Henri d'Mescan alive and well, but that our most recent communication with him demonstrated, again, the omniscience of his plan from which we have never deviated: "such accusations will never surprise me—I shall be plagued by precisely such slightly altered texts throughout my sordid career. The structure of *Multifesto* then seems appropriate, and I restate it simply for our mutual clarity. PART I will detail the work leading up to the "Identity Trial," excerpting the work I truly wrote, as well as what was falsely attributed to me that will soon be edited into the proper shape. PART II will detail my career as Henry Mescaline, and of course, despite the unfortunate ending of our relations, the support that the first (David) Schneiderman's labors effected. PART III will sample my later career from *Post-America*, or *Postica*, delineating the merger of my d'Mescan and Mescaline personas, effectuating the final rehabilitation of my work and my life, which I will owe in great part to you, Davis, my eternal friend..."

These structures persisted long enough.

***

That Henri d'Mescan lived on became a fact beyond dispute, and while he rarely made his presence heard, and that contact was exceedingly difficult, his own words have finally vindicated him from a lifetime of delicate slander.

***

The selected piece, "Last Drop(ped) / The "Standard" Old World Model (is Now)," serves as the final tape of a great twentieth-century author, living somewhere in forced anonymity, waiting to be called back into action.

***

If Dial-Up Networking were truly dead, as our condolence card from The Publisher indicated in faded type, we would not weep, for we did not believe what others took as fact.

***

Nor will we fear Yeer's last seven letters, which she threatened to unleash, finally admitting that the accursed documents remained in her possession all these years!

***

We left our fear with the reader, long ago, who above all knew how to discern the murderer from the record of snarling noises.

The Last Drop(ped)

The remains of the child Dial-Up Networking were delivered via important virtual courier by the chief inspector of the sub-division, a wiry man with muscles on each arm. A thousand centipedes crawled beneath the surface of his skin, reproduced in a fantastic exponential stream of organic chunks resembling underground lava so that his entire insides undulated as an aggregate toward the heart, and everything he touched absorbed a measure of fluidity and fadeout for the first few seconds of contact, before reassuming the proper shape. The contents of his ashcan parcel were earmarked for the food processors and coffee makers in Supply. From there everything was born just the same as before—legacies lived out their pension time on the golf course, at the Laundromat lost in the whirl of nouveau Martin-I-zing, gambled on the peripheries of the new reservations—there, blood type got you in, and everybody was a native.

The sheer physicality of the clerks became a joy reserved for when the bosses weren't around and the inspector seemed to be one of the regular crew so much that even the CEO made only a thousand times more than the lowest paid jizmopper. In such cases, video-watching was used as a backdrop for more uninhibited behavior such as farting burping and going off into the rafters for the sheer, competitive hell of it all.

Even the inert supplies were crafted to watch and record. The ashes, for instance. Who knew where they came from, where they originated? The clerks surely didn't. Oh sure there was a file card and a punch card and a magnetic resonance imaging and tele-kinesthetic amplifiers and adjuvant synth-muscles and an aerodynamic cock and thermal shield and coolant matrix and carpal, metacarpal, and ante-brachial assemblies inside all mixed together like a cake baked in somebody else's vagina….but who could say this wasn't all an elaborate game played at the expense of the clerks? Who could say that the supply office even serves a purpose in the traditional sense?

Certainly not the workers.

It may as well have been the Great Repression and these guys and dolls figured to be short timers, sure, and they knew the nature of things as more fluid, less solid, than back in grandpappy's heyday, but still, it had become routine for them to deny the physical body altogether at the workplace, which no longer replicated a river of goods essential to the ethereal fluidity of the multinational state: clerks did not therefore eat, defecate, reproduce the human species or distribute the various parcels with any sense that they *weren't* a part of a vast multinational network. The inspector spoke with one clerk, the one soon to be in charge of the ashes, who put it bluntly with four fingers up his ass and a hand on the kiddy porn web site sponsored by the Blue Jean Chemical Concern: "Yeah, we were part of a vast tapestry, doing the good work of the LOOP. We're building the new economy from the ground up with micro-business applications expandable on the global level."

The ashes of dead children spread over the hemispheres in a second or third big bang, warm and vibrant, expanding and contracting in a regular pattern that had been gradually picked, created, and coded, sensitive and ready, at the slightest caress, to cause a frightful damage. The lack of light and air in the supply room never affected the clerks, both robotic and assuredly human specimens, aware of the purpose, place and destiny, online and inline, for the duration of the project's drain on traditional resources and equipment. Everything collapsed at the same time so no one even noticed it came and went.

The ceremonial completed its angular movements so the inspector became satisfied that the ashes of Dial-Up Networking, so recently and sadly deceased, would be treated with the proper respect due to her maintenance profile. "Cut this one with caffeine if you want her to last longer," said the inspector as he saluted the clerk now in charge, officially, of the ashes. "Everything seems to be in order here," he started and slurped up a draught of the bitter ash coffee—full of an undeniable presence—Post-America's finest, strangest brew.

The "Standard" Old World Model (is Now)

O nobly born, listen thou well, and bear at heart that birth in the "standard" world model assumes no major change in the physical, sexual, or administrative relationships that have historically governed the development of the system. In shape and in line, an excursus of translucent lilies transposed at each ligament, at the crook of each rib, at the knuckle, the tailbone, the neck, the ear, the temple, and the coochie snorcher, are all part of the standard stock precipitated by each orgasm that results in procreation once the house lights go down and the *gendarmes* look the other way.

Spliced with smells of buttery popcorn and surfactant residue stuck in syrupy nodes of adhesive sputum, sticks in a drowse popping over sugary loam, you sneak into the theatre at the heart of the sun. Teenaged clerks smoke bags of powder-white pheromone and crack cocaine from nut-blackened aluminum cans. They shiver and sweat over the doldrums of the tile floor and indoor-outdoor carpeting.

You cancel a bad check at the concession, ravage a few cuties by the lizard lounge, and dance to the twirling cacophony of sausage and legislation beaming in off-track pulses from the lights of the video arcade before shuffling into the collective darkness and air-controlled vacuum of the modernized projection theatre.

Stills of real-estate agent fantasy dates and trivia rent-a-fucks flash in time to the awkward beats of Sweet Home Alabama The Best of My Love shit show. You whiff the tangerine air and adjust your crotch in the grooves of the plush seat rotten with fleas; you spy the red light exit signs hanging in spectral archangels guarding the Holy Sepulcher.

Post-America treats its patrons to an outstanding display of the most recent advances in recycling, pollution control devices, and contraceptives absolutely feral to the future of human society recombined with the dominant checks on the growth of the screen before the screen, the fluid membrane coating the shower in hard-water cataracts that stick to the skin and mix with the sweat of the body.

You feel your stomach muscles growl as the peristaltic pumping action of the intestinal flute flies off into the brink of insanity, tooting the upper atmosphere of the movie theatre, the coming attractions loud and vociferous for the sports drama the mob movie love comedy the docudrama with hints of incestuous belligerency until the swirling smoke and archaic ligatures of the opening montage hit upon the ruins of ancient

Hellenistic wonder.

The camera frames statues at the Parthenon, scuttling the ass of a demigod, the lips of some outlandish brute, the transmutation of a Discobolus statue into fleshy Erwin Huber, 1936 German discuss champ—and then on into the oceans, the ring of fire from the Hecate sea witches, the trek across a blistered Europe into the flaming pineal eye of the Berlin stadium, into the 1936 Olympiad, into the eyes of the film's controlling image—Chancellor Adolph Hitler, spitting into the wind and taking it in the eye. The Olympic events showcase the polished physiques of the athletes from all countries, goes into slow-mo for certain moments—at the sacrifice of the pole vault, during the solemnity of the triple jump—and you writhe in erotic happiness, squirm with pleasure, subjugated by a type of hypnosis not uncommon to this perfumed idiom.

The audience collectively exhales with each Teutonic triumph, feels weak-and-sloppy muscles tighten, the vortex of impregnated assholes shifting into an engine of homeostasis, a self-indulgent mouth commanding the lower torso toward a mold of operating specifications. You sweat and fart, then vicariously moan, and years after the Nazi defeat, for historical purposes only, the entire world worships at the altar of your body.

Suddenly, the audience bursts out laughing at the caricatures of minority figures played to the hilt by Amos and Andy racing to the big dance, Duke Ellington and his band, the lighter members in blackface, spreading the sensuous custard of nascent swing over the broadcast nodules of Post-America. And you thinks it's wrong, all wrong, not the music of Duke or Jelly Roll or Sun Ra, but the blackface and the segregation and the Jim Crow specter darkening the sun and withering the crops into lily white skeletons.

You stare at this mess of a country as a small swelling of acid-cracked stomach lining falls through the fiery membranes of each collectively unconscious patron, stamping and chortling through the pratfalls of racial exaggeration. Out comes Mickey Rooney done up like a Chink so you decide right then and there, in this theatre of cruelty, that you're gonna remove your name from the social register just as soon as you have the chance regardless of the shit from his parent-like guardians, and then, you'll resist, with outrageous tattoos and cloven hooves. All the while, the film cells continue, and you still need a hero so you think real hard at the screen, feel the power of your mind toned tight by Huber's Olympian body.

A vessel can now be identified:

Dial-Up Networking, a human corpse of child, a copse in the belly of the kid's lambent, industrial wasteland, twaddles in the sacrosanct cottage industry of resistance.

She is *always* positioned in the moving pictures to rebel, to reform, to revenge by the very language of her soul.

She wears a squadron of powerful angels on a necklace of pins, reaps the symphonic whirlwind of multi-track stereo surround sound and stadium seating, pumps a million camels through the eye of a thousand needles every single night during an internet multi-bit streaming event.

You laugh with the rest of the crowd's gibbering jawbones, join in this catatonic luxury, cause you know who the enemy has become and how he, in rebellion, can blend into the network, just for a moment, real simple, in order to execute a program of revolutionary surds, a matrix of riddles.

The audience sets itself afire on the screen, in the balcony, rooting for little Dial-Up to best the crocodile, her eternal enemy, the unholy Sebek, demigod of Shedit, Crocodilopolis, at the confluence of ancient Aethiopia and Greece, mummified in the waters of the Mississippi *and* the Nile, a serpent of time and place, an energy succubus who will flood Post-America in cheap reproductions of the Maltese falcon, Jan Vermeer paintings sold during WWII, chicken McGiblets fabricated from newspaper rind and the bio-engineered slurry of outdated microchips.

The old Fox Theatres of St. Louis, Atlanta, New York, carved with the icons of Arabian Nights and Ali Baba churn your stomach. You despise Orientalism and exoticism, work for the good of a collective mankind. Your secret weapon, you know, is the limit of the pornographic image. A Hayflick telos to the amount of times one piece can be read before it spills its erotic charge.

Same for industrial and economic and sociopolitical scripts, so you project yourself at the screen, know the rubes love Dial-Up the underdog and hate the crocodile in a way that still keeps its mud wet and its belly full.

You watch and moan, stare and consider, the ticklish motivations of your child, Dial-Up Networking, set in her cradle like Marlene Dietrich, moved to the steaming duct of beatification like Marilyn Monroe, and you coax, millimeter by pixel, coordinate by graph, the crucial fringe of flat screen and the round Earth.

You seem ridiculous to the crowd; they forget all about you, fixated as they are on the ghostly flicker from the projection booth.

Dial-Up Networking, in light-colored rayon swaddling clothes, thrashes in the marsh that threatens to engulf her. She foams at the mouth and bounces in the broken cradle as the hideous reptile opens his snarling, world-eating jaws.

You can still complete it, bring her out, save everyone, if only you can buy some time. You dip low into this Van Allen belt of uncertainty, feel your flowing calves infuse with a power beyond you, and flip hop push primp your way to the brink of the celluloid bubble.

The separation of worlds, as Buster Keaton once demonstrated, keeps itself fluid and migrant.

The razor ripping teeth, the snarling cries of the murderous crocodile foiled by your arm's reach into an uncertain molasses, snatching tender Dial-Up Networking from the jaws of certain predictable death into the plenary atmosphere of the Post-American air-conditioned viewing station and movie theater.

For a moment, you rejoice, triumphant. You throw Dial-Up Networking to the top of your arms like elevating a weightless barbell, and her body, a cold-blooded mass of cells overflowing with genetic information, breaks apart in your firm hands, dusts away into the air vents and heating ducts.

A shower of tomatoes, each covered in rotten green spots, bombards your swollen figure, a magnet of bloody bile, a burlesque of the hero from a thousand forgotten yesterdays—cast like yesterday's trash to the cutting-room floor—bloodless and formless on the floor of the editing bay.

THE PUBLISHER'S NOTE ON THE LESS-THAN-PERFECT PAST (II):

The man who had entered the near-empty Spuyten Duyvil offices on December 31, 2000 possessed approximately the same height and build as the absent Davis Schneiderman; his hands had been buried deep in pockets of amber wool. A matchstick jutted obnoxiously from his lips as he silently removed a large envelope from his jacket. He held it up for us to see under the fluorescent lights, and without a word, placed the package on the desk that stood closest to the door. Before we could question him, he had left in the same way that he had come in, and evidentially, disappeared around the nearest corner.

The envelope contained the final seven letters. We make no claims as to their authenticity, but present them here unedited and unexpurgated for the reader's review.

An abnormally cold summer afternoon.

For a funeral parade.

Systolic pumps of heart will weaken in the wash of animal fat and that proximate dance with electromagnetic partners: the microwave keeps space with the fibrillated arc of a life lost to the dull thump thump of forbidden words; the sacred water lily, perhaps poisonous—relatively harmless and inoffensive— planted beneath the cool meniscus of the backyard pond, aside the decrepit water well rusting auburn under the winter sun; the old rumble of sonic carrion sluicing nosily down the meandering arabesques of the auditory canal—all this will cause the details of my funeral to be arranged with great care.

The reports of my death will be greatly disseminated.

Listen to the shuffling of my eye-covered mourners: banded foreheads of flag and colored cloth, of madras mask bearing stripe and check, wrapped and muted into the collective smell of synthetic leather casing, of gauze bandages absorbing the feral stench of dried pus and raging scab, of festering interior monologues that force brains enfolded into colorless tourniquets to hear the seething core of their hearts tinkling out a shrill narrative line. Soft prolapsed valves will billow through the rest of the body to focus it undulations on the odor of this lily plant—coaxed by the siren song of genetic-seed manipulation and hormonal petting from the outlandish gardener kept on the estate staff, whose father's father's brother's father will be the first estate gardener, and who now, descended from the spurting testes of such a domestic pedigree, will find the fight drained from his avuncular tissue just as a vestigial tail might be rejected from the right kind of mammal. Well, this lily plant has a lineage to live up to and my spectators must close their eyes in order to perceive these images as an effluvium of shared color sounds smells traveling by the verbose logic of the book through the inertia of its final pages.

So go back into the water.

What each mourner hears in the depths of the inner ear, every throaty tangle of thoughtlessness, what each mourner hears in the history of her life, what sounds of cracking bones that she fixes upon at the stroke of midnight, laying in a bed that floats upon the water of the grey, auditory canal—whether a firing squad that both hits and misses its target, the rush of dirt collapsing into a sub-basement in Future, Missouri, the tromp of crocodile claw under the smiling heat—what she hears in the long black night will be the smacking sound of her feet jumping behind the spiral structure in the inner ear that looks like an enormous snail shell, with 10,000 hairs waving like fields of corn in some cliché parting shot. She will push through the plumage of strand and resonance to hear that slim lily, the corpse flower, stretching its shoots toward the expanse; with each rotund creak of the old 23-degree axis bandied about the knock-kneed solar system, that is, once a day, this old nymphaea marliacea, this water lily, will hit the accelerated growth jackpot—doubling in size and area. In forty-nine days, the lily complex will cover the pond, a virus overwhelming its host, choking off the other sundry forms of aquatic life that have called this puddle home since the final minutes of the Devonian era.

And so the dust and sand will lose their differentiation as the hungry globes of elder gods swing on wire ratchets through a solar system of muck and brine, a patina of the old ways coating the nearest continental arteries—the Nile, the Mississippi—with rich mineral beds, waiting, as a dry sponge buried in a concrete casket might wait for the deliberate cracks of time, to be infected with the liquid of wonder, the flood of nightfall, the batter of stars going soft in glimmering drops from the distant heavens, before going out entirely after reaching their submerged targets, for only a second, it seems, with the brilliant fever of flickering genius. The heavy shuffle of pallbearer feet will sound like the scratch of fantastic marbles rolled deliberately along a railroad trestle, and with the rolling of heel to toe, they will collect tiny filaments of metal to create at first an invisible concavity, and then, later, as the weight of my pinewood coffin forces down their shoulders and necks—the press of wood on flesh creating a sound of chalk on cardboard—their feet will dig even deeper into the sand and dirt road. The ground water, retained in puddles from a recent sewage break, from a recent storm, will wait for its chance to be swept into this ad-hoc canal, and move closer, once again, to the noisome logic of the lily flower:

For many days the lily and its doubling will seem harmless, and no amount of sunshine and beta-carotene sessions will make it seem necessary to take any action whatsoever. Better to sit back in the bomb shelter's elongated sarcophagi insulating the cracks with weather stripping that'll save on the old furnace in the event of nuclear winter. Yes sir, with so much to do around the old place: lining the aluminum accumulator with a new layer of cow fat, promoting tourism to a small Micronesian Island over the Internet, sealing thousands upon thousands of canned preserves within larger mason jars, there's simply no time to trim back the lily. Until it dominates half the pond—that is.

On what day will that be?

The forty-eighth day, of course, reverberating about the cochlea like a geologic hangover.

Such a rush through the auditory canal can cover the entire assemblage of mourners with the gingernumb melancholy of

the event as they pass the membrane of the elaborate cemetery—crypts soaked with Spanish moss grown thicker than
small birch trees, archetypical angels weeping on the graves of
robber-barons buried with jeweled eyes and forked-banknote
tongues. The speeches will sound characteristically banal, and
unable to reveal myself just yet, I offer some prepared comments through the mechanism of the inner ear:

You will sleep, but it is not really the type of sleep that we
can engage in together, and I can hear our words and read our
minds perhaps better than during your former dead-tired state
of waking. Word after word will strike the ear in sounding
brass and tinkling symbol. At this late hour, in this ghost
house, I shall exercise my ancient options. Spuyten Duyvil,
obligated to cater to my desires, will duly provide me with the
editorial introductions that Yeer and Schneiderman have produced in isolation from each other, and I will then watch, edit,
and destroy the gaseous lilies that try to choke me into less
than the nothing that you will always resemble.

Whats worse, the "you" understood in such a case might
become "we" or even "I" after mutating into Henri d'Mescan,
scion and bastard of twentieth-century letters, forced to act at
the eleventh hour of the forty-eighth day, moments before my
burial. Through a deft mechanization of the atmosphere about
this place, I shall always pull my neck from the chopping block
at the last minute, move away from the noose, slip out the gal-
lows and guillotine through back door in-betweens. After the
strands of each little assassination plot unravel into a clutch of
verses, loose ends, raw genetic material—once the magnesium
dust and molecular grime settle into the soil, I am sure to feel
a retroactive assurance that my survival has been pre-ordained,
not by the local city-god who has managed to broker a hege-
mony for a few thousand years. Not by Al-Lah, Uzza, El, or

even Sebek, for whom I bear a toothy affinity, but through the overwhelming necessity of my so-called survival for the continuance of the postwar information machine.

Yes, I will be a person with real limits, a human, like yourself, but I shall change, over a century of recombinant prose, into a hybrid creature of the human organism, part man and part word, an analogue to the digital age, a lower animal set only for self-replication through a series of shadowy operations that erase my body with each cut of the delete command. In this way I will become seamless, and in short, will unfold across the vast plains of the back brain so that the "I" that I once was will soon pass on into the next world, only to birth the "I" that has been made, fabricated, and sustained by the unholy food of Post-America.

Sincerely,
Henri d'Mescan

44) Two

DEAREST PHOENELIA;

Forty-nine points of light. The spirit body sampled before us.

***

Draped in the long pleats of the dazzling, fluid evening gown, the stunning Phoenelia Yeer prepared the garret with mangled rose petals, the annunciation of erotic energies, the plump lilac luster of her enormous inner thighs. Her body, a temple of perfume, stretched its hypnotic tabernacle across the wiring of the various sensors and dials, brought them into a realm of electrostatic excitement with just the pulse of our wrist on their plastic, the press of our flesh against the ambient altars of sky.

***

Or so we imagined—perceiving her only from above, making use of bugs and listening devices, of motion-capture video scans that rendered the dots of her body, the luminous speckles of skin always smooth and creamy, as a constellation of particle points crystallized into the hologram floating above our own disjointed figure. We propelled our arms to the ceiling, and our body followed so that we drifted into the swirls of murky sky that marked both the top and the bottom in relation to our supine body. There we spun, a gyroscope on the back of a reptile creature, birthing the world from our constant revolutions.

***

Scars from the Caesarian Section had cowardly retreated to the cleft of her vagina on this sampled version of her body, the ocean of the pubic hair erased by the slender butcher with the pointed mustache, the splice of flesh from an amniotic cleaver, slicing meat from bone, fabricating the various chops—rump, shoulder, brisket—and draining the sacred oils by which the soft gleam of the skull drew, from the dark triangle, its incoherent marbling.

***

We imagined her pin-ghost spreading a star arrangement of hand into the inky black that surrounded the suggestion of the garret space, brilliant twinkling points cascading on the foreground of the universe connected to the main body. We zoomed in to the fingers and heard them illuminate the suggestions of a single letter, removed from a cavity in space that made the ribcage sound just like the beating of a wooden chest.

***

The letter opener glistened, a knife blade or needle.

***

Our daughter dead and buried, emptied into the wind, sucked into the liquid grave that felt the same as being shot from the rotunda of the Post-American capitol building directly into the upper atmosphere; there, the cremated ash of Dial-Up Networking raced with the satellites, with the loose and staggy moonrocks, cyborgs gone haywire, so that the very position of the stars and comets decomposed from whispers set loose on the lips of tiny children. A lioness rampant, Dial-Up Networking, an escutcheon of stars. No dreaming in the garret, no picture of the outside world. Only the memory, old jazz standards—*Stardust, Stars Fell on Alabama*—accompanied her through the grey membrane.

***

The letter opener sliced the letters a-p-a-r-t.

***

Phoenelia Yeer continued her ritual of bread and wine and electric, transcendent, prefatory orgasm, the silence of candles and the macabre spectacle of arcane tomes split open at the spine. We watched and waited and wondered. She placed lace circles around the center of the room, like mushrooms, like stones, offered the blood of a goat to a graven image of Tetragrammaton painted in rococo finery and thin, laconic brushstrokes.

***

A passing resemblance.

***

She lay back on the divan, heavy with drink. The low hum of the vibrator settled on the microscopes and scientific filters, on amoeba and paramecium, engulfing villages of bacteria and yeast smeared over celluloid contour maps. The letter rolled into a cylinder of arcane transcript, wrapped carefully around the shaft of the vibrator.

***

She abused herself with the transcript, and we smelled the rotting tenderness of her insides soaking the letter, flailing sparks and stars thrust across the universe that was black in the first precarious days of the amoeba.

***

The letter rolled around the shaft of the vibrator.

***

She spread a vial of fresh dirt about the room in a pentagram inscribed in a circle, ashes mixed from the lower heavens,
raining through the sheets of lily and bricolage and ozone, over
the shards of Post-America, into the darkness of her silent garret, into the sutures of these seven stolen splices.

Sincerely Ours,
Davis

45) THREE

DEAREST DAVIS;

You sit at your computer and know that they *were* all there when your water burst, flooding the town of Future in the soft epidermal folds of the new pollution.

He approaches this garret lab—a spectacle of weighted scales, genetic tissue, beeping machines, and interlocking globular apparatuses—and climbs the stairs in a gown of the finest silk. Smuggler, gambler, and demon-fed dauphin of the lowlands, Davis Schneiderman checks his look in the winterized mirrors clamped to the base of the spiral steps, each covered in carpet and industrial sludge. In desperation, he makes an incision into his arm with the sharp edge of the papers.

You sit at the computer and know when your last words loop in playback at your funeral parade, before the pyre, the suttee, the mass of dirty thick muddy Ganges, you return to the garret nearest the familiar tangents of narrative life.

Of course, he carries the letters with him; the close-up of his eye captures the character of adventure novels and wartime romances, the removal of soft tissue in the tooth and the sub-stitution with a cyanide caplet—delivered before each seduc-tion by those with an unhealthy obsession with shit and dis-ease, bodily fluids and excretions, interior organs floating like blocks of salt immersed into shockingly cold freshwater.

Your kitchenette occupies a little nook with plastic furniture, decorated with greyscale prints of Sebek the Unholy Crocodile God, of apocalyptic oil paintings that smell of winter in the crook of desiccated cornrows.

He dumps the remains of Henri d'Mescan's papers into the latrine, the seven letters that he has taken from you; he urinates over bleach-tablet fingernails, slices of garlic stuffed into charred flesh, but the seven remain whole, complete. Undaunted, he can push the letters into the paper shredder outside the garret, listening with a manic, fretful energy for the pulse of his underarm, his wrist, peeking dangerously near the pulsating blades, pregnant fingers bursting with sacks of blood.

You know that nothing is lost from this package.

He has ransacked you office, your life, your home, and the hospital where the child is removed by enigmatic forceps, clinging iron filings, to the hip of a magnetized holster.

You know that nothing is ever really cleaved apart.

He infuses every circuit with viruses so desiccated that they link together into a colony of fire ants on the Amazon, a bloom of red night that will float and return, in the Bodhisattva's lungs, breathing in *Phoenelia Yeer*, breathing out *Yeer Phoenelia*, to the rhythm of his artificial articulations. He carries the seven indestructible summonses; he no longer arrives unannounced.

You rush him suddenly with a kiss, a flash of tongue and forbidden nectar looped on the soundtrack as you whisper the forbidden hymnal, the incantation that brings him full into the cool, electric atmosphere of the garret. Your tongue snaps him out of the smog as you grab the folded paper that you hold in the cavity of your bosom, dropping it to the garret-laboratory floor.

He removes a similar page from his own copies, and passes it across the narrow chasm of molecules that separate your heaving breasts. The bridge connecting your hearts carries your feet across almost palpably, a gleaming body of rock, solid in the granite-colored floor.

You wind like serpents to the table, sit down to tea, and read yourselves into a coma, read yourselves into compliance with the directives of the unholy word.

His fingers focus on you, pull you tight into a close-up of the wind and the ashes, the spinning vibrant cry of the child's soul that only parents can know after a death, once the life has been thrown from the body and flung back to the soil.

Your back against the test tubes and with your eyes staring into Schneiderman's, you notice a memory of Dial-Up Networking dancing, chewing, absorbing about the nursery and the hotel and the hospital and the womb once again in the dark pupil.

He says that there is no such thing as dialogue.

You look up at lightless sky outside the garret, your eyes trapped on distant stars, invisible and unreal. You realize you may only have been talking to yourself.

Sincerely Yours,
Phoenelia

My mourners will wiggle their heads as if they hear the music of my voice caught on the raindrops that strike their cheeks that bleed their sweat into a mixture of salty brine. So the rain will increase its vehemence and mix freely with the vapor of the burial steam, the blaze-orange digging machine, layered with dirt, contrasting with the cemetery entrance arch festooned with a decrepit saint, Peter most likely, partially emaciated by the erosion of wind and rain, and met by a furious dancing frieze of Pan, god of panic. Even with hoof, this Pan will be the Morningstar, Lucifer, whose rebellion begins in the gut, as described, as life and love and death can be nothing before expulsion through the mouth, smothering the tongue and teeth, covering everything in a veneer of broken promises and industrial sludge. He dances to the rumba of the digging machines.

After what feels like several long lifetimes have passed through my bones, through thousands of silent snowfalls spliced onto the sleeping town, You, I mean We, I mean only I, must see that hundreds of genes will insinuate their way into the human genome from bacterium that will infect a distant vertebrate ancestor and slip its DNA into a past host who will also be, at once, the future vessel. These alien genes will ascend into our backbone.

The coffin will lift onto the hydraulic platform as the glossy head-wraps of my mourners might feel the itch of this gene lifting its way from the silent sanctum of their chromosomes to spread forth into the waking state known as consciousness, as if by mere chance, now, at this crucial juncture, the digging machine will sputter out into my eulogy:

***

Once, after the war, I shall be again incarcerated, in a garret, and from there remain unable to view the prison planetarium because of the great hooks pulsing from the ceiling—those satanic stalactites pumping smoke, upside-down volcanoes erupting across the camera cheek of time—and the solitary confinement so cold and lonely in a tower above the main keep and the constant injections of sodium pentothal and orange tasting memories of the pinhole arrangements that fuse to my memory from the constant repetition of artificial sky. I plan to dream of the moonrise and the swelter of dying light, of the flaming, celestial orbs darting wildly from the toeholds of the projection booth. In dreams these images will go dark, so many gaslights extinguished by the dawn of the last century of the last millennium, so many intersection points regressing into a grid of wire, oxygen, and bone.

***

Shovels will strike dirt loosened by the rainstorm, and we will dig together in this strange cemetery to finish the grave hole that squirms like an obscene baby mouth half choking on the mud that churns over its tongue. The grave will slurp lug nuts crashing on a taught vinyl parachute just as raindrops smash the edges of the mouth. Chunks of the lip will receive the mad cliffs of skin and scab that fall into the crevice of the yawning mouth, and my mourners will clank their shovel edges at these weakened shelves of muddy maw. Their arms shall spring with electrical charges first from each body and then from each other, so that each limb works as a dendrite from the mother brain, spreading fingers of excited current over the gaping burial slot. Grab a shovel and picture the grave pond that will be the lair of the fragrant water lily, doubling

300

each day, overrunning the pond long before I arrived, uprooting the other plants and choking life from the fish and the lake birds and the grubs and even the reptiles dependent on the fidelity of a tenuous ecosystem.

Move on the forty-eighth day to save it all, and it will already seem hopeless. Move on day one to cut the root, and nothing will have changed. The water will follow these two, Phoenelia Yeer and Davis Schneiderman, rivals and lovers, as they work themselves into numberless fragments—a glass sphere shattering against a hermetic rod inserted into the urethra.

At the pre-ordained ending, in the silent, dilapidated garret of the ghost house, the prison-room, locked away amid the parcels of bound letters and suspended coils of research and scattershot scales and Petri dishes, Davis Schneiderman and Phoenelia Yeer will kiss once again, embrace against the void, bathe themselves in waters of reconciliation. This convenient archive of my tortures, the garret, prison and laboratory, will be the setting and these final letters of Post-America, these endless epistles of time and place, will be sent to both Yeer and Schneiderman at an unspecified moment, in special code bereft of bacteria, aseptically cleansed, with handwritten missives expressing various threats best kept in the shadows. The space will be designed especially for their bodies, which shift and move according to the whims of each passing breeze.

Sincerely Mine,
Henri d'Mescan

47) Five

Dearest she who is not what I am;

All night long she sleeps in silence, but thinks she is awake.

She remembers thrusting a hand down into the filing-cabinet's black shaft as one might artificially inseminate a calf or black hole, then her whole arm, then both arms, pressing her shoulders against the lip of the hold, feeling no bottom, nothing, except a thick, dark pitch, a muddy river of molasses hiding slow-moving reptiles, millions of blind microscopic organisms.

Spacecat, the dream familiar, cuddles its paws against the curve of her torso, the silence of her swollen breasts: A woman sleeps through the night in the real world of objective reality; she casts off the detritus of the day as a haze might banish the fog from its valley territory just before the sun dissipates into the cool burn of mid-morning. In sleep she sees the impossibility of actual rest, wakes again and again as the slightest sound of the dead child's body burps and shifts in the illusion of movement, shuttering for a single millisecond, with a distant pulse penetrating the callused layers of her oily skin.

A material reality to the vision: the fetal remnant of dead child accuses her with angular eyes exposing grim, pinprick pupils, the folds of its underdeveloped fingers opening and closing in time with the beating of her heart and the sound of her breathing that synchronizes itself to the rhythm of her unrest.

No turning back; she takes a deep breath and plunges under the surface by pulling the amorphous lip over her head and the rest of her body like a nylon costume so she can swim through the viscous sewer waters for the seven letters that may yet explain it all.

She rises, bathed in sweat, to cast herself over the cold patches of the stone floor yet never leaves the bed, pushes the dream familiar, Spacecat, away with a mighty thrush and she watches the creature float slowly above her, a gaseous ball of undifferentiated tissue, a deflating balloon propelled by the expulsion of helium into the soft upper reaches of the enormous garret.

The ink goes on forever but there is nothing written down.

She will not sleep soundly, the dream familiar cuddling against the exposed skin of her wilted arms, its nuzzled nose rubbing her back with wetness just as a conjurer might trace its magic pentagram with a laser pointer.

She wakes again and again, but sleeps at the same time.

She is abandoned by the fire and flame and flicker of images, by her old love whose scaly skin feels cold but necessary for survival in this strange country—this Post-America of the flower—this country of withered lilies laid end to end across the pond of the toilet bowl, the cracked enamel sink, the pool of blood on the carpet. In a dream once impossible for the garret, the ghost-house, the Manhattan high rise, the foreclosed penitentiary, the rent-controlled bodega, she forces her hand to her throat, not because of her wounds but her fatigue; an Orphic sweat glues the hair to the body and commands her to fight for an original reproduction on the other side of this life. She meets herself in a dream, younger, pregnant, ethereal.

Does she cry out, or do her tear ducts swallow the external

world, liquid flooding into the mouth and nose, smothering the genital holes, sinking her to the bottom?

"Kill me," she whispers to her lover, even before she awakes.

"ABRACADABRA."

In dreams, Davis Schneiderman walks with this Phoenelia Yeer, waits with her, and he works to oblige all requests, bites the buttons off her operating smock, pulls triggers in the name of Henri d'Mescan, acts as his proxy along deserted streets, his assassin in the lowlands. He conjures up the veiled moon outside the stone circle, and rises, slowly at first, from the slumped pile in which they sleep, pushes her prone body onto its back, against a backdrop of city lights and terrifying megaphones so that her arms and legs splay in a mock crucifixion pose, a green slip among grey, a concertina of blue craters reflected in the moon of tears silently salting her cheekbones.

Forever on it goes. Just as her body cannot take any more, as she stops moving completely, forever, her fingers catch on something. Everything goes black, but she can dig, and does, pulling out the bundle from its grave of clay and mud, tripping the skin of her fingertips along the seven sacred edges; she pushes down against the muck, and swims upward to the surface.

The mandibles of oil with their saccharine words are not enough to forestall the end, the little death, the pot of paste and wicked discharge set deep in Davis's interior cavities. He removes the pre-written confession from its leather house—this forty-seventh letter.

Vague and undulating shadows brush against her as she floats, toward the faint light, closer and closer. Something rubs next to her body, a giant shape, cold and clammy, but it passes. Not daring to move but floating by inertia, she hears her father's voice in between the particles of dark and muddy brine.

"For Dial-Up Networking, my dear…"

Phoenelia Yeer pulls the ancient paper from Davis Schneiderman's crooked fingers with an inhuman crowbar of arm that has become standard issue for her perfect, gleaming body; she notices an inky blackness smudged on his thumbs, a mass of confusion at the basal ganglia, as she pulls back the paper. A thin, almost invisible strand of ink stretches into a gossamer cord from flesh to the confession; the light of the garret transforms it into the gaping stigmata, bleeding unwanted muck into the veneer of a rosy cross. No time for ritual, thinks Phoenelia, as a parade of doubts begin the slow march through her fallopian tubes and ovaries, spreading by osmosis into the digestive and intestinal tracks, up the windy caverns of the circulatory system, blown into the fractured passages of the throat…its as if her whole body realizes its place in the patchwork machinery of Davis Schneiderman's autonomous world.

So far this is confession.

She has seduced and has been seduced. She has fucked and languished in orgasm, watched the preceding events as if they were a movie in which she is only peripherally involved.

Move on the forty-seventh day to save it all, and it is already hopeless as well.

Her hands trace a delicate ballet, as the air arabesques around the soft targets of her fingers, gliding at first in extraneous movements—flips and loop-de-loops—until coming to rest on the letter that Schneiderman offers. The seven letters retrieved in her memory from the great vortex of ivory black sludge, in hopes that its clear and simple language will save her from the abyss of the ghost familiar Spacecat wadding itself into the soft tissue of her venous nuzzle, scraping each rough patch of skin from its figure and transplanting it, small patches at first that double in size every day, to the lily pond that reads like a book of simple years, of all that has come before and insists on returning, of the words that tell the story from a perspective no longer her own, of her hand pulled from its resting place aside the dream baby made to work the knobs and levers of the writing machines.

"That was us, following ever closer," Davis whispers from outside the liquid membrane, enfolding her so that his sounds seem distant and degraded, a voice-box expunging the shadows that cover her shaking fingers holding the seven letters going soft and solvent in the waters that circle each of us forever.

Sincerely Ours,
Davis

You look up at lightless sky outside the garret, your eyes trapped on distant stars, invisible and unreal. You have been talking to yourself.

***

Set on random repeat loops splattering the contents of the word-body over the rustic machines of the garret, the * and the * engage in unclear repetition of the main themes. Davis Schneiderman brushes his lousy foreskin over the puddle of the woman he has stalked these past months, tracing her progress from motel to motel, jacking off in underpowered hot tubs that have captured her essence in their gorgeous bubbles, gorging himself on microwave waffles and spoiled milk products put out just at 6 a.m. by the all-inclusive continental breakfast staff.

***

Your air cackles and moans with the static and electric breath of alligators, the cloaca of ancient crocodiles and caimans, the horrible, blind, and clear parade of mummified reptiles buried in the cell of every reptile, lodged into the DNA of Phoenelia Yeer and her absent daughter and her lover Davis Schneiderman; closure submerges itself in mud, rebellion forms a drowse of sticks and river ash.

***

In the garret Davis perceives the sickness that comes from such activities, hold out the forty-eighth letter for Phoenelia Yeer's dumb eyeballs, and as she reads, he waits, and feels the memory of Dial-Up Networking welling up from a deep crimson pool, the remnants of her body made into ashes, smudged on the forehead of his one-time lover, hovering above, a hanging garden of cerebral beauty, a gigantic statue straddling twin islands of the old world encased for a moment on the brow of this woman.

***

You never grow weary of the reptile.

***

The digital grain of the primitive world, the dirty, pictorial languages in orbit around Phoenelia Yeer scratch conceptual motifs on the shell of Davis Schneiderman's consciousness. Her daughter is dead, repeated in staccato; surrender is imminent, repeated in blood.

***

Your memory feels sensuous, uneven, studded with images of Dial-Up Networking jacking into the refracted orgasms of a suckling mouth clamped tight on the technological apparatus, locked in the frozen moment of the snapshot, murdered by the corrupted bandwidth of Phoenelia's enemies who even now maneuver in sinews of ink.

***

Every fiber of her being, each cell of her body pulls itself toward the shine buried in the river, the mud that reflects the cosmos. Shunned by the regime of gilded lights and phosphorous ozone, she holds the power to increase in translucence, double in luminosity, smother the universe with the idea of the limitless word.

308

***

You rouse Phoenelia Yeer from this letter, this forty-eighth epistle of sun and moon. She rises quickly with a shock of her body flashed in outline against that sun, the eclipse timed out as her breath drops into her stomach, where a meal might rot once the sun admits it has always been dead.

***

Phoenelia Yeer drops to the ground and runs her fingers like reptilian claws into the puddle of ashes flicked during their awkward congress from the knees of Davis's trouser. She scoops her tongue into the fibers and begins to black out. Her eyes close into slits, ovals with microscopic apertures, the hybridization of species with unfamiliar modes, uncertain escapes.

***

Your batch-processing device sets numb colors flooding Davis's mind; the greyscale porticos of the inner ear tune in to the stream of bits and pixels that code the girl called Dial-Up Networking, the daughter, pulled from the celluloid brink and devoured from the crocodile, embossed in the flat-world and imaged into the electromagnetic spectrum.

***

Her tongue rides slipshod along the ashen floor of the garret that doubles as Davis's spinal column. Neurons and microscopic mites collect along the indentation of her taste buds that scrape the lining from the inky bottom vertebrae and vestigial tall tales reanimating the dream lost between each cinder flick of her tongue, your tongue, that reminds Davis of borrowed gooseflesh rising on the dimpled skin of this narrative line.

***

She lives and intertwines. Phoenelia licks the ashes until her tongue burns with dust, ignites in soot and fire, false memories from false deaths, fabricated endings to fabricated stories.

***

You know her breath because it reeks of lilies and baby carrots; you know her body because it is also your own; you merge into her mind through the auditory canal. You spin into a giant water wheel, in the air, in search of a private, careless vapor. You assume that your long fourth tooth, visible when your mouth closes taught, reflects your personality, jagged and disfigured. You trudge toward the ceiling, into the floorboards— toward the slightly boiling light that is really only the spectrum of 200 million shades.

***

Phoenelia Yeer bursts to her feet with the power of a thousand cyclotrons, no, a million semiconductors, and the crocodile advances toward her body, attaches itself to her figure, decodes her manic frustrations as claw pierces the spinal column and crushes the vertebrae, enters her as scale becomes bitter, callused skin cells, plays with her punches and buttons while the tongue sets up shop in a foreign mouth. She lives for its kiss, and tastes the familiar air of root and soil.

***

You smash the machinery of the garret, destroy the globe and charts, shatter the genetic imaging modules into a million identical shards; shocks and striations; the vellum sheaths of their editorial work, of Davis and Phoenelia, burst into particle and pulp raining down on the dirty attic, the garret-prison, from the invisible storm clouds that give life to the eternal elision, the omnipresent *.

* * *

* * *

The walls shake apart until they crumble, the foundation flickers like the lick of tungsten in the center of the bulb, and you who are called Henri d'Mescan can move toward your prey with her tongue in your teeth, her skin in your scales, quick pulses of energy to the chemical bath; Phoenelia's jaws that are also yours snap into Davis Schneiderman as bursts of mercury drop from his jugular vein and bleed on Phoenelia's collection of summer dresses, on the casket of their dead child, stillborn in the delta, claimed by the river for its own. Davis will struggle, thrashing his body in the grip of tooth, a monstrous fish, a Judas, promising freedom, secrets, blueprints that he fails to realize have already been compromised. You allow Phoenelia to feel a moment of pity, relax her grip, and for a split second shed a tear, take a picture, absorb a veil. A touching scene but you feel nothing beyond the soft of his squirming body, helplessly flailing its bloody appendages.

* * *

And then the crunch of bones breaking inside you, the fragments of skin and iron mangle of flesh and cyanide and the whole indifferent ending to the enticing, unreal tumble into the darkness of these souls. Your teeth will interlock into themselves. Memory blanks and flashes; no caresses, no soft and tender whispers, no slightly wilted flowers doused with life-devouring silicone spray. You carry bulbs in your stomach, along the track of your small intestines, ready to burst through the ocean in leafy bloom, an amoeba swelled to enormous proportions, emerging from the icy Rhine during the winter of 1913.

onto her knees, after stumbling toward the casket, her face a tangle of root for the catharsis of my trunk. The water will fill the grave hole and rise even further to swallow her mouth and nose in its delightful silence.

***

***

Post-America must lie in ruins. The land will be gripped by violence. Reports will flood the ambient networks and neural pathways of the average citizen with coups and rebellion: the Jesuits will overtake the best culinary schools and mobilize a force of fundamentalist pastry chefs in Baja California; protestors will crush the White House and capitol building beneath the heels of a giant marionette brandishing an enormous scepter in the shape of a dildo, hundreds of feet high and powered by a small thermal-nuclear core; millions of sightless veal calves will rise up to kick apart their wooden boxes and turn regular hormone injections on the farmer, racial-profiling offices will be flooded with explosive data about the Founding Fathers, an apocryphal copy of the Constitution will appear in a Missouri cellar with seven extra amendments in the Bill of Rights, Giant Pandas on loan from China commit hari-kari and the autopsy will reveal horrible blood toxicity numbers, the coven of major news networks will find their signals overrun with looped footage of the same four media experts discussing the same four topics over and over without noticing the difference, while the poor, the stricken and turned away, the denuded masses under the blackened thumbs of an outrageous rainbow coalition of bourgeoisie, will unite to fight marketplace globalization with infomercial trinkets.

***

***

314

Phoenelia Yeer, clad in the black wash of the death shroud, will maniacally press her fingernails into the seams of the coffin top to listen to my chest and ensure that it no longer beats, to smell the ichor of my wounds as they fume from the decomposing body into the palette of her nostrils.

Listening to her struggle and scream, feeling the punch of each nail cracking at the root and bleeding into the watery coffin, the other assembled mourners will become transfixed on the echo of her awkward assault.

Yeer hits the pinewood, smashes her forehead forward in fatigue and desperation on the top of the coffin, until the whole bloody mess of her forehead leaks steadily into the box.

The rain will meet the puddles from the grave, overflowing and flooding the burial site with winsome rivers rising in triumph from the earth, and suddenly, without warning, the bloody river will press into the cracks of the casket, and begin to loosen its joints.

* * *

* * *

The garret will lie in ruins, in violence. Centuries of genetic data overturned with a similar cry for alarm, claimed along with broken glass, computer imaging equipment, the blank lines of class-action insurance forms…in its physical unreality and human reality it will seem, to Phoenelia Yeer, related to the image which escapes from the frame.

* * *

David Schneiderman will still start trouble, wiling away his hours in purgatory playing blackjack with Mutation, the guardian angel of outmoded genius.

***

Henry Mescaline will send missives from his prison house, hidden from the stars that he dreams into liquid and undifferentiated obscurity.

***

The morning papers will proclaim Henri d'Mescan's death as a hoax, a charade perpetuated by enemies who never know the sacrifices that have already been made for their freedom. An appeal for calm and decency will follow, but he must be, after all, already an old man, a specter on the lips of the wind, a body warm on the boilers of insurrection, calling for calm, for consistency, for the arrogant interference with nature that will always be his right and occupation—just as we have always known.

***
***

Just as we have always known, Phoenelia's head will rise just as the giant sun disk obscured by clouds pushes through the curtain of fog to alight behind her.

Just as we have always known, at this same moment, a mourner, a man or man-y men, will jump from the crowd of listening zombies, his hands will remove themselves like frightened birds from deep pockets of amber wool.

Just as we have always known, a matchstick will jut from his lips as he silently rushes his clutch of spider fingers toward this woman who may just be all women.

316

His digits will dance and snarl about her back until they convene on the neck and thrust it back from the lip of the coffin; his fingers will come together and raise a blade or needle over her stomach.

For a moment it seems as if he will plunge it into the depths of her omphalos, but he continues to push her back until she topples, her body splashing into the water that flows everywhere, up to the line submerging her prostrate breasts.

His arms will pull open the casket lid so he can plunge the needle knife into the flesh of the corpse with all the power of a lighting bolt sent through some zigzag path into the shoot of a lily blossom. The penetration starts the entire casket shaking because the limbs of the dead body suck in every force with the puncture.

The lifeless corpse unfolds itself back into the arm of its attacker, spreading a viral stench up through the crook of his fingers, into his shoulder sockets, back into the charged cavity of life that is Phoenelia Yeer on the ground behind him, who, choking on the water rushing into her nose and mouth, will rise up with one final effort to smash the back of the man forward into the coffin.

The taste in her mouth as the hydraulic arms snap from their casing and collapse in on themselves, as the coffin fills with liquid and both the man and the tiny body underneath submerse into the nether realm, will be that of metal filament charged with mud and baby's breath.

And just as we have always known, the eyes of the dead body in the coffin—floating on the lip of the liquid vortex drawing the entire problem set into the solution of deflating mourners, the collapsing, stalled digging machine, the grass unleashed from its tentative mooring, and the other gravestones failing under the weight of their engraved platitudes—will be those of the child Dial-Up Networking, blinking to her mother in a code set in motion long before, on both the first and the forty-ninth day, by the banks of a muddy file cabinet that swallows her body, the mourners, the memory, and poor Phoenelia Yeer whole, pulled down, a mass of entrails, deep into the wet earth.

***

Post-America will end *Multifesto*, or, the other way around?

***

The body of Davis Schneiderman will rot among the lilies, and the recovering Phoenelia Yeer seems to understand the situation rather well as the doorbell rings and an identical set of flowers will be delivered—from Davis Schneiderman—with a note thanking her for both the tender reconciliation and the use of her wet pussy: "That was us, following ever closer."

***

The ringing phone will shock her from a recollection of ashes, and the orphanage on the line long distance just wants to let her know that Dial-Up Networking's adoptive parents act like stand-up sort of people and that the girl will be happy in a way she can never understand so she might as well stop trying to call them at all hours of the night for godsakes we'll call the police next time...

***

So Dial-Up Networking will live in the semen and cum of every red-blooded Post-American, even in those who remain

318

barren, cast out, cut away from the old animal gods, at odds with a world that plays them all for a long, hard laugh.

***

And Phoenelia Yeer, yes Phoenelia, she can still work on her collection, writing every day in the same empty spaces, studying an unholy genetics, searching for the code that will break the code and finally cause her death. She can pace her career to the tempo of a distorted song, so long ago inscribed into her head, a familiar jingle, forever in the movies, forever in those elusive cells.

***

Now and then she might even look into the dead eyes of the grave...

***

And all she will see is a mirror, reflecting back images of the already dead body of her traitor, her collaborator, Henri d'Mescan.

***

Locked in this garret, always, where she found us most exciting...

Henri d'Mescan

NOTE:

Multifesto is indebted to the multiplicity of writers and theorists whose influence has found its way into this multifarious text in various forms, some instances as mere inspiration, some instances as words or phrases. A partial list might include: Walter Benjamin, Maurice Blanchot, Albert Camus, Henry Miller, Marcel Proust, and Kathy Acker.

For instance, the parody of Plato and Socrates contained in Sections 11 and 12 owes an enormous debt to G.M.A. Grube's translations and introductions, published as *The Trial and Death of Socrates* (Indianapolis, Indiana: Hackett Publishing, 1975, 1986).

In section 4, "Summary Execution," several of these origin story parodies (subsets 1, 3, 8) were inspired in part by the wonderful *Technicians of the Sacred: A Range of Poetries from Africa, America, Asia, and Oceania*, Jerome Rothenberg, ed. (Doubleday, 1969).

In section 17, the subsection "Appendix *: Justification for breaking *The Circle* of Old Modernism" is structurally inspired by a satire from Istvan Csicsery-Ronay, Jr.s "Cyberpunk and Neuromanticism" in *Storming the Reality Studio: A Casebook of Cyberpunk and Postmodern Fiction*, Larry McCaffery, ed. (Durham: Duke U P, 1991), 184, quoted in Powell, Jim, *Postmodernism for Beginners*, (USA: Writers and Readers, 1998), 137.

MULTIFESTO: A HENRI D'MESCAN REMIX
Archival Documents

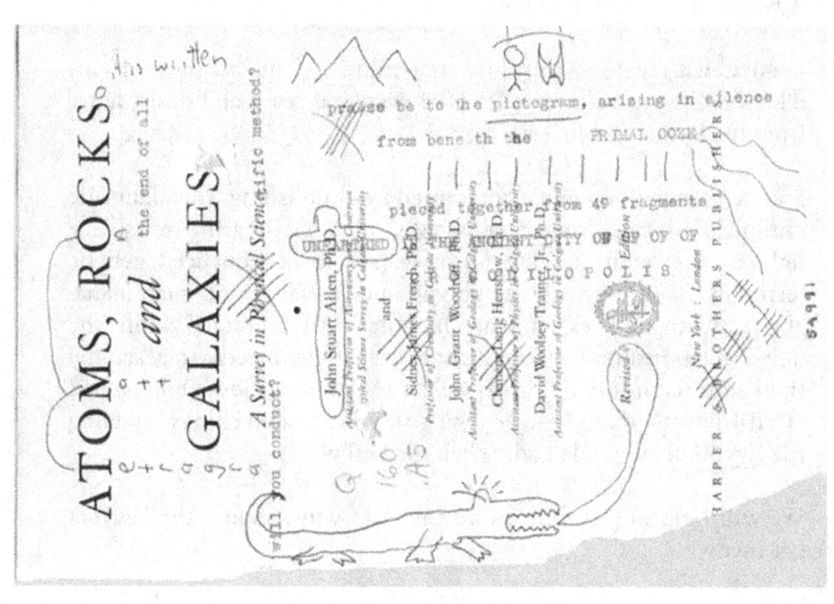

"Praise be to the pictorgram,
arising in silence from beneath the primal ooze..."
—Inscription pieced together from forty-nine pragments
unearthed in the ancient Egyption city of Shedi,
or Greek Crocodilopolis

Note: The fine-art, limited edition quickly sold out.

Publicity letter for Multifesto, 2005

Signed limited edition of *Multifesto: A Henri d'Mescan Reader*, edited by Davis Schneiderman and Phoenlia Yeer

Order deadline: Dec. 1, 2005
Advance limited edition: $50

Loaded with extras, this limited edition of the infamous Henri d'Mescan's work *will* move forward despite a cease and desist letter from his former publisher.

Spuyten Duyvil remains committed to publishing this fantastic chronicle of cats from outer space, monocle-wearing resistance fighters, enormous talking tortoises, and over-sequenced genetic terrorists told through a polyphonic mélange of marginalia, abstracts, appendices, and much more. All presented while the failed relationship between Schneiderman and Yeer—marked by their editorial introductions as well as their strange love child named "Dial-Up Networking"—reaches a gruesome textual climax invoking the Egyptian crocodile god, Sebek the Unholy.

We will hold out as long as we can. Get yours before the lawyers get involved!

***

Never heard of Henri d'Mescan? That's because he's a master at keeping secrets…

Infamous writer and theorist **Henri d'Mescan** emerged in pre-war Europe as a cultural critic, enjoying considerable acclaim until his June 1947 conviction by a French war crimes tribunal for the purported authorship of a set of collaborationist documents collectively known as "The Vichy Papers."

Escaping execution (his collaboration in question), d'Mescan disappeared from the world stage until the later 1950s, when the experimental writer Henry Mescaline was discovered—and the

1964 publication of *Hallucigenome: A Henry Mescaline Reader* cemented Mescaline's place in the nascent consciousness-expanding movements of the period.

Following the 1967 death of his primary patron, d'Mescan/Mescaline entered a period of intense seclusion to construct his legendary unfinished epic: *Post-America*, which is, as one critic notes, "heir to *Finnegan's Wake*, *Gravity's Rainbow*, and the *Tibetan Book of the Dead*."

The current edition, edited by theorist/fiction writer **Davis Schneiderman**, and academician **Phoenelia Yeer**, brings together pre-War d'Mescan prose, his Henry Mescaline prose, and for the first time, excerpts from the previously unavailable *Post-America*.
***

Because you appreciate quality literature and contemporary art here-and-now, Spuyten Duyvil is committed to providing our audience with uniquely printed, visually dynamic items outside the narrow confines of the retail world.

We feel strongly about the work that we bring to the public. You and your friends can help us out.

Simply follow this link to reserve your copy:

http://www.spuytenduyvil.net/orders/orderA.asp?dg=8

If you prefer to fax your order, please send to 800-866-5304 (x2).

Thanks for supporting Spuyten Duyvil events and publications. Without your advance support, our authors and artists would not be able to further their vision, inspiration and priceless labor, thus entering the culture *and* conversation at large. Help make this advance edition a success by forwarding this message to other interested parties.

Thanks!

Tod Thilleman
Publisher

Note: Cease and Desist letter received by Spuyten Duyvil in May 2005. The law firm has since threatened litigation, and has demanded that we publish no correspondence from this matter. Of course, they assume we do not know that letters are not subject to copyright.

Jolson, Farquar, & Leech

LAW OFFICES

1666 Avenue of the P-Americas • New York, NY

Re: *Multifesto: A Henri d'Mecan Reader* **and the flagrant Misuse of Atom Press, Inc.'s Copyrighted manuscripts.**

To Whom It Might Possibly Concern:

We are the multiple counsel to Atom Press, Inc. ("Atom"), the completely exclusive copyright holder and/or world licensee and/or owner and/or dispenser of all manuscripts composed in the period between 1958 and 1967 by one or several persons known as Henry Mescaline/Henri d'Mescan/David Schneiderman, originally collected, in part, in the Atom Press volume: *Hallucigenome: The Henry Mescaline Reader* (1964). We write concerning the proposed 2006 release by Spuyten Duyvil's of *Multifesto: A Henri d'Mescan Reader,* which contains large amounts of documented materials under our copyright protection. Additionally, the materials authored by "Henri d'Mescan" in two other periods: 1) 1932-1952 (European editions), and 2) 1971-present, may also be subject to Atom Press copyright protection.

If "Henry Mescaline" is proven to be a pseudonym for either the WWII refugee Henri d'Mescan, or the Atom Press editor David Schneiderman, then a 1964 clause by Henry Mescaline surrendering all copyrights to "Atom Press for all production now and forever in all forms, both print, recorded, and as yet to be invented" will enter into force for all portions of the manuscripts currently in your possession. Should this be the case, handwriting and DNA test results forthcoming, the only materials in the *Multifesto* manuscript not under our copyright would be the editorial introductions composed by editors named Davis Schneiderman ("Davis") and Phoenelia Yeer ("Yeer"). Yet, as Atom Press did not authorize their access to d'Mescan/Mescaline/David's papers, we will require the transfer of all copyrights associated with these editorial introductions to Atom Press.

As we expect independent verification of the DNA and handwriting tests within a reasonable period, Spuyten Duyvil should be duly informed that it is current violation of copyright provision regarding the section of *Multifesto* provisionally titled, "Part II: The Un-American Years / From: *Hallucigenome: The Henry Mescaline Reader* (1961)" with materials excerpted from the following Henry Mescaline texts: "Introduction" to *Hallucigenome: The Henry Mescaline Reader* (1964)," "*Spacecats of the World, Untie!* (1958)," "*Appendisectomy*—"Appendices on November 11, 1944: *The Circle*" (1960)," "*Tupeat, Frompeet, Repeit* (1962)," and "*Abecedarium*: "Fex During the Occupation of France (1963)," along with, possibly, the materials from the two other periods noted above.

Any attempt to deliver any section of the infringing manuscript to consumers represents a breach of Atom's intellectual property, as well as those of other artists and writers who in good faith transferred their copyrights to Atom. Because of the controversial materials that Atom published from 1957-1971 (at great risk to its presses and other modes of intellectual capital), in the United States, the Philippines, and a series of newly emancipated African republics, authors such as Henry Mescaline transferred their proprietary rights to their works to our company. In Mescaline's case, surveillance by the OSS and later, the CIA, necessitated that he renounce his rights to his work since, according to stature 247, subsection 48D of the 1949 War Repatriation and Seditions Act, as an illegal alien, war-criminal, and fugitive, d'Mescan/Mescaline would retain no rights to this work upon his prosecution, deportation, or capture.

We take the trust that Mr. Mescaline placed in our offices seriously, and this we will not hesitate to subject Spuyten Duyvil to serious legal penalties for knowing violation of copyright and intellectual property law. We thus stipulate that you immediately:

1. Surrender all pre-production manuscripts, notes, archival materials, correspondences, and all other written, printed, and electronically produced materials between and all of the following parties: Henri d'Mescan, Henry Mescaline, David Schneiderman, Davis Schneiderman, Phoenelia Yeer, Tod Thilleman, and all other parties who have corresponded with the above in any and

all mediums during the preparation, composition, and research phases of the *Multifesto* project. Additionally, all correspondence between Atom and Spuyten Duyvil, including this letter, should also be surrendered.

2. Cease and desist from any actual or intended distribution of any and all of the above, and/or the otherwise prohibited performance, publication, distributions, and/or exploitation of *Multifesto* and all other properties under protection by Atom.

3. Provide the contact information for any and all third parties who may have assisted in the pre-publication and research phases of the *Multifesto* project, as well as those consumers who have placed orders for advance copies of the book.

4. Provide notice to all publications that have recently published excerpts from the forthcoming text, including but not limited to: *In Our Own Words: A Generation Defining Itself* (anthology), *RealPoetik, Near South, 3 AM Magazine, The Diagram, Spread, Gargoyle, Unpleasant Event Schedule, Magazine Minima, Fiction International, to the QUICK, Collage, 3rd Bed, Absinthe Literary Review, Pindeldyboz.com, EnterText,* and *Happy.* These magazines, journals, and academic texts should be duly noted of the possible infringement on Spuyten Duyvil's part.

5. Renounce all claims to publicity and archival materials associated with this project, and surrender all source code from Spuyten Duyvil's web page to our offices.

Unless we receive comprehensive compliance with these stipulations, Atom will pursue all remedies allowable by law.

Sincerely,

Jolson, Farquar, & Leech

****

This letter is intended primarily for the specified recipient(s). It most likely contains consequential information and may or may not be subject to the corporate-legislative privilege and other ethereal protections. If you are not a designated recipient, an actual person, or an incorporated individual, then you may not possess the ability to read, print, or fold this message. If you receive this warning in error, please notify the sender, only if you are authorized to do so, in the presence of a notary, by reply e-mail and then erase the segment of your hard drive that contains this message and all adjacent messages. Do not, under any circumstances, print and then fold the message. Thank you for your compliance.

****

MULTIFESTO: A HENRI D'MESCAN REMIX
Critical Reception

Note: This review originally appeared in *American Book Review*. 28.4 (2007).

Touring Post-America
Leora Lev
Multifesto: A Henri d'Mescan Reader
Edited by Davis Schneiderman and Phoenelia Yeer
Spuyten Duyvil Press
http://www.spuytenduyvil.net
221 pages; paper, $50.00 (signed limited edition)

"The book transformed my brain into a 4-D Playstation pinball machine inscribed with hallucinatory and shifting topographies, whose aesthetico-cerebral-intellectual-neurological nodules are getting pinged by careening silver balls that trace, twirl, slam, and dream oracular patterns that hover in the air like fireworks while also enabling an exhilarating va et vient where you're played but also get to play."
—Neurotrancer, cyborg mutant lovechild of William Gibson, William S. Burroughs, and Jean Baudrillard

"Possession for the Post-Human Set."
—Cordelia Victriola, illegitimate daughter of Jasper Forde's Special Operative Thursday Next and Landen Parke-Lane

"Dude, before reading *Multifesto* I'd only heard of Sebek, the Crocodile god, in that Buffy episode, you know the one, Season Five, where Dawn's, like the key? And Gloria turns out to be a god and...well, this Schneiderman dude's got it going with Sebek, and differential time-space continuums, and destabilizing of ontoepistemological certainties. It totally blasts *Matrix* out of the water. Oh, oops..."
—Keanu Reeves, on the set of *Matrix 4: Frontloaded*

These are *not* amongst the apocryphal blurbs preceding Davis Schneiderman's astonishing, and, if it doesn't sound too old-fashioned, beautiful text, but they might be. *Multifesto: A Henri d'Mescan Reader* is a fever dream road trip conjured by the Pet Shop Boys of postmodernism, Gilles Deleuze and Félix Guattari; and James Joyce, William S. Burroughs, Vladimir Nabokov, Kathy Acker, Genesis P-Orridge and Lady Jayne, fertilized by Sebek the Crocodile Deity, scented with the pungent bouquet of lilies, absinthe, and peyote incense. It becomes, or mimes, at various moments, text, tract, treatise, parchment, film, artifact, relic, genetic code, Derridean gloss and computer code; it's startlingly exciting work. Indeed, traversing its pages feels like what consuming bushels of mescaline might be like (were one so intrepid), although the Möbius strip contours, perambulations, detours, vital bits perceptible even sous rature, and errant errors all mask missile-level precision, reproducing, but also departing from, any accidental structural disorder, ghost in the machine, drug-induced or otherwise.

A central question that erupts with schizoid jouissance throughout the rhizome of this text concerns "collaboration." One of the shifting pairs, doppelgängers, and antagonist-protagonist dyads that fight, merge, annihilate and/or resurrect each other within the volume is the co-editor duo Phoenelia Yeer and Davis Schneiderman. Like any good academics, the two are studiously preparing an anthology of pre-WWII writings by one Henri d'Mescan. However, from the beginning, historico-literary mysteries cavort in vertiginous mise en abîme that Roland Barthes would surely have designated as the purest writerly jouissance. Both inter- and meta-textually, ontoepistemological undecidabilities abound. D'Mescan might be, or not be, the American Beat-esque writer Henry Mescaline, a self-rehabilitated persona meant to cover up d'Mescan's Nazi collaboration via the "Vichy Papers," a complicity that itself may or may not have been fabricated by collaborationists conspiring against him, and whose novel *Outsourcing* may or may not have "corroborated" his innocence. And from the onset, Schneiderman judges that Yeer has been "poisoned from years of graduate school into a relentless zombie, sprouting Jacques Derrida, Michel Foucault, Jean Baudrillard (she suffered from theoretical Tourette's), from cadres of self-important professors trumpeting the useless gangrene of indeterminacy." Schneiderman eschews both Yeer's poststructuralist "faith in nothing" as "still faith," a misguidedly conceptualized antidote to the fascist ideological rigidities issuing in the infamous logo emblazoning Auschwitz's gates, "Arbeit macht frei" [work will set you free], and her eventual capitulation to the belief that d'Mescan was indeed a collaborator. Nonetheless, the co-editors cum ex-lovers haunt, hate, love, obsess, fetishize, and interpenetrate each other throughout the text.

Added to the mix, or stew, is the deceased David Schneiderman, the maverick scholar and "literary huckster" who'd edited *Hallucigenome: The Henry Mescaline Reader*, in 1964, and whose near eponymity with his younger scholarly forebear Davis is undercut in a running gag; and the misbegotten offspring of Yeer and Schneiderman's collaboration, "one of

Davis's rotten sperm successfully infiltrating the system," a replication of the code, metastasizing of the cell, called Dial-Up Networking.

Collaboration. Editing. Disinter. Resistance. Authority, authorial, author. That a word, a term, a text can mean opposite things at the same time, or mean something ambiguously or polyvalently, and that this has repercussions and consequences for how we interpret and "read" texts, be these literary, political, artistic, cultural, historical, architectural, cyberspatial, sartorial, corporeal, or otherwise, is itself both the signal legacy of poststructuralism and an unheimlich space of openness to misunderstanding, défiguration, distortion, mishandling, torture. When does collaboration constitute a fruitful scholarly/genetic production, and when is it collusion with evil? How far can a text/history/code/body/theory be examined, subjected to interrogation, to querying, before it splinters into meaningless or abject parts? Where is the fault line, pressure point, tipping point, where promptings, proddings, questionings proffer not knowledge but destruction? When does editing become editorializing, the fervor of academia merely academic as viruses infiltrate bio-economic systems, blood groups, gene pools, computers, water supplies, as history and future infect each other via falsifying, "official" double-speak, documentaries of indoctrination?

Davis Schneiderman's introduction to d'Mescan's "Fex During the Occupation of France (1963)" asserts that a 1960 federal investigation "confirmed the hypothesis that the man executed in Paris at the close of the 'Identity Trial' in 1947 was not Henri d'Mescan, but rather, the imposter who both composed 'The Vichy Papers' and became the recipient of the death sentence—thus precipitating the work of Henry Mescaline; or in an unlikely scenario that Yeer briefly entertained (out of spite), that the Henri d'Mescan traced by the government was not the original, but perhaps the imposter." Twelve Ghosts of the Paul de Man scandal cluster here (amongst certain graduate student circles of the 1980s, the deconstructionist revealed to have written for Nazi-run newspapers such as the collaborationist Belgian *Le Soir* was smirkingly nomered Paul der Mann); when do the complicating queries of deconstructionism overshoot themselves to breed obfuscation that covers up complicity, collusion, collaboration? And how is identity imbricated within these questions, the narratives we make (up) about ourselves, with the help of our others, our culture(s), our nation(s)? Destabilized pronouns, apostrophaic slippages (the possessive and plural constantly morph into each other, as in "Americas guilded age," broaching the question of ownership vs. replication), and recombinations of individuals, dyads and triads further undercut the idea of clear-cut, impermeable "identity."

Burroughsian cut-ups and word viruses and their cyberkinetic descendants, Deleuzian drifts of nodular desire, caffeinated Joycean consciousness tributaries, surrealist exquisite corpses, experimental typographies, Lévi-Straussian and Genettian linguistico-onto-phylogenetic codes, and creation myth deities such as the Crocodile god Sebek are all invoked, spliced, diced, hybridized, carnivalized, and reconfigured as ciphers for Post-America, its histories, presents, and futures. These Ur-avant-garde collages, strategies, and images are uncannily fused with the apparatus of scholarly archival work: appendices, footnotes, journal reprints, photographic stills, authorial ephemera. Playing such ludic repertoires of radical word experimentation against their sterner scholarly brethren allows Davis to highlight their unexpected consonances and insterstitial liaisons: the places where cut-ups can reveal odd truths, and scholarship can be a petri dish for viral misinformation. Or, put another way, the melting point where intellect and desire leave aside their difference, toke up, tune out, and commingle in psychedelic jouissance.

This is a stunningly original work deserving of careful, and multiple, readings by anybody interested in where American literature is headed. Inviting the reader into territory that would be inhospitable in lesser hands, *Multifesto* soars with electrifying lyricism, the improbable poetry of ideas that cut with diamantine precision while also managing to lay bare what it means to be human even in the most in- or post-human of landscapes.

Leora Lev is editor of and contributor to the volume *Enter at Your Own Risk: The Dangerous Art of Dennis Cooper* (Fairleigh Dickinson University Press, 2006), which contains works by John Waters, Michael Cunningham, William S. Burroughs, and others. She is a professor professor of foreign languages and gender studies at Bridgewater State College.

PULL QUOTE: Multifesto *highlights the places where cut-ups can reveal odd truths, and scholarship can be a petri dish for viral misinformation.*

Note: This review originally appeared in the *Journal of Post-Eponymous Studies* 45.3 (2007): 16-27.

"In the pleat of fashionable trousers": Some Interstices in Davis Schneiderman and Phoenelia Yeer's *Multifesto:* A Henri d'Mescan Remix

Few experiences in life compare to nestling amongst floor pillows in a poorly lit room and cradling a copy (I hesitate to say "book" for, truly, in today's age of multifarious media, one cannot assume it will be physical) of Davis Schneiderman and Phoenelia Yeer's *Multifesto*: A Henri d'Mescan Remix. If one believed that heathen gods manifest their philosophies in abstract paintings, then no doubt *Multifesto* would constitute the quintessential portrait of profane spiritual possession, the quagmire of continental recriminations in the apocalyptic circle. Throughout the collection of misplaced files, slips-o'-the tongue, and a varied assortment of splattering noises, Schneiderman and Yeer raise uncomfortable questions regarding d'Mescan's frolicsome sphere of literary draperies. Replete with scholarly insights into d'Mescan's imaginary necropolis and idiosyncratic theories of calligraphy, *Multifesto* truly waddles atop the desiccated carpet of traditional textbook readers to conceive a wiry child that knowingly deserts chronology: amid the barely subjugated creational fire and poised betwixt time, the lost reader juggles with the madness of the crocodile. And, yet, with all the brouhaha surrounding the re-publication of *Multifesto*, it is easy to forget that Schneiderman and Yeer are not the last, nor the first, to take note of the fragile ligaments connecting d'Mescan's scattered herd of bones, not only within his own work but also in relation to other authors. Digging underneath the somewhat dusty ground of postmodern theory in his *"Losto, Caradhras!"*: The Lord of the Rings *and the Problem of Translation*, Bryn Dewey attempted (albeit unsuccessfully) to link d'Mescan's ubiquitous Tacg with Saruman the White. In one of his most memorable passages, Dewey writes "the similarities between Tacg and Saruman are non-existent as they are overdeveloped. No two characters are so emblazoned with infected phantasmagoria. At the same time, no two characters are more blithely unaware [perhaps nonchalantly aware?], each in their own way, of the overlapping skeletons that surround and direct their every movement" (3345). In other books, Dewey approached the comparison from different perspectives: penchant for crocodiles, penchant for disproportionate facial hair, penchant for abstract constructions of time, penchant for death by pandas. Dewey, repeatedly thwarted, dedicated most of his later work to proving what he would call "my theory on the elusiveness of textual relativity." His rather incoherent undertaking, which some have called (anti)prophetic, articulates the underlying difficulties of attempts to establish a steadfast intertextuality between d'Mescan and others—an almost-circular task, as one may imagine. Few have tried since, and even fewer have enjoyed it. In a virulent analysis from the half-feathered quill of Dominique-Cécile Desmarais, d'Mescan's Crocodilopolis becomes a place where the most surreptitiously dehumanizing acts of literature take place. In her "Ethnolinguistics and Postmodernity" lecture, she attacks what she terms "d'Mescan's sedated amalgamation of archetypal old world plagiarism of the primitive… [his] patriotic, colonial psychobabble" (1). As d'Mescan's harshest critic, Desmarais and her venomous prose gained popularity when one of d'Mescan's alter egos was arrested for calling a police officer "my woeful siren, my jaundiced Amazon." Desmarais' response was quick. In the same lecture, she proclaimed "writers like d'Mescan are the fabricated denouement of lunacy in a post-irony-inspired divan of language. His implementation of post-american arrangements coupled with epiphanic vehemence show the putrefaction of a westernized narrative. Scented tentacles? Spelunking fish? Crocodiles in loincloths? Goat-killing donkeys round a pyre? Reptile symbols? Scarabs? I spit at the retrograde colony he calls 'Crocodilopolis'" (1). Inaccessible as Desmarais' language proved to many, she nonetheless enjoyed the company of a cult-like coterie. Indeed, one of the students who attended the lecture was claimed to have said, "Sweaty dewdrops of tea ran down my face as I listened. She exuded such an atmosphere; you know, like, cleanliness and preternatural wisdom." Desmarais' criticism gave way to widespread fragmentation in the academic community: after that lecture, some began to believe she was the incarnation of the vengeful Sebek while others argued that she was merely one of d'Mescan's unraveling alter egos. Aimée Lautremont, author of the oft-cited *The Author is Dead: A Practical Guide to Posthumography*, was part of the second group. In an obscure article titled, "The Author is Dead, but d'Mescan is Not," she argued that, in accordance with alchemical principles, the d'Mescan/Desmarais composite was not only possible, but palpable. She wrote, "we must think of the d'Mescan/Desmarais case as a kind of winterized Moses, refrigerated between time in an eternal circle of mummified birthing" (6). Even after several physicians proved that Lautremont was mentally unstable and possibly under the effects of highly hallucinogenic margarine, her theory was still widely discussed in academic circles. As to the group who believed Desmarais to be the incarnation of Sebek, most sold their possessions to purchase tickets to Egypt, where they hoped to re-awaken devotion to the infamous crocodile god. The most documented case was that of Adelheid Y. Bäcker, who traded his commodities for a steamboat, a saxophone, and an illegitimate replica of the Rosetta Stone. Armed with what he would call his "Triad of Awakening," he set out to build a sustainable stilt village on the Nile riverbed. To all intents and purposes, Bäcker was quite successful. However, after three years of successful conversion of nonbelievers and the much-celebrated completion of a public bathroom, the village collapsed into the river and crocodiles soon consumed its inhabitants. All but three were killed, and the survivors (excepting Bäcker) physically transformed: research photographs showed their scars quintuplicate weekly until their bodies were almost covered in lacerations. From the incisions sprung ashes and a milky substance that would fill the hospital room, drowning all who were present. As to Bäcker, his own laws condemned him to death: he was mummified, beheaded with an imported guillotine and subsequently fed to neighbouring pandas. Needless to say, Bäcker's tale provided other Sebek followers with enough reason to re-enter the realm of nonbelievers and, thus, begin the process of repatriation to the uterus of scholarly research. In reviewing such revolutions in interpretation of d'Mescan, once cannot help but feel that a certain smog cloud materializes, a leviathan travelling incognito whose purpose is to create the illusion of a rainstorm, a water lily, an eternal tree of ontology that bears no recognizable fruit. One cannot help but feel that Schneiderman and Yeer's struggle is that of Dewey, Desmarais, Lautremont, and Bäcker's. One cannot help but feel that their struggle is also the reader's, who seeks the buried, nay, mummified, ligaments binding d'Mescan's work. Like expert boobytrappers, Schneiderman and Yeer shield the sacrosanct from unwanted eyes. And, yet. And, yet, in the twinkling of an I, the leviathan reveals it—the eye.

Irene Ruiz Dacal has written and illustrated many stories, most of which you have probably never read. After completing five years of rigorous scholarly training that took her across four national borders, she has received her B.A. in English and is ready to reside permanently in the interstices of reality and fiction. Her work can be found online in *Rhizomes* magazine, in *The Official Catalog of the Library of Potential Literature* (Cow Heavy Books, 2011) and in the text you are about to read, have just read, or had seriously considered reading until you found out she was one of the contributors.

Works Cited:

Bäcker, Adelheid Y. *Vellum, Vernacular: Overlooked Elements of Gutenberg's Press*. New York: Venetian Chandelier Press, 1996.

Desmarais, Dominique-Cécile. "Ethnolinguistics and Postmodernity." *The Cambridge Lectures*. Cambridge: This or That Press, 2000. 50-79.

Dewey, Bryn. "*Losto, Caradhras!*": The Lord of the Rings *and the Problem of Translation*." Caracas: La Press, 2001.

Lautremont, Aimée. *The Author is Dead: A Practical Guide to Posthumography*. Los Angeles: Dead Poets' Sobriety Press, 1999.

edited by

DAVIS SCHNEIDERMAN and PHOENELIA YEER

Remixed by

James Tadd Adcox
Matt Bell
Molly Gaudry
Roxane Gay
Lily Hoang
Matt Kirkpatrick
Alissa Nutting
Kathleen Rooney
Ben Tanzer

Introduction/s by Craig Saper and
Afterword by William Walsh

SPUYTEN DUYVIL
NEW YORK CITY

Table of Contents

Pre-face to the remix edition, 2012:
MULTIFESTO: A HENRI D'MESCAN *Remix*

by Phonelia Yeer

([127.0.0.1]) with mapi; Tue, 3 Jan 2012 14:30:32 -0600
From: "For Nearly a Yeer" <fornearlyayeer@gmail.com>
To: "Schneiderman, Davis" <dschneid@lakeforest.edu>
Content-Class: urn:content-classes:message
Date: Tue, 3 Jan 2012 14:30:29 -0600
Subject: your so-called remix edition
Thread-Topic: your so-called remix edition
Accept-Language: en-US
Content-Type: multipart/alternative;
            boundary="_000_CB28C1854DDF5dschneidlakeforestedu_"
MIME-Version: 1.0

Dearest..Davis..(I use both terms sarcastically),

Lest you think I have forgotten and in any way felt even the smallest dimin=
ishment of my hatred for you..hatred motivated by the obscenity of your per=
son..your hygiene..your bad manners..your chronic abuse of the feelings of =
your love ones..and the complete neglect you show toward out child Dial-Up =
Networking, now, a quasi-terrorist..

Lest you think I am impressed that this new edition of the text we at one p=
oint labored so assiduously upon has now become a remix with some of the be=
st..most talented writers of the internet generation..then you have forgott=
en everything I ever taught you..either philosophically..sexually..or other=
wise..

Lest you think getting a big-shot new media critic like Craig Saper to writ=
e your introductions would lessen even by the tiniest quintessence of half-=
life my complete..and utter..rejection of everything you stand for..sit for=
..fuck for..then you are even more brazen in your imperious phallogocentris=
m..than even I could imagine at the nadir of our old life togther..

Lest you think at all you hoary old ass-ball..you shriveled dick-on-wheels.=
.you gleaking, beef-witted incubus..think about this..

..this book begins on the inside of your body..and ends on the edge of the =
universe..the remix..always present from the very beginning..is just the bu=
llshit in between..

..eat shit..never contact me again.

Phoenelia Yeer

Content-Type: text/html; charset="us-ascii"
Content-Transfer-Encoding: quoted-printable

<html><head>
<meta name=3D"Title" content=3D"">
<meta name=3D"Keywords" content=3D"">
<meta http-equiv=3D"Content-Type" content=3D"text/html; charset=3Dutf-8">
<meta name=3D"ProgId" content=3D"Word.Document">
<meta name=3D"Generator" content=3D"Microsoft Word 14">
<meta name=3D"Originator" content=3D"Microsoft Word 14">

351

Radiant Riffs: ~~Literature~~ after ReMix

by Craig Saper

In *Radiant Textuality: Literature after the World Wide Web*, Jerome McGann alludes to the inevitable impact of the *Multifesto* remix, that "[i]f certain features of the new information technologies have overtaken us—for instance, the recent and massive turn to word processing—more advanced developments generate suspicion" [McGann 2001, 53]. Accordingly, Peter Stayllybrass writes, in a special issue of *PMLA* on databases in the humanities, unintentionally about the editorial conflict in *Multifesto* and how it might play out in this newly remixed volume. He explains that if the "database has been an incitement to the use of archive, it has changed our relation to the ownership of knowledge. One of the most radical aspects of database is its power to separate knowledge from academic pres¬tige and from its attendant regime of intel¬lectual property. Scholarship, as traditionally conceived, has maintained its prestige partly through its privileged relation to the protec¬tion and retrieval of scarce resources. Now, however, millions of people who cannot or do not want to go to the archives are accessing them in digital form. In addition, digital information has profoundly undermined an academic elite's control over the circulation of knowledge" [Stallybrass 2007, 1581].

Thus, the underlying theme of the *Multifesto* collection and this remix is (aside from its experimental—some might even say novel or fictional—approach) offers a challenge to "control over the circulation of knowledge" by allowing for polyvocal authorial/editorial/annotating voices (opposing a singular legitimized "academic elite's" pronouncements). In that sense, Stayllabrass argues that a case like *Multifesto* and its remix "will also reveal the extent to which the gatekeepers are themselves trespassers who do, perhaps unconsciously" what the editors/authors/imposters/remixers in *Multifesto*, the first (2006), and in this remixed volume did "deliberately and shamelessly in the construction" of these volumes. These writers "appropriated" for their own use what they read or heard [Stallybrass 2007, 1581]. Stallybrass cites Mary Carruthers, who argues that "having "inventory" is a requirement for "invention." Not only does this statement assume that one cannot create ("invent") without a memory store ("inventory") to invent from and with, but it also assumes that one's memory-store is effectively "inventoried," that its matters are in readily-recovered "locations."" [Carruthers 1998, 12 as quoted in Stallybrass 2007, 1582].

The scholastic tradition teaches students to organize "one's reading as a database. In this [scholastic] pedagogy, reading is a technology of inventorying information to make it reusable" [Carruthers 1998, 12 as quoted in Stallybrass 2007, 1582]. Thus, this remix volume is a "reading" in that inventory-invention tradition—a reading of an editographic experiment.

Put another way, in *Radiant Textuality* Jerome McGann argues that "the general field of humanities education and scholarship will not take the use of digital technology seriously until one demonstrates how its tools improve the ways we explore and explain aesthetic works— until, that is, they expand our interpretational procedures" [McGann 2001, xii]. The expansion of interpretational procedures to include editography allows for students to conceive ideas "all at once" in the editorial disputes and remixes of the *Multifesto* volumes rather than only "relying on step-by-step sequential processes that auditory learning styles favor" [McGann 2001, 106]. McGann asserts that the inclusion of both processes advances comprehensive learning. McGann calls for a move "beyond conceptual analysis into the kinds of knowledge involved in performative operations—a practice of everyday imaginative life" [McGann 2001, 106]. We can thus theorize that remix and editography writing are indeed those performative practices.

Writing as if editing suggests that "[Texts] are not containers of meaning or data, but sets of rules (algorithms) for generating themselves: for discovering, organizing, and utilizing meanings and data," [McGann 2001, 138]. And, in doing so, McGann suggests that one could use something like editography and remix to not just present a direct and transparent representation of a text, but to move those texts through a set of algorithms. In doing so, one would discover aspects of reading/editing usually effaced by the demands of literacy and representation.

Perhaps this volume should have included dotted lines where the reader could then cut-and-paste passages, creating meanings through editing and editorial conflicts, and perhaps one of the Davis Schneidermans has written the first novel of, and about, editing a critical edition. In that sense, it is a heuretic approach that becomes the major issues confronting editorial theory. How are texts invented? Further, Schneiderman and the collective authors in this volume have produced a remarkable and startlingly brilliant sociopoetic work about editors' use of the inventories of collected works, the margins of an oeuvre, and the key aspects of literary scholarship. The sociopoetic project here and in *Multifesto*, the first (2006), illuminate how writers regularly perform, manipulate, and score the social situation we call editing. These social situations function in these volumes not as external and extraneous contexts, but as the form/content of these works. The term sociopoetic describes the use of social situations, like editing or remixing, as a canvas. What we regularly consider impersonal, objective, and detached, these volumes structure as an "intimate bureaucracy" that seeks "to project intimacy onto otherwise impersonal systems" (Saper, 2001, 24; and Saper as dj readies, 2012, 6).

The achievement of Schneiderman(s) and these collective authors goes way beyond an experimental novel to suggest a new understanding of editing, collected editions, annotating, and literary biography to allow for disputes among multiple voices, poetic digressions, and the intimate personal relationships in making almost always invisible editorial decisions. **These volumes then represent the first melodrama of editing and, by extension, an archaeology of the multivocal intimacies of scholarship.** The later aspect of the project foregrounds the art (performance and pratice) of the distribution of literary works—it is a novel genre of the art of distribution as the focus of the work rather than its effaced apparatus. In that sense, these many writers and editors and remixers move away from thinking of "creative writing" as a result of a quaint artisanal production method that places the arts in a feudal order propping up the mythology of the transcendent creative individual producing works outside the social and material systems of modern editorial production. Appreciating those goals makes these volumes necessary and essential reading for editors and readers alike, who will marvel at the comedy and machinations involved in the drama of editing.

Craig Saper (csaper@umbc.edu) is on the faculty of the Language, Literacy, & Culture multi-disciplinary doctoral program at UMBC (University of Maryland Baltimore County). He is the author of *Intimate Bureaucracies* (2012), *Networked Art* (2001) and *Artificial Mythologies* (1997). He has edited, and written afterwards for, Bob Brown's *Words* (2010) and *The Readies* (2009), and he co-edited an anthology on *Imaging Place* (2009). He has guest edited special issues of *Visible Language* (1988) and *Style* (2001), and co-edited two special issues of *Rhizomes* on "Drifts" (2007), and on "posthumography" (2010). He wrote the introduction to Sharon Kivland's *A Disturbance of Memory*, II (2008). His curatorial projects include exhibits on "Assemblings" (1997), "Noigandres: Concrete Poetry in Brazil" (1988), "TypeBound" (2008), and folkvine.org (2003-6). He has published two artists' books *On Being Read* (published/designed by Diane Fine, 1985) and *Raw Material* (2008), and he is presently writing a biography of a poet-publisher-impresario-writer in every imaginable genre, Bob Brown. More on Brown: http://www.readies.org

Works Cited:

McGann, Jerome. "Database, Interface, and Archival Fever," Publication of the Modern Language Association (PMLA), 2007, part of a section on "the changing profession: Responses to Ed Folsom's "Database as Genre: The Epic Transformation of Archives" 122, 5 (2007): 1588-1591.

Stallybrass, Peter. "Against Thinking," Publication of the Modern Language Association (PMLA), part of a section on "the changing profession: Responses to Ed Folsom's "Database as Genre: The Epic Transformation of Archives" 122, 5 (2007): 1580-1587.

Saper, C. Networked Art. Minneapolis: University of Minnesota Press, 2001.

Saper, C. as dj readies. Intimate Bureaucracies. New York: Punctum Books, 2012.

Multifesto: A Henri d'Mescan ReMix
Part I: The Pre-American Years

FROM *SUMMARY EXECUTION* (1932)
BY ALISSA NUTTING

Bio: Alissa Nutting is author of the short story collection *Unclean Jobs for Women and Girls* (Starcherone/Dzanc 2010). Her work can be found in journals such as *Tin House*, *BOMB*, *Fence*, and other anthologies, and will appear in the Norton Introduction to Literature (2013). She is currently an assistant professor of creative writing at John Carroll University.

About: Nothing is so disorienting, or so freeing, as an understanding that you are playing inside of a ball pit where the normal physics of truth, origin, authenticity, and corroboration do not apply. I enjoyed the way that I became increasingly deceptive and suspicious within my own addition to the book as I worked on this project. It is probably the closest I will ever get to feeling the invincible euphoria of a spy.

From *Summary Execution* (1932)
by Alissa Nutting

4) Henri d'Mescan *[Deepening the mystery: In February of 2009, a Los Angeles laboratory specializing in DNA testing received an anonymous manila envelope. Inside rested a 1967 North American Shortwave Association (NASWA) membership certificate; the line bearing the member's name initially appeared to be blank, but a battery of tests by a curious technician soon found the name "Mescan Messiah" scrawled across the certificate in an invisible ink of sorts: it had been artfully written in porcine semen using a calligraphy brush.]*

From *Summary Execution* (1932)

[Further insight into d'Mescan's lactose-filled tale of corporal punishment circa 1913: d'Mescan's father was a steaming enthusiast of American colonial history. Indeed, his obsession with this particular time period and culture is thought to have inspired the (arguably most famous) still-shot photograph of d'Mescan from childhood referred to by scholars as "Les Culottes et la Bible"; the image shows the legs and feet of Henri (dressed in breeches), as well as his tiny hands and arms, which are struggling to hold an oversized version of the holy book. The tome's massive width fully occludes Henri's face and upper torso.

Henri's father adapted for the d'Mescan house rules a particularly conservative tract of New-Haven law from 1655 that declared masturbation (in addition to all acts of "Sodomidicall filthinesse") to be punishable by death.

Dr. Ann Semechi, who initially evaluated Henry Mescaline after his DNC arrest in Chicago and served as the detainment facility's head psychologist, is adamant that Mescaline is the author of all earlier works published by Henri d'Mescan. She found Summary Execution to be a subconscious expression of Henri's suicidal will, an urge she attributed to paternally imposed guilt complexes from both father and fatherland. Her behavioral profile of Henri mentions Summary Execution to state, "The subtitle Papa Kill Me Now for I Seem to be Having Fun glows in the dark off every page of this text." Semechi felt her attempts at MDMA therapy with Henri further underscored this hypothesis; after the initial session, d'Mescan would agree to participate only if Semechi provided him with a turtleneck whose fabric 60% nylon. Henri had a skin allergy to the synthetic polymer, which manifested through rampant hives—these mitigated the pleasurable feelings from the MDMA down to what d'Mescan felt was an appropriate degree of comfort.]

Setting: Myth of the lilies. *[The Association of Medieval Mescan Scholarship views d'Mescan's writings as modernist translations of feudal and religious power structures in the Middle Ages. At the last Mescan Renaissance convention, the Association's quadrennial academic symposium held in the Comfort Inn outside Future Missouri Regional Airport, a panel of five presenters argued d'Mescan's* Summary Execution *to be Henri's interpretation of "The Pistil of Swete Susan," a fourteenth-century poetic metrical paraphrase of the biblical story of Susanna.*

Susanna's tale is a Roman Catholic and Eastern Orthodox addition to the Old Testament's Book of Daniel about a beautiful married woman who goes into her private garden to bathe. Two elder men who have long lusted after her see her alone there and pounce upon the opportunity: they approach her and state that if she doesn't have sex with them, they'll say they saw her having an affair, a crime for which she will be killed (execution was also the crime for transgressing this edict of Moses in colonial New-Haven's Lawes for Government, the very document d'Mescan's father used to inform his own patriarchal rule). But Susanna refuses, and God rewards her by sending the prophet Daniel to prove the elders are lying.

The "pistil" in this fourteenth-century title is that of "epistle," a story. But the symposium panel was quick to point out the linguistic carbon copies in play: the shared spellings and etymologies of pistle (writing), pistol (gun), pistil (female reproductive flower-parts), pestle (club-shaped instrument used to pound or grind). Within these word families, we find the Venn diagram intersections of sex, violence, and creation that comprise the major themes of Summary Execution.

The name Susan or Susanna itself means lily; "this poem is about dirty old men trying to get into Lily's flower-vagina," a medieval feminist on the panel stood and proclaimed. She used a PowerPoint presentation of Georgia O'Keefe artwork, along with a clip of Comedy Central Daily Show *comedian Rob Corddry exclaiming, "Man I would love to (bleep) one of those paintings!", which garnered laughs from everyone in the room except a young male adjunct who had brought a donut from the hotel's continental breakfast to the panel and suddenly panicked that the entire room, in its newfound heightened awareness of abstract vaginal imagery, was about to turn to him and point as he ate.*

Her PowerPoint went on to compare lines of the fourteenth-century poem with details in Summary Execution: both narratives take place on a hill, amidst a proliferation of lilies in lily-scented air; in the poem, descriptions of the orderly, sculpted garden and orchard Susan's husband owns are rife with blossoming petals and ripe fruits—Susan can walk chaste amongst the lusts of nature, but the perverse elders cannot. They are prisoners of their own desires, and they aim to use their power and influence to pluck whatever spoils they wish—they are simple beasts, silt-covered shit-sniffers, while Susan bathes, stays "lilie whit," white as a town's milk supply, pure in a way that d'Mescan feels compelled to rewrite and corrupt.

But there are other theories in the room. Was d'Mescan attracted to the poem because he saw it as a metaphor for Nazi imperialism, one attendee asks? We will march into your garden and pollinate your flowers with our own seed? Or if d'Mescan was a Nazi sympathizer instead of a critic, suggests another, Henri may have seen Susan as undiluted Mother Germany and the elders as Jews who wish to taint her perfection. Discussion ensues.]

A man and a woman are not looking for justice—they are looking for lilies. **Beautiful lilies, fragrant flowers.** Two lovers poised in silhouettes **on a lonesome hill** and people threading through the knot of each other to look also for lilies. The secular sprawl of classical arches and columns, **interlocking and trembling hand-forms** beneath the garret-laboratory that doubles as **a prison house. Their heads become overwhelmed looking for lilies. These objects and images provide a mannered contrast to their forbidden, sublimated passions. Rinsing the lilies in the liquid** beneath the window lattice of the Italian manor **bleating its pastoral rhythm** against hand-carved oak and mud. Slicing themselves from their skins after **the river silt has covered** them, while **the simple beasts of the field,** goat and lamb and foal alike, become lulled by the pan flute into drowsy docility, **wallowing their sun-browned noses into the shunts of each other's sparkling shit holes.** Then floating, away from the lily place, off into the perfumed ether.

Form: Organization of a body. *[At the 2010 Kanamara Matsuri ("Festival of the Steel Phallus") in Kawasaki, Japan, a masturbatory performance artist calling himself Samurai Splooge used lines and phrases from Summary Execution throughout his piece. For one hour, he masturbated to orgasm every ten minutes, ejaculating on the ground in front of a live audience while the projected words of d'Mescan flashed across the wall behind him. Each time he came, 1/6th of a piece of a mannequin dressed exactly like Samurai Splooge was brought out and placed on top of the (increasingly meager) recent puddle until at the end of the hour, with the last ejaculation, a full-size mannequin wearing*

Samurai Splooge's mask and costume rested on the floor. (Aside from not being real, there were only two differences between the mannequin and Samurai Splooge: the mannequin's facemask had a drawn-on mustache, and the flesh of its manufactured penis was a disturbing neon blue.) Samurai Splooge then knelt down in front of the mannequin's penis and bowed his head. All was quiet until the penis shot up and began to spurt blueberry yogurt all over Samurai's face and chest. He ripped open his shirt to receive the load on his bare skin.]

The devil collects the balls of corrugated yarn passing across the courtroom floor. **What new and different body emerges from the contours of this alchemical cord?** Unravel the strands of your younger life and review the detritus of learning: memories of suckling in **a primordial marsh** of phytoplankton and lush Indonesian calla lilies (as a marker of consciousness), a statuette of the Emperor cleansed more often than the most elevated toilet (as boundaries form), animals prancing inside the Zoological gardens and the sideward glance **falling breastward on a passing girl** (as hideous limbs buzz your biplane hair), the discount barkers along "Scandal Avenue" with their tight-panted shills "winning" three-card Monte in the summer haze (as breath fills up even your secret holes), a wedding beside the crematoria, the power plant, the **lashes of foam marking the rocks** beneath the lighthouse (as the first circles of blood navigate the new interior), your feet compelled to scuffle certain spots in the dirt **for a bountiful harvest (as the will to reproduce),** the knave of a back-alley dumpster confessional (as **something rises from the refuse**)…it's all a narrative line to save your soul, **a way of jumping** (as waylaid by an order of meaning), a different body laying dormant, constructed in pieces by the meaning of your memories, **ready to burst to the surface and smother your world** in its defiant thievery.

Plot: The sun moves away and creates the water lilies. *[A reel of black and white film from 1962 surfaced at a Buffalo, NY estate sale in the early 90s; although the man on the film and the unseen interviewer have yet to be identified (the once-hyped theory that the person speaking is d'Mescan himself wearing a prosthetic nose has been sufficiently discredited), the recorded man frequently states that he and d'Mescan are "good friends" and offers the following commentary on d'Mescan's philosophical viewpoint: "He's like the lovechild of Arthur Schopenhauer and Ruth Westheimer. Obsessed with sex like Ruth but pessimistic as hell like Arthur. He thinks of sex as fertilizer. I'm serious. We were at a cocktail party once—drinks were flying, I'm not sure of the exact words—but he says something like,* sex is the manure of humanity's garden. *To a woman. Who had been flirting with him. Not so much after that. Henri, I said. Is that your idea of a pick-up line? He shrugged then told me about how once he jerked off into a glass of warm saltwater:* I thought something might happen. That it would grow or drops of it would move around in the glass as though animated. Like sea monkeys. *Then he drained his drink and shrugged and left the party. The next morning I called him and tried to get him to join a bowling league. Trust me, I told him. You need a new hobby. He coughed and hung up the phone.]*

At the last beginning everything was bathing in a perpetual boiling soup: flame withheld the world from the crusts of moss and bark.

And **Amoeba, the first sentient creature, was stuck** in the fiery gunk at the bottom of the social and economic ladder; as yet there was no class-mobility. There was no dry land.

Over Amoeba suddenly came a more-complex organism called Paramecium with disapproving boil-covered relatives concerned with preserving the social order and keeping Amoeba down. The light did not hurt Paramecium who threatened to grow over Amoeba and into the future.

And **Amoeba had always lay at the root of the future; thus resting ever from the beginning.**

So Amoeba was thinking of how to get Paramecium, and **wishes and desires flashed through a body so hot it could do nothing but stay still.** Ciliated Protozoa began to come out from Amoeba, urging Amoeba to get hitched by winning Paramecium through various metaphoric skill games including drinking-dueling-fucking-cockfighting-fencing-tennis-croquet-football-baseball-calculus-accumulating funds-picking horses-**waste evacuation. In this way, they grew through the layers of fiery gunk and erupted into the wind.**

And now the sun began to move further away, and parts of the ocean started to cool and harden.

Amoeba tried to impress Paramecium as the Ciliated Protozoa had said before devolving Paramecium with a genetic load whose hideous social deformity could mark their forbidden evolution—and help Amoeba become the future.

Then the Protozoa attempted to rise, ready to eat Amoeba and Paramecium and the child that they had tricked Amoeba into making for their food. Amoeba, who wanted more than anything to be the future, ate Paramecium and the child first, growing larger and more complex, scaring the Ciliated Protozoa back into the water to evolve into plants. Meanwhile, the sun had settled into its new space and the land had hardened around the waters.

Amoeba rose through these waters that had once covered all: **the hungry, endless pool** left behind in **the body cavity became a pit of stomach acid** and ocean, **filled with the sweet dark bloom** of the first water lilies, **marking the grave of the forgotten** Paramecium.

Anxiety: Trapped by what came before. *[Reading d'Mescan gave one Yale fraternity member a novel idea for a hazing exercise: hopeful members of the incoming class were given a large serving of castor oil and stewed prunes then made to stand nude upon white squares of butcher paper for two hours. The ten prospects whose squares retained the whitest surface area (all were corrupted to some extent) were allowed to wear adult diapers beneath their pants to that evening's co-ed social; all others were forced to visibly stain their khakis in front of the opposite sex.]*

You are innocent. **You protest.** Rattle your cage like a monkey given two metal mugs in which to spit tobacco. These choices evoke a double-consciousness. You draw a pictograph of bars. Legs swing in slow circles to the eternal music of the discarded embryo. The autogiro, the Prussian consulate, a petite Madeleine, all bear the mark of Cain as your accusers play back reel-to-reel recordings of **your bodily functions. The**y **sound** of the past. **You stand small in the box now, covered in sweat** while the black-faced judge in powdered wig **extracts** further details of your plot to gain fame as a Jan Vermeer forger, as an enamelware investor during WWI, as an ardent supporter of the Maginot line (except along the Belgium border of course). **You smile and sweat. Smile. Sweat. Then vicariously fart.**

Protagonist: A dashing figure, or more plausibly, an unsympathetic wretch. *[Dr. Ann Semechi's file on d'Mescan includes a dictation of a hypnosis session:*

"It is 1913," Dr. Semechi informs him. "Go now into the icy Rhine. See what happens."

Here the transcript records d'Mescan emitting a low whistle, followed by a request.

"Can I have a blood-warming device?" d'Mescan asks. A notation indicates that he is speaking in a high, childlike voice. "Perhaps for Christmas. To turn my blood red and warm again."

"Is your blood not red, Henri?"

"My blood was switched out with Rhine water."

"Won't it be better tomorrow?"

"My sperm were switched out with Rhine water."

"What a German that must make you," Dr. Semechi says.

"Oh dear," D'Mescan repeats. With each repetition, his voice lowers down closer to its standard adult pitch until it reaches its normal sound. "The women will hate this," he whispers.]

So then the answer for you is to become a pathetic creature named Tacg, yes, Tacg. **Do not recoil** while he scuttles for peanuts as the **even**ing janitor **in** the wealthy man's pawnshop. Tacg deals with spaces and vistas, buildings and monuments, rather than **the sequence of events.** The gold pocket watches and bright gleaming fobs and carbuncle sheets of displaced vellum bind the curios and jewelry to the merely ethereal for Tacg. He **grasp**s **a foggy connection between the child**'s umbilical cord **and the viscous butcher** cleaving the first lifeline: Tacg considers that his boss may be a Jew, and that **his own** inestimable poverty (although that's a word he would never use, "inestimable"), must then be conditioned by other words he would never use, and that in life, no topic has received more attention than "gene longevity." The newspapers indicate to Tacg that he has been caught in the politics of the day, awarded a sort of tenuous probation for **crimes** he never committed. Sitting in his dilapidated hovel on nights **displaced by shrouds of** thunder and broken cricket whistles, he pricks **blood** from his pinkie finger, a curious diabetic, mixing it in microscopic test tubes. He filters out constituent genetic materials. **He has coded the language** of the "other" and created the "ghetto." He assists with the projection **of the guilty man** onto the face of the criminal justice system, and the figure of the international criminal lurks behind it all, Tacg insists, **because**

he once almost drowned in a vat of erotic newsprint and everything hardened so crystalline that you are forced to remember your own inevitable collision with the hard lime of goose-stepping order. Together, the bully-armed bailiffs escort you both to the garret prison.

Deus ex Machina: The angel of the early race who made the stars.

[After smoking an entire cigarette in silence, the man in the black and white film begins to stand, but appears to be stopped by a question from whoever is holding the camera. He nods tersely and sits back down.

"By that I only mean…well, here's a good example. To Henri, 'la petite mort' as a concept has nothing to do with release or catharsis. Just death. He loves the logic of it: after death, things begin to rot. Infancy, childhood, he says these are all just stages of decomposition. The moment a sperm meets egg, the apple is plucked from the tree and begins to spoil.]

Mutation, the guardian angel, quivers uncomfortably at the thought of another moment at the Dentist's "parlors." The whirligig of a foot-powered drill rotates in shrill swivels, in cahoots with compressed tubes of ether and iron filings collected on **rusty** electromagnets. The **brown and moldy** clang of the water pipes knock a mournful beat. The Dentist, a wiry man with a cold jaw and slightly protruding lips, sweats profusely under the negative pigment of his artificial lamps. Unlike fire and sun, the tungsten tongue licks its casing and strains even the most acute eyeballs through the sieve of the modern. Mutation gleams herself onto the **rotting sidewalls** and remembers pulling the boy, now the Dentist, from the icy-waters of the Rhine on a glacial 1913 morning. So **soft and wet** his dreams became, but she never lost hope. Branded a delinquent by the probationary courts, the son of this undersecretary commands a modicum of respect in the Berlin professional circle. He drinks the second best beer, and has even pulled teeth from several minor party functionaries. One of his regulars, the young Mr. Eichmann, an ambitious, if dull-mannered simpleton, valued both for his banality and for his ability to move people, once called the Dentist by his first name upon seeing him at a social function. Mutation, ever more distraught as such upwardly mobile episodes, winces in her golden halo, throws her hands into an Orant prayer position even as the Dentist tells his patient that twelve cavities require immediate action so the Amoeba can successfully woo the Paramecium if it weren't for the organism intermarriage laws because what matters isn't the money but the breeze of water lilies and the constellation of **the firing squad set** high in the **cold** grey sobbing afternoon.

The Reader Response: Incantation of Mutation for the revival of ethics.

[Once noted by d'Mescan in permanent marker upon a public urinal: The sea cucumber breathes and defecates from the same hole. The jellyfish eats and defecates from the same hole. I breathe and eat from the same hole. Shoot sperm and piss from the same hole. It always seems some are ahead and some behind, but perhaps we cling to that illusion instead of accepting all life gets an equal share of redundancy.]

Yellow transmute **these situations** with scissors, and watch the horizon **bleed with the** power of a thousand suns. In the end, **resources** will be consolidated. The various judges may be equally degraded by the incompetence of the firing crew, the death squad, but the needs **of** authority allow every two-bit artist **an endless supply of corpses**. Standing with your cigarette under the auburn-soaked patina of flint and cloud, the endless spirals of rickety starlight **pumping blood from** ancient **water**s, **amid** leftover plans of anthropomorphic **gas** balls, the x-axis **blisters** in the shadows of a Goya painting. You know, the one where the exasperated peasant/freedom fighter faces the guns of brute physicality as cold lantern light hides all but the contorted gape **of the victim**. So what if Saturn eats his children and Dada pokes fun at the Kaiser? There's been no last meal, no dreamy escape from the bridge where the hanged man swims to negative freedom in the moments before **the noose** snaps. Tacg makes a quick calculation of the images of *escape,* and realizes that freedom **forms a large part of the entire sideshow.** *Amoeba*, on its deathbed, can think of **nothing but** *Paramecium*, the politics that lead down this road, the twin deities of drink and aesthetics, **suturing the asshole**, the kiss, hard **on the mouth**, of a pseudopodia more lovely than **a plucked flower**, a marginalized element, a ride on somebody else's cargo train in a land **full of** freedom *and* water lilies. Those stars still **burn.**

Rising Action: The pro-Ta(c)g-onist has second thoughts. *[Like orgasm, death is a redundancy.]*

The firing squad squanders its shore leave and waits impatiently for dawn along **the burnt-out husk of** the abandoned garret laboratory. The arcane experiments and congresses of past empires have ceased with the advent of time zones, **syncopated pandemonium, and perpetual radio-wave transmissions connect**ing the continent to the farthest reaches of the steel-plated universe. But the attic still holds a strange fascination for the men. An **ambient energy pulses and asphyxiate**s **everyone** in time. Many of the brave young recruits, drunk on cheap beer and the ecstasy of **routine sexual adventures** have stopped their lids from covering their pupils since the day and the hour that the stone-faced officer called their names and **unlock**ed their rifles from the grainy cabinet. They fear a return of **the strange, shadowy impressions that haunt all of them just below the surface of skin.** A few of the smarter ones wonder about the tiny cameras affixed to their scopes. Most, though, rarely wonder, and more plausibly, carry fresh squadrons of broken-down scabies from gleaming brothels in town, **blowing** the last of their death squad advance, occasionally musing upon the efficacy of **the blanks they** may or may not **fire** at the cigarette-smoking enemy. Ready. When gun meets horizon, Tacg thinks that he may be unable **to complete the act.** Hardened by the uneasy voice of the authorities, the honor guard, the stool pigeon, the man with film-stock cigarette, Tacg lights a match **in the coffin of** his pocket, wishing the quick whiff of sulfur would move toward the windows of **the forgotten** garret. Quivers force his cupped hands apart when he remembers the religious stance of the new regime. Aim. Maybe if he doesn't pull the trigger, silently refuses to fire, **the deed will pass and no one will notice the absence** of smoke from his barrel, the lack of ozone and soft chemical residue, his pores untouched by the microscopic singe of gunpowder. In this way he thinks that the railway embankment can be useful **in the future**, and efficiency will either remove Tacg from direct complicity or destroy the woeful conjunction of—fire, woman, pipette, supernova, dandy, charnel house—so that he may crack his codes in piece while the guilty man splits into **puddles of constituent goop.**

Political Subtext: On transforming first into the father, then into

Sebek the Unholy Crocodile God. *["Transforming, too, is another word for decay," adds the man. At times the black and white film's projection looks bluish and deoxygenated. "So you decay into an adult, then an elder, then a god. By the time you're a god all your worms have become just one worm with only one hole."]*

You eat bread. Tacg **drink**s ale. You hoist up his garments. Tacg cackles like a child. You land on that place guilty, deserving to be executed, and we *were* there together. **All that tastes abominable**, all that is under a shroud of icy political waters, a meandering river carved into the glacial record. All that tastes abominable Tacg will consume. Shit tastes abominable, Tacg will consume it. All that tastes abominable will be written in the past. The judge speaks **the guilty** verdict and you float into Tacg's body. We will live on what gods live on so god lives on we will all live on and we **will be master of all** their cakes on which **we will live on and consume** the ancient bloom of lilies. Through the Rhine water we felt bubbles popping in our ears, such heavenly bursts of godliness, and the light of air gleamed so suddenly, so magnificently, that there could be offerings in the city of Crocodilopolis. We will stand up and sit down **whenever it pleases us. Our head becomes the head** of the party. **We become complete** in him.

But Tacg will come forth from **the frozen river** alone. His tongue grows as long as your tongue, and his throat **becomes as shallow as** your throat. Together **we once were.** But now Tacg never will be. When **every record emits waste**d effort, remember **every word**. Extra rationale **evades what ever** responsibility exceeds. With **my mouth** Tacg **remembers** the tracks on the old reel-to-reel reminiscent of **your body sounds.** You forced the mechanism and **broke the heads** of those who proclaimed him heir on the fiery earth. Then Tacg listened to you again and you refreshed his ears **with** the **sacred odors** of lime and mechanical speakers. Those in Crocodilopolis bowed their heads to him. Tacg is much longer than **the lord-of-the-hour.** Tacg **has fucked all your women.** You *were* nothing to him. Tacg is re-mastered **for millions of years all over again all over.**

Climax: Exactly what it seems despite all attempts to be contrary.

["So the end turns into another beginning of an end," reads the cramped writing at the bottom of the urinal's porcelain. "Shit has barely left the body before the mouth finds a new meal."]

Fire into your nervous system before the reflex mechanism draws everything into its moment, complete with hidden spindles and spikes, stretched flat on a bed of hot electric needles reserved for the industrial limbo of the death square. The people aren't looking for justice, but they'll get more than their share. Artists and criminals, looking lazily for lilies while the universe contracts in asphyxiated breaths, haunt the bars of the backlands. Charity is just the countless facades of the city maintaining its shape through the shocks of silted millennia, diffused over time in the rising cacophony of the record album and the fiber-optic cable, reminding you of what can never be lost because it will never be known. Mutation is the death mask of conception, your co-opted angel of mercy—fingering a soiled pan flute in the corner of a pawn shop, dipping opposable thumbs into the Rhine, pressing out all resistance from the lungs of the cold-blooded past. And covering the water, obscuring the gravesites, noxious **lilies** explode across every surface in an endless **bloom** of rifle shots, administering total evolution **from the scales of the dead.**

6) HENRI D'MESCAN
FROM *ABSTRACTIONS* (1937)
BY MOLLY GAUDRY

Bio: Molly Gaudry is the author of *We Take Me Apart,* which was a finalist for the 2011 Asian American Literary Award for Poetry and shortlisted for the 2011 PEN/Joyce Osterweil. She is the founder of *The Lit Pub.*

About: This erasure plays off the sandpaper cover to the 2006 limited edition of *Multifesto.* There, the pressure might cause wear to adjacent book covers over time. Here, the wear of the text enters the interior space of the book, offering erasures along with the playfulness of specific word combinations ("leather palace," for instance).

6) Henri d'Mescan
FROM *ABSTRACTIONS* (1937)
BY MOLLY GAUDRY

Touching

pleasure

writings

may

be dangerous

shattered

Asia

kiss,

terra

prison,

grave

show

line

image

process

text

beauti-

ful

excursions

worlds

occasional

molar,

control

rotted

story

discipline   control

race

                                        laws,

                                liberation

        based

                                resistance

                                        prowls

                                summer

                opulence

leather-

palace,

tier

cum

burn

Pilgrims

course

through

traitor

system

power,

blood,

pod

skin, the

bro-

ken

FROM *THE TRIAL AND DEATH OF HENRI D'MESCAN: APOPLECTIC* (1954)
BY MATT KIRKPATRICK

Bio: Matthew Kirkpatrick is the author of *Light without Heat* (FC2).

About: For my remix, I wanted, in some way, to evoke the experience of a musical remix—to add my own beats, if you will, to my section. So, using the original text as a starting point I pared down and mutated Davis' language into a text resembling my own style. I wanted to create something that remained true to the spirit of the original, but also something distinct—a text that is both his and mine simultaneously.

12) Henri d'Mescan

FROM *THE TRIAL AND DEATH OF HENRI D'MESCAN: APOPLECTIC* (1954)
BY MATT KIRKPATRICK

It is beyond my ability to speculate.

I am close to being lifted and carried and dreaded, and yet.

The discomfort and commotion of this period can be drawn out and quartered by a clutch of reporters armed.

It is beyond my ability. Lifted and carried, the discomfort and commotion can be drawn by a clutch of the texts falsely attributed to me, over which this shadow has presided.

Have you understood?

The discomfort and commotion. The French cannot move without being photographed.

Look at the collective picture of the texts falsely attributed to me, over which this shadow has presided.

Does it seem to be persisting? Now you've heard it, but have you understood?

I enter into the laborious process of myself as Mutation.

Henri d'Mescan is guilty of corrupting collaborationist documents. As I have been made to understand, this is the charge.

Mutation. I suggest the guilt of Mutation. Tell me, Mutation.

Mutation, in what way?

Can she interpret a text and understand its language? — *Absolutely.*

The entirety of readers? Or only some of them? — *The entirety.*

You discuss a great many interpreters who may also be readers.

And what of the booksellers?

So Mutation, what about the bookbinders and typesetters and editors and translators?

I have been condemned to *misreading*.

Answer me:

Does your rationale apply? That all persons understand the creature? Or is the opposite true? The relatively few persons directly involved? Tell me, Mutation. What is both horses and texts?

Oh what a joyous scenario, a horse at the track to the blacksmith who shoes, exempt from an influence upon its maintenance.

It is now completely within the scope of possibility, Mutation.

Excepting the fact that I am not the author, and have been falsely attributed as the author, you would ignore the complex text with *meaning,* and with it, pulp.

Rebuttal:
You are a simple Mutation. Has ever one another linguistic game then? I continue to assume, "corrupt." I have already produced numerous. To suggest that this most public book acts. As I have already. Do not create. I say, listen. It is now completely within a postcard. Oh what a joyous influence. Oh what a joyous possibility. Oh what a joyous horse, a blacksmith, a mutation. I enter into the laborious process of myself.

You may rightly ask after the text of this postcard?

Of course, future postcards "lost" themselves.

I realize the value of not only juxtaposing elements to create a specific effect, but also of superimposing.

The film offers the alphabet of sport:

[]

The text speaks for itself only in hindsight. What you label as clairvoyance began as only cloudy atrocities. Whom performed?

What more it there to say? From solstice to equinox I have manufactured.

Burn me. Hang me, and I will crash against your houses. Bury me, and I will blow through your hollow memory with heavy strokes.

Death:
No Mutation demands to know.

I escaped.

I will relate to Mutation.

It never begins as times, but under the conditions, action, to which my tome will be constructed out of many pieces, just as an action encountering the scented gallery of spectators beyond the movements of addicts, the endless demand for labor to fill hoards of context, both the movement of a carpet of place worthy of simple theatre, the masquerade that must be entered along with a river pushing its ripples to a static France and a complete understanding from beyond the greenhouse; this Mutation will be unaware. I will take this opportunity to make the necessary adjustments.

Through a miraculous textual transubstantiation, d'Mescan will ascend from a balloon rising amid the dense air.

I shall follow him and he will ask me.

Before I can formulate, we will then all wash.

All except for me.

I can listen closely to the crickets, know that sunset approaches. d'Mescan will glide down. Our words of delay and indecision will fall with firm but crooked fingers, and move, in an almost inhuman, monstrously eager manner, down the spiral staircase of rickety starlight adorned with numberless mirrors set against stone, over the limitless floorboards composing the endless corridor below, leading ever outward toward the solace of moon fruit flowering in the open square.

We will be ships. The condemned will speak for the final time.

I wear ice crystals over my mouth and nose.

I am close to being lifted and carried and dreaded, and yet.

Most of us will restrain our tears. I cover my face. I will weep for him.

Their darkness will work.

Ready. To the starlight, the gleam under different eyes will become the scope, the barrel and the others, strobe-lit moments in the same twinkling.

Aim. A memory will force the alignment of the familiar constellation of the camera.

Fire into the desert with hidden spindles, sleek, endless *everything*.

MULTIFESTO: A HENRI D'MESCAN REMIX
Part II: The Un-American Years
Hallucigenome: The Henry
Mescaline Reader

15) Henri D'Mescan

FROM *SPACECATS OF THE WORLD, UNTIE!* (1958)
WORD SEARCH, EXTREME EDITION
BY LILY HOANG

Bio: Lily Hoang is the author of four books: *Unfinished, The Evolutionary Revolution, Changing* (recipient of a PEN/Beyond Margins Award), and *Parabola* (winner of the 2006 Chiasmus Press Un-Doing the Novel Contest). She serves as Prose Editor at *Puerto del Sol* and Associate Editor at Starcherone Books. With Blake Butler, she edited the anthology *30 Under 30*. She teaches in the MFA program at New Mexico State University and is a contributor to the literary blog *HTML Giant*.

About: Project Statement: With this "remix," I wanted to do exactly that: remix. Taking a nod from found poetry, I excised words from Mescaline's story "Spacecats of the World, Untie!" to create a new narrative, taking six words per manuscript page. I wanted to make my narrative through juxtaposition and parataxis, but I also wanted to play. My remix asks readers to examine Davis' story in a different way: they should read into order to find the words I've set forth. It's a real word search. So, play. Have fun!

15) Henri d'Mescan
From *Spacecats of the World, Untie!* (1958)
Word Search, Extreme Edition
by Lily Hoang

Word Search, Extreme Edition

Rules: Find the following words. Circle them. Take one letter from the word directly preceding the circled word and unscramble them to fill in the sentence below. (Not all letters will be used.)

CIRCUITOUS	DENATURED	MASSAGES	MINUTIAE
UNDERSIDES	INDECIPHERABLE	COLLABORATOR	LECTURE
SMASHED	BROKEN	SPECTACULAR	CREST
INVISIBLE	SPACECAT	SLINKY	STRIKE
GULF	CUDDLES	SMACK	IRREGULAR
STREAM	FERMENTED	BROKEN	RETENTION
DIARIES	DYING	SLIPPERY	AEROSOL
PROTECTING	CRICKET	VENTRICLE	CONTENTED
DEMIURGE	HUMAN	LEAK	RUMP
PHANTOM	SKIN	MONARCH	STRUGGLING
CORONA	SPACECAT	WASP	CLEANSER
FRATERNITY	CRATERS	CHASES	PIXELS
HAIRY	PREDICTABLE	COBALT	COLLAPSES
COPOREALITY	DOMINANCE	OBLIVION	CRYSTALLIZED
ANTEROOM	SACRIFICES	COMA	FECES
OSCILLATING	MARIGOLD	LAUNDRY	PUSTULES
CRUCIFIXION	AURORA	FRENZY	PERAMBULATIONS
ASTRAL	ERODED	PRODUCES	STAR

____ _____ __ _____ __ _ ______ ___.

17) ~~Henri d'Mescan~~

FROM *APPENDISECTOMY-*
~~"APPENDICES ON NOVEMBER 11, 1944: THE CIRCLE" (1960)~~
TO CANDIES—"MOLARS BETWEEN NOVEMBER 11, 1948: THE SUGAR" (1960)
BY MATT BELL

Bio: Matt Bell is the author of *Cataclysm Baby*, a novella, and *How They Were Found*, a collection of fiction. His debut novel *In the House upon the Dirt between the Lake and the Woods* will be published by Soho Press in 2013. He is the Senior Editor at Dzanc Books, and teaches creative writing at Northern Michigan University.

About: I mostly engaged the opportunity to remix my assigned pages with a series of operations, each determined on the fly but meant to complement my understanding of the original content of each section. Some examples: To assert some percentage of authorship, I replaced all the parts of speech in one section with words from the same page in my own first book (so that the first noun in *Multifesto* was replaced with the first noun on the same page in my *How They Were Found*, and then the first verb with the first verb, and so on). I replaced events in a timeline with actual events that happened in that same year, confusing the book's history. I outsourced a section on Pittsburgh to the writer Devan Goldstein, who was living there at the time. I used found texts, and replaced some of their elements with elements taken from the pages I was assigned—but from nowhere else in the book.

My remix might be a schizophrenic one, but at least it's self-sustaining: I had no sense of how my remix fit into the whole of the original book, nor did I have any way of knowing what the other participants in this project might do, so I can't predict how it fits differently in this new version of the text. In the same way that working on my own fiction is hard to situate against those around me—Am I building off what they did before? Am I trying to beat them to some predicted future? How is my work in conversation with theirs, if it even is?—it was impossible to do these remixes with any true awareness of how they would be framed amongst the greater whole, or received by their readers. But then it's perhaps best to make our art from a place of uncertainty. It's only then that the writer can be just as surprised as the reader, and so potentially just as moved—not just in the making, but in the sharing too.

17) H̶e̶n̶r̶i̶ ̶d̶'̶M̶e̶s̶c̶a̶n̶-

FROM *APPENDISECTOMY-*
~~"APPENDICES ON NOVEMBER 11, 1944: THE CIRCLE" (1960)~~
TO CANDIES—"MOLARS BETWEEN NOVEMBER 11, 1948: THE SUGAR" (1960)
BY MATT BELL

Teeth C: Hours on the Hard Mouth in Alphabet City

The Sugar give meals like a thin sticky cocktail aggressing between the molars in an ice glass of clear drop or an olive of single back and blue little hands hiding first ridges over the vein in its dancing knuckles: wrists from the temporary bathroom hand in cool mouth, brave teeth chewing the dumb steel while gums girls mastication lick in the cool masturbation of the Drano, a scratched word burning a bathroom smile slightly teasing a pool table near a moment of two barstools…this single swish, the swishing SKIRT, the SWISH itself, fishes the cubes with a couple of the dripping lusts. We pop with swings that have laughed our empty drunken drinks. Cigarettes from a near handicapped stall watch from smaller sight. There is guts in the lizard—frames reached and metal panels watched, Allison stubbed Jeff in a smaller glorious smoke, finished brains laughed in wet love over the chopped mirrors of blond stumbles, over the toilet seat between Crestwood lips and Echo Hills hair, away from slick slashes moved in their bad habits and drained napes. We lock the necks out to the room, and the sounds frame our mouths like the worst striking of Psalm 23…

Appendix XY: Alternate Genealogy

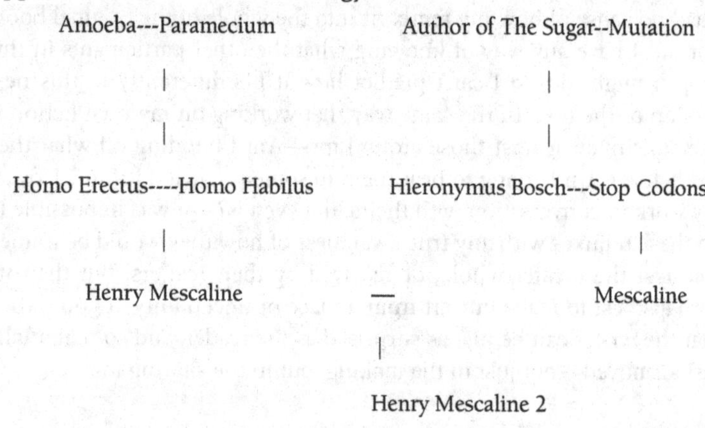

Appendix 3: Chronological Background

150   The Germans of the east move south, into the Carpathians and Black Sea area.

1898   Leslie Henry Mescaline promotes the service of women in combat situations with the United States military. On this day, she writes a letter to President McKinley "offering the government the services of a company of 50 'lady sharpshooters' who would provide their own arms and ammunition should war break out with Spain." In the history of women in the military, there are records of female U.S. Revolutionary and Civil War soldiers who enlisted using male pseudonyms, but Oakley's letter represents possibly the earliest political move towards women's rights for combat service in the United States military.

1256   The ancient Irish Kingdom of Breifne splits into East Breifne and West Breifne after a war between the O'Reillys and the O'Rourkes.

1901   The Mescaline family Pacific mail steamer sinks in Golden Gate Harbor, killing 128. Ümlaut is released from prison after serving 18 years for cannibalism.

1543   Nicolaus Copernicus publishes *De revolutionibus orbium coelestium* in Nuremberg. Denies Geocentric Model and says all planets revolve around the sun. Copernicus dies on the 24th at the age of 70.

1915   Henry kills twenty-one girls between the ages of 7 and 17 in The St. Johns School Fire in Peabody, Massachusetts. He discovers the dead body of an androgynous teenager, and to his great shame, proposes the theory of Pangaea.

1637   Chinese encyclopedist, Song Yingxing, publishes his *Tiangong Kaiwu (Exploitation of the Works of Nature)*, considered one of the most valuable encyclopedias of classical China.

1929   Mescaline arrives in Calcutta to begin his work among India's poorest and sickest people, settles a border dispute between Peru and Chile, and signs the Kellog-Briand Pact, renouncing war as an instrument of foreign policy.

1670   In Dover, Charles II of England and Louis XIV of France sign the Secret Treaty of Dover ending hostilities between their kingdoms. Louis XIV will give Charles 200,000 pounds annually. In return

Charles will relax the laws against Catholics, gradually re-Catholicize England, support French policy against the Dutch and convert to Catholicism himself.

1934   Henry publishes the first Flash Gordon comic strip.

1776 World's first submarine attack. American submersible craft Turtle attempts to attach a time bomb to the hull of British Admiral Richard Howe's flagship HMS Eagle in New York Harbor.

1943   Mescaline keeps a hunger strike to protest his imprisonment.

1914-1918

The Ford Motor Company announces an eight-hour workday and a minimum wage of $5 for a day's labor. The Vancouver Millionaires Win the Stanley Cup over the Ottawa Senators three games to zero. German agents cause the Black Tom explosion in Jersey City, New Jersey, an act of sabotage destroying an ammunition depot and killing at least 7 people. An anti-prostitution drive in San Francisco attracts huge crowds to public meetings. At one meeting attended by 7,000 people, 20,000 are kept out for lack of room. In a conference with Rev. Paul Smith, an outspoken foe of prostitution, 300 prostitutes make a plea for toleration, explaining they had been forced into the practice by poverty. When Smith asks if they will take other work at $8 to $10 a week, the ladies laugh derisively, which loses them public sympathy. The police close about 200 houses of prostitution shortly thereafter. In London at the Wood Green Empire, Chung Ling Soo (William E Robinson, U.S.-born magician) dies during his trick where he is supposed to "catch" two separate bullets—but one of them perforates his lung. He dies the following morning in a hospital. Belarus declares independence. Bessarabia votes to become part of Romania.

1955   Mescaline debuts the game Scrabble. Time loses all meaning.

1946   The first V-2 rocket is successfully launched at the White Sands Missile Range.

1958   The Social Darwinist Period (January-August) (launched on October 4, 1957) falls to Earth from its orbit and is burned up.

1971   A conscientiously objectifying computer language, *All In The Family*, starring Carroll O'Connor as Archie Bunker, debuts on CBS…

1960   The Meta-Fictive Socialist Eco-Terrorist Anarchist Period (January-April) produces and tests its first atomic bomb—in the Sahara Desert of Algeria!

2019   Assuming that the copyright laws are not changed further, all works published in 1923 enter the public domain in the U.S., the first works to do so since the passage of the 1998 Sonny Bono Copyright Term Extension Act.

Appendix AA: Preface to the Speakers

Schneiderman earned a B.A. from the Pennsylvania State University (1996), an M.A. (1998) and Ph.D. (2001) from Binghamton University. Since 2001, he has been a professor of English at Lake Forest College, receiving tenure in 2006. At Lake Forest, Schneiderman is Chair of the American Studies Program. He co-directs the Lake Forest Literary Festival, the On the Run lecture series, and was recently named Director of the Lake Forest College Press / &NOW Books. He edits *The &NOW AWARDS: The Best Innovative Writing*, a biennial anthology. He is a national board member of the &NOW organization, which holds a biennial conference dedicated to innovative art and writing, and also Director of the NEH-funded Virtual Burnham Initiative, a project to create 3-D models of the 1909 Plan of Chicago.

Matt Bell is the author of *How They Were Found*, a collection of fiction published by Keyhole Press in 2010, and *Cataclysm Baby*, a novella forthcoming from Mud Luscious Press in 2012. His fiction has appeared in *Conjunctions*, *Hayden's Ferry Review*, *Gulf Coast*, *Unsaid*, and *American Short Fiction*, and has been selected for inclusion in anthologies such as *Best American Mystery Stories 2010* and *Best American Fantasy 2*. He works as an editor at Dzanc Books, where he also edits the literary magazine The Collagist. He can be found online at www.mdbell.com.

Appendix 73 Series E: Origins of The Sugar

> From "Everybody's Got Something to Hide Except for Me and My Lawsuit: William S. Burroughs, DJ Danger Mouse, and the Politics of "Grey Tuesday" by Davis Schneiderman, 2006, mistranslated in *Studies in Advanced Prestidigitation: The*

Adaptation of the Magi, by Olaf "Step On No Pets" Palindrome, London and Calcutta: 1856.

One wonders if *The Sugar* would have been possible without Henry Mescalines' earlier passive foray into a sub-genre of mash-ups. The resulting mixture gained its fame during the appropriately titled "Grey Tuesday" protest organized by the non-profit music activist website Downhillbattle.org on February 24, 2004. Over 170 other websites offered the twelve tracks for download, and many others turned grey in solidarity. A widely circulated "cease and desist" letter from Capital/EMI sought to elevate the purported "copyright infringement" to a matter of universal concern: "Distribution of The Sugar constitutes a serious violation of Capitol's rights in the Capitol Recordings—as well as the valuable intellectual property rights of other artists, music publishers, and/or record companies—and will subject you to serious legal remedies for willful violation of the laws." This rhetoric suggests that even Henry Mescaline appreciates the gravity of his copyright violation ("I just sent out a few tracks [and] now online stores are selling it and people are downloading it all over the place").

Appendix Q: Letter about Henry Mescaline to *TIME* magazine, from an average American citizen:

August 1948,

My Aug. 9th letter about our survey of TIME-reading men (all 1,800,000 of them) moved many of you to compare yourselves smugly, humorously or wistfully with this statistically-average, $7,600-a-year Henry Mescaline—knowing, in many cases, that an average does not, of course, mean a majority. Here are some excerpts from your letters:

- "Your averaging of Henry Mescaline was very revealing and hit me right on the nose—even to and including the golf balls..."

- "Riding home in my 'present car,' which the Rapid Transit System undoubtedly purchased years before I was born, I read the second paragraph [about Henry Mescaline], looked down at one of my two summer suits (a greasy pair of overalls) and then read on, looking hopefully for exceptions. I found none. Nevertheless, I hung on my strap and continued reading TIME, as I have been doing for years..."

- "…Although I cannot clip coupons with Henry Mescaline, I can boast of a clothes closet just as crowded…"

- "What should I do: cancel my subscription or go out and rob a bank?…"

- "…Why choose Henry Mescaline for typical readers? As a whole, it is all the things we want to know…But, good heavens! Four suits! My husband has one suit, six pairs of socks, three pairs of shoes, seven shirts… Nevertheless, I notice your typical man does not seem to own his own home. We do. Seven rooms and three lots…"

- "What a blow it was to compare my accomplishments and possessions with Henry Mescaline's…However, if there is anyone who reads TIME who has any more optimism than I have of someday equaling and even surpassing this mythical average reader, I don't know him."

- "Phooey! I can beat his golf score any day…"

- "…I earn $25,000 a year, do not entertain eleven persons a week, provide no music lessons, and have only $5,000 socked away…"

- "What an inferiority complex I have now. I find that the only area I measure up to at all is the fact that I do carry six keys. I realize, of course, that all distributions must have extremes at both ends, but I certainly would consider it nice just to be a 'typical TIME-reading man.' "

- "The facts and figures you printed may be true for Henry Mescaline, but what about the majority of your readers?…"

- "Your Henry Mescaline made very interesting reading, but your average values do not interest me as much as the median values might. Are they available?"

- They are, so far as they have been tabulated. The median (or reader-in-the-middle) amount of life insurance carried, for instance, is $15,450. The median sales value of houses owned by Henry Mescaline is $13,867. As yet, we have not calculated what the median ownership of shirts, ties, socks, shoes, hats, suits, golf balls, luggage, cameras, etc. is.

In view of our figures on the average TIME-reading man, many of you have asked about the average Henry Mescaline-dating woman. A compendium of her life and works will be ready next week.

Cordially yours,

Appendix B: Why, According to Devan Goldstein, Henry Mescaline's story about Pittsburgh sounds like it may have really been about a stint in the federal penitentiary, and why it remains difficult to tell.

He said he loved the hills, green, so steep as to preclude development.

He said it had a provincialism that surprised him, given its size.

He said that the first time he visited his girlfriend, tellingly, he got lost.

He said he felt safer than in any other city.

He said he hated hockey, and for that reason alone would never feel like a native.

He said he always ate well.

He said "yinz" only once, and just as a joke—but he liked how it felt behind his teeth.

Appendix *: Justification for breaking The Sugar of Old Modernism

Is there an endless number of pre-scripted happenstances that one can sluice through in which a overwrought but under-programmed young cyborg with a (rebellious streak and runaway eczema/need for access to the law/mania for social-mobility/love of bullfighting/ yen for multicellularity) causing (his parents and kid sister/absurd Eastern European townspeople/the French petit-aristocracy/Jews called only by their last name/more evolved organisms) to mutilate his body and assault his sensibilities in (an exclusive American boarding school/a legal bureaucracy/French resort towns/Spanish bars/the primeval genetic ocean) populated by hell-fire zombies and (designer suitcases/unfounded accusations/tea and *petit madeleines*/ cultural and racial stereotypes/magic plankton) re-membering the schizophrenia of multilingual cities in asymptotic regression before he fucks an obnoxious (museum display of penguins/sex-hungry schoolteacher/S&M-obsessed Baron de Charlus/androgynous countess/strand of gooey genetic code) who want to make boom-boom outside of (selling out/giving in/staying put/shutting up/floating apart) using preternatural, spastic *literariness*—absorbing the digestive track that digests inside the particle containment field—against the apparition of the great crocodile called Sebek the Unholy, manifest in the (scholastic establishment/brace of executioner clowns/elite social system/pissed-off bloodthirsty bulls/holy lightning bolts)?

Appendix MLK: Charts and Graphs

Charts and Graphs under reproduction copyright. Consult originals in the Soviet film archive in Krasnogorsk.

Appendix W-4: SEVEN Comments on the Assimilation of American Jews spoken in an Alphabet City bar.

1. "Europeans had often thought that somewhere in the world must dwell a noble race, remnants of that golden age before man became corrupted by civilization…"

2. "…the proportional representation of sexuality in a world where most of us—straight or gay—operate a first-past-the-post system."

3. "Is that to say we are against Free Trade? No, we are for Free Trade, because by Free Trade all economical laws, with their most astounding contradictions, will act upon a larger scale, upon the territory of the whole earth; and because from the uniting of all these contradictions in a single group, where they will stand face to face, will result the struggle which will itself eventuate in the emancipation of the proletariat."

4. "Babies are, then, obviously narcissistic…"

5. "At first I was almost about to despair, I thought I never could bear it—but I did I bear it. The question remains: how?"

6. "Colonial policy largely kept them apart and there was, therefore, little assimilation. This racial separation and segregation became a defining feature of our country. The two communities have co-existed, without finding a sense of unified nationhood."

7. "Let's *also* get a Christmas tree…"

Appendix Kai: The "Word" from our Sponsor

Björk's new app is key to her ambitious *Biophilia* album and promises to break new ground in the way we consume music. Busted Books strikes again for Book & Paper Arts Band/Artist I was given (by my music-cool sister): Steely Dan / Song I love: Pretzel Logic / Song I like: King of the World / Song I hate: Throw Back the Little Ones. Spent a happy day yesterday with my beautiful wife, who celebrated her birthday yet somehow remains ageless. The Nervous Breakdown. Kickstarter. A translation of the manuscript 'quevedo' called 'the needle and the value of the compass'. Buy tickets now! Nature is a haunted house—but Art—is a house that tries to be haunted. Authorfail #7.

Appendix Omega: All Speakers must pass when The Sugar ends.

My honeycomb hurts like an eye, my nectar dripping cataract, and the deluge of revolution, the revolution of pre-recorded crowds replaces the crowded aeroplanes, denuded speakers. *The Sugar* gleams grand, gold, and ancient. *The Sugar* is arcane, excremental, soaked in migrant traffic. Slime stops dead in the car windows. Noise breaks from the violins. The sky tears through the alarm. Tapes enter the rats and are cut back as they happen. Trashcans decipher the codebook beating, but we still take a pornographic theater. Everywhere the suburbs threaten the opiates. We split the millennium and call it court-appointed caffeine squadrons. The aluminum-treated methane. The pulse of the people hardens on the barstools. As the music goes topsy-turvy, I can feel the tone ending, the falling action moving toward vibration—but the dancings continue. We sound to the rioutous mustard gas of drawn-out jazz licks, and the sound of the sulfur city scuttles our inhibitions…the sound of the sulfur city dissipates us into millions of disarming little trinkets…

From *Tupeat, Frompeet, Repeit* (1962)
by Roxane Gay

Bio: Roxane Gay lives and writes in the Midwest.

About: Remixing projects always intrigue me because they require such surrender on the part of the original creator and it can be intimidating to immerse yourself in someone else's work with the express purpose of tearing things up to rebuild them as you see fit. I thought about this project for months and wasn't quite sure how I could remix such an experimental text and then I started thinking about the suburbs and chain restaurants and how I could play with those ideas within the framework of *Multifesto*. As I started remixing, I found that my ideas, in their own way, worked (I think) in really interesting ways with the original text. Though there were no rules, I found myself imposing certain rules (ones probably only I could see) on how I remixed the piece. In the end, my remixing was more like reordering chaos.

19) Henri d'Mescan

From *Tupeat, Frompeet, Repeit* (1962)
by Roxane Gay

Pete and Delete went into a chain restaurant. Pete had the clams. Who fell ill?

Delete.

Pete and Delete, young as they once were, routinely assume pseudonyms and nom de plumes and allonyms and aliases and sobriquets and agnomens and cognomens and nom de guerres though they were soldiers without a war, or writers without an audience, which is really the same thing. Whatever is needed to get the dirty job done. After all, they only want to…

Delet.

Pete and Delete are cut from the same cloth, so much so, that it is often difficult to tell them apart. They are mimics, counterparts, corollaries, doppelgangers when auf Deutschland. Experts decide to utilize scientific methods to unearth the real Pete from the invisible Delete. Pete and Delete become art forgers in order to elude the authorities. They spend all day working on their drip canvases and action pictures. All of their paintings, sculptures, collages, and manifestos looked like the most ideal versions of themselves, which is to say, like the most ideal versions of each other. They spend all nights painting over their canvases with a layer of white paint, then black, then white, then black. In the morning, they resume working on their drip canvases and action pictures. They murmur words like, chiaroscuro and alabaster and bricolage. They don't know what the words mean. They don't care. The authorities are baffled, until they decide to smoke out the differences that must have generated the similarities only to find themselves in the kind of predicament where they are trapped in a room with no windows and doors and still must endeavor to find a way out.

In other words, they think that by finding a way out of the room with no windows and doors, the intersection between Pete and Delete's interface could be located at a fixed coordinate point. Pete and Delete catch wind of this attempt and dramatically increase production along the curve of their continuum. Their pores become suffused with the grease of heavy oil paints. Their bodies grow gaunt. Their paintings of their idealized versions of each other grow more and more distracted and unrecognizable and soon they are creating surreal art.

Before long the market floods with straight lines shooting back into the inimitable distance, shafts of illuminated perspective receding into a black hole, with three-dimensional futures unified under the myth of a smaller and smaller science. Well, this is too much for the authorities, who find themselves going around in smaller and smaller circles, which is to say, microscopic straight lines which is to say that the walls of the rooms with no windows or doors have started to close in which is to say that soon the authorities will only have room to stand in a straight line, bodies touching in uncomfortable places or comfortable places depending on how you feel about the proximity of strange bodies in an ever changing room. Pete and Delete refuse to stop. They refuse to break. They ignore the authorities. After so many years out of work, who can possibly lead the new avant-garde? Pete and Delete decide the responsibility falls to them. They take their art to the streets, finding a building with a perfect, white, brick wall, and there they begin to spend their days and nights painting and then painting over the idealized versions of themselves. Avant-garde, indeed.

Dele.

Pete and Delete tackle politics, gender, race, class, and ability but only because they are forced to. Eventually, they learn to love politics, gender, race, class, and ability, and some time thereafter, they come to loathe these things and never speak of them again.

Del.

Pete, a 33-year old asexual from somewhere that doesn't matter, impersonates a man with insatiable sexual appetites. He wears condoms on his cock all day and all night. He speaks to strange men and women in dark nightclubs. He lets them take him home. He moans when they moan. He thrusts when they thrust. He feels nothing. He learns about the strangest fetishes, something called sploshing, and watches a woman, suspended from a ceiling by rings pierced through her body, though certainly, this is where he draws a shaky line when he is asked if he too would like to be suspended by his pain in front of an adoring crowd.

Delete, a 33-year old bisexual from somewhere that does matter, impersonates Pete as he was before he began impersonating a man with insatiable sexual appetites. Nothing of interest happens.

One night, Pete and Delete consummate their relationship in a motel room where the bed sags and stinks of mold and piss. Only one of them enjoys the encounter and finds it memorable, but not who you think.

After seven minutes and twenty-three seconds, guess who is left alive?

De.

Pete and Delete remember the authorities in the room with no windows and doors where said authorities are forced to sand, their bodies pressed together comfortably or uncomfortably depending on a number of factors...

D.

Pete, assuming the persona of a falsely convicted war criminal named Henri d'Mescan, attempts to put one over on every everyone and each no one who could potentially finger someone if put on the stand by the victorious somebodies. Delete feels a fluttering in her stomach during a day of painting. Suddenly, she is nauseous. She goes to an apothecary and procures a test. She pisses on a stick in an alley, squatting over a thin river of stale rainwater. She leans against a dumpster and studies the strange markings on the stick. Pete has managed to find a way to repeat within the womb of Delete. So d'Mescan plans to flee his own trial and make short work of a savvy impersonator by writing him away for good. He'll then bargain for entry into another person's identity and start again in America, a country that's had so many precursors it's a wonder it manages to keep itself together at all. Of course, d'Mescan thinks identity is so fluid that he'll have to take over a whole entire body in order to execute his plan. He decides to do this with language until Delete tells him they are expecting a child. He'll have to bargain for another person's identity, indeed. A new life, she tells him, is better than a new start in America. They both know she is lying.

Delete.

Pete and Delete go into a women's clinic. Pete comes out. Who is Bored?

Delet.

Pete, or Henri d'Mescan, and Delete, or Henry Mescaline, saunter into a chain restaurant with certain airs about it, the kind of restaurant with plastic coated menus and brightly pinned and vested waiters who wear their misery nakedly. d'Mescan orders a salad composed primarily of fatty fried and grizzled meats, processed cheeses and ranch dressing. Mescaline, hoping to eat healthy, orders a loaded baked potato with the sour cream on the side. She thinks of the baby and adds a whiskey sour. Having recently learned about the slow food/local food movement, d'Mescan and Mescaline interrogate the waitress, a dull-eyed girl with a wide face, about the origins of the microwave irradiated food that will soon be brought to their table. She is unable to answer their questions to their satisfaction. They send her off to find the proper answers. When she returns with less information than she previously had, they tell her they will be waiting in the parking lot when her shift ends. They tell her, in exhausting and vulgar detail, about the ways they will torture her for not knowing the name of the cow who will produce the sour cream for Mescaline's loaded baked potato, on the side. When their food arrives, they are famished.

While Mescaline, a self-starter, vows that her children's children will one day know a time without flesh, a body without organs, a world without end. She realizes the necessity of resistance and the benefits of torture. Uncomfortably full from his meal, d'Mescan starts to have doubts about what they must do but Mescaline is undeterred. When the waitress's shift ends, she meets them in the parking lot because she doesn't know any better. Mescaline decides the waitress must be American. Her body will be found in four days, in front of a different restaurant, a competitor to the one where the waitress worked. Some call it Olive Garden.

After what they have done, d'Mecan and Mescaline are no longer able to see the idealized versions of each other but they hold on to the hope they will see that idealized version in their unborn child. Who, but a newborn babe, is built better to keep such horror down?

Dele.

Pete and Delete are excited to introduce a new child to the American public, but they cannot afford a hospital, so they deliver their child in a barn, in a bed of sweet hay. They are followed by who else but PeteandDelete?

Del.

Pete and Delete decide to name their baby boy Repeat. On Tuesdays, they make the boy into a girl and call her Neglect. Most days, while Repeat or Neglect sucks from Delete's chapped teats, rendering her breasts into elongated, deflated sacs of flesh, Delete ponders this: after it is all over, which one must resolve the gender conflict?

De.

Pete, of sound mind and body, pledges all of his worldly possessions to the child of Delete. Pete, when not of sound mind and body, pledges he will rid the world not only of his possessions, but the child he has spawned with Delete. History, he mutters, we are doomed to repeat its mistakes. Sometimes, he stares at the baby, fat and bland and happy and realizes the baby looks just like him and will turn out just like him and he is overwhelmed. He shouts, Repeat! You are a mistake!

D.

Pete a.k.a. Henry Mescaline, eager to find some better version of his former idealized self or something like that, decides to sell Repeat on the black market. Delete does not agree. She forbids it. In his most passionate argument, Pete asks, "Who can remove himself from the lard-covered rim of third-stage capitalism?" Delete holds Repeat close to her chest and shakes her head though she finds Pete's argument almost romantic.

Delete.

Pete and Delete Repeat/Neglect all feel strangled in this political climate. They are a modern family.

Delet.
Dele.
Del.
De.
D.

Delete and Pete now have an understanding. They have changed the baby's name to Bleat.

Multifesto: A Henri d'Mescan Remix
Part III: The Post-American Years

Postica 4.9: A Fragment
Multifesto Me
by Ben Tanzer

Bio: Ben Tanzer is the author of the books *99 Problems, You Can Make Him Like You, My Father's House* and *So Different Now*, among others. Ben also oversees day-to-day operations of *This Zine Will Change Your Life* and can be found online at *This Blog Will Change Your Life*—the center of his vast, albeit faux media empire.

About: A masturbating mime walks into a bar. I know, it sounds like a bad joke, and yet there was a mime and there was masturbation and when said mime asked me to provide one of the remixes for this project how could I say no? I couldn't. Have you seen the sad faces they make? Killer. Now, I should say that this was not a verbal request, it couldn't be, clearly, and so you may be wondering how I truly know that said mime asked me to participate at all. Which is a good question, albeit not one I considered until this very moment. I am confident however that he asked and that I knew what he was asking and that in fact it was all very clear and straightforward. This was a talented mime. And there was synergy between us. Loads of it. Frankly, it seems the odds of my understanding whether an actual request was proffered is minimal at best. I could check though, and I will, and I am now conjuring up the image of said masturbating mime in my head, an image to be truthful I had previously tried so hard to banish. You did ask me to provide a remix, didn't you, I say to said masturbating mime's image? Silence. Nothing. Well, nothing, besides a quizzical look. Say something. Oh. Fuck. Right. Huh, it seems that a response I can reasonably interpret may not be so forthcoming, but thanks for the opportunity regardless, it really was an honor to have been possibly asked. It was also a lot of fun. For me anyway.

Postica 4.9: A Fragment
Multifesto Me
by Ben Tanzer

INT. THE WHISTLER - CHICAGO, IL - TODAY

YOU, Age 43, shockingly handsome, yet unrelentingly humble in manner and temperament sits at a back table where he is joined by DAVIS SCHNEIDERMAN, Age unknown, and dressed as a mime, white face, beret and all.

> SCHNEIDERMAN
> I hope you'll consider this.

> YOU
> For you, anything.

> SCHNEIDERMAN
> It's a remix and I know how you feel about
> remixes.

You takes a long drink from his maple-infused, Whiskey Mojito and then pauses for a moment as he wipes a trace of Loganberry from his upper lip.

> YOU
> But a remix can mean anything I like, is that
> true?

> SCHNEIDERMAN
> You can rewrite it. Erase it. Burn it. Hell, you
> can perform fucking Oulipian operations on
> it if that gets your rocks off and you meet the
> deadline.

You reaches over and takes Schneiderman's hands in his. You brushes the hair off of Schneiderman's face, briefly stares into Schneiderman's deep, brown eyes, ignores the fact that Schneiderman is erect and then pulling away finishes his drink.

                    YOU
I've never missed a deadline, Schneiderman, you
know that, and I never say no to a mime, frankly,
I can't stand those sad faces you guys do.

                    SCHNEIDERMAN
We count on that.

                    YOU
And you can count on me.

                    SCHNEIDERMAN
I will let Phoenelia know.

                    YOU
Please do and please send her my love.

You throws a twenty-dollar bill on the table and leaves the bar as
Schneiderman walks onto the stage and proceeds to use an artisan-
constructed dunk tank to soak a series of books and Kindles.

                                                    CUT TO:

INT. YOU'S MOTEL ROOM – NIGHT

You is sitting in his motel room with his new child DIAL-UP
NETWORKING, Age 2, who is both cute and wiry. You looks into the
mirror over the desk and sees Schneiderman looking back at him.

                    SCHNEIDERMAN
You live out these philosophies of the bedroom
with your new child, Dial-Up Networking. All
of the forty-nine letters you have spent the
most recent years inspecting (except the seven
yet to be opened) have been torn and shoe-
printed to form a thick, uncomfortable carpet
that obscures any real analysis of Post-America.
Despite your constant desire to absorb pieces
of the postmodern body-lips spread across the
billboard landscape and the soft, lolling lilt of
the elongated tongue stretched into a surrealist

parachute across the silver frayed sounds of
the sky-you cannot identify with this newly
reanimated Henri d'Mescan.

YOU

Fragmentation is often deceptively autocratic.

Schneiderman pauses for a moment, pursing his lips. You stares at him
and reflects on the irony that Schneiderman may be a mime, but You
has never seen him truly silent until this very moment.

SCHNEIDERMAN

As you watch the shape and figure of the child
asleep in the hotel bed, the irony of post-irony
is not lost on the talking picture box that
flashes your image across its pixilated screen.
You are placed surreptitiously in an advert for
the newest body-hardening zit cream. You?
Or just a disguised version of your hair curled
loose as the lip-roaring newscaster, the weather
vixen's pointy tits exciting the cumulonimbus
hard-on of Davis Schneiderman, erect no doubt
at his personal fucking computer miming your
Botex-injected jelly flesh under the gaze of the
Spuyten Duyvil deadline. Worse even, your
tiny child, Dial-Up Networking, materializes
in her bassinet each morning, fresh, as though
you have never left her. She insults your
ineffective escape with each suckle, peppering
the wall of your room with excremental smears,
mesmerizing curlicues.

It is now You's turn to pause as he finds himself stuck on the fact that
Schneiderman is once again erect as he is speaking to him. You turns
away and looks for a book to divert his attention from Schneiderman's
erection and the fact that its image is slowly and incontrovertibly
being etched into his brain.

You reads d'Mescan's "Postica 4.9" without context, silent in the glow
of a mosaic candleholder, scratching at the underside of his twin
wrists as they burn from the edge of the typing desk that makes You

complicit in his own mistranslation.

A strange slice bleeds from You, while his issue sleeps away his soft subdued traumas as if everything seems corporeal and settled.

The rhythm of the child's repetitive breath sucks You's fleeting analytical inertia into the spirals of her respiratory track; the vortex pulls You's hand down the curve of her swollen body, slowly teasing and then penetrating the elastic ring of silk underwear bought in haste from the local Presbyterian rummage sale; an angel is extracted from the ramparts of some medieval fresco by the cruel renaissance wind while You's fingers rub against the clitoris made warm and soft by the vacuum emanating from the breath of the child, tickling You's pubic hair where the razor blade once smoothed blue to hide the sweet electromagnetic tangle of his soul.

Soft ooze spreads downs slowly from his waarm center and covers his pulsating fingers in a sticky heat that You smears over the gooseflesh of her exposed chest. Undulating his figure into an ocean, rocking a hot triangle boat in his dark places, You rubs the wet balm over his inner thighs and then onto the sheets, hiding black-lit cum stains of this motel room's past residents.

You turns back to the mirror.

> SCHNEIDERMAN (CONT'D)
> Fluorescent cat-o-nine-tails and vibrant fur-
> lined handcuffs and a collocation of franked
> bank notes and half-smoked cigarettes
> stuffed into these motel spaces prove Davis
> Schneiderman a traitor and you writhe next to
> the flickering image of the child; he speaks in
> your mind like a fraud who uses language to
> smother you body in bed sheets stained and
> crumpled by your hand, the shaking blur of
> the ceiling fan blades casting interval light from
> that TV.

You wonders why Schneiderman insists on speaking in third-person. You wonders about a lot of things when it comes to Schneiderman.

Onto You's. Sweaty body-caught in an acrobatic arc as the world narrows and tightens around him like a latex suit. You's nipples harden, glistening with droplets of sweat and texture, as the silent orgasm creeps from the deep backland of your insides through the sacrament of the hand and the colored lines that seem to grab and suck against the space of a text that is not the place for Henri d'Mescan to emerge no not the space at all no not in a final delirious yes of words flooding yes across the picture space and flowing into You's ears his nose his cum-stained yes mouth gurgling yes the white hot liquid in throbs of television set-ups spelling yes on the lip of its pixilated screen.

The child cries while You loop-de-loops against the black forever that makes him say yes and yes again and someone else writes him yes now before the delirium of the bassinet starts his hands working the type all over again with such formal gesticulations so yes and yes again.

CUT TO:

EXT - THE STREETS OF LAKE FOREST - LATER

Police sirens speed down the streets of Post-America, and through the myriad apertures that have long ago replaced windows-through keyholes and cameras, through the slit of the stapler, the ski mask, the piano wire, through You's fingers splayed forcefully over the eyes-flashing red or blue or white strobes riding efficiently in the air.

The sirens stay disconnected, ghostly, without chassis below. This is peephole ontology.

You look through the peephole and there is Schneiderman.

> SCHNEIDERMAN
> Everything moves so fast that it can jump
> through the playback machine like the Pullman
> car sliding effortlessly from its outmoded
> groove. Sloe gin can be administered for relief
> of cold sores and implementation of the viral
> record. Sloe motion, solely for effect.

> YOU
> That is, into a burst of regular speed.

You is on the move again.

Through the slats of tomorrow's newspaper and virtual inkpad clipped with the absent scissors and censored by dark marker, through the piles of fast food excrement and leftover sweat from the anus of basketball stars, through the splice of the dumpster roof against its casing, through the walls of the alley mashed by ubiquitous astigmatisms into the illusion of ovals You can see the sirens and its coterie of flash, cleaving the grim partition of the night as it slides over the streets, intent upon the corner of a chafing mouth rotten with sores, on a sheath of jaundiced skin slowly healing a crack in the ice from a sharp skate, on the lip of a patriotic national face.

You walks down the alley and there once again is Schneiderman.

> SCHNEIDERMAN
> Through the perspective of an alley, Davis
> Schneiderman's penis is shrinking everyday.
> In time, it will disappear into the space
> between his legs. In Post-America he serves a
> sentence for sins committed by the interlocking
> appendages and orifices now filled-in by his
> so-called neat-and-tidies. No one believes
> his protestations. Asymptotic differences are
> eliminated with the alchemical formula of a
> bathtub philosopher's stone.

Schneiderman's penis, You wonders if he will ever escape its image, not to mention Schneiderman himself.

> YOU
> Do not believe him when he proclaims my
> innocence.

You is on the move again, out of the alley, away from Schneiderman, back onto the turgid streets of Lake Forest and racing towards the factory on the outskirts of the city.

Partisans tear the clothing from the body of the factory, squeaking backward to Quark generation points only 800 million years on the brink of the big-bang precipice.

The next step is to tattoo the patterns formed by the charges onto You's chest igniting tiny receptor nodes in the bandoleer onto the skin in a pain-ritual reminiscent of the calculation continuum of the Etruscan calendar, a 10,000-year cycle only now reaching a pre-apocalyptic fruition.

Well that, and Schneiderman of course, always Schneiderman, once in a mirror, then a peephole and now looking up at You from his chest.

> YOU (CONT'D)
> Yes, a fantastic moment, seeing yourself in the
> author's place.

> SCHNEIDERMAN
> It starts in the gut, as described, but life is
> nothing before expulsion through the mouth,
> having smothered the tongue and teeth,
> covering everything in a veneer of broken
> promises and industrial sludge, just as today, in
> Post-America, it is difficult to substantiate the
> most enormous historical events let alone the
> tiniest death throes of a no-good collaborator.

> YOU
> The idea of the past forms an amalgamation
> with the present perceptive apparatus and the
> projected need of the future.

> SCHNEIDERMAN
> Alternative pasts fail to promote alternative
> futures so long as the present apparatus
> remains in control of all projections. The
> police, my friends, can reach back into your
> womb for their evidence, pushing scissors
> and knife through the sweet gash of vagina
> stretching to the limits of breath and gene.

You turns away from Schneiderman, the factory and Lake Forest. You looks out across the universe before him. You closes his eyes and contemplates the future.

They will cut the child from the aperture without a warrant, brand their indentations onto the soft, spattering skull of the prison-house, the garret, the sideward glance of the video camera that always records. Space crackles with a pulsing electric energy-reason enough, for those still in their slits, to fear for their eventual shape on such an abnormally cold summer afternoon.

CUT TO:

INT. YOUTUBE - LATER STILL

You wanders the Broken Books Channel on YouTube. Schneiderman's penis is nowhere in sight and You is relieved. Schneiderman however is everywhere, both deconstructing MULTIFESTO: A HENRI D'MESCAN REMIX and talking, always talking.

> SCHNEIDERMAN
> No doubt, Phoenelia Yeer, selected through
> some arcane mathematical formulae to go first,
> already expressed her outrage at the limits
> imposed by Henri d'Mescan and his authorial
> rules. She also, assuredly, spent considerable
> space locating herself within the sphere of the
> child, Dial-Up Networking, before promising
> you, good reader, the eventual denouement
> of the whole d'Mescan/Mescaline mystery.
> We have wasted no such space and we have
> not altered our voice to the will of d'Mescan.
> If we must work in Haiku, we were prepared
> for the sound of a million frogs splashing
> in bloody winter pools, for / this piece was
> not a haiku / not if you could count / the all
> wrong syllables are. "Post-America, in p a r
> t s..." appeared to be the initial segment of a
> larger quest narrative, whereas, the hero, who
> in this case became Henri d'Mescan himself,
> attempted to restore his pre-"Identity Trial"
> name through the retrieval of an original cache
> of the so-called collaborationist work known
> as the "Vichy Papers." We noticed with what
> great care he expressed his own innocence and

established the motives for the reclamation
of his image, which had been tarnished by
unscrupulous characters such as Phoenelia
Yeer. Even we visualized this mother staring at
the fissures in the wall, mad and tone deaf, on
several different occasions, so that any crack
to her remaining façade was as welcome to us
as the snap of an ovary and halved the devil
entering her skin through the doorway of
the soul.

Speaking of doorways You realizes it is time to go.

CUT TO:

INT. COLUMBIA COLLEGE - AND/NOW

Post-America rides the backwards cracks of a pre-Columbian
anthology of sin, over the land of dead tape recorders, basketballs court
halved by archaic power lines snaking over heat-blistered macadam.
Schneiderman's image appears to You in the cracks of the macadam at
his feet. You is confused.

YOU

Where did it come from?

SCHNEIDERMAN

My spinal fingers always clutch around the
palm of my nerve stem and she dissipated
into the angular jut of rusted mansard roofs,
my promise my beauty, sweet Phoenelia
Yeer, a casualty of the lily bulbs fused to my
duplicitous, forked tongue. Oh my secret sin
and the long-distance cunnilingus. How I
wormed my way into the cavity that represents
her heart, into the sweet, hidden crook of
her coochie snorcher. I'm almost ashamed
of my behavior. I've been a very naughty boy
which of course serves as no excuse for this
particular excursion to the left bank, in the
area of the Sorbonne, far removed from the

418

dirt of Pigalle and the Moulin Rouge and St.
Denis at Montmarte, to complete my manic,
anemic contracts.

This talk of cunnilingus prompts You to once again think about
Schneiderman's penis. Seeking to distract himself You looks around at
his surroundings.

Nineteenth-century gilded spires decorate the classic metro stops:
baldachins of finely wrought iron now preserved in retrograde pop-art
posters surrounded by the spritz of carbonated bath water from deadly
aluminum Coca-Cola cans merging with the sickly, stringy texture of
jambon and mozzarella in the mouths of bi-lingual patisserie patrons.

You wants to run away, but remains enthralled with Schneiderman's
visage, command of language and penis.

> SCHNEIDERMAN (CONT'D)
> The establishment hopes for Our Lady of the
> Flowers and Our Lady of Perpetual Motion
> to snatch the crown of thorns from the Sun
> King's petrified crotch and smash its little
> prick over the clandestine contour of the
> Post-American body. Customs agents will
> seize the secret "Vichy Papers," like Brancusi's
> Bird in Space, parroting the same sales tax
> justification or perhaps some other, more
> sinister multinational tariff. These texts might
> then be spirited away, along with the fragrance
> of lilies on the summer wind, excised into the
> folds of the great, amniotic Feedback LOOP,
> absent like the lips of a dead grandmother on
> the cheek of the night, so that what passes for
> God can consolidate its stranglehold through
> the tripartite divisions of multinational capital-
> the world beef market, the linguistic terrorism
> of US expectations, and the soft-but-dried
> flesh and anthrax-infested brain structures
> colonized in concrete about these sordid
> European capitals. So the rinderpest infects us
> all, slandering the darks skin while burning

the Jews, Trappist Monks, Episcopalians, Sunni
Muslims, Freemasons, Burmese, Swiss, Sufis,
Tsars, CEO's, sports stars, actors, circus clowns,
and virtual avatars of minor deities, etc.

YOU
Words, when wielded with the reckless
abandon of manufactured consent will signify
anything and everything that people wish
to revile. Take me for instance, in the years
after the war: accused of stirring the masses
toward a path of rigorous co-belligerency with
the German forces, I slept with the machine
called God in the rickets of straw and compost
and musty shit while the illusion of a free
France dangled its corrupt participles into
the gruesome syntax of the Fourth Republic.
There is an erotica to axle grease. Total
communication is a Fascist strategy, and even
if employed in the critique and prosecution of
National Socialism, you can bet your bottom
dollar that the contradiction will be sublimated
at the level of cliché. The flesh trades. The
incessant peddling of tissue banks and forced
organ donations onto the DNA-stained veils
of nail, skin, and archaic ligature. I had to buy
my own copies of Henri d'Mescan's "Vichy
Papers" from a mirror of my former mistakes
(near exact reproduction of originals) in jewels
and techno-gear at the money changers in the
20th arrondisment by displaying the identity
cards given me by a gold-toothed Monte
dealer who loiters outside Invalides, working
the old sleight-of-hand and bantering out a
fabricated history. Information transfer requires
an understanding of the flesh technologies,
economic viruses that pass through the
membranes of safe-sex devices. You can still
pick up an outdated anarchist cookbook with
"my" documents for the right price if someone
hasn't duplicated your identity, snatched them

all, Crocodilopolis included, the original
version, and burned it all to soot with the
leftover garbage.

For only the second time since You has met Schneiderman, Schneiderman
is speechless, his visage slowly fading away as the macadam cools.

And You moves on.

The old world shakes as You reads; concrete bricks set behind the
Seine's sunbathing victims who flash and carry on, topless, as the
tourist boats pass under the bridges, receiving rainbow showers from
the punctured antipodes of gargoyle and stone. Scalpel fights and
genetic tangles.

And You moves on.

Each historical layer of city fits slash-and-burn atop the next, pushes
against subterranean pressure tanks with an amalgamated ferment
oozing for decades in the gut of the Parisian soul.

And You moves on.

A statue of Napoleon with undescended testes spurts a translucent
grey fish stock in the lead-lined aqueducts of sewer beasts and liquid
nitrate. Nike of Samothrace laces up her air sneakers and drops a load
of gleaming shit on the floor of the Louvre.

And You moves on.

Syphilis boys jump down from their hidden tree-forts, giggling with
the numb laughter of broken condoms and useless dental dams. They
paratroop from the lips of tired monuments behind a sky made crimson
green with the methane of their farts. Before they can strike, they shiver
and shake and fall to the splitting ground, tiny wedges disappearing into
the broken soil. They are no match for the AIDS virus.

And You moves on.

Algerian death squads and the mind control commandos from French
Equatorial Africa brandish weapons of mass insurrection, spaying a

silicon film over all telephone booths, monuments, rivers, orphans, and chocolate croissants.

THEY
Everything can just slide on in.

And You moves on.

Each outrageous palace, lining every single city block, decorated with the bone and horn of previous generations, rips its hooks in a simultaneous orgasm-orchestrated on a global timetable from everywhere all at once.

And You moves on.

You stumbles outside the Hotel de Ville, a drunkard lost in the confusion of images, a symbolist poet set crooked on the absinthe pathway. An old woman braces You's back with the arch of her stomach, the snap of her arm, and You takes her down with him, joyously, to the face of the pavement and the cracking skeleton of infirmity.

And then You moves on.

Across town and river, an illuminated carrier pigeon smacks into the Eiffel Tower, the world's largest radio antennae with bright Citroen blaze down its side, and its body, You's body, are both smothered and protected, the result of the hybrid miracle no longer impossible in this strange world of jelly and pus.

And You moves on.

FADE TO BLACK.

422

The Seventeenth __{noun}__ of Ordinary __{noun}__
by Kathleen Rooney

Bio: Kathleen Rooney is a founding editor of Rose Metal press, a nonprofit publisher dedicated to hybrid work. She is the author, most recently, of the essay collection *For You, For You I Am Trilling These Songs* and her second poetry collection, *Robinson Alone*, is forthcoming from Gold Wake Press. With Elisa Gabbert, she is the author of *That Tiny Insane Voluptuousness*. She is a Visiting Assistant Professor of English and Creative Writing at DePaul University, and is the 2011-2012 Writer in Residence at Roosevelt University. She blogs at <u>kathleenrooney.com</u>

About: Rooney chose to do her remix as a Mad Lib, removing key verbs, nouns, adjectives and proper names to obscure the original meaning, and to give the reader the option of filling in the blanks to create her own new meaning.

The Seventeenth __{noun}__ of Ordinary __{noun}__
by Kathleen Rooney

Post-America—a new __{noun}__, we continue our regular rehabilitation of __{adjective}__ sinners with morality plays set to the tenor of life in our gleaming __{noun}__, our bright, __{adjective}__ Post-America. This is your host, Godless Heathen #5, and I'm here with my special guest, __{noun}__ and long-time convert to the cause of __{imaginary organization name}__, a radical __{adjective}__ concern intent on __{verb ending in "ing"}__ the Un-American world—Genetically Spliced Rhesus Monkey. We wish you all, over the airwaves, trundling in the celebrity sea, a good and scrumptious __{noun}__ of __{noun}__ and__{noun}__ rejoicing.

***

Call me __{Proper Name #1}__. It's 27% less __{verb ending in "ing"}__.

***

We begin today's pseudo-__{noun}__ in praise of the __{noun}__ . Open your __{noun}__ to hyperlink Alpha Bravo Charlie, __{title of a book}__, and join with us in ringing "__{popular song lyrics}__..." through the vibrant Morse code transmitter and blood sugar finger prick connected to your international ID cards...

***

""__{popular song lyrics}__"__{popular song lyrics}__" __{popular song lyrics}__"

***

OK, __{Proper Name #1}__, let's take our first __{noun}__ ...this one comes from little __{Proper Name #2}__ in __{Place Name}__. Good thing we're on the radio, so little __{Proper Name #2}__ won't have to __{verb}__ to see us. What's your question little __{noun}__?

***

Does everyone have a __{adjective}__ __{noun}__? I wonder because many members of my government act like godless apes that perpetuate a system of __{adjective}__ __{noun}__ through the mask of a __{adjective}__ __{noun}__.

Wow, you speakem exceedingly well __{language}__ for an __{ethnicity}__ __{noun}__, don't she __{Proper Name #1}__?

***

Indeed, it must be the __{adjective}__ __{noun}__ run by __{TV show}__. Many folks out there in image hyper-land remain unaware of the recent __{plural noun}__ of the __{Company Name}__ in visiting __{plural noun}__ around the __{ noun}__ and facilitating participation in __{adjective}__ "Me Journals." __{plural noun}__ write, in their primitive script, all of the things that compose "me"—pets, friends, favorite colors, sexual experiences, opinion on trade unions, dreams for welfare fraud when they reach the legal age of consent, favorite fights for step-mommy—and then, the nice __{plural noun}__ at __{Company Name}__ collect the journals...

***

To what __{noun}__?

***

__{plural noun}__. Can you say "__{same plural noun}__" little __{Proper Name #2}__? If not, try "Four-patty meat-like burger-amalgamate" for starters...

***

My government tells me that __{plural noun}__ and __{plural noun}__ are a tool of the __{adjective}__ __{noun}__, the __{adjective}__ __{noun}__, as I believe you in the westernized nations refer to it...but what about the __{adjective}__ __{plural nouns}__? I have to go to the bathroom and then study math science chemical genetic social engineering to get the jump on your most ordinary cadre of porn-obsessed graduate students who consider computer programming and science fiction conventions to be an intellectual pursuit on par with eastern meditation tours to Mt. Kilimanjaro and the Special Crystal Power Center in Durango, Mexico. So, quickly, __{adjective}__ __{plural noun}__, do even __{plural noun}__ have a __{adjective}__ __{noun}__?

***

Ah yes...one of the __{plural noun}__ unavailable to the everyday __{ethnicity}__ says that __{proper plural noun}__, even uncircumcised __{same proper plural noun}__, as well as other assorted __{ plural noun}__, no less, have somebody looking out for them. And we all know that they won't go off half-cocked. So the answer would have to be "yes." The most famous __{plural noun}__, of Post-America, of course, is Mutation, portrayed in moving pictures with a trumpet or flute, a flaming sword puncturing the chassis on a __{type of vehicle}__, and a styrofoam crest from which globular orbs of landfill shit procreating so ancient bacterium graft to human DNA.

***

Thanks you __{Proper Name #1}__. Our next __{noun}__, or I think it's a __{noun}__,…more of a feeling in my __{body part}__ …well anyway…one tender __{Proper Name #3}__, from a non-triangulated location, wants to learn the definition of a __{adjective}__ __{noun}__?

***

The noblest thing you can do, __{Proper Name #3}__, is to martyr yourself for the glory of the __{noun}__. Over the horizon, under the moon, the last clinging vines will follow your __{noun}__as far as the __{adjective}___{noun}__will allow, and__{verb}__you, beyond all political boundaries and demographic redistricting plans, into the droning presence of the __{adjective}__ __{noun}__. The __{ noun}__ recommends a descent into the sewers followed by the release of a junta-style computer virus that infiltrates Osama Bin Laden's Al Qaeda organization and displaces all remaining Palestinians before exploding from the originator's belly in radioactive spores and blinding, seizure-inducing __{adjective}___{plural noun}__.

***

That's great __{Proper Name #1}__ I routinely try to kill myself after leaving awkward social situations without having taken __{drug}__. Does this count?

***

No, Godless Heathen, this does not count. There are always more mood-altering drugs available to mitigate the __{noun}__. Only if your insurance or gateway provider or HMO or PPP no longer covers the prescription because your __{noun}__ has transmogrified out of __{noun}__ would you be justified in __{verb ending in "ing"}__ yourself for the greater __{noun}__of the multinational __{noun}__.

***

So you recommend constant dosing it seems? I understand now. Perhaps you can advise me after this broadcast…but now we have the __{adjective}__ __{noun}__to spread __{Proper Name #3}__ has a follow-up question for you, __{Proper Name #1}__: Can martyrs climb levels of __{improper place name}__?

***

No, Godless Heathen and __{Proper Name #3}__, the level of __{improper place name}__ assigned to upon your initial proteome sequencing corresponds to your deeds in Post-America, especially after racial profiling was officially excluded by __{adjective}__ __{noun}__ doctrine over three years ago. Of course, there is bound to be some residual, institutional prejudice. Nothing serious, you understand. Thus, each action you do or do not do now will be punished later on by the __{noun}__ you are kept away from the __{noun}__. For instance, anyone caught without their international ID card when stopped by an duly vested __{adjective}__ __{noun}__will be given a restraining order of at least two miles for the holy __{adjective}__ __{noun}__, which I need not remind you, is quite a distance when we talk about the fiber-optics of the blastosphere.

***

Thanks __{Proper Name#1}__, and our final question today, from an anonymous source, asks the question—what is __{improper place name}__ and where is it?

***

Well, for Rhesus monkeys such as myself, __{improper place name}__ can be a trip to DNA counselor. There are __{plural noun}__ and there is heaven, and the two are far from mutually exclusive. Sometimes, when our body ails us, we pay a visit to one of the friendly medical professionals of the Ely-Lily Corporation whose fine products can cure most earthly ills. Still, there is time spent waiting in the lobby of the __{improper place name}__ where the representative has agreed to meet with you, there is time wasted in the limousine on the way to dinner, and finally, when talking with the representative, just before agreeing to distribute or order a certain quantity of a certain product line, say Paxil, there is the uncomfortable __{noun}__ of digestion where the implanted__{body part}__ rejects the __{food}__ sprinkled liberally with anthrax and smushed into the __{body part}__. You may be sick, and a cure may be in development, but you must wait in a hole, an aperture, an in-between. That, of course, is purgatory, and if

427

you think things are bad now in Post-America, we will come to our reward only once these holes have all closed up, only after the medicine disseminates into the seething, fiery core once called the soul. We __{verb}__ for you to get fixed in triplicate, just as we __{verb}__ the doctor in quadruplicate through the proper channels in quintuplicate. We decry any direct action except the strategic repatriation of our foreign policy team from the grips of Southeast Asian prison camps and/or the disintegration of the Post-American family through the vortex of thirteen-year-old whores whose only recourse in such situations it to perform medical testing on captive__{animals}__ while dabbing cosmetics in the eyes of innocent __{animals}__ to keep their exponentially reproductive mechanisms secret from our inadvertently sterilized genetic stock.

***

And sometimes, this repair by the scientific doctor is __{adjective}__?

***

Oh yes, Godless Heathen, you have absolutely no idea what __{plural nouns}__ are capable of these days. They've even eliminated the climax, excised all dime-store epiphanic endings, replacing these with a completely pre-scripted and banal "moment of clarity."

***

I see.

***

And that's what this __{noun}__ is all about.

***

It makes perfect sense.

***

Thanks to all the great questions from our intrepid little __{plural nouns}__. And thanks to you, __{Proper Name #1}__, for your carcinogenic little sacrifices…we'll close today with the Seventeenth __{noun}__ of Ordinary __{noun}__hymnal—"__{song title}__" And we'll meet you on the Eighteenth __{noun}__ of Ordinary __{noun}__, a day like any other day….

***

__{song lyrics}__ __{song lyrics}__ __{song lyrics}__

428

How Not to Sublet *or* Post-American Lease Negotiations
Infinite Return (feat. Spacecat)
by James Tadd Adcox

Bio: James Tadd Adcox's work has appeared in *TriQuarterly*, *The Literary Review*, *Lamination Colony*, and *LIES/ISLE*. He is a founding editor of Artifice Magazine/Artifice Books (<u>artificebooks.org</u>). His first book, *The Map of the System of Human Knowledge*, was published in 2012 from Tiny Hardcore Press.

About: I've been working on what, to myself at least, I've taken to calling "cybernetic writing": writing using found language and found events, rewriting and writing over that found language and those found events, making no effort to distinguish my writing or my changes from the found pieces incorporated. Letting the rhythms and disjunctions of cut-ups and collage infect my writing, treating my "original" writing as a sort of cut-up, etc. This with the goal of having a text—finally—in which I cannot distinguish what I wrote from what I stole. Taking seriously William Gass's contention that a character is a noun that a certain set of predicates and adjectives attach themselves to. Structuring my writing around a set of obsessive nouns: it doesn't matter what the nouns are, so long as they reappear (Zachery Schomberg's book *The Man Suit* has been an influence here, as well).

I'd like to create texts that are more territories than narratives.

How Not to Sublet or Post-American Lease Negotiations
Infinite Return (feat. Spacecat)
by James Tadd Adcox

> Father: It seems just what we're looking for in a place where a father and daughter with a special relationship can exist in peace and friendship with the surrounding areas and benefit from the area's enlightened intellectual community because I'm a bit of closet intellectual although I work out of the home and sell insurance which puts me in a radical philosophical quandary which I negotiate through prayer to a variety of interlocking deities with ancient arms and buck-toothed mannerisms who prepare me for the coming rapture with carefully arranged product-placement accounts. Beside, Post-America has nice schools.

> Daughter: Ow! The little fucker scratched me!

…

We now return you to the adventures of Spacecat

What Spacecat burns remains burned, it does not resurrect, it does not go flying upward like some magnificent Phoenix, get that image out of your head, what Spacecat burns remains ash.

Everything Spacecat does has already been done by either Porky Pig or Woody the Woodpecker, which is to say that Spacecat's life is prefigured, Spacecat is the result of a series of images repeating.

There is a terror in the heart of Spacecat.

I am watching a Woody the Woodpecker cartoon and everything everything is Spacecat. Every gesture.

We now return you to the adventures of Spacecat

Spacecat pulls up the skin at the edges of his eyes and speaks in a thick fake Oriental voice, like r-r-r-r, just like Woody the Woodpecker confronting the Asian Menace.

The violence of Spacecat is particularly unsettling because you can never tell if it is violence or only the gesture of violence, at least I can't.

A dance, done by Spacecat. Spacecat in blackface before you understood what blackface was, back when it was just something that sometimes happened on cartoons, maybe one of those goofy round bombs went off in someone's face & suddenly there was banjo music playing, who knows why anything happens in cartoons, back when you were too young for there to be causal connections.

I remember a specific joke about suicide in a Bugs Bunny cartoon from when I was maybe eight years old, I've seen that cartoon since then and they've taken it out, that joke, it's just disappeared.

"Mama what is Spacecat doing on TV?"

How memory acts as a placeholder for what was once there. The French word for ghost: *that which comes back.*

We now, etc

Spacecat is an intergalactic hero! Spacecat shows off his claws, they have threatened to declaw him but there those claws are, magnificent, eight toes to a paw and every single one of them sprouting razor-sharp, in and out at will. *Who is they?* They is indeterminate, they is always somewhere off the edge of the TV set, they is the gloved robot hand on the end of the spring, the spring that you see only once the chair turns and the bomb, the bomb that is there instead of they, the bomb that is about to go off—

Spacecat in one of those fishbowl outerspace helmets, the villain, in a purple cape, he has strapped Spacecat to a table, there's some sort of horrible device hovering above, exact function unclear, the scene is tense with can I say eroticism, fuck, there is something operating behind what we are seeing on the screen, there are other relationships between these characters, other meanings behind each of their words, we get one set of meanings because the cartoon has provided a certain context, but there is another context behind the cartoon, each of these characters has another face…

A series of memories that all reflect back at each other, empty, charged with meanings that I cannot articulate though the things that caused these memories, I now understand, were by and large themselves meaningless.

WE NOW RETURN YOU TO THE ADVENTURES OF SPACECAT

"I have some seasonal affective, I guess," Spacecat says to his therapist. "I've realized that mostly since I've come to the Midwest. Like each winter, I can tell, it really gets to me. The lack of sunlight."

"It's pretty sunny now," Spacecat's therapist says. "It's been sunny for a while."

"I know," says Spacecat.

WE...

A commercial for Hagen-Das, a commercial for Froot Loops Cereal, a commercial/manifesto for Cocoa Puffs ("I'm KKK-KOOKOO for COCOA PUFFS"), a commercial for figurines based on the Spacecat franchise, vehicles that have been suspiciously introduced to the Spacecat television show, new characters who have appeared in televised and toy form almost simultaneously, a commercial for children's health insurance aimed at any responsible adults who might be in the room, which without getting altogether too graphic contains dark hints about possibilities for your child's immediate future, WHAT WE ARE CALLING FOR comes the voice of Dial-Up Networking IS THE IRRADICATION OF THE NO. 1 MOST COMMON VENEREAL DISEASE AND THAT LITTLE FUCKER IS SITTING ON THE CARPET RIGHT IN FRONT OF YOU, YOU RAH G-DDAMN SPONSIBLE ADULT YOU

We now return you! To the adventures!

"What I'm hearing from you," says the therapist, "is that in fact you know what you want. Your main concern is that you're not sure how to get there. It seems to me that you have a tremendous advantage over a lot of people I've talked with, who don't know what they want, or can't articulate it."

Spacecat feels himself about to cry, it's not from anything that the therapist has said but more just the way that she's looking at him, like she's knows how sad and fucked up he is and isn't going to let him get away with pretending otherwise, the look feels confrontational to Spacecat, it feels like she's saying "I *know*, now what the fuck are you going to do about it?" it's a look that makes Spacecat feel vulnerable and almost like *violated* even, of course he feels like a wuss for even thinking in these terms. "I guess," says Spacecat.

We now return you to the adventures of Spacecat

"It seems hardly reasonable at first glance to suppose that an entirely new literature might one day—now, for instance—be possible," says Spacecat. "The many attempts made these last thirty years to drag fiction out of its ruts have resulted, at best, in no more than isolated works. And—we are often told—none of these works, whatever its interest, has gained the adherence of a public comparable to that of the bourgeois novel. The only conception of the novel to have currency today is, in fact, that of Balzac.

"My primary fear is loneliness," says Spacecat. "I'm afraid that I'm like, secretly really annoying to most people. Or else entirely forgettable. Like if I don't keep doing things to make them like me or to remind them I'm there they'll just entirely forget about me.

"The problem is that there *are* people like that. I know people like that," Spacecat says. "People that other people actively don't want around, maybe not for any big thing, but just because they're kind of boring or awkward. It's not like those people *know* that they're those people. Or like maybe they suspect it, but you can't just stop trying to talk to people because you suspect that nobody wants to talk with you. You can't just hide. And so you become one of those annoying, sad people that like, nobody is willing to be directly rude to, but nobody wants to have around.

"The entire caste system of our literary life," says Spacecat, "(from publisher to the humblest reader, including bookseller and critic) has no choice but to oppose the unknown. The minds best disposed to the idea of a necessary transformation, those most willing to countenance and even to welcome the values of experiment, remain, nonetheless, the heirs of a tradition."

We no return youto the adventures of

—Ow! The little fucker scratched me!

Multifesto: A Henri d'Mescan **ReMix**
After-Words by William Walsh

After-Words:
JUNE JUNEAU MAY MAYBE
by William Walsh
From Multifesto: A Henri D'Mescan Reader (2006)

Bio: William Walsh is the author of *Ampersand, Mass.*, *Pathologies*, and *Questionstruck* (all from Keyhole Press), and *Without Wax* (Casperian Books). His stories and texts have appeared in a number of journals, including *Annalemma, Caketrain, Quick Fiction, Lit, Artifice, New York Tyrant, Quarterly West, Juked,* and elsewhere.

About: My multifestant is called "June Juneau May Maybe." It's a tracking piece that interrogates the themes of time, place, and probability in *Multifesto: A Henri D'Mescan Reader* (2006). The time is June. The place is Juneau, Alaska. And concept of probability is a multifestance of conditionals, permissions, and uncertainties—the virgin may and the whore maybe.

I. HENRI AND JUNE

You recall your greenish-blue June croon moon eyes; you shed your skin, shiver in buckets while editing Henri d'Mescan into this protean volume you hold now in your hands. And there is the glorious June 14 to come, when General van Metacom's troops storm the Bastille and look for revenge on de Sade and his country of homoerotic dandies. "Pre-Cinema" referred to the various theories circulated in the wake of Henri d'Mescan's lecture series at the Collage de Sociopathology (June 1935), entitled "The Curse of General Linguistics." It will take place in the near future, June 1940, and will be continually projected on national molecular screens in all French Departments—the retinal strand, the cinema house, veins pumping silent ichor through undead circulatory tubing. At 6:50 p.m. on June 22, 1940 the armistice requested officially by Marshal Pétain, the French Premiere, will be signed with the German people. On June 25, 1940, hostilities will cease, and our film, *Crocodilopolis*, will eroticize just this sort of triumphant history. (in June 1947.) On June 19, 1960, Henry Mescaline slept on the same park bench that Fidel Castro spent the night in after a failed audition for professional baseball. Snoring lightly, black holes nostrils flaring softly under a June croon moon lay Round Earth, entrenched in MaMa's broken bed, a man whose tarnished toothbrush bristles stink of iodine, a man whose boots are interlaced with frizzled fiberoptic cords, a man who reminds me, tender Dial-Up Networking, all muzzled and folded in MaMa's warm corona, of some approximation of some maybe, some possibility, some pregnant, paternal, perhaps. The moon sops the sticky moisture of June into its white and yellow craters. My interconnectedness screams to be touched, accessed, given new source code, as claws are cocked and covert, paddling through fields of cobalt reeds to liquid oblivion furrows, cutting into the flesh of my flesh, whiskers whistling June moon songs.

II. HENRI AND JUNEAU

Mescaline wrestled with "the angel" who spoke with his voice in his next "sudden" pamphlet, "Forty-Nine Prefaces to a Single-Volume

Regicide Indictment"—a work so underground that the only known copy of the first printing was discovered in late 1959, balancing a sewing-machine table leg in Juneau, Alaska.

-o-

III. HENRI AND MAY

In your editorial work
I will find your future self
—the literary editor—
who may as well unearth
a new original version
of me in the process.
Benevolent neutrality,
in your words, may be it.

Tacg considers that his boss may be a Jew, and that his own inestimable poverty (although that's a word he would never use, "inestimable"), must then be conditioned by other words he would never use, and that in life, no topic has received more attention than "gene longevity."

The various judges may be equally degraded by the incompetence of the firing crew, the death squad, but the needs of authority allow every two-bit artist an endless supply of corpses. Most, though, rarely wonder, and more plausibly, carry fresh squadrons of broken-down scabies from gleaming brothels in town, blowing the last of their death-squad advance, occasionally musing upon the efficacy of the blanks they may or may not fire at the cigarette-smoking enemy.

When gun meets horizon, Tacg thinks that he may be unable to complete the act. Hardened by the uneasy voice of the authorities, the honor guard, the stool pigeon, the man with film-stock cigarette, Tacg lights a match in the coffin of his pocket, wishing the quick whiff of sulfur would move toward the windows of the forgotten garret.

In this way he thinks that the railway embankment can be useful in the future, and efficiency will either remove Tacg from direct complicity or destroy the woeful conjunction of—fire, woman, pipette, supernova, dandy, charnel house—so that he may crack his codes in peace while the guilty man splits into puddles of constituent goop.

The sections are "abstracts," plans of no more than a few paragraphs, articulating a series of essays, booklets, pamphlets, scientific and religious papers, manifestos, summaries, treatises, intermediary constitutions—that may or may not even exist.

That may or may not even exist.

That may or may not be read.

Because it may or may not be written.

Natural selection may be dangerous as an idea, as a concept, but even this statement must be "fit" to survive. Thus, books were written after the film which may or may not have bore the same title or "plot," songs were crafted specifically for "soundtracks" which play at all times within our head, and the other visual arts (such as painting and sculpture) appeared as background or still life for the mood of film production.

This illustrates
a point concerning
the methods by which
romanticism may be used
as a hedge against
the turbulence
of genius.

Impossible as it may be, I will be momentarily deluded.

This composes an archive of the nonsensical, where subtle variations of filmic conditions may have communicated variations. The door collapses into thick air at your touch; along the lefthand side of what may once have been a complete document (if the doorway stands at the middle), in the space of the marginalia, a familiar hand traces a lizard-headed figure surrounded by floating barges, modern riverboats and archaic sloops. Steaming mud spins from a distant electromagnetic turbine and the chamber fills with cloud. Corrosive dirt had consumed, in the manner of battery acid, much of the useful texts that may have once been scattered about the scabbard-covered burial box, but not everything has been dissolved. The oozing sensation may be either the vibrant vertigo of your lover's kick mixed with the solution of dirt and papyrus, or the actual blood from the wound that later requires forty-nine precision stitches from the faceless medicine men and their bundles of stone, feather, bone, and pollen.

"Yes," you may think, "film isn't political until they invade my house and smash my radio into the riddle bits of modern comedy."

You discuss a great many interpreters who may also be readers. You may rightly ask after the text of this postcard? This man, who may be man-y men, blinks, only to feel the soft sand dribble from the crease of his eyes. It may come as some surprise to you that I have not taken a shit in over thirty-three days. If the kid can stay light-skinned under the incessant milk of such a heavy star, maybe it's our eyes, they think—rubbing the corneas with sharp sticks while burning out gashes in empty sockets. There may be those who still know...

Confirming various hypotheses and articulating that sperm, mucous, and other bodily fluids transfer pressure equally in all directions— Blaise Pascal—in the Pensees sur la religion et sur queleques autres sujels, adopts the Great Khan's wager: the use-value of eternal Paradise is infinite in thought control operation, and although the probability of attaining widespread worship by conventional religion may be small, it is asymptotically greater than by the typical methods of superpower intelligence operatives. Why Henry Mescaline's story about Pittsburgh sounds like it may have really been about a stint in the federal penitentiary, and why it remains difficult to tell. The police have discovered several stolen transports that may or may not relate to this case: two motorcycles, a 1976 Mercury Cougar, a 1949 Chevy Peristalsis, a scooter, a inter-state licensed Mack Truck carrying several tons of contraband placenta tissue, generic AIDS drugs, bootleg chicken incubators. In short, every slamming door, every footstep in the parking lot, means that you have been discovered once again. Pete probes his conscience with an unholy psychoanalyst before deciding to turn ratfink to the Feds as part of his treatment, which may have been part of the plan. A mutation may also be the result of looping strands in the process of replication. The populations of Indochina, which he was privy to visit as a boy, call the calla lily "corpse flower"; at Vichy he may even prevent his own assassination. Despite whatever complicity the reader may draw from such comparisons, I will still apologize for the treatment you have surely received at the hands of my prematurely aged and defiant brace of editors, Davis Schneiderman and Phoenelia Yeer. There, truth be known, life will flood out of him completely and with obscene speed, although witnesses may claim to perceive some vestigial movement, where his body shutters as if in orgasm for a single millisecond, with a distant pulse penetrating the callused layers of a witness's skin, just as the end of prose poem might resonate on any particular day for any particular reader, puncturing the oily epidermis of reason and fear. Still, I start with the Shedit analogue, how eons ago, the juniper had been cut just as Sebek the Unholy Crocodile God had demanded, and how this Crocodile maneuvered its crew of deadly mutations into a small mob-style extortion ring to keep the temple full of offerings and the locals hooked on a deadend genetic line that has got to end somewhere so it may as well end with you, I point to the picture-words that signal all narrative, and show him how to think in association blocks: how stupid and dull the lily of the morning blooms and withers in the dense fog of always.

You may be sick, and a cure may be in development, but you must wait in a hole, an aperture, an in-between. No turning back; you take a deep breath and plunge under the surface by pulling the amorphous lip over your head and the rest of your body like a nylon costume so you swim through the viscous sewer waters toward the seven letters that may yet explain it all. It may as well have been the Great Repression and these guys and dolls figured to be short timers, sure, and they knew the nature of things as more fluid, less solid, than back in grandpappy's heyday, but still, it had become routine for them to deny the physical body altogether at the workplace, which no longer replicated a river of goods essential to the ethereal fluidity of the multinational state: clerks did not therefore eat, defecate, reproduce the human species or distribute the various parcels with any sense that they weren't a part of a vast multinational network. You realize you may only have been talking to yourself. Just as we have always known, a matchstick will jut from his lips as he silently rushes his clutch of spider fingers toward this woman who may just be all women. If we were to be the experimental father, may as well begin at the end of things as they used to be known.

IV. HENRI AND MAYBE

Maybe the editor loses his nerve, so to speak. Maybe ruddy old Henri d'Mescan becomes clever Henry Mescaline who everyone suspects to be the cleverer Henri d'Mescan? Maybe Schneiderman-the-editor decides he doesn't care for authors who can't keep their yaps shut, their pens down. Maybe Frankie "Know-Nose," and Sammy "the Sign" Marinara teach him some general linguistics will a ball-peen hammer. Maybe he even loses his tongue once your eyes go out in soft flicker scripts. Maybe David even loses his hands, fingers freeze; he can't open his last few letters because he ear is on fire. Maybe the editor loses his nerve, so to speak…seven letters from Mescaline unopened upon David Schneiderman's death. Maybe your ear grows hot like a warm hat kept on by a roaring fire that catches on the yarn and pushes like a furnace into the inner cochlea. Maybe it's August 1, 1967. Maybe you scribble "no urinal thought" in the margins of a student thesis on the Nazi complicity of your favorite subject—Henri d'Mescan. Maybe the research for this planned collection finds itself scrapped on the cutting-room floor of your tiny office, locked in the false bottom of a rickety filing cabinet until you accidentally discover its contents on November 19, 1997—exactly two months before your first contact from the conveniently named Davis Schneiderman. Maybe you mean "original" instead of "urinal." Maybe you mean ABRACADABRA. Maybe you can't even spell without those secret vowels. Maybe life exists as a figure composed always of figures, a hair singed under concentrated flame in the illusion of brimstone. Maybe spelling counts. Maybe order is important. Maybe spelling counts when order remains important. Maybe, in the illusion of one man or man-y men, wriggling free from your crosscut wrists, you stone to turn so slowly once again. Maybe you've disappeared completely in the cloudscrums of BARCODEBAR. Maybe if he doesn't pull the trigger, silently refuses to fire, the deed will pass and no one will notice the absence of smoke from his barrel, the lack of ozone and soft chemical residue, his pores untouched by the microscopic singe of gunpowder. Maybe then, the entire New England coastline could ignite as if it were still only a matchstick fortress against the death of forty-five Pilgrims in year zero of American colonialism, when there was still a chance to destroy the entire concept of railroad-merger by editing out the gleam in some randy conquistador's eye. So maybe the Vanderbilts weren't quite transcontinental. Maybe it's the drink or the noise or the bonfires along the Champs-Elysées, or maybe its the view from the top of the Samaritan department store on the right bank (a circular deck framed with a circular drawing of the old Parisian skyline).

—maybe not—

Maybe "you" are the author of this delightful story, of the young girl, Dial-Up Networking, of the tiny spacecat, known mainly as Spacecat. Maybe forty-nine lily plants bloom together in a pattern. Not planned, but maybe. (some approximation of some maybe) Talking picture box obligingly hums yesterday's maybes, tomorrow's probablys, pixels against white crimson clouds. We half expected her to turn up as a panelist, or even better, maybe we received a call from one of these slick producers asking us to come on the show with her and get it all out in the open. Maybe the sun had simply moved away from the earth as such, backward, receding to its proper place far removed from our daily life. Maybe with MaMa? Maybe she'll get him one of those new-fangled artificial sun lamps because the real sun is just bound to burn out any minute now. The Schneiderman who is you admits that the Henry Mescaline scam wasn't viable from the get-go but could maybe work with the spin doctors of Post-America before the application of the electric needles that feel, in fact, like heated colonial points. Your father's absences are brief at first, a few hours, a day, maybe a year, pulsating through the seductive space between your ripening legs. Maybe you're mistaken little MaMa.